FIND VIRGIL

A Novel of Revenge

Frank Freudberg

Published in the United States

Inside Job Media
Wayne, Pennsylvania.

13: ISBN: 978-0-9845945-8-0
10: ISBN: 0-9845945-8-2
www.FindVirgil.com

To my mother and father

Acknowledgments

I would like to thank Dylan Garity, Carol Thompson, John Harten and Charlee Redman for their assistance and creative insight.

Revenge! That feral justice,
Suited more to beast than man,
Yet it furies through the human heart,
And knows no other clan.

— Jennie Rose, *The Beast Within,* 1899

(*Find Virgil* is based on Frank Freudberg's
1995 cult classic tale of revenge, *Gasp.*)

PART ONE

Philadelphia

1995

Gas prices average $1.09 per gallon
Forrest Gump wins Best Picture at the 67th Academy Awards
Google, eBay and DVDs do not yet exist
O.J. Simpson is tried for murder
Bill Clinton is President of the United States
Philadelphia journalist Martin Muntor is diagnosed with lung cancer

1

Friday, September 29, 1995
Martin Muntor's row house
Philadelphia

For a man with less than a year to live, seven days had been too much time to lose.

Martin Muntor took two weeks to prepare everything, twice as long as he had intended.

Now, all that was behind him. He was ready.

Despite the dull, relentless pain in his chest that radiated down into his lower back, he felt good. He felt great. He hadn't felt this good in months. Maybe years. Maybe ever. He believed the Lord helped those who helped themselves, and this was the proof.

In a matter of days, Muntor would be assuming a permanent place in the history of the world. Then, no one would ignore him. No one would ever again succeed in pretending he didn't exist.

But Muntor couldn't rest quite yet, and so he rose wearily from the worktable in his living room and stretched. He paced. He opened dusty blinds and leaned against a window to see the sky.

A perfect day, he thought when he saw the slate-gray clouds. *Dark and ominous. God is the best set designer you could want.*

Muntor sat down once more, anxious to complete his task.

He needed to seal another twenty or thirty envelopes, and then that would be it. All seven hundred packages would be finished.

Twenty minutes later, he was finished. He got up from his chair and caught a glimpse of himself in the mirror that hung on the wall over the living room sofa. Drawn, nearly emaciated. Older than his fifty-six years.

Not a handsome sight. It enraged him to see it. He had taken care of himself. The body was a temple, a belief he had taken to heart at a young age. A lifetime of maintaining his temple, and now this.

One thing was missing from the reflected image, he realized. There was no evidence of absolute evil. *I don't think I look like the monster they're going to say I am.*

Each morning for nearly two weeks, the dying man had been getting up before dawn to seat himself at the worktable. Nothing was more important to him than this project. The early hours had proven the best. He was strongest then. He'd make coffee and have high hopes of how many packages he'd be able to finish that day.

But most mornings, after only a few hours of effort, he'd lose steam. The dexterity left his fingers. The muscles in his back stabbed at him. And then, his eyes quit focusing on the close, exacting work despite the assistance of the illuminated magnifying glass mounted on a swivel arm and clamped to the edge of the table.

On those few mornings, Muntor felt he was able to work through the pain and discomfort. His body resisted him with another barrage of difficulties. Catching his breath required more and more effort, the dull pain in his chest tightened its grip, and the coughing fits became increasingly violent. Some days, Muntor would find the strength to work three or four hours, but that was his maximum. Then, he'd have to quit. Getting to the sofa a few feet from the worktable seemed like crossing the Serengeti, but he'd get there, ease himself down, pull up a blanket, and sleep for hours.

Now that Muntor had finally finished the most taxing part of the project, the assembly work, he felt better. The physical troubles had less impact on him. The tedium was over, and there, on the floor next to the worktable, was the fruit of his labor — six large cardboard boxes holding seven hundred FedEx envelopes. Each one stuffed and sealed with a form attached that would direct the envelopes to addresses all over the United States.

Once more, Muntor did the mental calculation he'd done many times before. Thirteen dollars to ship each package. Times seven hundred packages. Nine thousand, one hundred dollars. That was going to be the most money he'd ever spent at one time. In his pocket, in the wallet with the fake identification, he had a cashier's check for the exact amount of the shipping charges. He had called FedEx. No, he had been told, he wouldn't need to set up an account. No, the seven hundred envelopes all at once weren't a problem. Sure, they'd accept a cashier's check from a local bank.

I am going to go through with this, he kept telling himself. Nothing was going to stop him, although he had good reason to give up. He'd been in pain, extreme pain, but he had a way around that. Muntor would give himself an injection — a homemade combination of prescription pain-killer and amphetamine crushed together by a mortar and pestle in his kitchen, mixed with water and injected into his arm.

But he felt that was cheating. He had never used drugs — they defiled the temple. And if he started giving himself injections now, what would he do when his physical condition deteriorated even more and he really needed them?

For the first time in his life, he found himself obsessively committed to something. All throughout his school years, they had called him a quitter and a loser. And they had been right.

He grew up in a run-down Philadelphia suburb. He kept his few friends at a distance. His family had no money and his father was a loudmouthed, chain-smoking drunk. The house was shabby and reeked of the stale smoke that caused Muntor to cough himself to sleep most nights. Who needed the other kids to know about all that?

Muntor's father worked as a pipefitter in an oil refinery, commuting by bus. A neighborhood church sometimes dropped off grocery bags of food at the house, but nothing very good. Almost-stale bread, cans of beans and vegetables, Jell-O mix. Most of his father's paycheck went for Marlboros, Budweiser and lottery tickets.

Muntor's mother cleaned house for a neighbor every Saturday morning so that she could have a little cash to take her only son to the toy store or get him a birthday gift. She'd hide her small stash of neatly folded bills in a sock tucked in the back of a dresser drawer. If Muntor's father found the money, he'd piss it away by the end of the night.

And there were arguments. Muntor's mother would beg for her husband to stop drinking, smoking and gambling. She didn't mention his pushing and shoving and cursing. That would be too much to ask. She made her pleas almost daily, and almost daily he'd curse her and storm out. Muntor felt relief when he'd hear the door slam. Children

7

need consistency and Muntor had it. The day before payday — when his father had no ready cash left — had always been hellish.

That all ended one afternoon when he was eight. Muntor came home from school to find his mother laying face up on the couch, barely breathing, foam collecting at the corners of her mouth. An empty vial of prescription medicine had fallen to the floor near her dangling arm.

"Mom? You okay?" he said. She did not respond.

The child walked past his mother's near-lifeless body, went to his bedroom, grabbed a yo-yo and six marbles — the only ones he owned — and spent the next couple of hours playing with them out front, alone on the sidewalk. Within minutes of his father arriving home, an ambulance and police cars arrived. As dusk settled in, the boy stood with the neighbors, watching as his mother's body-bagged corpse was carried out.

Later that week, the official autopsy report indicated the cause of Mrs. Muntor's death was suicide and that she had died of a barbiturate overdose. Muntor never understood why she'd intentionally leave him so alone. And another thing troubled him. His mother had taught him many things from the Bible, including the idea that suicide was a sin. Muntor blamed his father. From that day on, he referred to his father only as "her husband." He never again thought of the man as his father, only as "her husband."

You loser, his father had said, *you didn't know enough to pick up the phone and call someone, didn't have enough sense to run for help? You could have saved her life, but look what you've done. What kind of little fool are you? You sat and played with those damn marbles while your mother lay in the house dying. You could have saved your mother's life. I'm ashamed of you, and so is everyone else. You're nothing. You don't exist.*

Muntor thought of those words as he slipped the last pack into its envelope and struggled with each heavy box, carrying them one by one and piling them by the front door. He wanted nothing more than to get to that sofa, to sleep, to rest his burning eyes, if even for only a few minutes.

But he had learned in almost six decades that if he couldn't exorcise his father's voice from his head, he could at least answer it back. *Go to hell, old man. I am what you made me, what the world made me. I spent my life pushing back against the way you programmed me. I worked, and I was good at my job, even if those shitheads in management never appreciated me. I had a family and took care of them. I took care of myself. And where I am today is despite the life that I was born into. I don't deserve to die, not from cancer, but others do, and I'm going to take them with me.*

Muntor loved the story of Jesus throwing the moneychangers out of the temple. His mother would read it to him often. He liked to imagine that not all the priests were corrupt, that there might have been at least one who understood the temple was a holy place.

He was fond of thinking he was like that too.

He wanted to rest, but he couldn't.

Not now, not today. Not quite yet.

Martin Muntor had one more thing to do.

2

The Executive Suite
Old Carolina Tobacco, Inc., World Headquarters
Asheville, North Carolina

A telephone rang on an immense mahogany desk in the Executive Suite of Old Carolina Tobacco, Inc., the world's fourth-largest cigarette company. Without looking up from the quarterly financial reports he was studying, W. Nicholas Pratt, president and CEO, switched on his speakerphone.

"Yes?"

"Mr. Pratt?"

Recognizing the voice, Pratt grimaced, cut off the speaker, and picked up the receiver.

"Why aren't you calling on my scrambled line?" It wasn't a question. Pratt's voice was icy. Valzmann should know better.

"I'm at a pay phone up in Pennsylvania, sir, in the mountains, looking for a site, and my cell phone won't work up here. Your private number is on the cell phone's autodial, and so, I had to call..."

Pratt silenced him with a derisive laugh. "You commit that number to memory."

"Yes, sir."

"Now what do you want?"

"It's about Tom Rhoads. I've just gotten a report from one of my men. He's gone three days without a drink. Been to two AA meetings."

Pratt pursed his lips, exhaled, and thought. He leaned back and ran a finger between the tight shirt collar and his neck. Even on Saturdays, Pratt wore a suit.

"That won't do," Pratt said. "I need him out of control, acting wild. We need a ready-made chump. Eventually someone's going to come up short one research scientist. If Rhoads straightens up and flies right, we won't be able to use him." Pratt paused, fishing for an idea. A moment later, he found one. He sat up straight and snapped his fingers. "I know what. I want you to start in on him, wear him down. Aggravate him. Drive him to distraction. Chase him back into the bottle. It won't be difficult. What's that piss he drinks?"

"One-hundred and fifty-one proof Bacardi rum," Valzmann said. "Straight. It's like drinking rubbing alcohol, just not as flavorful."

"Put the Pennsylvania project on hold and come back. I want you to see to it that Rhoads's life here in Asheville becomes one big unbearable cesspool of frustration. Think about how you're going to do it and call me back. On my secure line, Valzmann. And I do not want Rhoads to know someone's dicking with him. Everything you do has to be subtle, plausible. Things that could happen to anybody on any day. Understand?"

Pratt knew Valzmann enjoyed the dirty-tricks assignments. They provided a break from the other illicit things Pratt had him do. Valzmann had told him the dirty tricks brought back memories of his days as a CIA man in Brazil when he served as liaison with the military regime that came into power there in 1964. He'd think of something good to do to Rhoads, something to help justify the two or three hundred thousand in cash he managed to get out of what Pratt called his "special projects" slush fund every year.

"I'll call you back," Valzmann said to his boss.

Later that day, a different telephone rang in the Executive Suite. This one sat inside a locked drawer in Pratt's desk.

Pratt put a gold Mont Blanc fountain pen down on top of a stack of proposed magazine ads. At Pratt's request, Old Carolina Tobacco, Inc.'s ad agency had prepared a campaign to attract first-time smokers. The telephone rang again and he unlocked the drawer, pulled it open, and picked it up. "Yeah?"

"I've got it," Valzmann said.

"I'm listening." There was no hint of forgiveness in the CEO's voice for the earlier error of calling in on the wrong line. The demerit would remain on the books Pratt kept in his head, and Pratt knew Valzmann would know that.

Pratt had been an army officer in Vietnam. He had been captured and kept in a river, hunched over in a partially submerged bamboo tiger cage, for fifteen months. About once a month, he had once told Valzmann, the VC commanders would come around and announce he was to be executed the next day. Sometimes, to amuse themselves, they'd bring in an interpreter and have him dictate a farewell letter to his family. Then early the following day, they'd drag him screaming out of the cage, put a pistol to his head, and pull the trigger, or tie a grenade around his neck and pull the pin. Then they'd laugh and spit and urinate on him.

Occasionally they'd put the cadaver of another American in the cage with him and leave it there for weeks. The only visible scar Vietnam left on Pratt was an upper lip tic that, when active, bared his canines like a dog about to attack. Pratt was a private man, but he knew sharing this part of his past with Valzmann had convinced him that he was not someone to be toyed with. He knew people thought of him the same way they thought of John McCain, a man he admired. People might not like his style or the plans he came up with, but most of them wouldn't push back because they knew he had been a P.O.W. People figured there was no way he could be cowed, and on some level they feared what he might do if he were pushed.

"Next time Rhoads eats in a restaurant," Valzmann began, "which is just about every meal, we'll slip something into his food. Visine works great. Puking, violent diarrhea, the whole mess. That'll lay him up for a few days. When he finally feels that he can get more than ten feet away from a toilet, he'll want to go somewhere. But then, his car won't start."

Pratt thought about this.

"No flat tire," Valzmann said. "Too obvious. Something electrical."

"Okay. What else?"

"The gastrointestinal thing will have kept him up nights. He'll be exhausted. He'll need sleep. A little trash fire on his floor around three in the morning to set off the fire alarm. Wake him up. Maybe even cause a building evacuation."

"Good," said Pratt. "He'll be inching closer to a drink by then."

"That's not all. Eventually he'll get his car fixed, and when he's ready to return to work, on his way to his office, what if someone rear-ends him?"

Pratt laughed.

"Cockroach infestation in his kitchen," Valzmann continued. "We know he's scared of them, so where will he go to hang out while he waits for the exterminator? A bar, probably. And to add to his misery, we'll also be loading a bunch of unauthorized charges on all his credit cards, Visa, MasterCard, American Express, Texaco, the department stores, his long distance company."

"He might not see the statements for a month."

"No. We'll put enough charges on them so that he'll be over his limit all the way around. Then, when he keeps getting declined, he'll call the credit card companies, screaming. When he denies that he's made the purchases or that he's lost his wallet, they'll cancel all his cards. What a migraine."

"Good. I get it. Make it happen." Pratt hung up, slid the drawer closed, and took out his calculator to perform his daily ritual. He looked at a computer screen that displayed yesterday's New York Stock Exchange closing price of Old Carolina Tobacco, Inc.'s common stock. Two hundred and fourteen dollars per share, up 7/8 of a point. He multiplied the share price by 825,000 — the number of shares he owned.

"One hundred and seventy-six million and change," he said out loud in the empty suite. "That'll keep me in Biltmore Forest at least until payday. Not too shabby for the skinny kid from St. Raymond's orphanage. Not too shabby at all."

Pratt took a deep breath and went back to the proposed ads. He decided to reject them. They weren't bad, but the subliminal message they were supposed to convey, *you're eighteen now, you can smoke if you want to*, didn't come across quite loudly and clearly enough.

3

Raising two small children by herself made Millie Jenkins's job at Tunn's Tobacco Shop in the mall seem like a leave of absence. She enjoyed every moment of it. At 9:30 each morning, she arrived at the shop. At 9:59 she unlocked the glass doors, plucked the occasional dead fly or moth out of the display in the store window and opened for business.

A little before 10:30 on Monday morning, the FedEx delivery man stepped into the shop and rapped his knuckles on the glass case that displayed a variety of imported pipes and lighters.

"Millie."

She looked up. "Hey, Greg." She liked Greg. He had that blue-collar-model look of so many FedEx drivers, and she had been flirting with him for a year.

"Something for you today." She wrinkled her brow. He handed her the FedEx envelope and a clipboard.

Then she smiled. "Wow, for me?"

"Sign right here."

Millie signed, taking care to make certain her name was legible.

"Alrighty then," Greg said. "See you." He retrieved the clipboard and returned to his dolly stacked with other packages.

"Can't wait," she said, wanting to sound interested but not desperate.

Millie carried the envelope back into the stockroom, poured the tepid coffee out of her mug and refilled it with fresh. She tore open the envelope and shook the contents out onto a desk.

Out tumbled a pack of Easy Lights rubber-banded to a disposable lighter, a regular envelope marked "Survey Enclosed," a cheap pen and a letter addressed to her on the stationery of Old Carolina Tobacco, Inc. Millie knew the company's regional sales manager. That was probably why the package was sent to her. She pulled the personalized letter from under the cigarettes and lighter and smoothed it out on the desk.

September 29, 1995

Ms. Millie Jenkins,
Assistant Mgr.
TUNN'S TOBACCO SHOP
Bay View Mall
Boston MA 02109

Dear Ms. Jenkins:

Thank you for taking the time to read this letter. We are conducting a consumer survey because we've changed the taste of Easy Lights and want to know what consumers think about the difference.

Complete the enclosed survey form now, and you'll be $100 wealthier in just a few minutes! Old Carolina Tobacco, Inc. will mail you a check within five business days.

We need your feedback right now, so our offer of $100 applies only to the first 250 respondents. We have sent surveys to 500 tobacco retailers via overnight mail, and so by midday Monday, all participants will have received them. May I suggest you complete the form right now? It's simple. Here's all you need to do:

- *Open the enclosed pack of Easy Lights and enjoy one cigarette as you would any other.*
- *Complete the survey. We've even enclosed a pen for your convenience!*
- *Immediately dial the 800 number listed below. One of our opinion researchers will ask you to read your responses.*

- *Provide our researcher with your name and address — work or home, whichever you prefer — and we'll process your $100 payment today.*

Thanks and please keep enjoying Easy Lights, Primos, and other fine Old Carolina Tobacco, Inc. products!

Matthew Doran
Vice President, Product Development

P.S. If you are not over 18, if you are not employed by a tobacco retailer, or if you do not regularly smoke cigarettes, please discard this survey.

Millie checked her watch.

10:26. *I'm getting me that hundred bucks, honey. The good Lord knows I can use it.*

An occasional smoker who had never tried Easys before, Millie knew her survey responses would be of little value to Old Carolina Tobacco, Inc., but she didn't plan to mention that when she called in so she could get the one hundred dollars.

She removed the cellophane from the pack, took out a cigarette, and put it to her mouth. She flicked the lighter and brought a bead of flame to the cigarette.

Millie inhaled deeply. A vicious cough burst out of her throat.

The smoke had blistered her mouth, throat and lungs. Her eyes opened wide and the burning cigarette dropped into her lap. The room spun so fast she saw nothing but a whirl of muted color. She coughed again and a choking sound came from deep within her chest. Still on the chair, she doubled over, gasping. Her diaphragm convulsed, forcing air into her lungs. The current burned the back of her throat like a blowtorch.

She panicked, as if submerged in water without warning. She tried to scream, but couldn't. *What's happening to me?* Her respiration became a staccato series of violent grunts and snorts. Furious coughing hammered her chest. She swallowed air spasmodically. Millie, no longer able to breathe, could only choke. Eight or ten seconds after lighting the cigarette, the poisoned smoke had annihilated her respiratory system. Her lungs had been rendered incapable of harvesting oxygen from air.

Millie's jaw locked open, and she fell thrashing, wild-eyed, onto the floor. Her body jackknifed, every muscle contracting then relaxing, contracting then relaxing, in pantomime of the gasping mouth of a caught fish fighting for air. Her fingers spread wide and went rigid. Her hands jerked up in front of her as if to stop an oncoming truck. Her bladder and bowels convulsed and emptied. At the moment of death, an agonizing spasm wrenched Millie Jenkins's back into a shape it had never known in life.

For another half-minute, her body continued to jerk, writhing sideways on the unswept stockroom floor, crashing into steel filing cabinets, smashing into boxes, the overturned chair, and finally, a cinder-block wall.

4

Monday morning, October 2
Tom "T.R." Rhoads's apartment
Asheville, North Carolina

At forty-two, on a good day, preferably one slightly overcast, Tommy Rhoads could be mistaken for a handsome man.

He was tall and wiry, his hair curly and brown, his gait agile.

Rhoads's face was angular and awkward. He had the habit of leaving his mouth slightly unhinged. And his nose was a bit hooked in that jagged Anglo-Saxon way and too long. Bright light didn't flatter it and it cast a giant shadow. Beneath the skin of his face was an ensemble of expressions coiled and ready to spring. At any moment, Rhoads's face could contort itself into a firestorm of rage or become the source of an inappropriate laugh.

On a bad day, like this day, after the bout with food poisoning and his search for relief in a bottle of rum, Rhoads could look like hell. The ensemble wouldn't show up, and his face would recede into dark gloomy pockets under his eyes, and that was all you could see.

This morning, he was too hungover to go to work, too embarrassed to go in and pretend not to see his employees avert their eyes while thinking, *Look what Rhoads did to himself again.* The three employees at his private security and investigations firm were loyal and devoted to him, he knew, and that's why he called in, saying that he was working in the field all day. He knew they were worried about him, and he couldn't bear to face their concerned looks. It had been this way since his wife died, months of sobriety alternating with weeks of showing up late, bleary-eyed and exhausted. His clients were always happy with the work the firm did, but in times like these, he leaned heavily on his people to make sure nothing slipped through the cracks.

Instead of showering and dressing, Rhoads paced slowly back and forth through the rooms of his small apartment in a high-rise in the heart of Asheville. Rhoads had hardly furnished the place. When he had moved to Asheville from Philadelphia years earlier, he installed expensive off-white wall-to-wall carpeting and bought a dozen large indoor trees. Ficus and avocado and Norfolk Island pine. When the flora didn't produce the dense woodsy effect he was after, he went out and bought six more. That had done it. He used a water bottle with a spray nozzle and misted the trees three or four times a week. Large windows flooded the apartment with sun for most of the day.

Eventually, Rhoads replaced his futon with a real bed and bought bar stools for the breakfast counter in his kitchen, along with a big television, VCR, and audio system. He didn't own much more than his clothing and what he had in the apartment. He drove a Taurus — reliable and not flashy, the impression he wanted to give of the firm itself.

Rhoads sat down at the breakfast counter and dialed his secretary's voice-mail number, letting her know he was working on the latest case — a corporate security analysis — from home.

After leaving the message, he called his younger brother Teddy who lived in Cherry Hill, New Jersey. The two Rhoads brothers had always been prone to drink — a family trait — but Tommy hadn't given in to it until his wife of three years died. She insisted he call her Janet, but he preferred to call her Jan. Now that she was gone, it was Jan. She had died too early — complications from a congenital heart defect that kept her side-lined from sports and exertion her entire life. Her heart simply gave out, and now Rhoads's only family was Teddy's.

Teddy hadn't done as well as Rhoads when it came to pushing back from alcohol. Rhoads loved his brother, and since he and Jan hadn't had kids, he loved Teddy's like his own. Teddy's life had been falling apart for years.

His descent was accelerating. When Rhoads couldn't get to his office, he had employees who worried about him. When Teddy didn't make it in to work, all he had was a belligerent manager who was no doubt building a file for Human Resources detailing his erratic performance. Tommy knew it wouldn't be long until Teddy and Kodak were history.

The phone rang in Teddy's den. He answered Rhoads's call, and as soon as the "how's the family" talk was over, Teddy asked, "You ready?"

"Ready for what?"

"Plan B, big brother. I found us our boat."

Rhoads and Teddy, years before, had come up with a plan to strike out on their own. They would buy a fishing boat and run charters together off the coast of southern New Jersey. For Teddy, it was a way to escape the disapproval of his bosses and take control of his life. Rhoads was ready to leave the P.I. business, which was mostly a seedy and depressing world where he could make a living but never get rich.

But mostly he had always thought of the charter business as a way to keep an eye on Teddy. They would work together every day and, though Rhoads knew he had little hope of keeping Teddy off the bottle, at least he could keep him from going too far. They had talked over their Plan B for years, but Teddy could never come up with the money for his half of the boat. Teddy's sudden declaration that it was time made Rhoads immediately suspicious.

"What happened?" said Rhoads.

"Nothing happened, man. It's just time. I'm done with working for corporate America."

Rhoads smiled. Their father had been a mid-level manager for an auto parts manufacturer and a union rep. He was the picture of middle-class American success and compromise — a responsible employee who had dreamed of earning a living as a jazz saxophonist. Somehow he had adopted the resistance vocabulary of the sixties counterculture and regularly made ironic commentary on his life, a life serving "the man" that was bearable only because of his union work, which he considered "fighting the man."

"How's work?" Rhoads asked Teddy.

"How's work? Work blows. The man is after me, you know that. But I've got twenty-five grand to put down on the boat, so who cares how work is?"

"You win the lottery or something? You haven't been gambling again."

"No," Tommy insisted. "I cashed out my IRA, okay? We've been talking about this for how long? Years and years. I just realized we have to put our money where our mouths are."

"You cashed out?" Rhoads said. "Are you still employed?"

"It's not looking good for me at Kodak, okay? Maybe my boss is after me more than usual. It's time to do it. You want to go for it or not? Are you ready to bail out of your business?"

Rhoads suspected that Teddy had been fired, but it didn't matter much. If that was the case, Rhoads would have to find some way to support his brother's family, something he was happy to do if he had to. But if Teddy didn't have a job — about his last reason to stay sober — then, within months, he'd inevitably go into a fatal alcoholic spiral. Plan B was Rhoads's best hope of keeping his brother alive and intact. Rhoads understood the irony in all of this. He was barely holding it together himself.

"Let's make it happen, brother. I'm in. Tell me about the boat."

"There's a big-ass fifty-two-foot steel Can Grande trawler they're going to auction off tomorrow. It's already rigged for charter fishing and probably within our price range. It'll be perfect."

"Well, let's have a look at it together," Rhoads said.

"Outstanding," said Teddy. "We're going to name it *Plan B*."

"I like *Second Chance* better, but we can figure that out later."

Rhoads felt relieved. It'd take him a couple months to wind down the P.I. business, but the charters would mostly be on the weekends anyway, so that shouldn't be a problem. He and Teddy had talked about their Plan B for a long time. That it was finally happening made him happy. *A drink to celebrate would taste good right about now.* He thought about it for a long minute. *A thousand excuses to take a drink, but not one good reason.*

He leaned back in his chair and thought about blue water and standing behind the wheel of his own boat, his brother at his side.

5

Monday, October 2
Philadelphia

Surrounded by ceiling-high bookcases in his living room, Martin Muntor sat quietly in a worn, green leather recliner and faced a blank, large-screen television. A sleek cat jumped up out of nowhere into his lap, formed itself into a ball, and closed its eyes. Muntor put his hand on the cat's back and felt the heat under the fur. Without warning, he began coughing — deep rasping coughs that startled the cat that jumped off his lap. Muntor felt the absence of its warmth.

So, that's how it's going to be, he said to himself as he watched a tail disappear into the kitchen. He sipped some water and the coughing subsided.

Twenty years earlier, Muntor had made the living-room bookcases himself. He had used boards of redwood and fastened shelves into the frames with brass screws. He owned more than fifteen hundred books on almost every imaginable subject and organized them by subject. Physics and chemistry, classic literature and cheap thrillers, political philosophy, biographies, music, the media, westerns, popular psychology, and different versions of the Bible and books about God and spirituality. Each volume was cataloged in a spiral notebook he kept in the basement in a fireproof safe. In the event of a fire, he could replace the books with the insurance money.

He had read every one of them. No book got onto the shelves unless he had read it entirely. That was one of his rules. Newly acquired books he hadn't yet read remained stacked in a small pile on the Oriental rug next to his recliner.

Muntor's cat, Bozzie, a rare-breed Bengal male, jumped up onto one of the shelves and rubbed its black-spotted, reddish fur against the clock that Muntor used to separate his collection of Thomas Berger novels from his autographed set of Mark Twain's works. When Bozzie finished and moved away, Muntor looked carefully at the clock.

10:40.

It's happening now.

Wherever it was Eastern Time, overnight deliveries had arrived, and the shipments to other time zones wouldn't be far behind. People were already beginning to die.

He thought, *It's happening. Smokers getting what they deserve. And the cigarette companies are next.* He regretted that his targets wouldn't experience the daily pain of lung cancer, emphysema or the other diseases smoking caused, but the thought of their folly being paid in kind gave him fierce satisfaction. He had done everything right. He kept himself in good shape, ate right, took care of his family, went to church, worked hard. And yet there he was, unemployed, dying and alone.

Some days he was convinced that it was the sheer number of people who didn't treat their bodies like temples that had made him sick. The smokers, the druggies, the ones too fat to see their feet. They were everywhere, like a poison in the air that had infected him. The American dream was a lie — people didn't necessarily succeed just because they did the right things, worked hard and persevered. Sometimes, maybe usually, the deck was stacked.

He had seen them every day of his life, starting with his father, the people who threw their lives away, wasted years chasing excesses. He had lived like a monk — the accusation his wife had thrown at him when she left with his children — and others who had wasted their lives had done better and would live long after he was dead.

Muntor was going to make a point, wake people up to the opportunity they had been given. Until he had gotten sick, he had exercised twice daily. He wore the same size thirty-two pants he had worn when he graduated high school. And through all the years that followed, he watched as everyone around him got fatter, sicker, and older, victims of their own appetites. *Weak,* he thought. *Every one of them.*

His wife had grown enormously fat. She smoked two packs of unfiltered Camels each day, most of them in the house, generating clouds of smoke that floated through the rooms like smog. The thick air caused Muntor to cough all night. Year after year he pleaded with her to smoke outside on the front porch. She refused, citing the weather and the inconvenience. His daughters smoked too, both of them, even though they were in their teens — his wife had permitted it.

He couldn't prove it, but Muntor was convinced the years of breathing second-hand smoke contributed to his lung cancer. His doctors didn't disagree.

His few friends had drunk themselves insensible like his father had. They had thrown away their lives, yet he was the one who was dying. He felt like an unwilling Christ, made to pay for the sins of the world, as if all the damage they had done to themselves had been visited on him.

The average American reads five books a year, mostly bullshit recycled pop-psych disguised as self-help, and romance stories. By his own count, Muntor read over two hundred books a year and could have qualified for several PhDs by now. And it was he who was dying. The fat, lazy and ignorant lived on, like cows chewing the cud of the Madison Avenue and government propaganda that had replaced intellect in American life. But he wouldn't go alone. He would take some of the herd with him. Not as many as deserved it, but he was only one man, and he could do only so much. But he thought it would be enough to make his point.

Muntor dressed in black jeans and a black turtleneck. He made a big pot of coffee, and the aroma filled the small house. He wondered how long it would take for the news frenzy to begin. That would depend on how long it took law enforcement to connect the dots — make the connection between all of the deaths that were to take place within hours, minutes, seconds, of one another.

During the past ten days, Muntor had used his video camcorder and a tripod to film himself at work on his tobacco project. He was making a documentary. *A great documentary,* he hoped. *Perhaps the greatest documentary ever made. And it will show the world that there was more to Martin Muntor than met the eye. Martin Muntor was more than the little boy who played outside as his mother died inside their apartment. Martin Muntor was more than the loser who had to wear hand-me-down clothes. Martin Muntor was more than the loser his father had been, more than his colleagues at the new service were: Martin Muntor was an example of a life well-lived, a life of restraint, care for the body he had been given, and of superior intellect.*

This morning, in his living room, while waiting for the first news bulletin to interrupt the all-news station, he wanted to keep himself busy by editing his documentary. Next to his chair were several videocassettes containing scenes of him preparing for the first series of attacks. Earlier, he had reviewed the tapes and decided which scenes to keep and which to discard. He found he could use almost all of them.

As he worked, he kept an eye on the old but functional television he kept on an antique table in the living room. It was black and white, a gift from his mother. It had been rare for him to receive more than a shirt or socks, so a gift of a television, albeit small, was something to cherish. It wasn't new when he received it. Some teacher, feeling sorry for the family, had given it to his mother.

It was only a matter of time before some talking head broke in with the first bulletin. He could barely wait. Muntor wanted to be sure that he was awake and alert when the first bulletin broke, so he began the exercise routine he had devised decades before to keep his body strong.

He knew he wouldn't be able to finish even half of it due to his increasing frailty. But it was a ritual he wouldn't give up even now that treating his body as a temple didn't matter anymore. He made it through three sets of squats and some pushups before the coughing took over and made it impossible to continue. He didn't berate himself, for once. He was sick, and even as sick as he was, he had done more to maintain his body today than most of the cows that populated the world did in a year.

Muntor rose to get more coffee. On his way back from the kitchen, he stopped at the printer set up on the dining-room table. The printer had been there for a year. No loss. No one visited him at home anymore, even though everyone knew he was sick now. The kids hadn't been by for dinner or Sunday lunch in years. From the printer tray, Muntor collected a dozen pages of script he had written as narration for the documentary.

Before settling back into the worn green recliner, Muntor crouched by the VCR and picked up a cassette marked "Paradiso." He slid it into the slot and turned on the machine. Then he sat down and pressed the mute button on the television's remote control. He would use his larger, much more modern television, that sat nearby his trustworthy black and white one, so that he didn't miss the breaking news.

He picked up the portable tape recorder, pressed the record button, and held the microphone in his left hand and the pages of the script in his right.

He planned to read the script aloud, keeping the words in sync with the images that were beginning to appear on the television across the room. Once he finished reading the entire script, which might take days, Muntor intended to dub his tape-recorded voice onto the videotape's audio track. It would be worth the effort.

This was his documentary, this was his life's work, and he intended to produce the best record of it he could.

On the coffee table next to the recliner, Muntor's telephone rang, startling him. It was Lori, his daughter. She almost never called, and he did not want to be interrupted now. He told her he was drying off from a shower and asked politely for permission to call her back later. They both knew he wouldn't.

Muntor pressed another button on the remote, and an image jumped shakily onto the screen — a close-up shot of a computer monitor. Off-screen, someone typed. Bold, italicized capital letters appeared one at a time, spelling out the title *MUNTOR'S LAST STAND*. Under it, perfectly centered, a subtitle. "The Greatest Documentary Ever Made." There were no production credits.

He had considered calling it "Muntor's Masada," but he was afraid that the average person wouldn't understand. Maybe, Muntor thought, he'd put the credits at the end. His one indulgence in his life had been a devotion to film. He had learned a lot from watching them, and more from reading about how they were made. He knew he was going to be remembered as one of history's great filmmakers. He read the words as they appeared on the screen.

Based on a story conceived and executed by Martin Muntor.
Script by Martin Muntor.
Produced by Martin Muntor.
Directed by Martin Muntor.

The title shot faded, the screen now pitch-black. Muntor turned on the tape recorder and began to read into the microphone in a slow, almost mocking deep bass voice of an announcer.

"It's payback time ... (pause). For hours, those words kept whispering themselves to Martin Muntor as he worked to set everything up exactly as planned ... (pause). It's finally payback time ..."

He pressed the stop button on the tape recorder. Click.

Muntor watched the television as an image appeared, an over-the-shoulder shot of a man at a worktable facing away from the camera. Muntor had shot this sequence the Friday before, the day he delivered the seven hundred envelopes to FedEx. For most of the scenes, Muntor had mounted the camera on a tripod set up in the doorway of the room. He had kept a small remote control in his pocket and turned the camera on and off as needed. If the script called for a panning shot, Muntor had done that manually.

He couldn't be recognizable in those shots unless he panned by a mirror.

As he watched himself now, he realized his hair looked shaggy and reached past his shirt collar. When had it grown so long? He needed to get a haircut. And he had lost weight and was thin, too thin. He could clearly see his shoulder blades as they pressed through the white shirt that hung on him as it would a scarecrow. The figure leaned back against a bookcase and folded his arms.

That was Muntor's cue. He turned on the recorder and again began to read.

"Muntor stood back finally, arms folded, with the calm confidence of a Christian holding four aces. Sunlight and the low rumble of traffic penetrated the Philadelphia row house through open windows as he surveyed the assembly-line setup in his living room. Outside, a few paces beyond a tiny rectangle of lawn, another rush hour had begun to leave its yellow gray smog on Roosevelt Boulevard."

Click.

He kept a finger at his place on the page, observed the images and waited for his next visual cue.

The previous Friday, an hour before he shot the scene he was now watching, Muntor had laid out everything he needed across the surface of two side-by-side aluminum card tables. It had annoyed him that the dented tables wobbled when he brushed against them. *That won't look good on video*, he had thought. *Martin Scorsese would never put up with a wobbly table.* So he went upstairs into one of the empty bedrooms and found some duct tape in a dresser drawer.

He remembered now how musty the room had smelled.

While up there, a pang of homesickness yanked at him. He walked out into the hallway of the house he had lived in since a year after his mother died. It had been his grandparents' home, where he was sent to live when his father, arriving home late and drunk one night, had missed the bathroom and wandered into Muntor's room. The elder Muntor had urinated on his son. The next day, when the teacher took him aside and asked him why he smelled so bad, Muntor embarrassingly told her what his father had done. Following two days in a foster home, the court had awarded Muntor's grandparents legal guardianship.

His grandparents had tried to soften it. His father had been drunk, they said. It was the alcohol, not him. He didn't mean it. Muntor knew it was all true, but what he concluded from it was that anyone who gave himself to drink or any other untoward appetite was less than him, maybe even less than human. He knew then what his life would be — an example to others of what a gift it was to be born in a healthy body with a powerful mind.

In the decades after, he had learned that people were too stupid and weak to understand the lesson he presented to them. They polluted their bodies and minds with physiological and intellectual poisons — drink, drugs, cigarettes, ludicrous TV shows, books aimed at the masses. He had hardened himself, become even more of a model of human potential. His body was a temple, and he was the high priest. The more people failed to respond to the lesson he delivered merely by walking out the house each day, the more he became devoted to his mission. In the end, he knew that the cows would never learn.

He knew it was time to thin out the herd.

Years later, he would own the home in which his grandparents had raised him. It had become his sanctuary, his escape from the shabby neighborhood, his escape from his father, the inner sanctum of his faith — a haven of books and an exercise regimen that would shame a Green Beret.

It would also become the home where he had totaled a marriage and tried to raise two girls. This was the house where he now lived and had slept without human company for a decade.

During the divorce, Muntor's daughters, then seven and ten, had clamored to live with their mother. That crushed him. He had been the attentive one, the affectionate one, the one who encouraged them to eat right, to educate themselves more than their underfunded public school could ever do, to keep their bodies in top shape. He had been what his own father had never been. It was important to him. Martin Muntor's children had never experienced the wrath of growing up with an abusive father, and they had been given the secret of living a life worthy of the bodies and minds with which they had been gifted. But their mother had turned them against him. She was like all the others — a fat cow that crammed her body and mind with toxins and gave her children permission to do the same.

For years after his wife had taken his children away, he lived alone, until he decided to get a pet, something he had been denied as a child. He chose a cat, the animal that most closely resembled him and his approach to life. Well cared for cats were lean, fit, and clean. They were the opposite of the cows he shouldered his way past when he had to leave the house. Cats seemed to live their lives with purpose.

The wobbly table was just another example of the difference between him and the herd. Most people wouldn't notice, or, at best, would shove a matchbook under one leg. Instead, Muntor took the duct tape and, for stability, wrapped layers of tape around the offending leg and affixed it to the table's corner. When finished, he slapped the tabletop with his palm.

"There you go," he had said, satisfied the table was sturdier.

On the television, the camera began panning objects on the worktables. Muntor glanced again at the clock on the shelf. Five minutes past eleven and still no news bulletin. His eyes returned to the script.

"Today was the day. Muntor knew exactly what to do. He had rehearsed the procedure in his head a thousand times. His first task was to organize all the pieces. He placed the FedEx envelopes, the regular envelopes, and the shipping labels on the table to his left. His computer had printed out the cover letters on counterfeit stationery, and he stacked them neatly on his right, next to the survey forms, pens, a box of paper clips. He didn't like being cramped. He left plenty of work space in the center."

Click.

Next to the boxes on a steel typewriter table, Muntor had placed a stoppered glass test tube upright in a wire rack. The tube contained a solution as clear as spring water. Next to the wire rack on a folded bath towel lay a syringe, a portable hair dryer and a box of latex surgical gloves.

The close-up of the gloves was his cue. He turned the recorder on, found his place in the script, and picked up where he had left off.

"No more putting it off. He had to get going. Thinking about what came next sent a shudder through him. Muntor felt the familiar clenched fist of pain behind his breastbone. Whenever he momentarily lost his confidence, that pain would return, reminding him, prompting him, spurring him. He had a purpose — to teach the world about the gift they had been given and that they squandered. No amount of pain would deter him. He was like Jesus on the cross — unbroken."

Click.

Now the on-screen shot changed. Shooting from the living-room couch, Muntor aimed the camera at the worktables.

He could remember shooting this particular sequence as if he'd done it five minutes ago. Despairing thoughts had come to him while filming. He realized he had been stalling, delaying his project, not working as fast as he could have, finding distractions, exaggerating pain. This dawdling had rung a familiar bell. Muntor had a history of rarely finishing anything he started. The corpses of things he had begun and later abandoned cluttered his life the way trash blows down dead-end alleys and stays there.

He had realized early on that living a perfect life was impossible. There were too many things to work on, too many improvements to make. This had often resulted in him beginning projects that were never finished — books about nutrition, a Guinness World Record for the greatest number of pushups completed, a health-food business. But none of that mattered now. He was older and wiser. Much wiser since the doctor had pronounced his death sentence — and he focused on what he could do: illustrating that the wages of sin were, in fact, death.

When the images on screen panned away from the worktables and moved unsteadily up the carpeted stairs and through the rooms on the second floor of his old house, he picked up the microphone and began reading.

"Muntor had been a quitter, giving up easily and often. One of Muntor's specialties had been half-painted rooms. But his greatest escapes involved people — an ex-wife, two daughters and countless employers to vouch for his unreliability ... (pause). For Muntor, there had always been something else to do, somewhere else to go. There was always another distraction more worthy of that special vein of genius he knew be possessed but had never been able to apply. Until now. Now, finally, it was payback time."

Click.

On the television appeared another close-up shot of a computer screen. Letters appeared again, typed out one at a time.

7:15 a.m.
Friday, September 29.

On screen, Muntor walked into the shot, steam rising from the hot coffee he had poured himself in the kitchen. He walked out into the living room and sat down, back to the camera, sliding his chair in, his emaciated abdomen against the edge of the table.

His hand reaching up on screen to adjust the magnifying glass was the next cue.

"Muntor began to treat the cigarettes, the most demanding step of the operation. A simple procedure, really, but time-consuming and painstaking. Hours passed while be used the fine narrow blade of an X-ACTO knife to slit open the cigarette packs. He made three slits along the bottom of each pack in order to expose the ends of a few cigarettes. He mangled a half-dozen packs — a casual glance and anyone would have known something wasn't right — before he found the trick was just to go slowly. Muntor had never bought the 'be patient' argument, regarding patience as nothing more than a lesser form of despair. Today, though, he was going to do it right."

Click.

At that point in the filming, Muntor had turned off the camera, disgusted with himself. Things were going slowly enough and stopping frequently to shoot scenes for the documentary wasn't helping.

After a few minutes of pacing, he went back to work. Being nearly finished gave Muntor a newfound energy. His production rate accelerated. With a gloved hand, he took pack after pack from the box on the floor. Then he swung the adjustable arm of the illuminated magnifying glass into position. Using the knife, he cut through the cellophane wrapper, the cardboard, and finally the paper-backed foil inside the pack. Muntor's design was to lay bare the ends of the three cigarettes at the extreme right of each pack. He had used flip-top packs instead of soft packs. Flip-tops have a front and back, and therefore a right and a left. He had observed that when most smokers opened packs, they took cigarettes from the far right.

Later, when his body needed to shift positions, Muntor moved the tripod-mounted camcorder in and focused the lens on the close work. He filmed his hand using a syringe to inject the sodium cyanide solution carefully into the end of a cigarette, making sure none of the solution seeped out and stained the cigarette paper. The chemistry stuff was easy. He learned all he needed by reading.

On screen, finishing one pack and reaching for another was his next cue to resume reading from the script.

"The latex gloves were difficult enough to use, but worse, Muntor's hands perspired profusely inside. The sensation made his skin crawl, and the trapped moisture impaired his sense of touch. After treating a pile of a dozen packs, he would stack them with the bottoms open and exposed and dry them with the portable hairdryer. At first he had used the high setting to speed up the process. The cigarettes dried in three minutes, but the heat caused the cellophane wrappers to crinkle. To avoid that, he used the low setting. That took six or seven minutes per batch."

Click.

The last part of the procedure had been to reseal the packs. Muntor did that with meticulously placed droplets of quick-drying clear glue. For quality control, he compared the bottoms of adulterated packs with those he hadn't touched. They looked good. His handiwork would not stand up to a close inspection, but it was more than adequate to fool the typical consumer. He'd done a great job.

Again, letters appeared on the screen.

11:20 a.m.
Friday, September 29.

The camera panned the living room where the worktables had been set up. This was not a tripod-mounted shot. Muntor had shot this live. No one, except Muntor's cat, was in the scene. Muntor had zoomed in on the wall clock.

Again, he read from the script.

"Even though the FedEx office on Market Street stayed open for drop-offs as late as 7:30 p.m., Muntor wanted to be downtown and parked sometime between 5:30 and 6:00. At that hour, the facility would be a madhouse, and he'd stand out less. It was early in the

*day, but he needed at least several more hours to finish all the ciga-
rettes. If he'd work fast, he'd make it."*

Click.

Last Friday, Muntor finally put down the last pack. His fingers ached,
his neck seemed permanently cramped, and his back felt as if someone
had taken a swing at it with a baseball bat. Hunching over the worktables had caused all of the muscles in his upper torso to knot. During the
assembly and packing procedure, he had risen and stretched frequently
to relieve the strain. Very little could have stopped him, not even the
pulsing throbs of pain behind each of his weary eyes. Every heartbeat
sent spears there. Through all the discomfort, he had kept going. When
he had finished treating the packs, he used a mantra to get through to
the end.

*Stuff the envelopes, seal them up, take them into town. Stuff the enve-
lopes, seal them up, take them into town.*

A small pile of paper strips from the adhesive on the back of the
FedEx envelopes lay curled like birthday-present ribbons on the floor.
Then, all at once, there had been no more packs left to stuff. Muntor had
finished the assembly procedure. He had not eaten all day. He chided
himself, even though it didn't matter anymore. His research had convinced him that a regular and exacting diet was necessary for maximum
health. His insistence on eating the right things at the right times had
been one of the many contributing factors in his divorce. Now, though,
his mission took precedence. Eating well wasn't going to save him. The
only thing left was to teach his lesson after he was gone — those who
did not respect their bodies would pay, and in dying, they would educate
the rest.

He set up the camera to shoot from the living room through the
dining room and into the kitchen. He committed to making up for his
failure to follow his dietary regimen by providing an example to his
audience.

The on-screen image showed Muntor in the kitchen, arranging a
healthy and nutritious meal on a plate: slices of avocado, an orange, a
handful of nuts, some sliced chicken.

Muntor read from the script.

"A proper diet is composed mostly of greens. Fat and protein should be consumed in moderation. Avoiding processed sugar and artificial ingredients is critical."

Click.

The camera, now set up in a corner of Muntor's bedroom, showed the emaciated man dressing. Muntor read again from the script.

"After toweling off, Martin Muntor selected from his closet the prop he needed, a generic uniform purchased two days earlier at Sears. Perfect for a deliveryman. He had washed it twice to give it a worn look. Khaki pants and shirt and a brown cotton twill jacket, the name 'Arnie' — he stitched it himself with blue thread — on the pocket patch."

Click.

A close-up of a digital clock on a dusty nightstand.

5:25 p.m.

"On his way out, Muntor petted his cat, Bozzie. He was less than an hour away from committing a crime, a federal offense, of unprecedented proportion. At any time after he left his house, in theory, he could be arrested. There was a slight chance, very, very slight, but real, that he'd never see this house or his Bozzie again. He left an envelope addressed to the twelve-year-old son of a neighbor. The envelope contained two hundred dollars in twenties, a letter describing how to care for Bozzie, and a dozen KatCrunch cat food coupons. Just in case."

Click.

Muntor carried the packages in heavy boxes to his car. It took several trips. Once inside the car and driving, Muntor propped the camcorder on the passenger seat, aiming the lens to shoot across him, past his face and out the driver's side window. It was the first time he allowed his face to be seen on camera. The camera also picked up passing images of his ride down Roosevelt Boulevard, on the Expressway along the Schuylkill River and into Center City Philadelphia. The camera's microphone picked up the sounds of traffic and Muntor's troubled breathing.

Once in town, at a traffic signal, Muntor swung the camera around and pointed it at the clock in the car's dashboard.

6:11 p.m.

Next, he edited in a shot of the computer monitor displaying three words.

Center City Philadelphia

There was a sloppy edit, some choppy white static, and shots of Muntor riding around Nineteenth Street, up Sansom Street, and right on Twenty-Second, looking for a parking spot.

He couldn't find one until he pulled onto a side street. Once parked, he turned off the camera.

All that had happened three days ago, and Muntor recalled it with vivid clarity. He remembered that while he had been in the car, he had to squirm out of the light blue windbreaker he had worn and into the brown deliveryman jacket. He had looked into the mirror on the sun visor, then outside. No one had seemed to be paying any attention. Muntor had opened the glove compartment and pressed a large gauze bandage on his chin. Earlier, he had dotted the underside of the bandage with iodine, and a little splotch of brownish-red seeped through. Perfect. The prop would draw the clerk's eye to the bandage, he hoped, not his features. He put on a cap and tugged at its bill, bringing it low on his forehead. He put on a pair of sunglasses.

"Hey, is anyone alive under all that?" he had said out loud. Muntor climbed out of the car and deposited two quarters into the meter. A slight tremor, a vague fear, had run through him. He noticed it in his shoulders and chest when he raised his arm to check his watch. 6:20.

He remembered thinking, just as he had locked the car door behind him, *This is the first lesson.*

Muntor had tried to take a deep breath but had to choke back a cough. He was learning that deep, satisfying breaths were a thing of the past. A light breeze caught his jacket and flapped it at his waist. He had bent near the rear of the car and wrestled in the open trunk with the hand truck he had buried under the cardboard boxes.

People had walked by, the sidewalks busy with workers heading home. No reason for anyone to notice the colorless little man wheeling boxes down the street. He watched them, fat and unhealthy, the stupid herd rushing here and there, the only thing on their minds the TV shows they would fill their evening hours with before retiring.

He rounded the corner onto Market Street, the hand truck rattling over the sidewalk. Low clouds gathered and moved easterly toward New Jersey, obscuring Muntor's view of the statue of William Penn atop City Hall.

The FedEx office had been mobbed, but the line moved quickly. When he was next, he set the hand truck down, took a thick sheaf of shipping labels from atop the top box and handed them to the woman behind the counter.

"I'll need a receipt for this, please," Muntor had said, placing a cashier's check on the counter.

The woman glanced at the check and then up at Muntor. Her eyes fell on his bandage. She looked back at the check while another employee removed all the envelopes from the boxes on the counter and put them in a processing bin. The woman tapped her keyboard and looked at the check again.

"You got the exact amount," she had said as a receipt materialized at the printer. She tore it off and handed it to him.

"Do me a favor?" she had said, pointing to the six now empty cardboard boxes that had held the envelopes. "Take those with you."

Muntor had nodded, not saying another word. He put the boxes back on the hand truck and strode out of the office and back onto rush-hour Market Street. People moved by, traffic stalled.

He remembered having checked his watch. It had read 6:33.

He had gotten into his car, switched on the camera, and pulled out into traffic.

Muntor read from the script again.

"It was official. Six thirty-four p.m. and the war had begun. Martin Muntor had just fired the first, long overdue salvo. The missiles would fly all weekend long, taking serpentine paths to seven hundred targets with all the stealth of a cat on a moonless night, and the first ones would begin landing midmorning Monday. The death that the smokers — the cows — had been seeking for so long would find them."

Click.

6

Boston

"Unit three-four to dispatch."

"Dispatch to three-four."

"Unit three-four. Priority request for a supervisor to our location. Tunn's Tobacco, west side, Bay View Mall."

"Do you need me to launch LifeFlight?"

"Unit three-four. Negative."

A moment later, the fire department's East Division captain picked up the radio microphone in his car.

"Charlie One to three-four. What do you have there, Gerry?"

"Unit three-four. You'll need to see this, Captain."

"Charlie One en route."

7

Philadelphia International Airport

The USAir flight from Asheville had landed at Philadelphia International at 1:31 p.m.

Something about the airport bothered Rhoads. En route to the Avis counter with the pea-green duffel bag he used as a carry-on, he realized what it was. *I've been using this airport for thirty years, and every time I'm here, it's under major construction.*

Rhoads rented a car and headed east into New Jersey to his brother's house. He was sober now but still in high spirits. He and Teddy were about to make their dream come true.

The *Deep Blue* was being auctioned tomorrow. A big, creaky charter fishing boat hiding under a fresh coat of deep blue paint. Auctioned tomorrow at noon, and they were going to buy it, rename it *Second Chance*, and spend the rest of their days laughing their asses off, fishing, and overcharging tourists.

A little over an hour later, Rhoads pulled into Teddy's driveway in Cherry Hill. Before he could turn the car off, Teddy's wife Linda stepped out of the house. Rhoads immediately felt a sense of dread. Linda met him at the car as he stepped out. She hugged him and said, "Teddy went to Atlantic City." Her face displayed only a token sadness. The tears of disappointment she might have shed had been exhausted years before.

"What?" Rhoads said. "Why?" But he knew.

"Come on, Tommy."

"Shit," Rhoads said. He knew Teddy: when he was up, he could always be counted on to try to capitalize on his holdings at the craps table. Years before, Teddy had agreed Linda would have control over the money, but obviously the lure of cashing out his retirement had been too much.

Linda said, "I don't know what we're going to do. He lost his job, you know."

Rhoads hugged her again and said, "We'll figure it out. We always do." But he didn't know if that would be true this time. If Teddy didn't have a job and gambled away the boat money, what then? Rhoads's business made enough to keep him afloat, but it wasn't nearly enough to support Teddy and his family. His half of what the boat would cost had wiped out his savings, and if he was honest, the business wasn't doing too well. He had always been a great salesman, but his disengagement lately had left the firm without new contracts going forward.

"Come on in. The kids want to see you," said Linda.

Rhoads opened the car door, grabbed the gifts he had gotten them and followed her inside.

8

Asheville

In the office of W. Nicholas Pratt's executive secretary, a large television peered out of a massive, elaborately carved teak credenza. Someone had turned the volume up too high. The CNN news anchorman's booming voice filled the room.

"... deaths now reported in Cincinnati, Boston, Boca Raton, New Orleans, San Diego and Tacoma. And as we've said, additional reports continue to come in. There is no way at present to know the full scope of this disaster. The FBI has issued a preliminary statement warning all consumers that cigarette packages may contain lethal poison. To this moment, however, we can confirm only that the 122 known deaths, and many, many injuries, are thus far associated with the Easy Lights brand manufactured by Old Carolina Tobacco, Inc., of Asheville, North Carolina. An FBI press conference has been scheduled for ..."

Executive secretary Genevieve DesCourt, a trim older woman in an expensive dark blue suit, stared, flustered and aghast at the screen.

The intercom on her desk squawked, startling her. "Have you located Rhoads yet?"

"No, Mr. Pratt, but I have gotten hold of one of our pilots, Jack Fallscroft. He and Rhoads are close friends. He said to tell you he has an idea about where Rhoads may be. He's checking. And Mr. Pratt? The men from the FBI, they're getting impatient. I told them..."

"All right, Genevieve. Send them in."

She rose and started around her desk to lead them to Pratt's office, but Deputy Director of the FBI, Oakley Franklin, stopped her with a wave.

"Additional agents will be arriving," he said to her. "Tell them I said to wait here."

He took a moment to check his watch, then crooked a finger at another FBI man. The two walked across the office to the oversized red-wood door that separated Pratt from the rest of the world.

The Deputy Director was built like a linebacker, big, black and humorless. The other agent, no more than twenty-five, was forgettable, average in looks, weight, and height. His name was Brandon. His father was a congressman from northern California, and he was part of an experimental fast-track FBI training program. Franklin found him annoying but efficient.

Franklin motioned for Brandon to step in ahead of him. The two men strode toward the huge desk at the far end of the room. It was a considerable walk on the thick carpet.

Pratt stood staring out the floor-to-ceiling windows, silhouetted against the darkening skyline of Asheville and the Smoky Mountains. He looked as if he was born with the title of CEO. Tall, sleek, with skin bronzed by many hours on the back nine of the most exclusive golf courses. His gray suit fit as if Pierre Cardin himself had been his tailor, and his shiny-as-steel silver-and-black hair looked good atop the dark face and dark suit.

Pratt shook the Deputy Director's hand perfunctorily and ignored the junior man.

"I'm Oakley Franklin, Mr. Pratt. Deputy Director of the FBI. This is Special Agent Ben Brandon. We flew in from FBI headquarters in Washington."

"I'm not particularly pleased to meet either of you." Pratt swallowed as if pained by a severe sore throat. Then he looked behind Franklin at the woman with the double-take legs seated on a couch. A stack of manila file folders weighted her down. "This is Anna Maria Trichina," he said, "one of our assistant vice presidents."

"So, what do you have?" Pratt said as he sat down. The two FBI agents remained standing.

Franklin looked at the woman. Trichina, a voluptuous redhead with shoulder-length hair, had been out of sight on the couch until Pratt stepped aside and introduced her. She began to move the folders from her lap to get up and shake hands. Pratt preempted her by waving the FBI agents to the chairs on the other side of his desk.

Franklin spoke. "Well, Mr. Pratt, Ms. Trichina, what I have is a mess. Apparently, someone has injected packs of your cigarettes — we believe hundreds and hundreds of them — seven hundred to be precise — with a sodium cyanide solution and shipped them all over the country. It looks as if they've arrived at tobacco shops as some kind of consumer opinion survey. The packages came with a cover letter. A cover letter that had been printed on your company's letterhead and signed by you."

"Mother lover!" Pratt whistled as if he'd just seen an interception against a team he had a big bet on.

Trichina rose. She seemed offended by Franklin's report. "Old Carolina Tobacco, Inc. letterhead and signed by Mr. Pratt?"

Brandon snapped open a soft-leather portfolio he had tucked under his arm and handed Franklin a flat sheet of paper enclosed in a clear plastic evidence bag.

"You tell me," Franklin said, handing it to Trichina. "An agent had to use a letter opener to pry this out from between the thumb and index finger of a cadaver in Annapolis about ninety minutes ago. Don't open the plastic."

Trichina held it up to the light.

"The logo looks good," she said, addressing Pratt. "But this isn't ours. The watermark is wrong. This paper is Philamy Linen. Old Carolina Tobacco uses Strathmore Writing, twenty-five percent cotton. And that's definitely not Mr. Pratt's signature."

"Relax, Anna Maria." Pratt said to her. "He doesn't think we did it or that I'm involved. He's simply trying to acquaint us with the situation."

"That's not entirely accurate, Mr. Pratt. At this moment, I have no idea who did it. The only thing I know for sure is that I didn't do it. That leaves five-and-a-half billion-minus-one potential suspects."

Ben Brandon's cell phone chirped in his pocket. He turned away when he answered it, spoke for a moment, closed his phone, and turned back to the conversation without saying a word about the call.

"At this point, Ms. Trichina," Franklin said, "it is the policy of the FBI that we don't rule things out. We rule them in. We have over one hundred dead, seventy-two critically injured — and word is many, if not most, of them will die — and reports of new fatalities and injuries coming in every time I turn around. We're looking at a nationwide panic. And who knows if this is a single isolated attack by overnight mail or if poisoned cigarettes are right now sitting in cigarette vending machines and on retailers' shelves all over the country?"

Pratt looked as if he'd been punched in the gut. He spoke quietly. "Who's on the top of your short list as of now?"

"Mr. Pratt, again, the list is almost six billion people long. This investigation is about three hours old. And all we know for sure is that whoever is behind this is an intelligent, crafty individual with at least some knowledge of how you test market your products. Perhaps a disgruntled employee, or maybe someone else with a problem with your company."

"Oh for shit's sake, Nick," Trichina abruptly interjected, holding up the letter in the evidence bag. "Did you read this? Any Intro to Marketing student could think this up."

Pratt ignored her and spoke to Franklin. "You're saying it may be an inside job? An employee? A former employee? Someone like that?"

"As I've said, there's no reason to rule it out. What I want to do right now is talk to whoever heads up corporate security here. He may have someone in mind already."

"Gary Dupree," said Pratt. "He will, of course, give you whatever it is you'll need. And, of course, so will Anna Maria and I."

"We'd also like to talk to your previous head of security, Thomas Rhoads."

"Rhoads was just a consultant, and he hasn't worked for us for nearly a year."

"I'm aware of that," said Franklin. "We'll still need to speak with him."

9

Asheville

In the orderly master bedroom, a green oxygen tank on wheels sat beside a single bed by an open doorway to the hall. Vials and bottles crowded the nightstand.

The shower hissed as Mary Dallaness, thirty-four, entered from the hall and walked quietly toward the bathroom. She was barefoot and wearing jeans and a tank top. She stood just outside the bathroom looking in. Her husband, Anthony, was barely visible through a foggy shower door.

"Why didn't you call me before you got in there?"

"Probably because I don't need a nursemaid when I'm taking a shower."

But you do, she thought. "Why aren't you sitting on the folding chair, at least?"

A telephone rang in another part of the house. She looked in the direction of the ringing, then back at Anthony, torn over whether to answer or not.

"The telephone's ringing, Ant. Stay put. Don't try to get out until I come back. Do you hear me?"

"No," he rasped. She could hear the emphysema in his voice.

Mary jogged around the banister to another bedroom. Hers. A bright, multicolored comforter, half thrown over a nearby rocking chair, lay in disarray on a double bed. Stacks of magazines and books and a compact stereo on the dresser cluttered the room. She hurried to pick up the telephone.

"Hello?" She listened. "Yes, this is Mary Dallaness. Mr. Pratt?" She listened again. "Goodness, no! I took a personal day, and I've been tied up with my husband and the doctors since this morning. Wait a moment, I'll put it on."

She crossed the room to a small television and pushed the power button. A news anchor was talking in front of a graphic luridly titled "CIGARETTE TERROR." The sound was low.

She picked up the receiver. "I have it on, Mr. Pratt. I can't believe it." Mary watched the screen as she listened to Pratt. "No. No, sir, no reporters have contacted me. Of course I won't speak to them." She listened to Pratt. He spoke in urgent bursts. "Yes, all the Level Three documents are totally secure. No, sir. Nobody can access a Level Three file without my knowing about it."

Pratt asked her if the computer database kept a record of everyone who requested the top-secret documents. She told him yes, the system did that automatically and kept those names in another Level Three document called "LTD-PULLS." He sounded relieved. Immediately his voice tensed again. He asked if there was a way that anyone, anyone, could access that document and erase names of those who have seen Level Three files.

"Yes," Mary said, and then added, proudly, "Only one person not including you and Ms. Trichina is cleared to see LTD-PULLS. Someone I know you can trust. Me."

Pratt said that was what he was hoping to hear. He thanked her.

"Do you need me to come in, sir?" Mary asked, hoping he'd say no. "All right. Yes, sir. First thing in the morning, then." She paused, and Pratt said something else. "My husband?" She lowered her voice. "As well as can be expected ... but thank you for asking, sir."

After hanging up, Mary Dallaness stood still in the dark of her bedroom, listening to herself breathe.

Something about Pratt's call left her unsettled. She had never trusted him to do anything other than protect the shareholders' profits. A call like this had to do with much more than finding out who was poisoning people who smoked Old Carolina cigarettes.

10

Across town, Nick Pratt had just said good-bye to Mary Dallaness and hung up the telephone in the living room of Anna Maria Trichina's luxury condo in North Asheville.

A black leather L-shaped couch stretched across two adjacent walls. Track lighting highlighted framed prints of several views of Monet's water lilies from his garden at Giverny.

Pratt and Trichina, both dressed in the business attire they had worn earlier to World Headquarters, sat on separate sections of the long couch. Pratt looked at his watch, picked up the telephone, and checked his messages.

"Shit," Pratt said upon hearing the call from the company's investor relations manager. The manager had reported that huge blocks of sell orders on Old Carolina shares were already piling up for the opening bell tomorrow at the New York Stock Exchange. That on top of a four-and-a-half point loss on enormously high-volume trading earlier that day.

Trichina was still thinking about Pratt's call to Mary Dallaness.

"Did she sound suspicious?" Trichina asked.

"Not at all. In a crisis like this, it makes sense that the CEO would be on damage-control duty."

"I'm surprised you have any confidence that you can count on Mary Dallaness." Trichina flashed a bratty schoolgirl smirk when she mentioned her subordinate's name. "She's so ... so subservient. Anyone in authority can manipulate her. I wouldn't be surprised if a tough-talking meter maid could badger her into divulging top-level corporate data."

"That's what I like about you, Anna Maria — your tolerance when it comes to other people's frailties."

"And the other one you have to watch out for is Rhoads," she said. "He's a fuckup waiting to fuck something up. He's a drunk and a bum."

"Sometimes a drunk and a bum is exactly what the doctor ordered. You should know that." Pratt smiled at Trichina. She looked away.

"Every problem brings with it some benefit, even if it's hard to recognize," he continued. We should have more devastating crises around Old Carolina, Anna Maria."

"What do you mean?"

"Ever since we learned of this product-tampering nightmare this afternoon, you've had the most adorable furrow in your forehead. It's quite..."

"Oh, Nick. Not now. Please."

Pratt tuned out her voice and looked at her. He wasn't smiling. His eyes narrowed on her like a predator spotting game. Still seated at the other end of the couch, Pratt reached for one of the round white leather throw pillows. He remembered paying the credit card invoice for them. Trichina had bought six of the pillows for ninety dollars each on a business trip in Chicago and had them shipped to Asheville. He dropped the pillow on the floor between his shoes. He closed his eyes and indicated "come here" with a slight jerk of his head. Trichina pretended to miss the cue.

Pratt waited half a minute. He heard no sound of her moving toward him. His eyes remained closed.

"All right, Anna Maria. I'll try it in English. Why don't you come on over here?"

Pratt leaned back against the couch. He patted his knee three times. Trichina hesitated a moment too long before she began moving. Pratt heard her slide along the leather to him.

Fetch, he thought to himself as he interlaced his fingers behind his head and suppressed a grin. *Fetch, girl.*

11

In his limo on the way home, Pratt picked up the secure line and pressed a button to call Valzmann.

In a remote part of Old Carolina Tobacco, Inc.'s World Headquarters subbasement, a small room existed, lined with advanced electronic equipment, walled in cinder-block and devoid of any natural light. The room did not appear on the floor plans on file with the Buncombe County's Emergency Management Services nor in the building's architectural blueprints. Officially, the room didn't exist.

In that room, a telephone's soft electronic tone hummed.

"Yes, Mr. Pratt," the voice said.

Pratt was on fire. "This tampering shit. Rhoads's name is on the letter but the Feds don't think it's him. The signature didn't match, the title's wrong and if anything, it's somebody that has a grudge against him, but that could be any number of people. You know, Benedict's name is going to come up sooner or later. I know it. The government never contacted us about his little telephone call to the Justice Department. You know why?"

Valzmann said nothing.

Pratt kept roaring. "Well, I'll tell you why. Because the Feds were just waiting for their chance. And, now they have it. I'll bet you money they start in with Benedict. *Where's Benedict? What happened to Benedict? Could Benedict be behind this?* And of course, we can't tell them why we know it's not Benedict. We ought to make damned certain those documents are secure. I've already begun. And I want you thinking about the logistics of tying Rhoads to Benedict."

"I'm working on it," Valzmann said, making a note on a lined pad. "Mr. Pratt? Can I ask you something? Why do those documents still exist? Why do we even have them?"

"I wish they didn't, but they were logged in on the auditor's schedule long before they became a problem. Getting rid of them would be a red flag. It's better to keep them buried in the archive database."

"Then why are you nervous?"

"Because there's always the human element."

"As in ..."

"As in Mary Dallaness."

"The name rings a bell."

"You don't know who she is?" Pratt seethed. "Mary Dallaness, idiot. In the corporate documentation division. You keep an eye on her. She and her husband are buddies with him."

"Rhoads?"

"Rhoads."

"How do they know each other?"

"Don't you bother reading the reports your own investigators write for me? Rhoads used to be a cop in Philadelphia. Mary's husband Anthony has a brother. He was a Philly cop with Rhoads. She was the one who recommended him as an outside security consultant."

"Small world."

"Yeah, and I think we're going to need to find a way to make it a little smaller, by two."

"Why are you worried about Mary Dallaness? What's the problem with her?"

"She's unstable. Her husband's dying. Chronic pulmonary emphysema, from smoking, of course. That makes her susceptible to pangs of conscience. You know, we had one like her not so long ago."

12

After Pratt left, Trichina poured herself a glass of Merlot, sipped it once, then took several larger swallows and topped off the goblet before heading to the bedroom. She stripped off her clothes, removed her makeup, and reclined on the bed.

Closing her eyes, she exhaled deeply, almost a sigh. Images like film clips moved in slow motion through her mind, images of Rhoads and those many nights not so long ago when he lay there curled up next to her, so large in the bed she was used to sleeping in alone, and so strong, so dumb looking, asleep with his mouth open. The memories were a lullaby she sang to herself. Not sadly, though. Fondly.

Trichina knew the tampering chaos presented an opportunity to her. Her father had always insisted that she be on the lookout for opportunity, and when she saw it, she was to seize it. But he was gone now and it was up to her. She remembered his corny saying and the way he smiled when he said it. *You have to take responsibility for what you do in this world, Anna Maria. You have to know the ten magic words that make anything possible, that can make anything come true.* Then she remembered the little thrill she experienced every time he said those words. Because he wanted her to hear them, he said them very slowly, very carefully. He would take her tiny hand in his rough one and say, *If it is to be, it is up to me.* Then he asked her to repeat them with him, and they'd say the words together. *If it is to be, it is up to me.*

The wine had bathed every nerve in her body. She felt carefree.

She knew she performed her job honorably, and she earned fair day's pay for a fair day's labor. Her father certainly would have understood that. No, there was nothing in the world wrong with that. At all. She didn't force people to smoke, she didn't even ask people to smoke. People had smoked for thousands of years before she was born, and she knew, no matter what, that people would smoke for thousands of years after she was gone. So, if she could take advantage of this situation and rise within Old Carolina Tobacco, Inc., she was going to do it.

And once she got to the top, or near enough, she'd be able to influence company policy.

She could make a difference. A positive difference.

Plus, she could buy herself one hell of a Jaguar.

13

Atlantic City

Night. Almost cold. Maybe forty, forty-five degrees.

The salty breeze that blew in from the Atlantic Ocean across the south Jersey beachfront made it colder. Crisp and clear. Wave crests picked up the glitter of starlight. Rhoads finished his cigarette and tossed it out the car window. He turned the key and steered toward the police station.

They had gotten the call the day after Teddy disappeared. Atlantic City P.D. had arrested him on a drunk and disorderly. One more arrest and Rhoads worried Teddy might have to serve some real time.

It took Rhoads an hour to convince the cops to drop the charges. In the end, it wasn't that he had been a cop, or the names he told them that they might know. An older sergeant had stopped by as Rhoads tried to figure out what else he could say to the arresting officers who sat there stone-faced.

One of them, Bellini, said, "He's got a sheet, Rhoads. I don't know how you do it in Philly, but Atlantic City's a quiet town. We have rules."

The sergeant said, "You're Rhoads? Philly P.D.?"

Rhoads always tensed when someone brought it up. "Not anymore."

The sergeant stuck his hand out. Rhoads shook, confused.

"I knew Michael Flynn."

Rhoads smiled and shook the sergeant's hand harder. "You knew the Mick?"

"He went to school with my brother. Hell, he dated my sister. Mick was a good man."

"The best," Rhoads said. "Don't believe anything they say about him. Mick was my training officer. None of that shit's true."

"You don't have to tell me," the sergeant said. "Anyway, I heard what you did for the Mick. That your brother in the tank?"

"Yeah. Sounds like he had a bad night. He didn't hurt anybody, though, just being loud."

The sergeant pointed at the two cops. "Cut him loose."

"Come on, Sarge. Guy puked in my car."

"You two are going to be good cops someday," the sergeant said. "But today you're young, and you don't know shit. Cut him loose."

As Rhoads led Teddy past the squad room, he saw the three cops talking together and waved. The sergeant waved back. He went to the desk to get Teddy's personal effects. As he watched his brother filling out the forms, he heard the other young cop say, "Bullshit, Sarge."

"I'm telling you. When he wouldn't take it, they went after him. He and the Mick might have been the only honest guys in the district. Rhoads didn't rat, but he wouldn't give in either. But when the Mick died — they said it was suicide, but no way — Rhoads lost his shit. He went to his lieutenant's house with a bat and jumpstarted the guy's head. And then he went after two of the detectives running the racket."

"So what's he doing walking around?" Bellini said.

"They were going to put him away on felony assault, attempted murder, the whole thing, but Rhoads had files. Said he was going to go to the press. So they dropped the charges and gave him his pension and he walked away. This was like six years ago, so you guys would have been too young."

"Shit," one of the cops said, "I know what you're talking about. My pop wouldn't shut up about it. There was this article, something like 'Hero cop fights corruption' or something. That was Rhoads?"

"That was Rhoads," the sergeant said. "The papers got hold of the story, but it was just a story. Without Rhoads's files, there was no way to prosecute. Story goes that he's just holding onto them so they don't come after him or his family."

"Jesus," Bellini said.

"Yeah," the sergeant said. "Not someone you want to piss off. One of those guys that don't know how to stop once he gets going, is what I hear."

Teddy had heard it all too and looked at Rhoads. "Come on," Rhoads said.

14

American News Syndicate
Washington, D.C. Bureau

AMERICAN NEWS SYNDICATE
SLUG: CIGARETTES TAMPERING-ART
ALL MEDIA: MAJOR STORY UPDATE: MONDAY, OCTOBER 2, 11:42
P.M. EST WASHINGTON BUREAU
ART AVAILABLE: 8 COLOR CRIME SCENE PIX. NATIONAL.

1. *Crime scene. Tobacco shop in mall. Seattle, WA.*
2. *Crime scene. Tobacco shop taped off by FBI. Memphis, TN.*
3. *Victim's distraught wife, children comforted by friends and police. Memphis, TN.*
4. *Antismoking protesters with signs at AmeriLeaf Tobacco, Co. distribution center. Long Island, NY.*
5. *Hospital spokesman, Fisher Memorial Hospital. San Bernardino, CA.*
6. *Close-up of Easy Lights package w/ arrow indicating point of tampering on cigarette pack. (Xmit FBI photo)*
7. *Crime scene. Victim under sheet in front of tobacco shop. Orlando, FL.*
8. *Massive media turnout at FBI press con. Washington, D.C.*

309 DEAD, 132 HOSPITALIZED AS OF 9:00 P.M.
By Fred Bird
American News Syndicate Staff Reporter

Monday, October 2 – Washington, D.C.

The estimated death toll in today's mass poisoning of Easy Light cigarettes has reached 309 as of this evening, FBI spokesman, Special Agent Herman Litts, said tonight. Litts also told a packed press conference that 132 others have been hospitalized as a result of the tainted cigarettes.

"The investigation is intense and we are pursuing several promising leads," Litts said. "Hundreds of FBI agents, augmented by state and local police and officials from state, local and federal agencies have been mobilized. The operation is being managed by the FBI's Event Response Center here in Washington."

In Philadelphia, a FedEx spokeswoman confirmed that the company delivered 697 of the suspect packages Monday. Exactly seven hundred packages were shipped from Philadelphia, but three had been inaccurately addressed or shipped to tobacco shops that had gone out of business.

Two FedEx employees who handled the transaction say a Caucasian male, age fifty to sixty, weighing 150 to 160 pounds and dressed as a deliveryman, dropped off the packages early Friday evening. Investigators say that although that individual is the focus of their search, he may have been an employee of a legitimate courier service that unwittingly delivered the deadly packages. Other sources speculate the man may have been the perpetrator who intentionally poisoned the cigarettes contained in the packages.

15

Atlantic City en route to Deer Mountain, Pennsylvania

The route Rhoads took wound him around upstate dairy farms and stands of pine trees and ranch houses with huge picture windows set way back on two-acre front lawns. Bleary-eyed, he took sharp turns too fast, tires crunching gravel and shooting it out into ditches like bullets. On the winding roads, his headlights illuminated everything but the asphalt. In Rhoads's mind, the trip from A.C. to the redwood cabin was being made in one great careening sweep. He stopped only once to use the restroom at a rest stop.

Rhoads exited the Northeast Extension in Carbon County, trying to figure out how to salvage this. He had called Linda and told them he was going to dry Teddy out at their uncle's cabin. He had called the office and said he had "family business," and to hold down the fort. He heard Dale's concern and suspicion over the line but didn't say anything. They were wrong about him for maybe the first time, and if they thought he was on a bender, that wasn't unreasonable. He hadn't had a drink since he left Teddy's house, and he knew that the next few days were going to be almost as hard on him as they would be on Teddy.

But he could handle that. He had done it before. The money, though, that was the thing. Teddy had lost it all. He pounded the wheel in frustration and looked over at his sleeping brother. Fifty-eight thousand dollars in a single night. Teddy had tried to tell him the story — he had been ahead at the tables, and then things had turned sour. Rhoads stared him into silence and told him to sleep it off.

How was he going to manage it? Chances were Teddy wouldn't be able to get another job, at least not soon. Rhoads knew everything Teddy and Linda had was going to their mortgage. They had bought the house during one of Teddy's years-long good spells, but they bought at the top of the market and there was no way to unload it now. Rhoads had his pension, but that was about it. The business was in the black, but just barely. He didn't have enough to support Linda, Teddy and the kids.

Rhoads had done the math on the charter boat obsessively, and it all worked out. It would keep them employed and make more than the security business ever had. But for now, the boat was out of the picture.

He realized he was too tired to get any closer to a solution and just let himself ease into the drive. He followed his headlights through the dark and thought that Jan would have known what to do. She had always been smarter than he was, and she had the talent of seeing the bright side of things — something most cops lost in their first few years on the job.

Rhoads and Teddy made it to the cabin in one piece. Once inside, too weary to find the linens and throw them onto the bed, he helped Teddy to the bed and then collapsed onto a crummy sleeping bag a previous guest had left on the floor.

In the middle of the night, he awoke, half the sleeping bag wrapped around him. He unzipped it, got in, and pulled it up. The cabin door, ajar, inched back and forth, creaking in the cool, mountain wind.

Rhoads rolled around, semiconscious, both sweating under the thermo-lining of the sleeping bag and shivering where his skin was exposed to the cabin air.

He fell back asleep to half-dreams of warm sun and fishing boats and the thumping putt-putt-putt of a diesel engine.

16

Amherst, Massachusetts
City Desk, *Amherst American*

"Carney!" Geoff Gavin, the night editor, screamed. He chomped his cigar so tightly his teeth met. "Where in the hell is Carney?"

Carney came sprinting from the vending machine area, two minutes into her first break in six hours. "Yes sir?" she said. She was an intern from the University of Massachusetts working general assignment.

"Where'd you get these tobacco facts for the tampering story sidebar?"

The girl looked nervous. "From the current almanac and from a UPI story. Is that all right?"

"You didn't tell us that. Always use attributions."

She nodded.

"Let me see," he said, scanning the story on the computer monitor. "Tobacco is a fifty-one-billion-dollar-a-year industry?"

"Yes, sir."

"Americans smoked four hundred and eighty-six *billion* cigarettes last year? You sure that's not four hundred and eighty-six *million*?"

"Yes, sir."

"Ninety-two percent of all lung cancer cases result from cigarette smoking?"

"Yes, sir."

The editor kept reading down the list she had prepared. "Now here's one I can't believe," he said. "'The cigarette industry continues to zealously dispute any scientific evidence that links smoking to health problems.' That's preposterous. What's your source on that? MAD magazine?"

"UPI quoted that Pratt guy from Old Carolina who testified earlier this year before the House Subcommittee on Health and the Environment. And here's another one I found in the *New York Times*. Just as absurd. Seconds after being told that users of snuff were fifty times more likely to develop oral cancer than abstainers, U.S. Tobacco's CEO said, 'Oral tobacco has not been established as a cause of mouth cancer.' They asked another guy if he knew that cigarettes caused cancer, and he said, 'I do not believe that.'"

"Who said that? Attributions!"

Carney flinched. "Um, Andrew Tisch of Lorillard."

"Okay," Gavin said, grinning. "Here's what we're going to do." Gavin screamed for the front-page man. "Fisher! Get in here!" A man appeared. "Fisher, what do we have for the first edition headline?"

Fisher held up a banner that read, "300+ CIGARETTE DEATHS."

"Good," he said. "Now, make me up a nice big box with bold black mourning borders. Lead with the Tisch quote about cigarettes causing cancer. 'I do not believe that.' Then Carney's cigarette facts beneath it — with the attributions. At the *Amherst American*, we always use attributions."

17

Tuesday, October 3. Early, a.m.
Deer Mountain, Pennsylvania

Around dawn, Rhoads went outside to check on the day. He could already feel the need for a drink. He knew that once he had been off it for a few days he'd sleep better, but now he was wide awake. He could hear Teddy snoring through the open door of the cabin and thought, *Yeah, sweet dreams, Teddy.*

He went back inside and made coffee. There was always coffee at the cabin, but he knew he'd have to go into town for food later on. He looked in the fridge and found three lonely beer bottles. He took them outside and threw them as far into the woods as he could. He heard one smash and nodded in satisfaction. Teddy was still asleep at nine, and with the beers gone, he couldn't get into any trouble, so Rhoads drove into town.

He bought enough supplies for three days. He planned on getting Teddy through the worst of the shakes and then checking him into a rehab clinic not far from where Teddy lived. He knew that a month there would wipe out a lot of the cash he had set aside for the boat, but there wasn't anything to be done about it. How he was going to keep the family in food and the mortgage paid in the long term was still a big, black question mark, but obviously things with Teddy were worse than Linda had told him, and family had to come first.

When he woke, Teddy was in turn sullen and ashamed. He tried to apologize a couple times, but Rhoads cut him off. "I don't want to hear it. Let's just get through this and then we can talk about all that idiocy."

"Fine," Teddy said and looked around for something to do. Rhoads knew that without the possibility of a drink, Teddy was suddenly faced with the long emptiness of the day and the days that would follow. Rhoads was feeling it too, but at least he had Teddy to worry about.

They made a big lunch, played cards, drank a lot of coffee and read the dog-eared paperbacks that had collected in the cabin over the years. They didn't say much to each other. Every once in a while Teddy would get up walk around outside. Rhoads kept an eye on him from one of the porch chairs. He had the keys and Teddy's wallet. Town was miles away, so he wasn't worried Teddy would make a break for it, not without any money, at least.

Over dinner Teddy said, "Dad would have hated this."

Rhoads swallowed. "Yes. But he would have understood. You know what he told me when I went to the academy? He said, "Watch out. It's in the blood."

He had said more than that, Rhoads remembered. *You're going to be a cop, so you're going to have some beer with your partner, with your friends. But you watch yourself. This thing, it's in our blood. You know what Uncle Mike is like. Man can't help it. That don't help his family, but it also don't make it his fault. Just something we got stuck with.*

"He said that?" Teddy asked.

"Yeah. Just like that. 'It's in the blood.' He had his own troubles, you know."

"What do you mean? Dad didn't drink."

"Not by the time you came. But before that, I think. I remember being four or five — you were a baby still — and him and mom fighting, really fighting. And then one day the fights stopped. And after that I never saw him take another drink."

"God damn. I always figured he just thought I was a screw up."

Rhoads snorted. "Well, maybe he thought that too. When you chucked your scholarship to spend two years crewing charters in Florida, he was pretty pissed. But I think he got it. Man worked hard his whole life to put food on the table, but you know dad. All he ever really wanted to do was go fishing and play the saxophone."

Teddy smiled and did an impression of their dad's voice: "Son, when your heart is right, the fish will come to you."

Rhoads laughed. He was happy remembering his father, and that made him want a drink. "Seriously, he used to tell me that —"

"I know! All the time. What does that even mean?"

Rhoads shook his head. "I have no idea. Never did. Maybe it's a metaphor. We get our hearts in the right place, things are going to work out."

"Shit, Tommy, I hope so."

The next day, Rhoads was outside trying to get the ancient riding lawnmower to start. He had left Teddy asleep in the bedroom, his breathing shallow and dark circles under his eyes. He looked up at the sound of a helicopter the way men always will and watched as it came closer. Soon enough he pushed the mower back into the shed. It was obvious the pilot was going to land it somewhere on the acres of tall grass at the front of the property.

The Old Carolina Tobacco, Inc. Bell Ranger landed a hundred yards from Rhoads.

The pilot, Jack Fallscroft, shut down the helicopter, jumped out, and crouched to make his way beyond the still-whirling blades. He reached Rhoads and shook his hand.

"Well, well, well. What have we here? This certainly is not a fishing trawler. No, I think I recognize it though. Oh, yes. Now I have it. Thomas Rhoads, also known as T.R. Hi, Tommy! Where's your boat?"

Rhoads had kept in touch with Jack when he quit working for Old Carolina. They had talked about the boat a few times, and Jack was all for the plan. "Sunk," Rhoads said. "Off Atlantic City."

"Sunk, huh? I think you projecting. You're sunk, T.R. A moron who quit the easiest, highest-paying job he'll ever have."

"I don't work for crooks. You know that. We're different in that way." He smiled. "I'm kind of busy here, Jack, so why don't I just tell you no and you can take Pratt's toy back to North Carolina or wherever you park it."

Jack waved his hand at the helicopter. "It's not right to make fun of my baby, T.R. It's like telling jokes about your mom. Who," he added, holding up a finger, "I banged last night."

Rhoads pasted on a smile. "My mom's dead. Anyway, it was great to see you, Jack. You can go away now. Actually, don't just go away. Go away mad."

"I would, except that Pratt summoned you. Can't go back empty-handed to the boss," Fallscroft said, reaching for a pack of cigarettes in one of his aviator jacket's zippered pockets.

"Why are you here? If I knew you'd come here looking for me I would have put a bag over your head last time you flew me up here."

"Best fishing in the whole area. I'm not likely to forget where it is." Fallscroft's tone turned serious. "Something not good happened, TR. They wouldn't tell me exactly what. Just said to dig you up, wring you out, and bring you back. Right away."

"Huh? What could have happened so bad that they'd send you to find me?"

"They want to talk to you about it in Asheville, T.R. It's big. It's FBI."

"If the FBI wants to talk to me, you tell them where I'm at. I'm kind of busy."

"What are you doing here?"

Rhoads squinted at the horizon. Jack was a good friend. It was time to quit screwing around.

"My brother. I'm helping him get back on the wagon. Couple days up here and then he's going to rehab."

Jack nodded slowly. "What about you?"

"Yeah, I'm off the bottle too." He held out his hand. It trembled. "See? Steady as a rock. So whatever Pratt wants, now's not a good time."

"What happened to the boat? You said you guys were finally going to do it."

Rhoads sighed and poked his thumb over his shoulder. "Teddy went to A.C. and lost his half. No boat. But I have bigger things to worry about now. He's in a bad way, Jack. I have to take care of him."

"I'm sorry to hear it, man. But you know that was coming for a long time."

Rhoads sighed again. "I know, but I thought the boat — you know. I'd be there with him all the time. We'd be doing something we always wanted to do, no shitty boss that makes you want a drink with lunch, you know? Well, no point in whining about it now. We're on to Plan B."

"I thought the boat was our Plan B."

"Plan C, then. Sorry you wasted your time, but I hope flying here cost Pratt a lot of money."

"All right, T.R., you want to know why I'm here?" Jack said. He took a newspaper out of his deep jumpsuit pocket, unfolded it to the headline, and held it for Rhoads to see.

A giant headline screamed:

CYANIDE CIGARETTES SLAY 341 ACROSS
U.S. 200 MORE SERIOUSLY INJURED
Doctors Say Many Are On Life Support.

"World's full of crazy people, Jack. What's this got to do with me?"

"This crazy must know you. He signed your name and Pratt's name on the letters that went to the dead people."

"Like I said, if the FBI wants to talk to me, they can drive up."

"Yeah, they could do that, but they're not going to buy you a boat."

"Quit screwing around, Jack. What are you talking about?"

"Pratt wants you on the case. He says you're one of the best, and he knows you can't be bought off, so he says he can trust you. He's offering $1,000 a day to run an internal investigation into why Old Carolina's being targeted. And if he's offering $1,000, you know you can drive him up to twice that, and there's a bonus if you catch the guy. See what I'm saying? Boat money."

Rhoads ran his hands through his hair. "Shit. Let's wake Teddy up. We need to make a stop on the way to see Pratt."

Two hours later they had landed at a small airfield in New Jersey. Linda was there to pick Teddy up and take him to rehab. She hugged him, crying a little. Teddy said, "I'm sorry."

Linda didn't answer him.

Rhoads kissed her on the cheek and said, "Try not to worry too much. We're going to fix this."

"If you say so. This is the last time, Tommy, I mean it."

"I know," he said. "Let's just get through this and see where we are. I have a plan."

Teddy came over to him and before he could speak, Rhoads said, "I'm sorry, Teddy. I have to do this thing. Just keep your head down, do your time, and we'll go boat shopping in a month."

"Thanks, man. I promise you I'm going to beat it this time."

"I know you will."

Jack waved to him and Rhoads got back into the helicopter. Jack had a short conversation with the tower and they were on their way to meet the company Learjet in Philadelphia.

18

Pensacola, Florida

It had taken Muntor two hours to find Oscar's, a coffee shop on the west side of town.

Good. The last one on the list, Muntor thought when he saw it from his car. He was spelling out a five-letter word and had already taken care of the other four.

He circled around and parked a block away.

Before getting out of his car, he reached behind the driver's seat and felt for the McDonald's bag, ostensibly filled with litter. He used it as camouflage for the various packs of cigarettes he brought with him. He grabbed a pack and looked at it.

Winstons. He slipped the pack into his jacket pocket, locked the car, and headed for Oscar's.

The short walk caused pain in his feet. He couldn't wait to get out of the size twelve shoes he had purchased and padded with terrycloth to make him appear inches taller than his five-seven.

Inside the busy little shop, a half-dozen customers sat at the counter. Most of the booths were occupied. Only one waitress and a cashier were visible. The cashier smiled at him.

"Pay phone?" Muntor asked in a deep voice.

"Sorry. Too many kids in here raising hell. We had to take it out." She pointed through the plate-glass window onto the street. "One right outside, though."

Muntor spun to see, as if he really cared whether a telephone was there. "Okay. Thanks," he nodded. He looked back and over her shoulder at a rack behind her. "How about a pack of Winstons then?" He pointed with his eyes.

"That I can help you with," she said and took down the white-and-red pack and set it on the counter for him. He paid her, said thanks, and picked up the pack with his right hand. As Muntor turned to leave, he made sure his left shoulder was blocking her view of his right jacket pocket. He dropped the pack into his pocket and, using only his Band-Aid-covered thumb and index finger, pulled out the other pack, the treated one he had brought in from the car.

"On second thought," he said, turning fully toward her, "mind if I get a pack of Carltons instead?" He put the Winstons on the counter. "They cost the same?"

"They're all the same except the generics," she said, handing him a pack of Carltons and returning the Winstons to the rack.

Muntor nodded again, pocketed the Carltons, walked outside, and faked a fast call at the pay phone.

19

FBI Headquarters
Tenth and Pennsylvania
Washington, D.C.

Brandon waited until the others left Franklin's office. "May I close the door, Oak?"

Franklin looked up from the stack of messages on his desk and nodded.

"I always thought Rhoads's personnel file from Old Carolina looked a little too clean," Brandon said.

"So you thought you'd dig up something negative."

"I did some research. There was a problem when he was a Philly cop. They kept it quiet, but some of it made the papers. Thing is, there's two stories. Sources in Philly P.D. say Rhoads was crooked and some people think he killed another cop, one Michael Flynn, who was going to turn him in."

"What's the media say? It's going to be a balmy day in hell before I trust Philly P.D."

"The paper said Rhoads was clean, and Flynn died in 'mysterious circumstances.' The investigation said suicide, but there are doubts."

"What did Rhoads say about it?"

"Nothing. He took his pension and went private. Some kind of deal was made, but it's hard to say if it was to protect the department or Rhoads, or both. A few years later he landed a consulting job with Old Carolina, worked there for three years and abruptly quit. I talked to some cops I know in Philadelphia. Rhoads was an exemplary cop before it happened. Supposedly a decent man, but it's hard to imagine that based on what we know about Rhoads today. Word is he's an alcoholic, shows up, does the job, and then goes home and drinks himself stupid."

"What's that about?"

Brandon said, "Looks like it runs in the family. He's got a younger brother, Theodore, and the guy's a mess. A couple DUIs and he just got fired from his job. Rhoads had a wife, and after she died, it sounds like he never got over it. A couple guys I talked to said before his wife died Rhoads spent every weekend as a Big Brother."

"Volunteer work for fatherless kids. I had a Big Brother when I was growing up in Columbus." Franklin pointed to the clipping. "What do you want to do with this?"

"Bury it in the back of the file?"

Franklin nodded and handed the clipping back to Brandon with an inward smile. He had never before seen any evidence that his subordinate had a heart.

20

Fully dressed and reclining on a saggy king-sized bed in the Beachwood of Pensacola Motel, Muntor snacked on nuts and celery while he watched CNN. The news anchor announced that the network was preparing a special report to air in half an hour on developments in the cigarette-tampering story.

"Courtesy of one Martin Muntor," Muntor added to the announcer's statement. He'd tune in then. He had seen all he needed to see for now.

Yet, he kept watching.

Then, a thought, a joyous, uplifting thought came out of nowhere. *Even if I drop dead here and now, they'll soon learn who did it and why. I've already succeeded. The rest of what I'm going to do? It's just icing. And now that the FBI's involved, they'll dig deep enough to find out what Big Tobacco's really been up to.* He smirked. Killing people who were killing themselves with cigarettes was justified — and a lesson the world needed to learn. But using an arm of the government that had protected the tobacco companies for decades to destroy them was an entirely different level of satisfaction.

Exhilarated, he flipped through the channels until he found another network working the story.

The images and sounds that came from the screen, the newspaper articles, the conversations he'd be overhearing in restaurants and in line at the supermarkets were the world's acknowledgment of his might. He tried to control the agitated thrill that rushed through him, excited as a kid running home from school on the last day of classes.

While he daydreamed, the television image switched from the head-and-shoulders shot of a news reader to a recorded shot of a swarm of reporters in a residential neighborhood.

"He's gone. He was the one who cared about me," cried an elderly woman grieving over a lost grandson. "Of all my grandchildren, he was the only one who visited." A crowd of reporters and cameramen hovered around her on a lawn.

"Oh, my!" Muntor said in falsetto, putting his hands up to his face in mockery. "If only he hadn't thrown his life away on cigarettes!"

The network cut to a reporter posing in the dusky light on the steps of the Lexington, Kentucky Federal Courthouse. He summarized what was known thus far in the investigation, but Muntor was too distracted by his own thoughts to hear it. The reporter then introduced a Kentucky State Police commander. Muntor listened attentively. The commander said tersely, "We can't say very much until our laboratory analysis identifies the substance we recovered from the crime scene."

"Oh, go ahead, tell us anyway!" Muntor said to the screen. "We're dying to know." He caught himself again.

The reporter promised more information as soon as it was available. Muntor's heart rate picked up when he heard that a press conference was scheduled in Washington later that day at 3:00 p.m.

Then the report ended and the network cut to commercials. Muntor's face fell.

He turned one of the shabby armchairs toward the picture window. Beyond the glass, his room afforded a view of Pensacola Bay, obscured in part by a Texaco station and its revolving sign. He watched the sun reflect a prism of color on the water. A humid breeze blew in from the Gulf of Mexico and jangled the wind chimes not far from Muntor's room. He was tired. The chimes annoyed him.

He dozed off for a moment, but his slouching position caused his chest to compress, and that made it nearly impossible to breathe. He straightened up, and his head cleared. The events of the preceding twenty-four hours marched through his mind like troops returning on a soggy road.

Muntor had taken a red-eye just after midnight from Philadelphia to Mobile. There he rented a car and drove the hour to Pensacola. The fake ID he used had worked perfectly, and paying cash for the airline ticket, car rental, food, and fuel wouldn't leave much of a trail.

The flying and driving, and finally the running around once he arrived in Pensacola, exhausted him. He had spent the hours after daybreak walking in and out of convenience stores and restaurants, dive bars, and supermarkets. The "W" and "Y," contrary to what his research led him to expect, were easy enough to find. He knew from the Free Library of Philadelphia's telephone book collection that there'd be plenty of "H"s and "D"s. The stumper, at least for most of the morning, had turned out to be the "O." When he finally met with success at Oscar's, he knew his salutation would soon be heard around the world.

Muntor was enjoying the mental travelogue and regretted not taping some of it for the documentary. Then yammering from some talk show that had replaced the news on television intruded on his thoughts. He got up, found the remote, and tapped a button a few times to lower the volume. He dropped onto the bed, rolled onto his side, and reached down underneath. His hand found the McDonald's bag containing his cigarettes and other supplies. He patted it like he'd pet his cat. Reassured, he rolled over again onto his back.

Fatigue tugged at him like an undercurrent, but he fought sleep. He wanted to be awake when the CNN report came on. He closed his eyes, hoping he'd rest a bit, but even rest wasn't available. Muntor could not stop thinking about what had happened at the office a few weeks earlier.

It had been a Tuesday. Tuesday was payday, and the New York brass of the American News Syndicate, Muntor's employer then, had decided to close its Philadelphia operation, laying off Muntor, who had served as an editor and beat reporter, and the rest of the five-person staff. Rumors had been circulating for months. Creditors pressured the company to close six of its thirty-six U.S. offices. New York assigned Philadelphia's responsibilities to the Harrisburg bureau.

The bad news came by telephone from the Information Services vice president.

"Marty, I'm calling you unofficially," Cal Timonowski said. "I have some bad news. Although we hate like hell to do it, we have to close the Philadelphia bureau. You'll be getting formal notice sometime next week. We know you've done one hell of a job, but we're in big trouble. Just this morning the *Denver Post* and *Sacramento Bee* both non-renewed us. I'm truly sorry, Marty."

Muntor listened and made no other comment than a deep rasping cough for a moment. He could picture runty Timonowski sitting in his office on Forty-Seventh Street with a list of calls that he needed to make before he could go home. He said, "I almost won a Pulitzer, you know."

"I know Marty, for the tobacco company piece. It was great reporting."

"For all the good it did. I handed them the truth, and nobody gave a shit. No trial, not even an inquiry. You think they don't know they're killing people?"

"I know it Marty, I hear you. It was a crime, but —"

Muntor knew this was why he didn't have friends at work, but once he started in, he couldn't stop. "They're killing people, and nobody cares. Not even the papers. All they care about is celebrity and political scandal."

"Well, look, Marty," Timonowski said, "I just wanted to call and tell you myself. You've done good work, and I didn't want you to find out in a letter. So look, I have some other calls —"

Muntor had almost hung up on him. He said, "Yes, I know." He knew the call, the one that savaged the only real accomplishment of Muntor's life, an exposé on tobacco companies that demonstrated they had known all along their products caused cancer, was just one minor item on that list.

At fifty-six they do this to me. Buggerers. He clenched his teeth. A tiny ripple of pain radiated along his jaw and up into his temples. He put his tongue between his teeth to force himself to relax the muscles in his face.

Timonowski kept talking. Muntor wasn't listening. Muntor had been the odd man out forever.

The best that Timonowski could offer was a take-it-or-leave-it early retirement package. In his case, with only seven years on the job, the deal amounted to monthly income of about $600 until age sixty-five. Then, good luck and Social Security.

"Sure. Sure, Mr. T," Muntor said, coughing again. "Whatever you say." Muntor had heard a rumor that ANS was in default of its health insurance premiums and that everyone was walking around without coverage. With what Timonowski was telling him now, maybe there was something to the gossip.

Timonowski wished him well. Muntor laughed and hung up. He cleared his throat and stared off into space.

It had been a struggle for his grandparents to send him to college. Although Muntor barely made it out with his journalism degree, he did it, and his grandparents were proud. His father, on the other hand, didn't bother showing up for graduation. It was probably for the best. Muntor was spared the embarrassment of what surely would have been the only boisterously drunk parent in attendance.

Muntor leaned out of the window thinking. *Two weeks' notice. I'll see them in hell.* He went into the break room, grabbed an empty cardboard box, and packed his things. He looked at the framed picture of his mother. *Why didn't I run for help? Why didn't I pick up the phone?* Loading it carefully on top of his other belongings, Muntor tried to shake the guilt.

He sealed the box with a few strips of tape and took one last look around. *Well, you were right daddy-o, I'm a loser. An unemployed loser.* Muntor hadn't attended his father's burial. There was no need to. They had been estranged for years. Muntor learned of his father's death when the obit came across his desk. *Survived by his only son, Martin, of Philadelphia, and two grandchildren.* Muntor had red-lined the sentence and replaced it with *No known survivors.*

Muntor had no idea where he would get a job or what he would do. He did a quick calculation. He owned the row house. It wasn't worth much in the deteriorating neighborhood, maybe $40,000 or $50,000, then again, actually selling it was a different matter. And thanks to his lifelong, grandfather-instilled habit of putting a few bucks from every paycheck into one mutual fund or another, he had almost another $40,000. Getting a job wasn't something he had to worry about right away. Realizing that, he relaxed.

Before he went to bed, he made a telephone call. He reached an acquaintance who supposedly knew about layoffs and health insurance and employee's rights. The man told him that it wasn't possible for ANS simply to terminate his health insurance with only thirty days' notice. The COBRA rules protected employees. But, the man warned, if Muntor had been procrastinating seeing a doctor, even for something minor, he had better get an appointment pronto.

"Get it checked out and onto the books," the man said. "Then, no matter what happens, your insurance company will have to take care of it."

Muntor had been coughing with increasing frequency, and something ached in his chest. Why not run up a bit of a tab while he still could? Stick it to American News Syndicate while he still could.

The next day he made an appointment on an emergency basis and subjected himself to an examination, a battery of tests, and X-rays. Three days later, a diagnosis. Stage 4 lung cancer. And a prognosis — he'd survive for six months at the most.

Pensacola rushed back in on Muntor like a wave crashing over his shoulders.

He had nodded off thinking about his unceremonious termination. He opened his eyes at the sound of the standard theme music that heralded a CNN Special Live Report.

He reached for the remote and turned up the volume.

21

En route to Asheville

At the Philadelphia airport, Fallscroft and Rhoads shook hands and separated.

In the Learjet, waiting to take off, Rhoads sat forward in the seat closest to the pilots. He was the only passenger. Rhoads guessed the pilots weren't told much about their mission, just that something big was going on and that Rhoads figured in somehow.

Rhoads made a few attempts to converse with the pilots but they weren't too responsive, so he buckled his seatbelt and settled in.

"How long is this flight going to take?"

"You have about an hour," the pilot said, checking his watch.

"Okay," Rhoads said. "Shout back and wake me before we get there." They gained on Asheville while Rhoads slept.

Fifty minutes later, the huge red-brick-and-glass edifice that was Old Carolina Tobacco, Inc.'s world headquarters squatted like an Aztec pyramid on a grassy hill in front of the Great Smoky Mountains. A minute before touchdown, they woke Rhoads. The Learjet landed on Pratt's private mile-long strip.

As the airplane taxied in toward the ground crew, the sun blinded Rhoads. He squinted and looked out at Old Carolina Tobacco, Inc. He wasn't quite able to believe he was back a year after quitting.

A minute later, Rhoads heard the banging of the ground crew as they clamped the exit ladder in place. The copilot got out of his seat and unlatched the door. It swung open.

Rhoads stood up, rumpled. "Thanks, you guys."

Rhoads exited and took the service elevator down to the Fitness Center in the basement of WHQ. He needed a shower and a change of clothes. He smiled, thinking he'd buy a couple nice suits and charge it to the company.

Twenty-five minutes later, when he stepped into the elevator in the basement en route to the fifth floor, Rhoads was dressed in the same clothes he had worn for three days, but at least he was clean-shaven.

22

Asheville

The fifth-floor lobby reeked of arrogance and power.

A full-sized marble replica of Blind Justice, the scales of which contained a display of Old Carolina's various cigarette brands, towered in the lobby, greeting visitors. Fifty feet of polished marble floor led to the reception desk. Two uniformed armed guards were stationed at either side, their posts manned twenty-four hours a day.

As Rhoads exited the elevator, three men brushed past him and entered. Rhoads then pushed through the huge plate-glass doors that led, on one side, to the board of directors' conference room, and on the other to an expanse of computer workstations.

In the workstation area were rows of file cabinets and a sign that read "Corporate Documentation Division." From an office beyond the computer workstations, Mary Dallaness entered, striding briskly, her wavy brunette hair cut short and bouncing as she approached. She moved with the quick grace of a dancer.

Rhoads hailed her, and she waved back. They had never had any official business between them but they knew each other through her brother-in-law and years of bumping into each other at WHQ. Once, Mary and Anthony Dallaness had invited Rhoads and a date over for the Fourth of July. It had rained like hell that day, he remembered.

"T.R.!" she said. "You quit. Without saying good-bye. And you never even called me."

Rhoads crossed the terminal area and greeted her with an affectionate one-armed hug. *If only she weren't married.* He didn't want to pursue that line of thinking. Her husband was dying.

"Okay. Goodbye," he said. And in a whisper added, "Spur of the moment thing, Mary D. Trouble with Pratt. But I'm back now for a little bit. They want some help with this guy who's killing people. Apparently he's distributing the product without a proper resale license."

She didn't smile. "It's nothing to joke about. We just heard six more of the injured died from complications. The company's a zoo, especially here in Documentation. I can't figure it out. Some lunatic starts killing people, and all of a sudden, everybody needs irrelevant documents that are years old."

Rhoads squinted. The cop in him reacted to something that didn't add up. "Archived documents? What kind?"

"What do you think? Level Three, naturally. The kind nobody can authorize but me. At three o'clock in the morning, at eleven at night. Any old time. And there's a certain redheaded party who's about one irritating telephone call away from ..." Dallaness stopped herself.

"Really? Who might that be?" Rhoads was aware that Mary knew he and Trichina had been together, and that she didn't like it. There had always been something between him and Mary, but as long as she was with Anthony, Rhoads wouldn't make a move. And still he felt bad about Mary's jealousy.

23

In Valzmann's room in the World Headquarters subbasement, an enormous array of color video monitors, green and amber lights, switches, reel-to-reel tape recorders, telephones, and other devices squatted on shelves and lined the walls.

Valzmann, who wore a tiny ivory stud earring in his right earlobe, stared without expression at Video Monitor #65. Without taking his eyes off the screen, he reached out and slid a glide switch forward, causing a ceiling camera on the fifth floor to zoom in on Rhoads and Dallaness in conversation. He tapped a key that activated a directional microphone as he pulled a headset over his ears.

The sound quality was tinny but audible. He clearly heard Dallaness's response to Rhoads's question.

"Your ex-boss, Trichina," she said.

"Don't worry about her," Rhoads could be heard saying. His back was to the camera. "She always likes to get her hands in everything. She's probably just trying to find an excuse to run to Pratt with some kind of brilliant idea. She may actually think she'll crack the case by reviewing the list of people who've been reprimanded for parking in the 'Executive Only' lot."

24

Rhoads grinned goodbye to Dallaness and walked back past the reception desk to the Executive Suite entrance. The two guards, formerly his subordinates, nodded.

As Rhoads moved toward the closed boardroom door, what could only be an FBI agent moved to block him. Rhoads attempted to squeeze by but was again blocked.

From inside the boardroom, Pratt opened the door and shouldered the agent aside.

"Rhoads," Pratt said. He ushered him in as if he were a VIP. The room was half the size of a football field and dominated by a long walnut conference table with dozens of matching chairs.

Clustered around one section of the table were Trichina and two FBI men. From a wall paneled in burled cherry, another two FBI agents removed a gold bas-relief sculpture of a tobacco leaf. In its place, they tacked up a huge map of the United States upon which Rhoads assumed were tampering death locations marked with bright red flags. Also on the wall was a giant enlargement of the counterfeit consumer-opinion survey letter the killer sent with the poisoned cigarettes.

"Good of you to join us, Thomas," Trichina said.

Rhoads ignored her.

Pratt turned to the FBI agents. "I'd like to introduce our former chief of security, Thomas Rhoads. He's broken off his vacation to be with us." The agents nodded, but Rhoads sensed that Pratt knew about Teddy and probably the boat, and he knew that put him at a disadvantage. Pratt introduced Franklin and Brandon. The men nodded at each other, but Rhoads didn't offer to shake.

"Have a seat, Thomas," Pratt continued. "These fine gentlemen don't believe it was you who sent the letter. Obviously you aren't, and have never been, in our marketing department."

"That's not even my signature," Rhoads said, staring at the letter with bewilderment. "Hell, I might not have the greatest handwriting, but I don't chicken scratch like that."

"Right now this investigation isn't focused on you. Handwriting samples run through analysis indicate it's not your signature," Pratt said. "We were just discussing a former employee. Loren Benedict." Pratt's eyes bored into Rhoads's.

Benedict had gone missing in the last weeks of Rhoads's employment with Old Carolina. He had had access to sensitive documents, and Pratt had sent Rhoads to Denver to find him. In the end, he didn't find Benedict, but he had learned enough to know he couldn't work for Pratt any more.

Pratt said, "The FBI has put him on their most-wanted-to-interview list. For one thing, they've discovered evidence that he received psychiatric treatment during the period that he was in our employ. It seems an improbable connection to me, but then I'm not an FBI agent."

Franklin spoke to Rhoads. "Perhaps you can help us. Information about Mr. Benedict seems to be in short supply. The fact is, there's no record of him anywhere after he left the company. Does this ring any bells for you?"

"I remember the job. There was nothing suspicious about Benedict except the way he left. Suddenly and without notice. Which doesn't strike me as a crime. It happens."

"Yes. It does happen," Trichina said. "Sometimes people just drop out." She shot a quick glance at Rhoads. "Don't they?"

Rhoads saw that Franklin had picked up on the static between them.

"I'm sure you're right," Franklin said. "But here's our problem. Employee files in your HR department list him as being the lead in a research project you all called 'Midas.' That's all there is in the file. No CV, no address, no performance appraisals. Nothing. And there's no explanation of what Midas is."

"I've told you," Pratt said. "Midas never went anywhere. Midas has nothing to do with this tampering problem. It was some pie-in-the-sky new product effort. These marketing guys have a thing about secrecy.

Whatever it was, it was a bust, believe me, or I'd remember it. We withdrew funding. That's probably why Benedict quit. The documentation division manager is looking for the Midas files now. Last year we had a computer blowout. That cost us a lot of archived data. We still have the hard copies, but they're not at our fingertips. You'll get them as soon as I do."

Brandon turned to Rhoads. "Do you have any recollection of the Midas project?"

Rhoads knew what to say. He had signed a confidentiality agreement with Old Carolina, and whatever he suspected, he couldn't say anything or he'd be sued until he had nothing. He turned to Brandon.

"I didn't have any contact with Benedict personally," Rhoads said. "At one point, after he left, we wanted to check his office. I went to Denver, boxed up his files, and shipped them to documentation for safekeeping. If anything had been missing, I'm sure I would have been notified to take follow-up action. But I never got any such call. That was the first and last of Midas, and Benedict, as far as I'm concerned."

"Then," Franklin said, "I guess we work on other ideas until your documentation people find the Midas files. Unless, Mr. Pratt, there's somebody here in Asheville or back in Denver who was involved with Midas."

Pratt tried to mask a sour expression. "I won't know who was assigned until our archivists come up with the files. I assure you, I'll have that information very shortly."

25

A cell phone chirped in Brandon's pocket. All turned to watch his reaction. As he listened, his eyes opened wider. To Rhoads, it looked like bad news.

Brandon mumbled something into the telephone, hung up, and pulled Franklin aside.

He looked at Franklin, who nodded that he could share it with the room. "Chief, two things just came in to FBIHQ. One's bad news. Five new deaths reported, and not FedEx envelopes — cigarettes sold over the counter. All in Pensacola, Florida. The field team says it looks like our man, not a copycat. The other thing may be good news. A man claiming to be 'Cyanide Sam' called minutes ago. The call came from Pensacola. Caller says he wants to talk to Rhoads. Says he's going to call HQ again at two o'clock."

Franklin nodded expressionlessly. He said something quietly to Brandon who in turn issued instructions to the other FBI agents in the room. Then Brandon left.

"I need to get back to Washington," Franklin said. "If you don't mind, I'll borrow Mr. Rhoads here so we can continue our interview in the air. He may know of some characters we should be talking to. And Mr. Pratt, Ms. Trichina, I'll trust you will call me as soon as you find any information about Mr. Benedict and the Midas project."

"Of course. Of course," Pratt said, "I understand. And, yes, take Rhoads if you think he'll be helpful. But might I have a word with Mr. Rhoads before you go?"

Franklin had Rhoads by the elbow and was already half a room away from Pratt. Rhoads, puzzled, looked back at Pratt and gave a small shrug.

Franklin turned back, too, still moving. "I'm sorry, Mr. Pratt. We're in quite a hurry."

"Yes," Pratt said. "I understand. Thomas?" He raised his voice to be heard by the departing men. "Give me a call as soon as you get a moment."

26

Asheville, en route to FBI Headquarters, Washington, D.C.

The pilot and Brandon sat up front. The Blue Ridge Mountains flashed by below. Franklin and Rhoads were strapped into two rear seats. Franklin glanced at Rhoads, who was looking out the window. He didn't know what the FBI really wanted, but he knew it wasn't his help with the case. The Feds didn't work that way. He had decided to go along for the ride. The payoff and the boat depended on it. He knew the FBI Director would come on friendly at first and then try to ambush him later, but he didn't mind. He knew how it worked, and he had nothing to hide.

"This thing's a real bitch, isn't it? Guy killing all those people. Makes me wonder," Franklin said.

"Doesn't make me wonder," Rhoads said, "People are out of their minds." He could as easily have said nothing, made Franklin work for it, but what was the point? He wanted to get to whatever Franklin planned on surprising him with as soon as possible. Let the man play his games. Then Rhoads would know what Franklin really wanted and he would be in a better position to know how to play it.

"Something I wonder about in particular though —" said Franklin.

"It's funny," Rhoads said, interrupting and looking around the interior of the helicopter. "Pratt's chopper is bigger, better, faster and has more range than yours. Costs two or three times as much. Now he has that, but he's not exactly running around trying to catch psycho serial killers and save lives. He uses his to pursue dollars."

Franklin went on. " — is why one of the world's preeminent CEOs, a guy who *Forbes* magazine says is worth a quarter billion dollars, would be so determined, I mean I'm talking about a smart guy who's facing the greatest crisis of his career — you with me on this, Rhoads? — would bend over backwards to press into service a total fuckup. Like you."

Rhoads smiled. Franklin had overplayed his hand. The FBI didn't hire stupid, and he didn't believe for a minute that Franklin believed anything that Philly P.D. or Pratt might have to say about him. Rhoads's record spoke for itself, and he wasn't going to be rattled by an offhand insult.

Franklin wasn't finished. "Can you explain that for me? I mean I can only think of about eight thousand more qualified guys than you that Pratt can have with the snap of his fingers."

Rhoads was starting to see where Franklin was going.

"I couldn't say," Rhoads said. "Maybe you should ask Pratt. Except Pratt's not the kind of guy that would tell you the time unless he got paid for it, and you don't have any leverage with him. He's got too many friends. Maybe he's friends with your boss, or your boss's boss. So no point in going to him for the truth. So what's your play? You looked at my file, and you made some calls. You can read between the lines, so you know that I'm not bent, no matter what Philly P.D says. But you figure you can make me think that's what you believe."

Rhoads raised his hand when Franklin opened his mouth to say something. "I got it — you heard I was a drinker. Maybe you talked to my lieutenant. He told you about how my wife died, and maybe my employees let something slip. You know the lieutenant's a piece of shit, and you know I did some reconstructive surgery on his head with a bat, so you know he's full of it. But you want me to worry, to think about all the bad things I've done. Cause I'm a drunk, and drunks have secrets. I start sweating now and you figure all you have to do is lean on me until I spill, and then you own me."

"Rhoads —" Franklin said.

"No, it's not a bad plan," Rhoads said, "The only problem is that there's nothing to hide. You know the truth about when I was a cop. I drink, but I've never done anything dumb while I was drunk, nothing you can use. You know about my brother — hell, you probably know about the boat, and you know I need the money. But sure as shit you know I quit consulting for Pratt because he's a crook. So really, what do you have? As I said, it's not a bad approach. But it assumes that there are skeletons somewhere in my closet, and there aren't."

"I don't think you're understanding me, Rhoads."

"Oh, I think I am, and I think you know it. But I don't mind. It's the same game I played every time I arrested some scumbag. Look — let's just skip to the end. You want to know why I'm here, why I signed on with Pratt, even though I know what he is. It's the money. You know that, but you think maybe there's more. I need the money. I have family to take care of. The deal is this: I help catch the guy, I get the money I need. If I have to work with Pratt or you to do that, I will. So why don't we just get to the part where you tell me what you want and threaten me if I don't agree to deliver. It's going to be real awkward if we don't finish this conversation before we land, and I have to tell you, I need a nap."

"You don't have a family, Rhoads," said Brandon. "You're wife's dead, and as far as anyone can tell, you haven't done a thing to keep your brother from falling into the bottle."

Franklin shot a severe look at Brandon and started to say something.

"I bet you're a good agent…"

"Special agent," said Brandon.

"See," Rhoads said, "there you go again. I bet you're a good agent. You're not stupid, and neither is your boss here. But you have to watch the older guys, read the signals. Franklin here knows that his plan just went out the window, but you're still a step behind. You think that insulting me is going to make me mad, make me say something that gives you an edge. But it's not going to happen. It's a game. You know it, and I know it. When we're done with this case, you want to say something about my wife — my dead wife — then we can have that conversation. You and me in the parking lot behind the Federal Building. But we both know that's not going to happen. And not because you don't think you can take me — you're wrong about that, but I wouldn't trust a man that didn't take that position — but because it's a game. So look, Special Agent Brandon, I admire the go-team attitude, I really do. But it's not going to work. So can we just get to the part where you tell me what you need?"

Brandon looked away, reddening. He looked at Franklin, and Franklin nodded. "I apologize, Mr. Rhoads. I was out of line."

"I accept, Special Agent," Rhoads said. "I get it. It's not personal."

"It looks like I misread you, Rhoads," said Franklin. "Let's start over."

"Sounds good," Rhoads said. "Let's start with the threat. What are you going to do to me if I don't do what you want?"

"Come on, Rhoads," Franklin said. "It's not like that."

Rhoads turned away and pillowed his head on his arm. "Okay. I'm going to take that nap. You can figure out how you want to play it while I'm out."

"God damn it, Rhoads," Franklin said. "All right: the killer put your name on the letters. Why? Are you helping him? Do you know him?"

"No and no," Rhoads said. "But you know that too. I mean, maybe I knew him. How do I know? I know a lot of people. But you know I'm not helping him. If you thought that, I'd be in cuffs. What else?"

Franklin thought for a moment and said, "It's Midas. Pratt's lying about it, and my gut says it's central to the case. We're not going to get anything from Pratt, and you're the only one who knows anything about it."

"That makes sense," said Rhoads. "Benedict didn't just quit, that much was obvious. He had some serious problems with whatever Midas was. I chased down every lead I could, but I didn't find any sign of him. That was the extent of my involvement. I don't doubt Midas is something Pratt doesn't want the FBI to know about, but I don't know what it was. I looked for Benedict, and I didn't find him."

"And then you quit. You're not telling me everything, Rhoads."

Rhoads nodded. "I don't have anything you can use, but I'll tell you what I think." He looked out the window to gather his thoughts. "Do you have a pretty good idea about how my business works?"

"You're a P.I., and most of what you do is chase the big-paying clients," Franklin said. "Corporate security, that kind of thing. But business hasn't been that good lately. You're taking on divorce cases, bottom-feeding to pay the bills. Getting the Old Carolina account was a big win for you."

"Right," said Rhoads. "You did your homework. So we do corporate security, risk assessment, but yeah, we also do skip traces, security for the rich, that kind of thing. When we don't have a big account, a lot of what we do is finding people. You know how that works?"

Franklin frowned. "Of course. You trace people. Credit card statements, interview friends and family, phone records, the whole paper trail."

"Right," Rhoads said. "That's what we do when there's nothing better. But when a client comes to me and says, 'I'm looking for whoever,' the first thing I do is a background check on the client."

"Why on the client?" Brandon said.

"Because it's not just bail bondsmen and jilted wives who want people found. Sometimes it's the bad guys, and if you locate people who don't want to be found, they could end up dead."

"That makes sense," said Franklin. "So you think Pratt wanted Benedict dead."

Rhoads nodded. "I do. I don't have any evidence of it, but Pratt's not as subtle as he likes to think. Maybe there are reasons to find a high-level employee who drops off the map. Maybe you want to make sure he's okay because it makes the board happy. Maybe you want to keep tabs on him in case he leaks proprietary information so you can sue him. But beyond a certain point, it's money down a hole. I looked for Benedict everywhere the leads took me. Flights, hotel rooms, paying snitches, you name it. Almost fifty thousand dollars in expenses on top of my salary, and nothing. But Pratt didn't want to quit. So I figured that he didn't just *want* to find Benedict, he *needed* to find him. In Denver, I saw Pratt's lackey Valzmann tailing me, and I realized I was the sucker. I was supposed to find Benedict, and Valzmann was there to deal with him."

"That's a serious accusation," Brandon said. "You're saying this Valzmann is a murderer for hire."

"Come on, Special Agent Brandon. You know what I know, most of it, and I know it. You know who Valzmann is. Pratt's got himself an attack dog that does off-the-books enforcement. Why don't you pick him up?"

Brandon looked at Franklin.

"You can't find him, is that it?" Rhoads said. "Well, I understand how you decided I was the weak link, but I don't know any more than that. Valzmann and Pratt are dirty, but I don't have anything for you. If I did, I'd be the first one to give it up."

"So you say," Brandon said. "But the fact remains that you're being paid by Pratt."

"And you know why I took the job," Rhoads said. "My brother's got problems. That's no secret. But he's my brother. I'm going to do what I have to so I can take care of him and his family. Pratt's paying the bills, but that doesn't mean he's my buddy. If we catch this guy — and that's wholly aside from your interest in Midas — I get a bonus big enough to buy my boat. So that's where I'm at. Now what do you want from me?"

Franklin cleared his throat. "We want you to help us catch the killer, but we also need you to report to us anything Pratt does or says that might help us run down the Midas leads. Maybe Benedict is our guy, and maybe he's not. But the FBI is interested in Pratt. He's hiding something, and we want to know what it is."

"I'll do what I can, but I don't know anything about Midas," Rhoads said. "If you guys are holding back, it's just going to hurt the investigation."

Franklin nodded to Brandon. Brandon took out a file and opened it. He said, "Old Carolina runs lots of projects, hundreds of them. This Midas thing, I guess, wasn't a very big one. Didn't work out, they cut off the funding, and it just went away. That's Pratt's story — everybody keeps telling me how big Midas wasn't. But it had a project roster of twelve scientists. Five of whom are PhDs. And an annual budget of $4.1 million. The real story, what we know of it, is this — Midas was a sixty month-long scientific study designed to determine the optimum level of nicotine dosage needed to insure and maintain addiction to cigarettes. Project technically successful. Officially terminated when project leader Loren Benedict threatened to reveal analytical data to various federal agencies."

Rhoads's jaw dropped. Brandon flipped forward a few more pages.

"Benedict disappeared January, two years ago," the FBI agent read, "three days after telephoning an official of the U.S. Department of Justice and agreeing to meet to discuss some sort of conspiracy-in-progress at Old Carolina. Only problem was, the guy never kept his appointment. The DOJ official wrote a memo and forwarded it to us. To date, we have insufficient evidence to pursue prosecution of any party."

"I can't say I'm surprised," Rhoads said, "So it looks like I was right."

Franklin nodded. "We think so. We think Pratt silenced Benedict."

Rhoads knew Franklin was avoiding accusing him of leading Valzmann to Benedict, and he appreciated it. Rhoads was happy with the thought that he would collect Pratt's money as well as help to put him away.

"You agree to avoid doing anything that will jeopardize my payday," said Rhoads, "and I'll give you whatever I can." He held out his hand to Franklin.

"Agreed," Franklin said. They shook.

Rhoads turned to Brandon. "You're not as much of a jackass as you want people to think. But you mention my wife again, and we're going to dance. Agreed?"

Brandon nodded and stuck out his hand. "Agreed."

27

Seacrest, Florida

In Seacrest, a suburb of Pensacola, Muntor entered the Mr. Turkey restaurant lobby. On the street, it was warm and humid. Inside felt better — the air conditioning made it easier to breathe.

Two pay phones were installed on the wall next to a rack of giveaway newspapers. Neither telephone was in use. Muntor went to one, dialed a long-distance number he had written on a three-by-five card, and when instructed by the digital voice, began dropping quarters into the slot.

He silently rehearsed his lines. He cleared his throat to warm up for the voice he planned to use. Muntor took note of the lightheadedness that accompanied the sudden rise in his blood pressure.

His chest ached, too, and he felt a swell, like indigestion, burning behind his rib cage. His hands and fingers quivered. Heat built up under his scalp, and a thin film of sweat developed on his forehead.

Muntor had cause to be excited. For the first time in his life, he was about to claim the upper hand. For the first time in his life, he wasn't a loser, no matter what his father and wife had always told him. He had something to teach the world, and he had the means to make sure they learned.

If Dad could only see me now.

28

Event Response Center
FBI Headquarters
Washington, D.C.

In the huge Event Response Center — the ERC — on the second floor of FBI Headquarters, a dozen special agents and half as many support personnel sat at computer workstations. They moved about with files and faxes and photocopies. One woman monitored the FBI telex terminal that agents called the hot line.

In another room nearby, Rhoads was being briefed and instructed by FBI forensic psychologists about what to say, and what not to say, to the subject if and when he called in. Agents and assistants answered telephones and made calls. Every few minutes one would dash from one end of the auditorium-sized room to the other with some urgent communication for one of the supervisors.

Two agents, their fingers working furiously at keyboards, were logged onto NCIC, the National Crime Information Center network. They were seeking matches on a series of known-violator variables that the Behavioral Sciences Section in Quantico and the Identification Section in Washington had prepared. Among the search targets were previous offenders in tampering cases, those who made threats of violence against corporations, and those who, by virtue of employment history, had access to dangerous chemicals.

That was just the start. As more field data became available, the search experts would be able to sharpen the focus of their queries by polling for matches on increasingly specific variables.

At a large conference table in the same room, Franklin and several other FBI officials sat talking. Telephones rang and support people answered them. When warranted, an assistant would tap the appropriate shoulder, fast whispers would be exchanged, and the call would be taken. For any call that was not urgent, pink callback slips were hastily filled out.

A telephone rang somewhere in the background. A moment later, an assistant rushed to Franklin's side and whispered to him.

Franklin stared down at the multiline telephone on the table as if it was a water moccasin. He picked up the line the assistant indicated and listened for a moment to the FBI switchboard operator.

"Okay, everybody, headsets on," Franklin said. "Here he is."

He waited several seconds for everyone to get the headsets in place. Then he spoke to the operator. "Put him through on line four."

A second later, a light began blinking above the fourth button on Franklin's telephone.

Franklin clenched his teeth. Then every discernible facial expression evaporated. He took a deep breath. Calls like this sometimes come only once in a career. He stood up, the telephone still pressed to his ear, and snapped his fingers hard, once, for silence. Everyone looked to him except the one he needed most, the communications tech busy at a terminal.

"Dan! Line four!" Franklin shouted. The tech spun around.

Franklin gave him a sharp nod and pointed with his free hand to the telephone, signaling the tech to trap the incoming call. The tech's hands grew busy at the keyboard.

Franklin put his finger on the line-four button but did not press it. He closed his eyes and slowly eased himself into a chair. Then he pressed the flashing light and was on the line with a man who, less than one minute earlier, had told the FBI switchboard that he was the person the papers were calling Cyanide Sam.

"Deputy Director Franklin," Franklin said, measuring his tone.

"Howdy, Mr. Franklin!" a hoarse voice said, almost jovially. A rush of vehicles in the background suggested an outdoor pay phone. That could be faked, was Franklin's immediate thought, and could be a sound effect.

A few feet away, the technician assigned to trap the call reacted to something that appeared on his terminal. He picked up a telephone and, pressing his finger against the screen so as not to lose his place, he spoke excitedly in quiet tones.

Franklin, distracted by the tech's activity, turned away and closed his eyes. "To whom am I speaking?" Franklin asked. "And how may I help you?"

"Oh, yeah, my name? Walter Winchell. I didn't know you were a comedian, too. Anyway, you'll want to know it's really me. Here's a hint. My salutation. Have you deciphered it?"

Franklin turned around to those monitoring the call. *What salutation?* he asked with his eyes and a hunch of his shoulders. Then to the caller, "I do not know with whom I'm speaking."

"I issued a greeting," the caller said, still speaking through a hoarse voice, "to demonstrate the lengths to which I am willing to go to accomplish my goal, which is to educate people about the value of the gift of life."

The man, whether or not he intended to, succeeded in confusing Franklin. "What do you mean by salutation?"

"By salutation I mean greeting. What else would it mean? Check the names of the establishments in Pensacola where people recently went to quit smoking. First letters only. But you'll have to add the letter 'O.' If the news is reporting it accurately, the little trick-pack I planted at ... at the mystery spot must have been a dud. Then you'll know I'm me."

He still didn't know what the caller meant. Franklin turned again to the people listening in. With his eyes, he asked them if they understood.

"Pratt got your tongue, Mr. Franklin?"

The caller had scored one against him. "No. I'm here, sir."

"Then, if you want to resolve this ... matter ... as expeditiously as possible, I'll want to talk to that fellow who works as a security executive at Old Carolina down in Asheville. His name is Thomas Rhoads. I'll tell him, Rhoads, what I'm up to. My advice is to get in touch with him right away and tell him I'll call back at this number at, oh, let me take a little ride now, say four p.m. sharp. Today."

"Sir, we have Mr. Rhoads here now, ready to..."

"How about if I stay on this telephone for another couple of hours, chatting with him? Would that be okay with you? Tick tock, four o'clock."

The subject hung up.

Franklin stood motionless.

"Let's have it," said one of the agents who had not had the benefit of a headset.

Franklin looked to the tech.

"A public telephone in Seacrest. Number 11 Lightwood Street," the tech said.

The communications computer had locked the location of the subject's telephone into the system the instant the tech tapped the appropriate key, but the system took another thirty-one seconds to find and display the exact address. The caller didn't stay on the line much longer. The call had been clocked at seventy-two seconds.

"He didn't want to stay on the line. He said he will call back at four today to talk to Rhoads," Franklin said.

Franklin then turned to address everyone in the ERC. "Here's what the caller said." He paraphrased the conversation. "He said, '… you'll want to know it's really me. Did you decipher my salutation?' and then, '… check out the first letters of the places in Pensacola where people went to stop smoking, and add the letter "O" because that one must have been a dud.' Then he said he will call back here at four p.m. today."

Then, much louder, "Damn it!" Franklin slammed his beefy hand hard and flat on the conference table. The Director, who had entered the room during the call and stood behind Franklin, jumped back, startled at the outburst.

Franklin saw the movement, then realizing it was the Director, quickly said, "Excuse me, sir."

People began scribbling on pads and scraps of paper, asking each other about the different names of the retailers who sold the Pensacola cigarettes.

"W-H-Y something?" a female agent proposed, working from her seat at the Serial Criminal Profiling Section terminal.

"'W,' Wilkens Pharmacy. 'H,' the Heart and Soul Bar, 'Y' for the vending machine at the YWCA. What was the other one?"

"Davidson's, the grocery," someone said.

Franklin, standing now, listened. He said, "And then add an 'O,' he must have planted one in somewhere that begins with the letter 'O,' only no one smoked it."

"Yet," the Director said and turned to an agent. "Eddie, get on the phone. Let Pensacola PX know there may be a live pack out there in some establishment whose name begins with the letter 'O!' Then put a summary of what just transpired on the hot line. ASAP. I'm not happy about releasing the details, but we may save a life."

Everyone in the room doodled on pieces of paper for the next minute until the agent who suggested "W-H-Y something" sent a chill up the spines of everyone in the room.

"I think I have it," she said hesitantly. "At first I thought it could have been an interrogative — 'WHY DO?' But I'm afraid that's not it. I think it's in this order. Heart and Soul, then the 'O,' Wilkens, Davidson's, and then the YMCA. This guy, whoever he is, he's greeting us. He's saying 'HOWDY.'"

"Howdy?" Franklin asked almost inaudibly. His brow furrowed like he was trying to remember something. Then he rose from his chair, slowly, like a time-lapse film clip of a daffodil sprouting. "Howdy?" he repeated slowly. "Howdy? Like in hello?"

No one answered him.

To the Deputy Director with twenty-three years of experience, the one-word salutation sounded like a message from a madman indulging a freshly whetted appetite.

29

Association of Tobacco Marketers
New York

At Franklin's directive, a special agent in Washington called W. Nicholas Pratt and told him what the FBI had learned about the Pensacola incidents. At the end of the conversation, the agent was to inquire about the status of the search for the Midas Project files.

From Pratt's perspective, the Pensacola incidents were good news. The FBI had reason to believe that none of the tainted cigarettes were Old Carolina products, though that left the question of why Pratt himself was being targeted by the maniac.

"We're almost there," Pratt said to the agent's question about the files. Then he hung up.

Pratt called Bill McGarry in New York. McGarry served, at Pratt's whim, as the executive director of the industry's effective trade and lobbying group, the ATM, the Association of Tobacco Marketers.

"We have a serious, serious problem, Billy," Pratt said. "You've got to call the others. The FedEx thing was bad enough, but at least it was self-contained. People only had to avoid cigarettes that were delivered. Now with the Pensacola deal, we're going to have the FDA or the ATF or some other agency pulling cigarettes off the shelves. In Pensacola, the guy used brands from four different manufacturers. I was left out this time. That is no accident. The guy's showing us he'll target whoever he wants. Plus, my common stock is off another two points."

Someone entered McGarry's office, interrupting him. "Not now!" he said. Then, back to Pratt. "Okay, I'm sorry, Nick. Go on."

"Anyway, my damage control man here thinks we can get a recall restricted to Pensacola itself, maybe the county, or at worst, northwestern

Florida. And possibly for just a few days. I want you to call the other CEOs. Organize an invisible meeting. And I mean invisible. We can't have the public, and especially this lunatic, seeing us circling the wagons. If any of the others give you any friction about attending, tell them it's my idea. Tell them to fantasize about a nationwide product recall across all brand lines. They'll show."

"I imagine they will, Nick," McGarry said.

30

Pensacola, Florida

Two senior FBI agents boarded a United commuter flight in Washington and landed a little after 2:30 in Pensacola. They were met at the airport by Special Agent Lewis from the FBI's Pensacola Resident Agency office. An unmarked Florida Highway Patrol car and trooper sat in the Authorized Vehicles Only lane waiting for them.

"The FBI doesn't have access to its own vehicles in Florida?" one of the men from FBI Headquarters asked.

"Yes sir, but my van is being used as surveillance on another job," Agent Lewis said. "The corporal here has kindly offered to escort us today."

Twenty minutes later, the four men pulled up to the prefab three-bedroom house on Avelina Court. Two unmarked cars blocked the entrance to the driveway. Just beyond them, flowers and framed photographs marked a spot on the asphalt. The news crews had been kept back half a block under some thin crime-scene pretext.

Earlier that morning, Jack Stein, fifty-five, a chain-link fence installer, had lived there with his family. By 11:00 a.m., he was dead.

Stein, the first known HOWDY victim, had purchased a pack of Kools after supervising a tricky fence installation at an under-construction residential development in Sunaville. Local police had learned Stein's wife and two daughters had been hounding him for years about smoking. He had ignored their pleas to quit. Instead he promised he would quit smoking inside the house.

For weeks, he had faithfully kept his word, standing with one hand in his pants pocket, smoking openly in the driveway.

Stein's wife thought the display had been designed to elicit some guilt from any family member who happened past the large kitchen and living room windows that looked out onto the lawn and driveway. The first evening that Stein's own home had become one large no-smoking section, his family made him a dinner of steamed lobster and sautéed asparagus, his favorites, as a show of support.

The corporal stayed in his vehicle, and the three FBI agents walked up to the house, pausing briefly to look at the spot where Stein had died.

Lewis knocked on the front door of the residence. A young woman answered, dressed in shorts and a Grateful Dead T-shirt. The men identified themselves, and she immediately began talking.

"Daddy died right there where we set those flowers in the driveway," his daughter Donna said, tears building, pointing over the agents' shoulders. "If we hadn't a hassled him so bad, he might have taken sick right inside, where we could have called 911. I think me and Mom and Mary are as guilty as the man who did it to my dad."

"But you couldn't have helped your father — you weren't home at the time. That's what we understand," Agent Lewis said.

En route from the airport, Lewis had shown the other agents the crime-scene Polaroids and the initial incident reports. Stein's face and extremities had turned cobalt blue, and he died with his mouth open, gasping for air.

"Cyanide does that. You can breathe air in, but your lungs don't absorb any oxygen," the corporal had said on the way over. "Did you ever watch a fish flop around in the bottom of a boat trying to breathe?"

"Well, it might have turned out different if we would have left him alone," the teenager said. "Is smoking really that much of a crime?"

Lewis asked Donna if she could think of any reason why someone would want to hurt her father.

"I don't know anything that I haven't already told other detectives."

"Donna, sometimes you can know something that doesn't pop up in your head right away," one of the men from Washington said. "Like when you have a dream and forget about it until something happens during the day that reminds you."

"That's why we want you to call us, anytime, even in the middle of the night, any day of the week, if something does remind you of something you think may help us. You just call my number here, collect." The agent took a card from his inside jacket pocket.

"Okay, I'll put this with my collection," she said, reading the card and running her finger over the gold-embossed FBI seal. "Can I tell you something about my daddy?"

Lewis nodded.

The wet in Donna's eyes ran in rivulets down her cheeks.

"My daddy couldn't read anything harder than a stop sign. But when me and Mary were little, he wouldn't let one night pass that he didn't read us a storybook. He did it just by looking at the pictures and making up words to go with them."

Back in the car, the corporal asked the FBI agents if they learned anything they didn't already know. His intent, most likely, was to determine if the two men from Washington succeeded in finding anything his own organization had missed.

"I think we are beginning to see that these murders are random. No pattern, just a lunatic with a chip on his shoulder."

The corporal said, "Yeah, if there was anything to get, we'd a got it first time around. In a case like this, everything gets quadruple-checked."

Most cops love to rub it in to the FBI when they get a chance.

31

Franklin ordered a surveillance team to observe the pay phone in Seacrest at the site where the first call originated. Getting lucky there would be a thousand-to-one shot. Chances were slight that the subject would use the same telephone for the second call, but missing him if he did, Franklin knew, would be unjustifiable.

If the caller was not the actual perpetrator, but instead a malicious prankster, then he could conceivably be naive enough to think that it would be safe to call from the same place. Or, if the man who called was in fact the subject but was deranged or delusional, he might arrive at the conclusion that the FBI did not know where the call originated, and he might use the same telephone again. Most psychopaths, however, are paranoid. Neither scenario was very likely.

"Still can't locate Sorken," an agent informed Franklin.

"Well that's nice," Franklin said, rubbing his eyes with the heels of his hands. "Try the locals."

Dr. Myron Sorken, a forensic psychologist widely published in the field of linguistics and dialects and on the staff of the psychiatric board at Johns Hopkins University in Baltimore, could not be reached at his office or his home in Columbia, Maryland. Franklin had wanted him present for the first call. Now Franklin wanted him to hear the tape of the call and to hear the second call, if it came. Once, Sorken had successfully listened through a kidnapper's feigned southern accent and directed investigators to focus on suspects whose early language development had been in the Great Lakes region. One of a score of suspects in the case had attended elementary school in Benton Harbor, Michigan, and that suspect turned out to be Mr. Right.

The FBI asked the Columbia police to find Sorken. Two city detectives worked quickly and located him at the Rosewood Golf and Country Club not far from his residence. Sorken was sped by the detectives to a service station near the Beltway where he jumped into a waiting FBI sedan for the rest of the trip to FBIHQ.

Others, experts in product tampering, serial murder, schizophrenia, and other disciplines, were being contacted and rushed to the ERC as rapidly as possible. Franklin wanted to have a big congregation on hand at four o'clock. He realized there wasn't much that could be done with such short notice. Various special agents briefed the invitees as they arrived. Many experts had not yet been located, but Sorken was the one Franklin desperately wanted.

At 3:35 p.m., Franklin and the Director entered the room to join the group of nearly forty FBI agents, staffers, and consultants. They stood at the head of the room, stern-faced and greeting no one. Franklin saw Rhoads at the edge of the room, keeping his own counsel but watching the others carefully.

The Director tapped the microphone. "Being called in like this without notice is a terrible inconvenience, I know. We are grateful you could make it," the Director said without introducing himself. "The FBI appreciates your presence, and so does the president of the United States, with whom I just spoke. He asked me to thank you personally for interrupting your lives to help save others. That's a quote. But enough of the preamble. Let me get out of everyone's way. Most of you who have worked with us before know Deputy Director Oak Franklin."

The Director moved back. Franklin stepped forward and cleared his throat. "Good afternoon. We are calling this investigation CYCIG, as in cyanide cigarettes. The individual whom we believe is responsible for the hundreds of tampering deaths thought he would give us a call this afternoon. Our preliminary profile of him can be found on your information sheets. I spoke with him myself, by telephone, less than two hours ago."

A murmur rolled through the room.

"Ladies and gentlemen, this man, again if it is him and we think it is, is a cold, casual killer. He spoke to me as if he were ordering a pizza. He was calm and flippant. This case presents numerous complications for us, and one of the most frustrating aspects is that the subject has a practically limitless window of opportunity. About fifty million packs of cigarettes are smoked every day, day in and day out, in this country. That's approximately one billion cigarettes daily.

"The problem is this, it would be almost impossible to apprehend a litterer who did not want to be caught. And by dropping a pack of sodium-cyanide-injected cigarettes here and there, this subject is not doing much more than littering. All he has to do is be patient and cautious. An apprehension during the actual commission of the crime, unless we get extremely fortunate, is remote. We're going to have to take this one by figuring out who he is. That's why you have been called here."

The Director nodded in agreement behind Franklin.

"What we hope to get from you are your subjective observations for the purpose of enhancing our SCRIPS profile of him. For those of you haven't helped us before, SCRIPS is our new artificial intelligence Serial Criminal Profiling System. Anything you can contribute about age, mental status, educational background, regional clues from voice and language, all are incalculably valuable.

"Don't be bashful about wild guesses, intuitive feelings, gut reactions. We want, we need, them all. Candidly, we are all hoping his stated agenda, 'to save lives,' is the setup for an extortion attempt against the tobacco industry. At least then we could look forward to an eventual point of contact. Without that, we will have to rely on our Investigative Support Unit, the Behavioral Science Section, supported by the SCRIPS system, and what you, our consultants, can contribute."

A multiline telephone and headset sat in front of everyone present. Another dozen or so telephones were at the far end of the table.

Franklin glanced at his watch. "We have about twenty minutes until four o'clock, the time the subject said he would call. In the first call, he spoke in a gruff voice, probably contrived. Some of you have already heard the tape of that call. As far as we can determine, the subject didn't attempt any other voice modification. He called from a public coin telephone in a Mr. Turkey at 11 Lightwood Street in Seacrest, Florida. The telephones are in an alcove between the street and the dining area. Restaurant employees pay little attention to people on public phones, and not surprisingly, none of them specifically recall seeing anyone use the phones. We have a team on the scene now, just in case."

Franklin looked around the room. "What we'd like you to do is this. You will all remain here in this room with headsets on. The subject told us he wants to speak to Thomas Rhoads, a security official for Old Carolina, headquartered in Asheville, North Carolina." Franklin introduced Rhoads with a quick nod. "Mr. Rhoads is a former Philadelphia Police officer and had some media attention due to his work there. Following retirement, he spent three years working as a security consultant for Old Carolina. Ironically, it is that publicity that may have led the subject to target the company. There's also the possibility that he and Mr. Rhoads may know each other.

"Rhoads will take the call in Lab C on this floor. That's down the hall. You can feel free to speak among yourselves. Any urgent ideas, notes, or questions you have during the call should be written down as quickly as possible. Staffers will be in the room with you. Hold your pad up in the air, and someone will bring your comment or question in to me immediately, though it's not likely the caller will stay on the line long enough for us to evaluate your ideas and use them. In the first call, he hung up after seventy-two seconds elapsed. We hope he planned on no more than sixty seconds but let himself get carried away. That tells us he may not be in complete control of himself. That's better than being up against someone with the precision of a Swiss watchmaker."

Franklin sipped from a cup and cleared his throat again.

"Any questions?"

32

Fifty yards away in Lab C, Behavioral Science Assistant Section Chief Juan Estevez advised Franklin and Rhoads on strategy for the expected call.

"The best thing to do is to go with your gut, Oak. These are just general guidelines," Estevez said. "Picking up the telephone the instant it's transferred to you demonstrates a posture of urgent attentiveness. I don't think we want to be that servile. Especially with a guy like this. Waiting for two or three rings communicates a concerned but casual interest. Answering in the four- or five-ring range suggests a nonplussed attitude about the caller's status. Not a good idea. I recommend you pick her up on the third ring."

Franklin, listening to Estevez and doodling on a notepad, wrote the numeral "3." He drew a series of concentric circles around it until no more could fit on the page.

Rhoads peered over at Franklin's pad. "Feeling a bit boxed in, Deputy Director?"

Franklin frowned, his brown face growing darker. He dropped the notepad on Estevez's desk.

"These are circles, Rhoads. Boxes are square."

"Same difference," Rhoads said. "Anyway, your caller's probably thrilled about what he's accomplished so far. But he's put a hook in his own mouth. Best not overexcite him until it's to our advantage. Let's let him run it out a bit."

33

Pensacola, Florida and Washington, D.C.

At 4:03:16 p.m., Muntor picked up an outdoor pay phone and dialed the FBI Headquarters number he had now memorized.

When the telephone company's simulated female voice requested $1.85, Muntor began dropping quarters into the slot with his white-gloved hand. Nervous, he lost count of the coins deposited.

"Thank you. You have forty cents credit toward your call," the voice said.

The call came into the switchboard and a telephone center supervisor switched it to Franklin in Lab C. The telephone began ringing.

Franklin picked it up midway through the third ring.

"Deputy Director Franklin."

"Hello!" The voice was gruff again, the tone familiar, but different this time.

"To whom am I speaking?"

"Howdy, Deputy Director." The distinct whine of a tractor trailer flying by. "Rhoads present and accounted for?"

"Yes. Would you like to speak to him now? I know he wants to speak to you."

"Time's a wasting. Eleven seconds down the drain."

Franklin nodded to Rhoads, who pressed the button putting him on the line. Franklin tapped the receiver button to make an audible click but stayed on the line to listen.

"This is Tom Rhoads. They call me T.R. Hello."

"Mr. Rhoads. Thanks for coming."

"You're welcome. Do I get a name to go with the voice?"

"When I let you arrest me, I'll show you my driver's license, but until then, the name's Virgil. Now, listen up. I can't stay on this line gibber-jabbering with you all day." The caller's pace quickened. "We're going to launch a little public awareness campaign, you and me. You watch — it'll be quite educational. Now, what I want to do is this. I want to make a trade. I'll cancel the next event I've planned if you can get your boss, W. Nicholas Pratt, to do me a little favor. I need him to make a personal appearance. Help kick off the campaign. Tomorrow night. He'll have to spend some of the company dollars, though."

While the man who called himself Virgil continued his prepared speech, the communications tech spoke quietly to someone on the other end of his telephone.

"The Denny's at service plaza I 2-N, southbound on the interstate, north of Pensacola," he said to a Florida Highway Patrol dispatcher.

Rhoads listened to Virgil.

"... and he'll need to buy sixty-second spots on ABC, CNN, CBS, ESPN, MTV, and NBC." The caller was speaking so fast he was slurring words together, not sloppy, like a drunk, but hurried. "At nine o'clock p.m. It doesn't have to be precisely nine, but it should be within a few minutes. Don't keep me waiting long. I'm one guy you don't want to piss off. I'll be a big star burning bright while I'm waiting, and I don't wait patiently. I want to hear him, Pratt — no spokespeople, you understand? — read aloud an excerpt from page 345 of *The Surgeon General's Smoking and Health Report to the Congress, Third Revised Edition*. He's to read the third full 'graph on that page. It enumerates how many lung cancer deaths there were in the U.S. last year and then goes on to state that ninety-two percent of all lung cancer cases result directly from smoking. This ... this reading, constitutes Pratt's confession on behalf of the entire industry. And it must be delivered that way. Solemnly, contritely."

Everyone in the room listened silently.

"I've timed it — it can be read easily in under a minute. Now, let's say Pratt balks. We got trouble, big trouble. I go to plan 'B' — something I like to call 'Back to School Night.' Whoa! I'm looking at the second hand on my watch." Virgil spoke even more rapidly now. "Let me tell you something, Mr. Rhoads, they say that in life, pain is mandatory, suffering is optional. I like that saying. Don't you? Here's how that concept applies to us. See, I have got a grand finale planned for all of this, something spectacular, a little ways down the road. It'll make the Kuwaiti oil field infernos look like campfires. That's pain, the mandatory part. That will happen. But this 'Back to School Night' thing? Hell, we don't have to go through all that. That's an optional one. And it's Nick Pratt's choice. We'll see what he does. But I warn you, Mr. Rhoads, you won't like 'Back to School Night.' That much I guarantee. That is all."

An FBI agent handed Rhoads a note.

He paused half a beat to read it.

"Mr. Virgil, what do you mean by 'Back to...'"

"It's not Mr. Virgil, jackass. Are you Mr. Tom? It's just Virgil. Don't make that stupid mistake again, because I can spell 'RHOADS' as well as I spelled 'HOWDY,' except that one extra poor son of a bitch will die. R-H-O-A-D-S."

The sound of the subject's voice and the rush of background traffic ceased suddenly with a solid click. A dark quiet, as thick as night fog, eased out of the telephone and into all the listeners' ears.

Rhoads said, "He's a writer, maybe an editor or reporter."

"What," Franklin said. "How do you know?"

"He said 'graph' instead of paragraph. It's journalist jargon. I had a source in Philly, a reporter. He loved to say graph instead of paragraph to let me know he was a pro."

Franklin turned to Brandon. "Make sure that's in the profile. Narrow the search. Find Virgil. Find Virgil."

34

Dozens of state troopers' cars, lights flashing, sirens screaming, roared toward the Denny's. Emergency vehicles swerved past motorists, careened across tree- and shrubbery-lined medians, accelerated up both exit and entrance ramps.

Troopers and rifle teams boiled from the vehicles, surrounding the plaza and closing in on a bank of telephone booths. A helicopter arrived, but the commander ordered it back. Its rotors chopped so loudly the men on the ground had difficulty hearing their radios.

Police took up tactical positions, terrifying confused civilians.

In one of the phone booths, the handset of a telephone dangled, swaying in the breeze.

Florida Highway Patrol, Pensacola police, and FBI agents used dogs and helicopters to scour the service plaza and an adjacent gas station and surrounding woods. They immediately erected roadblocks on all highways within a fifteen-mile radius of the pay telephone.

Zero.

35

FBI Headquarters

Franklin slammed down the telephone. "We missed him."

"Oak," Brandon said. "Something here you ought to hear. This is Dr. Ertmann. Doc?"

A rail-thin, gray-haired man in a three-piece suit seated in a wheelchair rolled up and turned to face Franklin.

"You the top man?" the doctor asked in a nasal squeak.

"No, but in this investigation, I'm the next best thing," Franklin said, barely looking at the man. "To me Director of the FBI is the top man."

"Right," said Dr. Ertmann. "I don't want to be telling this story to lots of different guys. I'll say it once, do with the information as you see fit. I've been a respiratory specialist for forty years. Let me speculate and make a diagnosis based on what I've just heard. This Virgil fellow? He is, in all probability, in a very late stage of malignant carcinoma of the upper respiratory system. You send a copy of the tape of that phone call to my office, and I'll have some fellows listen to it, see if they get the same thing I did."

"Take it from the top in English, Doctor. Are you telling me he's dying?"

The doctor nodded.

"How soon?"

"Can't say. Could be very soon, could hang on for a couple of years."

"Which team would you bet on?"

The doctor thought for a minute. Franklin waited, desperate to hear good news.

"Well," the doctor said. "I'll tell you. Wild guess only. His shallowness, the faint wheeze, the suppuration, the way he stridulates. Let's put

114

it this way. I own stock in CIGNA, the insurance company. For this guy, I wouldn't want them to write a life insurance policy."

Everyone within earshot in the ERC listened and absorbed the information. Tentative smiles became broader as the implication sank in.

"Could it happen inside of a week?" an agent asked.

"I said I can't say. Possibly, but that's a little too ambitious. But, in light of the strain he's under, it could happen quickly. But I couldn't say how long even if he were sitting here in my lap. If I'm right, and I usually am, it'll take him very fast from here."

A couple of agents at the periphery of the crowd around the wheelchair-bound physician erupted spontaneously in shouts and cheers. Franklin glowered at his subordinates, and they immediately calmed down and assumed straight faces.

He looked at Rhoads, and Rhoads nodded at him. He said, "We're getting closer. He's careful. He's a planner. But since he's obsessed with bragging about what he's been doing, he can't help but give us clues every time he calls."

"Rhoads is right," Franklin said. "Whatever we have to do to get him to call, we'll do it."

36

Philadelphia

Muntor arrived home after his flight from Florida nearly incapacitated by exhaustion.

In his second-floor bathroom, his video camera sat perched on a tripod straddling the sink. A tiny red LED glowed next to the power button and the videocassette inside rolled silently, recording the scene.

The lens pointed at an ornate, claw-foot bathtub in the middle of the tiled room, bolted decades ago into the floor. Next to the bathtub, Muntor had placed a three-legged wooden stool.

The bathtub was surrounded by a ring of candles in red globes.

The candlelight drenched the room in the color of blood.

Minutes earlier, before beginning to film, he had cradled the camera in his arms like a newborn. Then he turned it on and held it up to his eye and slowly panned the room, preserving every detail. He had recorded the images of an orange crate just outside the ring of candles, piled high with newspapers, newspaper clippings, *Time, Newsweek, U.S. News & World Report*, and others. The one visible page showed a screaming headline about the cigarette murders. The camera's microphone had picked up Muntor's labored breathing and the musical tone of his wheeze. Between breaths, the mike recorded the steady dripping of a leaky faucet at the sink.

Muntor stopped recording and screwed the camera into the mounting on the tripod. After adjusting the angle, he flipped the switch back to "On." With the camera rolling, Muntor walked into the shot. It had been only five days, yet he appeared more emaciated than in the first scene he shot of himself preparing the seven hundred FedEx envelopes. His thin hair was even longer, and he was wearing nothing but baggy

116

white jockey shorts. His features were twisted, his skin stained by the candlelight.

Later, Muntor would hold pages of script in a shaky hand and record the text over this scene.

"Act II. Scene Four. The Anointing ... The One who has chosen himself has also chosen to wreak vengeance for the murdered millions. He must be initiated on his path. There can be no return. The commitment is final. The self-chosen one must be strong. Only sacrifice will convince the many to change their lives."

The next shot, Muntor would later see, came from another angle and showed him walking into the bathroom carrying a large plastic bucket of ice. He dumped it into the water-filled tub. He reached back and pressed a button on a boom box. He got in the bathtub, showing no sign of reacting to the cold, and sat down. Strains of music rose from the boom box and Muntor reached toward the wooden stool. Again using the remote, Muntor clicked off the camera.

The next camera angle was not perfect. Some of Muntor's figure was too far to the right and out of the frame. What could be seen most of the time was Muntor's arm being tied off with rubber tubing. From a paper bag on the wooden stool, he took a syringe and held it up to the candlelight to see it better. The camera showed it filled with milky-white liquid. Muntor jabbed a bulging vein in the middle of his inner elbow. The plunger sank slowly.

A tentative serenity grew across Muntor's face as the drug rush caused synapses to fire riotously. At the same time, the music reached its crescendo. Muntor, filling with numbness and energy from the Biphetamine and Dilaudid combination, began to straighten up, giving the effect of levitation, as if drawn erect by the ecstatic surge of energy. He stretched his bony arms out. He raised them slowly and evenly until he held them straight up, fingertips stretching for the ceiling. Then he brought them back down, again, slowly, steadily. When they reached his sides, he repeated the motion. All the way up, all the way down. And again. And again. Each time, faster and faster and faster until it became clear what he was doing.

He was flapping. His wings. The ice sloshed around in the bathtub and splashed over the side as Muntor maniacally flapped and flapped, trying to become airborne, paradoxically levitated by the effect of the drugs and weighted down by the cold of the ice and the water.

"Into the eternal darkness." Muntor cackled. "Into fire," he screeched. "Into ice."

Muntor opened his mouth wide. Several seconds elapsed before a long, shrill shriek rose from his gut and rattled the bathroom. Loud enough for the neighbors to hear, the sound twisted and turned like a snake in a sewer and finally gave in to what it was, a hideous laugh.

PART TWO

37

St. Ignatius Cemetery
Boston

A long line of black limousines, passenger cars, flower cars and a hearse wound through the narrow paved pathways of the rolling burial grounds under a blue sky. Television cameras and satellite trucks were set up on every patch of open grass or driveway. Throngs of spectators and uniformed police were visible outside an improvised rope fence around the gravesite.

A female television reporter stage-whispered a live broadcast no more than thirty yards away from the freshly dug grave.

"This morning the eyes of Boston and the world are mourning the terrible end of a human life," she said in pretentious solemnity. "And one which marked the beginning of a tragedy that continues its death march as I speak. For grade-schoolers Dolly and Brian Jenkins, though, this is not a symbolic or national event. It is the funeral of their mother, diabolically murdered seventy-two hours ago by a madman who glibly calls himself Virgil. This funeral ceremony honors the first of the killer's victims. But the sorrow of everyone here is compounded by the knowledge that there will be at least 361 other funerals in cemeteries throughout the United States. How many more there may be, no one wants to guess. The mandate is clear. Somewhere out there is an indifferent killer who must be found and stopped, and soon, for the sake of all the Dollys and Brians in America … This is Evelyn Townes, On-The-Spot World News, live from Boston."

The reporter stared into the camera with an expression of barely controlled rage for several seconds. Then she drew an index finger across her throat.

"How was that?" she asked the cameraman as she pulled a cosmetic mirror from her pocket to see if her false eyelashes had stayed put this time.

The cameraman responded by singing some Elvis. "I'm all shook up," and bent to pick up a coil of audio cable.

"Really, Bob, I'm asking you. Was it any good?'

'Yep, it works. Let's get something to eat, Evie.'

'Not so fast, pudgy. I want to make sure to shoot all the bigs. The Director of the FBI is here officially, and over there,' she pointed to several blue vans, 'I'll bet lunch, are the Feds doing surveillance in case Smokey's a funeral peeper. Shoot them as tight as you can. And I want you to get the kids looking down into their mom's grave. I want a sweep of all the tearful citizens, and get in tight when you see one with a hanky. And real important, the CEO of Old Carolina is here. I'll give you a hand job if you can get a shot of him by the casket with an arm around the dead lady's kids. His PR dork's already turned me down for an interview, so you get video no matter what.'

'Which one's Pratt?'

Evelyn Townes pointed across the lawn to the tall thin man in the black suit, flanked by a group of raincoat-wearing security men. A few yards away stood Rhoads and public relations consultant Arnold Northrup.

"I've had about as much of this as I can take," Pratt groused. "I'm going back to the airport."

"As your PR man, Nick," Northrup said, "I have to tell you how important it is for you to stay. It's not going to look good at all for you to exit before the finale."

"So I pat the kids on the head, pay my respects, and do thirty seconds with CNN to say that it's a very private loss for the family and I don't wish to intrude? Oh, come on, Northrup. The media have made it enough of a circus already."

"You don't need the media antagonistic toward you, Nick."

Pratt exhaled deeply. "Yes, Northrup, you're right."

reporter who covered breaking stories in New England. Northrup promised Danielson the exclusive graveside interview if Danielson would promise not to bring the tobacco-cancer issue into it. Danielson agreed with a quick handshake.

"...are you accusing the media of exploiting this event? Is that what you mean, Mr. Pratt?" The interview had been under control until Pratt let his temper intrude. His upper-lip tic kicked in.

Pratt came to himself. Smoothly and with an air of great dignity, he replied softly, "Daniel, you know better. This is hardly a time for us to argue about things we've always argued about. In my opinion, we should all be thinking only of the two bereaved children who have been orphaned by this Virgil maniac."

"And what of all the children who are orphaned by your products every day, Mr. Pratt? Do you feel for them, too?"

Northrup gasped and stepped between Pratt and the camera and deftly pulled his client out of the interview with muttered apologies and a quick tap on his watch.

The boiling CEO ducked inside his waiting black limo and slid onto the leather seat. Northrup attempted to get in, but Pratt waved him away. Pratt signaled to an assistant outside.

"Get Rhoads." Then Pratt made a quick telephone call to check on how the Old Carolina common stock opened.

A minute later, a piece of paper appeared in the fax machine on the seat next to the driver. He opened the window that separated him from the passengers and handed the page to Pratt.

Old Carolina Tobacco, Inc. Common Stock
Last, 206 –1 1/4, Volume 6,880,000
Third most active stock

Rhoads appeared a few seconds later and got into the limo, perching on the jump seat facing Pratt. He lit an Easy and took a drag. He liked Camels better, but he was with Pratt. It was the kind of petty thing Pratt noticed and didn't forget.

"Did you see the interview? That Northrup's incompetent." Pratt took a quick breath, a master at the quick change of mood. "Anyway, here we are alone at last. Fill me in, T.R."

The limo moved away from the curb near the gravesite, snaked through the hills of the cemetery, and pulled out into traffic.

"Like I told you when I called from D.C., the FBI is playing it pretty close to the vest. They keep asking me about Midas, even though I've told them I don't know anything about it."

Pratt remained expressionless, but his eyes flashed interest. "Do they have any idea when they're going to apprehend this gentleman? Or are they thinking they'll just bumble about and wait for him to die?"

"I don't know, Nick."

"But that's what I'm paying you two thousand dollars a day for, TR., and that seventy-five-thousand dollar bonus you talked me into, if he's caught in thirty days. And that's a big if, the progress you're making. I need to know what the FBI is thinking."

"My guess is they'll start to open up a little more once we satisfy them about the Midas-Benedict thing. Half of them think it's Benedict, and for all we know, it could be. When we give them the files that will show them we're not holding anything back. Trichina's people find it yet?"

"Trichina's digging all the project-related information out of the archives."

38

Newark, New Jersey

Muntor knew from *Who's Who* that W. Nicholas Pratt had grown up in Newark, New Jersey.

Between nine and ten o'clock, while glaring at the television screen, he had made up twelve trick-packs on the TV tray in his living room. He talked to himself the entire time.

That son of a bitch ... If I didn't have to keep a low profile, I'd short Old Carolina stock first thing tomorrow ... Mr. Limo ... I'll say the magic word and — bingo — it'll be a hearse.

Muntor put on his coat and made the trip in little more than an hour, hitting only normal traffic on the Jersey Turnpike.

While driving, he used a flashlight and peered at the Newark street map on the seat next to him. He lost his way after exiting the turnpike and ended up driving around inner city Newark for twenty minutes. He erred in assuming that the map's points of interest legend would include public schools. Finding a phone booth with a telephone book intact proved no easy matter. He finally did outside a supermarket. He looked up the schools in the city government blue pages and tore out the section with the addresses of the schools in the Newark Public School System.

He arrived at the first one, West Side High School, on Sorrell Street, just after midnight.

Under the map on the passenger seat, the twelve trick-packs sat in his open eel skin briefcase. Should the police ever stop him and examine the briefcase, the jig would, doubtlessly, be up. *C'est la vie*. Muntor believed he would never be in that situation. He was prepared with his delivery service decoy props — clipboard with pencil tethered by a piece of dirty string, a receipt book, a counterfeit delivery-request slip lifted from the inquiry desk of Fast and Faster, a Philadelphia courier service, and a suitable destination, Newark General Hospital.

The maps scattered on the passenger seat added just the right insinuation. As such, the props were more than adequate. If drawn into interaction with police as a result of a minor accident, mechanical trouble, or other unforeseeable incident, he would have a reason to be in Newark. A cop would think, *Here's some sorry old sap, confused, driving all the way from Philadelphia to make some stinking delivery for probably six bucks an hour and no benefits.* Muntor knew with a grimace that he could cut a convincingly pathetic figure.

On Sorrell Street, on his left, a line of row houses sat in the dark on raised tiers of lawn opposite the school's main entrance. On his right, the junior high school. Inadequate street lighting was his ally. He slowed to a halt at the stop sign in the block before the school. He picked up two trick-packs. He intended to make only one pass, hit or miss. He looked up the street and, in his rearview mirror, down it. A quick scan of the houses. Most were dark. No dog-walkers in sight. He lowered the passenger-side window and drove by the school slowly, but not too slowly.

When he reached the approximate halfway point between the corner and the wide cement steps that led up to the school's entrance, he winged the two packs at once through the open window, flicking his wrist in a Frisbee-like toss, aiming them to land at the base of the wrought-iron spiked fence that separated the sidewalk from the school's lawn.

Muntor had intended to repeat the operation at three more schools, but he couldn't bring himself to do it. He knew that most American kids would end up like their parents — fat, unhealthy, addicted to cigarettes or alcohol or drugs, but this was a lesson, not revenge. Some would have to die, but just some. He didn't have to kill dozens of children to make his point. Chances are, the ones who would find the trick-packs and smoke the cigarettes were already compromised. A good kid, a smart and healthy kid, would never do it. And if some children had to die, it was only the ones that would grow up to be the sick sacks of meat he passed walking down the street every day.

39

From the front page of the *New York Post*:

Retribution for Failing to Make
Televised Announcement?
Tainted cigarettes found in schoolyard
"Virgil" Targets Tobacco Exec's Hometown

Muntor was pleased that the trick cigarettes were found by an alert student and turned into the school principal, who immediately contacted the police. *There's one worth saving, one who will understand my lesson,* he thought. It was just enough to send a panic throughout Pratt's hometown. Muntor hoped that it would be enough to scare Pratt into making his televised announcement.

After reading the front-page story three times, Muntor closed his eyes, weary from a sleepless night. Since beginning his conquest, his mind had been racing nearly non-stop with thoughts of his next move, what he had accomplished, and, of course, thoughts of being caught. Sure, the day would come when his terrorism would end, but he wanted it to end his way, on his terms. And not until his lesson had been delivered and understood — the body was a temple. Ignore that at your own peril.

As Muntor lay still, his mind wandered to the past. How perfect a scenario. He could accomplish two goals with one act. The tobacco companies would lose millions at the least, and if Rhoads was who Muntor thought he was, they might lose everything. Pratt and his posse would suffer, and Americans would wake up to the poisonous lifestyle people like Pratt had been selling them.

Muntor read the papers and clipped stories about his work and put them in his scrapbook. That would be part of the documentation he would leave for the ones who would study him, the ones who would spread his name and his message after he was gone.

He also cut out two articles about Rhoads. *Rhoads is almost as much of a hero as I am.* Muntor was a good judge of people. He had always had that talent, and being a reporter had honed it. Even having never met Rhoads, Muntor knew he was a man who wouldn't be turned aside. Muntor read the title of an article about Rhoads from years before that he had found on microfiche at the library and printed. The headline was "The Last Honest Cop in Philly?" Muntor knew the story by heart. Rhoads had refused to take bribes, and he had gone after those who did. In the end, the machine had kept Rhoads from bringing down the corruption in the department, but Muntor thought that now Rhoads had much less to lose. He had quit working for Old Carolina for a reason, and perhaps working with the FBI would give him the chance to bring Pratt down this time.

40

Every now and then during Muntor's travels, the wind would blow up, fall leaves would swirl, and the sky would darken before a storm. These scenes filled him with a profound homesickness, such an ache to be with his daughters, to see them giggle and hear them argue. And that longing counterbalanced with the dead weight of emptiness and the knowledge that he would probably never see them again. Visions so emotionally overpowering that he'd have to pull off the road to cry, to watch the rain if it came. He wanted to see them, but he feared the possibility too. Who knew how his wife had influenced them. By now they were probably overweight, nicotine and alcohol abusers just like her. The thought brought rage. He had failed to teach his own daughters the most important lessons. He would not fail again. He would make up for it by teaching the entire nation. Scratch that. The *world*.

The end was near. Coughing and working for breath, Muntor hadn't been able to sleep well.

He splashed cold water on his face and took a videocassette from his briefcase and slid it into the VCR at the swank motel he had been staying at since the time he made the call.

He lay down on the bed and watched.

After a flurry of video static, Muntor saw a moving shot of a deserted business office. When the sound of the voice-over came on, too loud, he rushed to find the remote to lower the volume. The camera panned a bleak room, lingering on objects as he mentioned them.

"Act One"

Muntor's voice came out of the television solemnly. He loved watching the parts of the documentary for which he'd already done the voice-over recording. It made it so real.

"Scene Nine. Crimes Against Martin Muntor. The End of a Career. His good deeds always misinterpreted, slighted, undermined by the jealousy of others. Martin Muntor was a Pulitzer nominee and recipient of two National Society of News Editors awards — the only true talent in an insignificant office of a second-rate news service. All of his power and intellect was anchored to this battered desk ... this backbreaking chair ... and this file cabinet, the drawers of which refused to open ... His only confidant, a Mr. Coffee that never quit, could heat water, but the water never reached the temperature of his scorn for what the nation had become ... slaves to poisonous appetites, hardly more than animals seeking death. This bulb-eating light fixture . . . And finally, this telephone. The telephone he used during eleven years of caring about the stories, eleven years of dedication, eleven years of unpaid overtime — until he was flippantly dismissed by a New York yuppie ... And, told he no longer had healthcare benefits."

Next came some jerky camera work and static intervals between shots. The next image to appear was a moving shot of a medical office building, photographed through a car window.

"Act One. Crimes Against Martin Muntor. Scene Ten. The End of a Life."

On the video, Muntor switched to a mincing, nasal voice.

"I have your X-rays here, Mr. Muntor. It's not just emphysema. It's cancer, I'm afraid. Lung cancer, Stage 4, inoperable. Now, tell me again the name of your insurance carrier."

Another interval of static.

The exterior of a suburban Philadelphia hospital complex. Also, another moving shot through a car window. At the lower left-hand corner of frame, a cat's tail swept briefly against the window.

"Act One. Crimes Against Martin Muntor. Scene Eleven. Why?"

There was a genuinely pathetic puzzlement in his tone. This wasn't contrived emotion for the narration.

"A mother who shouldn't have died. A father who never missed a chance to have something else to do. A child without a chance, you could say. Fifty-six years of misery that ends with the death of Martin Muntor. But out of his dying body is born his avenger. Out of his dying body rises ... Virgil. A new man, a man with a lesson to teach."

41

Friday, October 6

Anna Maria Trichina, on the bed in the white-carpeted bedroom of her condo, sat cross-legged, in jeans and a T-shirt, flipping through a stack of Midas Project files. Her reading glasses had slipped low on her nose. She pushed them back into place and focused intently on something she had just discovered.

Her hand trembled slightly as she held a document captioned, "Post-Allocation Budget Request." Her finger ran down a column of entries until it landed on "Amount: $200,000." Then her finger slid across the page and stopped at the words "Approved by W.N. Pratt."

Trichina pulled herself upright and looked in the mirror. She shook her head to tousle her hair. She knew she could look good even after a long, besieged day, and for the first time in quite a while, she smiled. She rose and padded into the kitchen, poured herself a full goblet of Amarone and returned to her bed. She sipped the wine while thinking about what she would do with what she had discovered.

Several minutes later, an idea hit her. She sat up, gulped the rest of the wine, turned the light back up, found her three-year-old edition of the Confidential Employee Directory in another drawer and dialed Mary Dallaness's home telephone number.

"We think — no, we know — there's a leak," Trichina said. "Mr. Pratt personally told me that you were the only one in the company who I could trust. Someone in the treasurer's office, we're not sure, may be working with a reporter from the *Los Angeles Times*. Corporate Security's looking into it, of course, but in the meantime, we —"

Mary didn't try to mask her suspicion. "Who's 'we'?" *I need to get in touch with T.R. He'd help me sort this out.*

"Me and Mr. Pratt," Trichina said. "What we need you to do is this. Under the strictest of security, with only me or Mr. Pratt present, you are to make one, and only one, paper copy of every Midas-related document. Then permanently erase all the computer files. *All of them.*

"Then we're going to cause the computer system to crash, only for a few minutes. That way, if the *Times* or who knows who comes looking for the documents, there'll be a record that the system crashed. We'll be able to say that the files were actually destroyed, lost forever, and no one can prove otherwise. Those are proprietary company records. No one else's business. Old Carolina has every right to protect them."

A moment of quiet on the line.

"Ms. Trichina, our system was designed by Metro Computer Consultants in Princeton. They're the best in the world. You were on the contract-award committee. You should know. The system's been designed to back up everything. Something like what you're describing can't ever happen. Never."

"Do you want to tell that to Mr. Pratt and his attorneys? This is the plan they devised, so if you …"

Mary shivered at the thought of being in the same room with Mr. Pratt.

"No, Ms. Trichina," she said in a small voice. "I'm sorry. It's just that we worked so damned hard to build a computer system that was fail-safe, that would never …"

"Mary. Relax. No problem. Tomorrow morning, even though it's Saturday, a courier's going to deliver to your home a copy of the memo to me from Mr. Pratt. Call him directly, if you really feel you need to disturb him at a time like this. That'd be okay with me, if you're uncomfortable with the … the validity of the memo. It spells out all the details. But time counts. We both have to drop everything and get this done first thing to-morrow. I have a meeting I can't get out of, but I'll be free by ten. Okay?"

"I understand," Mary said.

"Good," Trichina said, stabbing the word into her. "Good."

42

The telephone rang late, and Rhoads answered it.

"T.R.?" the voice said.

"Mary?"

"Yes," she said. "Listen. I need to talk to you."

He sat up in bed and turned on the lamp. Light filled the room, and he noticed one of the ficus trees had dropped a lot of brown leaves. It needed more sun. "Go ahead, Mary."

"No. In person."

She can't mean now, he hoped. *It's not a come-on, not Mary, while Anthony is still alive.* He wanted her, but clean, legit. After Anthony was gone. "Okay," he said. "First thing in the morning? You usually go into work Saturday mornings. Meet you for coffee before. Name the place."

"No. Now."

"Now? Can't you tell me what this is about?" *Please don't invite yourself over here to tell me your troubles,* he thought.

"About halfway between your building and where I live is a little pizza joint called Slice O'Heaven. On Cadwalader near the movie theater. I don't care if you have a girl there in bed with you. It's important."

"Okay ... okay," he said. "And I'm alone."

Thirty-five minutes later, Mary had told him half the story and started on the first of two slices of pizza and a small Pepsi in front of her. Rhoads played with a plastic cup of lousy coffee. *God, she was perfect. Not beautiful, not even pretty. Just some primal attraction. Magnetic. That's what it was. It was like the force you feel when you hold two powerful magnets apart.* It reached out and seized him and it wouldn't let go, and he didn't know what to do with it. She was the only woman he had looked at that way since his wife died, but he knew he couldn't have her.

"Sorry," she said, tucking her hair behind one ear and leaning forward to blow on the still-too hot slice. "But I get ravenous when I'm nervous." The mozzarella steamed, and she dropped the slice back onto the paper plate.

"Why are you so nervous?" he said. "You're taking orders from the woman you report to. If she's forged a document, then no one is going to hold you responsible. You're just a cog in the wheel."

"I know that. But I'm not at the top of my form. Anthony's dying, and taking care of him's killing me. I can't seem to control my mind. I worry and worry about everything. And what I'm worried about with Pratt is that he knows, or thinks he knows, that I know what's in those files. If it's something bad, something he doesn't want anyone to know . . . well, you've heard the rumors. Who knows how far he'd go?" She looked through sad eyes at Rhoads and let him see her looking. "Okay, let's say I do what you said. Make an extra set of disks before I erase everything. The disks won't protect me unless Pratt knows I made the copies, and if he knows, then he'll definitely do something about it. It's a Catch-22, and I'm the one who's caught. I'm frightened. Really frightened."

"At the police academy they taught us that any time you're in a situation and you have to draw your gun, you've already made about ten mistakes. But that was just smart-ass twenty-year guys spouting off. The truth is, there are plenty of times you're minding your own business and things just happen. Those are the times when you're glad as hell you remembered to bring your gun. So I recommend you make those disks. You may never need them."

"Then again ..."

"Then again, you may be glad you have them."

"Let's say I do it. What do I do with them?"

"First, let me see what's on them. You're not wrong about Pratt, but Midas is his Achilles heel. We're both involved in Midas, if only peripherally. But if Pratt is as bad as you think — and I think you're right about that — our only leverage is knowing what he knows and what he's after. Once I've seen them, you hide them. Hide them very carefully," Rhoads said.

"What if I get caught making the copies?"

"Can't you fix it up so you don't? And if you do get caught, you can always say you weren't sure that Trichina was acting legally, and you kept a set to protect Old Carolina while you tried to figure out what to do, which would not be a lie."

"But it's illegal to make those copies, no matter what bull I make up to explain it," she said.

"Let me tell you something. Have you ever heard the expression 'impersonating a police officer'?"

"Of course."

"You think it's illegal to impersonate a police officer?"

"Of course."

"Wrong. It's only illegal if you get someone to do something they otherwise wouldn't do because you made them think you're a police officer."

She stared at him. "And your point?"

"You make copies of computer disks and just lock them up somewhere, it's not too much of a crime. It's not like you're selling the information for personal gain. You're not damaging Old Carolina. That's what law boils down to — did one guy cause another guy injury."

Mary nodded.

"Or," Rhoads said, "if you want, give the disks to me." His mind started churning, and he had a second thought. "The thing is, you'll have to get in tomorrow and quick make a copy of the disks before Trichina comes to Documentation."

"Wrong. You can't copy Level Three documents that easily. It's a complicated, time-consuming process. I'll need hours."

"How are you going to do it with Trichina standing right there making sure you don't make a second copy?"

"Already thought of that." Mary smiled, pleased with herself. "That'll be the easiest thing in the world."

"How?"

"Simple. First I have to print out a hard copy of everything."

"She'll be standing right there watching every keystroke."

"Then, after I've printed everything out, she's going to want me to delete every single Midas document from the computer."

"She'll be right there watching."

"So when the computer asks me which group of files to delete, I type in …" Mary took a pen from her bag and wrote on Rhoads's napkin. In all capital letters, she printed MIDOCS. "That's the computer's shorthand for 'Midas Documents.'"

"That'll delete them, right?" Rhoads said.

"Wrong. Take a look at the '0' in 'MIDOCS'." Rhoads did.

"Yeah?"

"It's not the letter 'O.' It's a zero." She drew a narrower character. She drew "0." "As far as the computer is concerned, it's totally different."

"Won't the computer flash an error message or something to alert you there's no such set of documents to erase?"

"Not if I create a MIDOCS directory with a zero instead of a letter 'O.' Then it will have something to delete. That I can do quickly."

Rhoads studied the napkin. "All this is a little over my dinosaur head. You're sure it'll work?"

"If I don't have a heart attack or shake so hard that the computer tilts." She spoke lightly but was being brave. Rhoads could see her hands tremble.

Rhoads wanted to touch her. He wanted to reach across the table and take hold of her hand, squeeze it. Maybe kiss it.

Instead of taking her hand, he complained about his coffee and tried to flag down the restaurant's only waitress, who was busy laughing loudly and jumping back every time the guy making the pizzas grabbed at her.

"It'll be all right. You'll see, Mary."

She shrugged and picked up a slice of pizza, finally finding a place where she could take hold with her teeth, negotiated a bite, and struggled with a long string of cheese.

"I hope you're right," she said. "But something Pratt said is what's got me super nervous. Maybe I'm just paranoid."

"That's easy when you work at Old Carolina. What'd he say?"

She leaned in a few inches and lowered her voice. "He asked me, when he called me at home Monday night, he asked me if someone could access the Midas files, then change the log that reports who's seen them."

"That's a good question. What's the answer?"

"Besides Mr. Pratt and Anna Maria? I'm the only one who can do that."

43

Saturday, October 7
Philadelphia

"Dr. Trice?"

She looked up from her desk. "Mr. Rhoads."

Rhoads, wearing a suit, stood in the doorway to the cluttered office of Beatrice Trice, MD, PhD, professor at the Hospital of the University of Pennsylvania's Department of Psychiatry. He was there at Franklin's request. It was busy work, but Rhoads was happy to play along. He knew Franklin didn't trust him completely, not yet, but as long as he wanted to keep him close it was fine. Once Rhoads had his hands on the Midas documents, he'd be in a position to deal.

There was a lot to juggle, to be sure — he had to find the killer to collect the bonus from Pratt and get the FBI off his back. He knew Franklin knew he didn't have anything to do with Midas, but that didn't mean Rhoads wouldn't get roped in and tainted if it became a political necessity.

Franklin wanted to take Pratt down almost as much as he wanted to catch the killer, but that would be a tough job. Pratt had people in the halls of power on his side, and if Franklin thought the best he could do was hurt Pratt by offering up Rhoads as an accomplice of sorts, Rhoads knew he'd be tempted to do so. Rhoads had to catch the killer to help Teddy, and he had to deliver something substantive to Franklin to save himself.

Mary was the key to that.

Rhoads would hold on to the Midas files until he knew exactly what Franklin was willing to do to get at Pratt. Federal whistleblower laws allowed inside informants to recover a percentage of the payout if a

Federal case was successful against a corporation, so there was another possible payout on the back end. A long shot, but something to keep his eye on. Until then, he played along and went where he was told to go.

So here he was at Dr. Trice's office. In a letter transmitted to the FBI through U.S. Senator George Brackenham's office, Dr. Trice had suggested that she had possibly divined hidden meaning in the published accounts of Muntor's call to FBI Headquarters. Rhoads figured Franklin thought it was a waste of time, otherwise he would have sent one of his own men. But Franklin had to cover all his bases in case it all went wrong.

Ceiling-high stacks of medical journals, files, reports, newspapers, and notebooks decorated the room. An overgrown Wandering Jew hung in a plastic pot from the ceiling.

Dr. Trice was a small, plump woman in her seventies. She dyed her hair an attention-getting shade of red that nature hadn't thought of. She sat, visible only from the shoulders up, behind her desk.

Dr. Trice used a spoon to scoop something out of a plastic container. Rhoads could not determine what it was. He walked in and sat down, opened a small soft-leather portfolio and removed a notebook. He turned to a blank page and took a pen from his breast pocket and clicked it open. He wrote "Interview with Dr. Trice" at the top of the page.

"Thank you for contacting the Bureau, Dr. Trice. I understand you have a theory regarding the cyanide killer."

"Until I complained to George Brackenham, no one at the FBI seemed very interested in hearing me out. Nevertheless," she sighed and took another scoopful of whatever she had in front of her, "what inspired my call is the published transcript of Virgil's communication with the FBI."

"What about it?"

Dr. Trice scraped inside the container. "Don't tell me the FBI actually thinks Virgil really revealed anything about himself in that call. Or do they?"

"I'm the one who's supposed to be asking the questions, Dr. Trice."

Dr. Trice smiled and made eye contact. "But I'm a psychiatrist. Even the FBI can't stop us from asking questions. And please, call me Bea."

"Okay, Bea. Here're my answers to your next ten questions. 'Don't know.' 'Can't say.' 'That's classified.' 'Don't know.' 'Can't say.' 'That's classified.' 'Don't know.' 'Can't answer that.' 'Can't say.' 'That's classified.' Now, please go on."

"Virgil's message is disturbing. That's why I called. To make certain that the FBI understands, fully understands, the extent of the problem Virgil presents."

"Disturbing. You mean, apart from the fact that he's smart, devious, doesn't seem to mind killing hundreds of people, and probably has a legitimate reason to hate tobacco companies?"

"Yes," Dr. Trice said. "Normally, if you'll excuse the use of that term in this situation, people who behave as Virgil behaves are seeking attention, and therefore, whether they acknowledge it to themselves or not, they have a desire to be caught. Getting caught generates a lot of attention."

Rhoads gave her his full attention. He doubted she had more to offer than the entire FBI profiling division, but he knew that a good investigator didn't prejudge new information.

Dr. Trice continued. "People who do the kinds of things Virgil does want their pictures in the newspaper. They want to be interviewed on television, even if it has to be from a prison cell. They want to be talked about. That proud child who brings home a pretty picture from kindergarten for all to praise. Such people rarely have the personal resources to endure the level of stress Virgil must be under for any extended period."

Rhoads shifted in the seat again. "And you think Virgil's an exception to this."

"No. I'm convinced he's an exception to this."

"So, he's not looking for a forum?"

"Oh, no, he is, and he's already found it. The media. He seems to know a lot about the media. He's already impressed me with his skill at manipulating them. The exceptional part is that I'm afraid Virgil has no desire to be caught. It's even likely that the stress he's feeling is for him a positive experience, almost joyous. He has finally found the thing at which he excels. Mr. Rhoads, how will you feel when you finally find the thing that feels right for you? And if my idea that Virgil's dying is correct — and I imagine it is — finally finding the thing he's good at in his last few days on Earth is a powerful discovery. It will spur him to heights of accomplishment he's probably never imagined."

"What makes you so sure?"

"For one thing, as far as I know, Virgil hasn't asked for money or anything which would benefit him personally. That means that his compensation derives from what he's already doing. And his behavior tells us exactly what that is."

"Which is ..."

"Which is his control over the situation. He can make the CEO of a major corporation into his own marionette and he commands the attention of the entire nation. He has a player and an audience, so we just need to discover what story he wants to tell. That will be one of the keys to finding him ..."

"Pratt's his puppet."

"Yes. And no matter how advantageous you think it may be to humor him and obey his commands, don't. He will punish you anyway. That's what he meant when he called Pratt's reading of the Surgeon General's Report a 'confession' and said that it had to be delivered that way. Nothing will be contrite enough to satisfy him. First you confess. You've admitted guilt. Then he metes out justice. My guess is that Virgil's not a member of the Forgiveness-of-the-Month Club. Body bags will be needed no matter what you do. Does the FBI understand this? No. Virgil is not a political terrorist or a consumer-product tamperer. And if your apprehension strategy is based on the supposition that he is a terrorist, you'll be in more trouble than you are now."

"Well, not to contradict you, Bea, personally, I do see him as a terrorist. He's getting something he wants through the use of terror. Now, what do you call that?"

"Virgil is, in his mind, an avenging angel. He has a lesson to teach."

"Okay, Dr. Trice. Then who, in your opinion, should we be looking for?"

"I believe there are two different personalities to consider. There is the personality of the man Virgil was for most of his life. And there is a second, I will say, 'super' personality that has come into being through planning and executing this crime. The original personality is that of a petty, resentful man, who has always felt that his abilities were slighted and unrecognized, someone who believes he has never gotten what he deserved."

"He's getting recognition now."

"Yes, but that recognition is for who he has become, not who he was. To look at him, you would think him an ordinary, perhaps rather unpleasant person unworthy of much notice. The super-personality is dangerous because the abilities he imagines he has, are, in some sense, real."

"You got all that from the transcript of a quick telephone conversation?"

"No, Rhoads, I got all that from forty-four years of sitting in offices like this, from working with thousands and thousands of people. I'm a scientist, and I can tell you that the test of any scientific theory lies in whether it can predict a specific outcome. I'm prepared to predict a specific outcome that will enable the FBI to assess the value of my insights."

"You've got my attention."

"He gave you a hint about additional murders he'll commit before the next broadcast deadline, which is ... when?"

"Wednesday night. He gave a hint? What is it?"

"I can tell you where it is in the transcript. He used it once in a call and once in the tape he left at the phone booth in Newark. Deciphering its specific meaning requires me knowing more than you are willing to share. But here it is anyway." Dr. Trice hesitated. "It's his use of the word 'star.' He jimmied it into his speeches."

Dr. Trice picked up a document that Rhoads recognized as a copy of the transcript. Rhoads reached into his briefcase to get his own copy. She flipped through several pages.

"What page are you on?" Rhoads asked.

"Page four, beginning at line number fourteen. This comes in where he states what time he wants to hear Pratt read the confession: 'It doesn't have to be precisely nine, but it should be within a few minutes. Don't keep me waiting long. I'm one guy you don't want to piss off. I'll be a big star burning brightly while I'm waiting. And I don't wait patiently.'"

"'I'll be a big star burning brightly while I'm waiting,'" Rhoads repeated. "That means something to you?"

"If I'm right about who he is, it sure as hell does. Listen, and read that line again."

Rhoads read it to himself, moving his lips to show her he was doing as asked.

"Now, doesn't that line sound a little forced, a little out of context?" she continued. "I think he had planned to work that line into the call. If only I could hear the tape. Then I might be able to say. Without more information, I can only guess. I think it's clear that until he gets what he's asked for from Pratt, he's going to keep burning. But the word 'star' is the tip-off. I had to think about it for a while. 'Star' has special significance.

"Listen to the tape again, and tell me if you don't agree. Probably 'star' has something to do with where he's going to strike. Too vague to help you now, but after he commits his next murders, we'll all see that he had already told us about it, how clever he's been."

Rhoads wrote "star" in his notebook. "Okay, Dr. Trice, you ..."

"Bea, Rhoads. Bea."

"Okay, Bea. You've been honest with me, now my turn. I know you're a smart woman. Unfortunately, a lot of smart people turn out to be, no offense, crackpots. Well meaning, well intentioned, but crackpots just the same. You'll have to give me something a little more concrete to take back to the boys in Washington. They're a black-and-white bunch. Super-personalities and burning stars. What can I do with that?"

"Rhoads, I can't give you anything concrete. I haven't enough information. The FBI probably doesn't either, or they wouldn't have sent you here, even as a practical joke in which you are the victim. But keep your eyes open for the 'star' hint."

Rhoads clicked his pen closed. Dr. Trice looked disappointed.

"Okay then, Bea. Thank you for fighting the bureaucracy and trying to get through to us. I'll write my report and describe your theory. I'm sure someone will get back to you soon."

Dr. Trice stood up and walked around her desk toward Rhoads. She wasn't much taller than when she was sitting. Rhoads saw her as a kind of Dr. Ruth, only heavier. She tossed the empty yogurt container into a wastebasket ten feet away. She didn't watch to see if it landed in the basket. She knew it would.

She looked at Rhoads's notebook. He had made only the one note. She studied his odd, childlike writing, big block letters. Then she looked up.

She pointed her finger at Rhoads. The friendly demeanor had disappeared along with the yogurt container.

"Let me warn you, in no uncertain terms. Virgil is a merry-go-round nightmare, and he's not planning to let anyone get any sleep. You know he's playing with you, right? What a sadistic, powerful opponent does is give you hope. He wants you to keep trying. It's entertainment. 'Star' is a valid hint. Virgil wants you to realize he's given you the hint after the fact. He's not counting on the FBI putting together some kind of 'star' angle now. This is your personal opportunity. He may not give you another. And while you and the FBI boys are trying to figure out whether or not I'm nuts, Virgil will be proving what he is."

Rhoads closed his notebook, stood and shook Dr. Trice's hand. She had impressed him. And if "star" was too vague a clue to follow without more information, it was a start. The FBI was covering what they considered to be the high-probability angles of the investigation, so he'd just have to work with Dr. Trice's clue. It wasn't much, but it was all he had.

44

Martin Muntor sat watching television in a drab motel room in Scranton, Pennsylvania.

Bozzie curled in my lap right now would be nice, he thought. But it wasn't loneliness that bothered him. It was the loss of his spotlight.

For the second consecutive day, the ongoing FBI manhunt for Virgil had slipped from the top news spot. Last night, Muntor had noted, the major networks led with news about a secret Middle East peace summit in Geneva attended by leaders of Hamas. And now this evening, CNN led with a breaking story about a National League sports-betting scandal.

Muntor knew what he needed to do to regain the media's attention.

He had no appetite, so instead of eating, he made a quick stop at a local library. A reference librarian provided him with a tour guide to Europe. In it, Muntor found the name of Davidoff, a famous Swiss tobacconist at number 2 Rue de Rive in Geneva.

Back in the motel room, he packaged six packs of Easy Lights. He left again and bought a *Congratulations!* card at a Hallmark shop. "Please consider adding this terrific American brand to your shop's inventory of first-class tobacco products," he wrote. He signed the card "Nick Pratt," but presumed the store manager in Geneva would know who sent the package and notify the authorities there.

The U.S. Post Office provided Muntor with a padded envelope and airmail postage. He left the post office content that he'd soon be the primary focus of headlines and newscasts throughout the world once again. And as a bonus, he grinned, he'd probably be the subject of an Interpol investigation.

Why should Hamas guerrillas have all the fun? he asked himself on his way back to the motel. *Geneva's a big enough town for the both of us.*

45

Monday, October 9

Muntor was growing increasingly anxious. He was no longer taking the top news billings, and in fact, he wasn't even getting blurbs. The media hype completely died and the international package had yet to make breaking news.

The lull aggravated Muntor. He thought of his father. *You'll never amount to anything.* Those words, spoken by the elder Muntor time and time again, had become haunting. The nationwide panic was subsiding. Pratt must not have been too concerned with his hometown school being targeted. The announcement hadn't come, and likely wouldn't come, because public calm was being restored. And that meant people hadn't learned the lesson.

Damn the media, Muntor thought. If these reporters were true journalists, they would hunt down new information, any information, to keep the story alive. Why aren't they reporting anything? Why isn't there a cigarette recall? Muntor thought for sure that by now the news would be trumpeting a nationwide recall. Nothing. There had been nothing.

He drew a deep breath. He coughed harder than he had in the past. His time on earth was drawing to a close and Martin Muntor would die with little fanfare.

It was time. Time to reset the alarm. Time to reset the panic button. *Martin Muntor will not die an obscure loser.*

46

Washington, D.C.

Pratt's lobbyists worked overtime on Capitol Hill to prevent even a temporary recall of tobacco products. They called in favor after favor. Favors due from insiders at the Food and Drug Administration, favors from the Federal Trade Commission, favors from sympathetic legislators.

Pratt's key lobbyist, Joel Chankron, even dug in and made some headway at the Bureau of Alcohol, Tobacco, and Firearms.

Chankron was after "pressure," he said to the ATF official who quietly agreed to meet with him. "Oppose any cigarette recall ideas as soon as you hear them. The story should be that a recall is exactly what the terrorist wants, and that is exactly why there should be no recalls."

Chankron felt the insider would be cooperative. He paid for the meal and the drinks, and it paid off.

"Listen, Mark," he said. "The Patriot Booking Agency in Boston is always looking for articulate people like you who might like to make speeches every now and then about, hell, anything that interests you. You're a golfer, right? Why not call this number," and he presented the business card of a Patriot Booking Agency executive, "and set up a tee time with this fellow here in Washington? I understand they pay a twenty-five-thousand-dollar fee just for signing up, making yourself available in case anyone ever needs you to make a speech."

The way Chankron was going, the booking agency exec was going to be playing a lot of golf.

"Plenty to be optimistic about," Chankron reported to Pratt. "And I can guarantee we'll know about anything before it happens."

"What good is it to warn me about something I can't doing anything about?" Pratt bellowed. Chankron didn't have an answer.

Pratt thought that for $400 an hour, Chankron owed him one.

47

Deer Mountain, Pennsylvania

A light fog hovered in the woods around Rhoads's Poconos retreat in Deer Mountain. There were no nearby neighbors, but had there been, and had they been watching, they would have seen little more than the red glow of Valzmann's brake lights when he slowed for the gravel driveway of the Rhoads family cabin.

He drove the car as far around to the rear of the property as the driveway allowed.

He got out and opened the trunk. With some effort, he lifted an oversized canvas duffel bag. Something heavy and rigid inside clunked against the rear bumper as Valzmann struggled with the bulky bag. Leaves crunched loudly under foot as he hoisted it over his shoulder.

Rhoads's cabin sat nestled under a grove of blue-green spruce trees. The man carried the bag about fifty feet into the woods and dropped it, caught his breath, and tried to pick it up again. Getting the dead weight back over his shoulder was more difficult than expected. Valzmann half-carried, half-dragged the bag. He made a mental note to obliterate the tracks he and the bag made.

He spent nearly an hour digging a hole in rocky soil with an awkward folding Army surplus shovel. When satisfied with the depth of the pit, he used his feet to shove in the duffel bag. Refilling the hole took only a few minutes. *So long, Benedict.* He removed his work gloves, pocketed them, and returned to his car, obscuring traces of his footprints and the bag as he went. He drove away over the bumpy one-lane county road.

With a sense of completion, Valzmann turned on the car's CD player and twisted his neck back and forth, stretching to relieve the strain from the digging. He was glad to be rid of the body once and for all. It'd been a pain caring for it for two years.

Keeping a stiff in cold storage always carries with it some risk, and while what Pratt paid him made it worth it, he was glad to be done with it. He had earned his money on this one, and then some.

48

En route to Washington, D.C.
Tuesday, October 10

Rhoads, coming from a meeting in New York with other tobacco company security men, sat in a crowded Metroliner, his briefcase open and papers and documents scattered on him and the adjacent empty seat.

"Union Station, Washington D.C., next stop," the conductor shouted from a car-length away.

Rhoads leafed through papers one last time, a U.S. map partially unfolded in his lap. Too close to the seat in front of him, Rhoads couldn't get a good look at the map, so he positioned it against the seat back facing him. He was working, trying to make a star shape somehow fit the crime-scene sites. It wouldn't quite work. In frustration, he pounded the map.

The woman sitting in front of him leaned around and glared. "Do you mind?"

"Sorry."

He sloppily folded the map and jammed it into a folder. As he did so, something fell out. It was the 1994 Old Carolina Tobacco, Inc. annual report. He absently thumbed through its glossy pages. He got to the last page and was about to put it back in the file folder when an idea barked at him.

He opened the annual report again, looked at each page carefully, not knowing why. What had he missed? He remembered Dr. Trice's warning to pay attention to nagging feelings. He turned page after page, his mouth ajar. Suddenly, his head darted forward in recognition.

A two-page color spread described Old Carolina's recent acquisition of StarCity Properties upscale hotels. Two beautiful hotel complexes in Princeton and Atlanta. There, on the right side of the spread, was a sky-blue map that marked both cities with the yellow stars of StarCity's logo.

Although he did not quite understand how he could use the information, he felt he had stolen a march on the FBI. Pratt's bonus hung on Rhoads being instrumental in catching Virgil, and this was his shot.

49

Wednesday, October 11

Prompted by Rhoads's brainstorm on the Metroliner and reinforced by the FBI's models of likely behavior patterns and the computer-generated Probable Vectors analysis, the Investigative Support Unit believed the StarCity Properties' Princeton and Atlanta locations were the two most probable targets for any attack Virgil might attempt. Both were immediately staked out.

One day into the surveillance, nothing had happened.

Rhoads and Franklin sat talking in Franklin's sedan in the parking lot of the StarCity Hotel on Route 1 in Princeton.

Franklin thought Rhoads's idea wasn't bad, but that, at best, crossing paths with Virgil was a long shot. And if the FBI had any decent leads to pursue, they wouldn't have used more than one hundred agents to stake out the two properties. Benedict was a dead end, and until they could learn more about Midas, it was likely to stay that way.

Bored, Franklin said he would stretch his legs by taking a walk around the hotel complex. He wore a maintenance man's uniform.

"I'm going in with you," Rhoads said.

"No thanks," Franklin said. "Look, Rhoads. Every bellhop, clerk, cashier, janitor, and half the guests in there are on my payroll. What do you think you can do in there besides get in the way?"

"I don't need your permission," said Rhoads. "For one thing, this is property owned by Old Carolina, where I'm a security consultant. And for another, I'll be the only one in there who's not looking for Loren Benedict."

"Okay," Franklin said, taking an official tone. "I think you had better go back to Asheville. Because you're getting ready to stick your ass somewhere it doesn't belong. And if you do that ..."

"I know, I know. Two hundred and sixty-seven thousand, eight hundred and forty-four counts of obstruction of justice. You're so dull, Franklin. It's interesting, though."

"What is?"

"I'm usually a good judge of character. I had you wrong. We made a deal that I'd help you out and you wouldn't get in the way of my payday. But all you've done is try to freeze me out."

Franklin bristled. "The deal was that you'd be my inside man and get me something on Midas. Until you deliver, I'm doing you a favor letting you tag along."

"Then I hope your birthday's coming up soon, because in a couple days, I'll have something that will be the greatest present you ever got."

Outside the hotel, and at nearby intersections as far away as a mile and a half, scores of unmarked federal agents' vehicles in every conceivable configuration — taxicabs and ambulances, beat-up wrecks and a limousine, a plumber's truck and a tow truck — idled impatiently or circled blocks, ready for the unlikely signal that Virgil had been spotted.

Martin Muntor, wearing a safari jacket and white Panama hat, was in the car of a ReMax real estate agent, a young woman, heavyset. Muntor told her he needed to make a pit stop. The car was marked with the agency's magnetic placard affixed to both the driver's and the front passenger side doors.

"Come in with me. I'll buy you an iced tea, and you can try to tell me again why condo maintenance fees are really to my advantage." Muntor coughed. "And I'll sit there with as straight a face as humanly possible."

The real estate agent laughed politely. "I'll come in and get a seat in the coffee shop while you're in the restroom." She eyed Muntor warily. The man looked ill, and she hoped he didn't have that coughy flu that had been wiping out everyone at the office.

She pulled into a parking spot and they walked across the lot toward the lobby.

Inside, Muntor livened his step at great effort. At once he saw several people who could have been agents, but he ignored them. And they ignored the little dandy with his seemingly lively step, fancy briefcase, and chubby associate. They were looking for a haggard man, wild-eyed and wheezing.

He walked her to the coffee shop, making himself available for scrutiny. Therefore, no one would bother. The hostess seated the real estate agent and he headed for the restroom. Near a bank of pay phones, Martin Muntor entered a men's room, locked himself in a stall, and, still standing, removed his belt. He took off his jacket, snagged it on the hook, and, white hat still atop his head, rolled up his sleeve. He sat down on the toilet seat, reached up and from the inside pocket of his jacket, and removed an envelope containing a syringe partially filled with a milky-white substance, a Band-Aid, and a wad of alcohol-soaked cotton in a folded square of plastic wrap.

Muntor used the belt as a tourniquet around his left biceps. He made a fist of his left hand and slapped at his inner elbow with his right to anger the veins there. Two popped up right away. With cool, clinical efficiency, he swiped the cotton across one, jabbed the needle into his flesh, and slowly, almost erotically, depressed the plunger.

Muntor's blood energized and coursed through his veins with a hot fury. His diaphragm contracted involuntarily, and he drew in a sharp breath full and rich with the oxygen he'd been cheated of. Within moments, he felt lighter, stronger, fiercer.

He stood up now and snapped the belt from his arm. He quickly threaded it through his trousers belt loops, pulled on his jacket, and took another deep breath. He dropped the cotton and square of plastic wrap into the toilet and flushed. He put the syringe back into the envelope.

In a flash, Muntor was out of the men's room, exhilarated and striding briskly in the direction of the parking lot, away from the coffee shop and the waiting real estate agent. Yes, the news wire would come alive once again.

Rhoads pushed through the doors and into the main lobby.

He was noticed but rejected as a possible Virgil by the numerous agents who didn't know who he was, and those who did rolled their eyes or shook their heads. In the pre-shift briefing, they had been told about Rhoads and told to keep an eye on him. The assistant team commander referred to him as a troublemaker pressed upon the Bureau by tobacco industry lobbyists with Justice Department connections.

Dead ahead, Rhoads saw the StarLight Lounge. To the left, the StarDust coffee shop. And, to the right, the StarBright gift shop, through whose entrance he could see the salesclerk and behind her, shelves packed with cigarettes, junk food, and condoms. He headed straight for it. The carpet changed color inside the gift shop. He walked to the over-the-counter section and examined bottles of painkillers.

Standing a dozen feet away was a man who appeared to be in late middle age, wearing jeans and a bulky beige cable sweater.

Rhoads observed him out of the corner of his eye. The man picked up a copy of *Scientific American*, leafed through it, and put it back in the rack. A moment later, he pulled it out again, turned to a page at random, and appeared to be reading.

Rhoads wanted a closer look at the guy. As he took a step toward the man, he felt a tug at his jacket. He turned and looked behind him. No one was there. He spun around and looked the other way. No one there, either. He tensed. He looked down and saw a boy, perhaps five or six.

"Hey mister," the boy said, "The man said to give these to you." The boy held up a pack of Winstons. "He said to see if you say thank you."

This took a second to sink in. Then Rhoads grabbed the boy's wrist and squeezed.

"Drop those cigarettes right now, son," Rhoads ordered.

The frightened boy yelped in pain and tried to pull away. Then he did as instructed.

The man in the cable sweater spun toward Rhoads and the boy.

Rhoads crouched down to get a closer look at the pack without touching it. He turned the pack with the temple piece of his sunglasses and saw immediately that the pack had been tampered with.

Rhoads looked up at the child. "Where?" he said. "Where did you get these?"

The boy shivered then cried. His fingers quivered, and he tugged at his lips.

"The man," said the boy, pointing toward the lobby doors. "Out front. In the parking lot."

"What?!" Rhoads stood up. "A man. What was he wearing? What did he look like?"

The boy seemed paralyzed.

"Look, son, I'm a policeman. I need to find him. What was he wearing?"

"He was old. Had a hat, a big white one. A kind of tan jacket with things here," the boy said, indicating his shoulders.

Rhoads began to rise but felt a powerful hand push down on his shoulder. He was startled to see how many undercover officers had materialized in the shop. Most of them were men, a few were women. One male agent, made up to look aged, complete with a walker next to him, put a large silver handgun in Rhoads's face.

"I think that's Rhoads," someone said.

"Get out of my way," Rhoads said, twisting away from the heavy hand and getting up. He figured the shortest distance between two points was straight up the middle. "It's Virgil. He's here!"

And he charged.

He rushed the crowd of agents and burst through them. He ran furiously through the lobby, burst out the front door, and looked wildly to the right. He saw nothing, no one. He spun toward the left. Six or eight agents, guns drawn, shouting into hand-held radios and cell phones, hesitated for a moment near Rhoads, then, as if on cue, splintered off and sprinted in different directions. Cars screeched and peeled out, horns honked.

At the far end of the vast mall-like parking lot, Rhoads spotted a figure, possibly a man.

That shape could be right, that could be him.

Immobile for a split second, the shape — now Rhoads could see it was a man — seemed to gaze back at him. The two were separated by one hundred yards, but to Rhoads, their eyes met and flashed at each other. The sun glare from all the windshields in the parking lot seemed dull in comparison.

Rhoads broke into a run but jumped back not an instant too soon. He had come inches from darting out in front of a Greyhound bus that was pulling up to the front of the StarCity main entrance. Rhoads lost his balance, fell backward and to the ground by the bus's exhaust pipe. Coughing, he was up in an instant. The bus had stopped, blocking his way. He sprinted around behind it and headed toward the corner of the parking lot.

Nothing was there. Not a man, not a car. Just black asphalt and white lines.

Franklin stood in the parking lot under a bright noonday sun and screamed at Rhoads. "What in the hell do you mean you didn't notice what kind of car?"

"It happened in an eighth of a second, Franklin. It barely registered in my brain before the bus tried to kill me."

Two agents hustled over with the real estate agent. Another had the boy.

"Deputy Franklin," one of the agents said, "This woman may have been with Virgil. She said he came into her office an hour ago and ..."

Franklin listened to the story of how Virgil posed as a prospective condo buyer, said he needed to the use the restroom, and never returned. When the woman inquired about all the commotion, hotel security brought her to the FBI.

"Where's your car?" Rhoads asked.

She looked around, confused. "There it is. The white Mazda." She pointed.

"Her car's a crime scene," Franklin barked to a subordinate.

Rhoads elbowed in closer. "Ma'am. Describe the kind of gloves the man was wearing."

"You're right. He was wearing gloves. I thought that was odd, but he said he had bad circulation and that his hands were always cold, even when he lived in Florida."

50

On Wednesday afternoon, the duty officer at the FBI's ERC received a faxed transcript of a portion of a conversation on *National Talk*, a call-in radio show that had been broadcast live earlier that day on National Public Radio.

In a cover letter accompanying the transcript, the show's producer said he had taken a call from someone claiming to be Virgil on the 800 line.

"SOP to record it," the producer had written. "The caller's voice is so muffled it was a chore to get even this much. We have no idea whether this is real or a prank. In transcribing, we found two brief unintelligible segments, each less than a couple seconds long. We think one was just a laugh."

The partial transcript read:

1:40 P.M. WEDNESDAY OCT 11, 1995
HOST TONY LOPEZ: And here's Walt in Fort Myers.
CALLER: Hello, Tony. My name's not actually Walt. I'm more popu-
larly known as Virgil, which I can prove. But I do have an intriguing
question even if it isn't exactly on the subject, Tony. How do you
think they will ever catch me ... [THIS IS WHERE WE TOOK HIM
OFF THE AIR BUT KEPT RECORDING] ... unless I lead them to me?
Which I will, as soon as I've made my number. That number is, by
the way, 430. It represents one one-thousandth — that's one tenth
of one percent — of the 430,000 people who'll die this year from
smoking-originated diseases. Just one year!

Anyway, practically half a million men, women, even children.
I'm just starting a backfire is all, combating a huge fire with a
few well-placed little ones. I'm a saint just about, a folk hero, and

they can't stand it! Ambitious, yes. Doable? I think so. Stealth is my watchword. I'm smart. I have no criminal record. And not that I'd let them have one, but I don't even think my prints are on file anywhere. I'm relatively sane. I'm motivated. I feel, no, I know, my small crimes combat larger ones.

I'm fully justified. Listen, I have taken responsibility for my life, and I have treated my body as a temple. Why don't the tobacco companies take responsibility for spending six million dollars a day advertising their poison? [Unintelligible.] My so-called victims are already smoking, voluntarily destroying their own lungs and themselves in slo-mo. I'm just expediting. Is that such a crime? [Unintelligible.] I'll answer that. It's not a crime, not if it teaches people a lesson. The body is sacred — that is what this country needs to learn.

Unlike most people, I'm going to accomplish something of real value before I die. What I'm doing will absolutely raise people's consciousness about smoking and about their other deadly habits, habits that are killing them, habits that companies make their money on. Hundreds of thousands of others may quit, or better yet, never start.

Once I've hit my number, then they can have their way with me. Don't worry, I don't plan on killing myself and leaving you hanging. Suicide is nature's severest form of self-criticism, and Tony, no matter what they say, I'm not down on myself. Okay, now, Tony, sayonara. And make sure this tape gets to a fellow named Rhoads, care of the F-B-I. The tape's evidence. Even if you think I'm not me, you have to report it.

51

Tucson, Arizona

The anchor on WTCR-TV Tucson began the six o'clock newscast with a local angle.

"The impact of cigarette terrorist Virgil has struck near home for the second time. A long-haul trucker was shot and killed when hijackers commandeered his United Tobacco truck early this morning . . . near the I-17 on-ramp north of Phoenix. The body of Jacob Edmundson was discovered just after dawn by the Arizona Highway Patrol in the Interstate's east-bound lanes.

"An Arizona Highway Patrol commander in charge of the investigation said as the threat of a nationwide cigarette recall increases, he expects more cigarette-related violence."

The newscaster's image disappeared and was replaced by Commander Harold Lamphreys at the crime scene. "People are addicted to nicotine. If the recall goes into effect, cigarettes will be selling for ten, fifteen, twenty dollars a pack. We'll be seeing robberies like this one every day."

52

Asheville

Nick Pratt decided it was in his best interest to go on the air and read the statement Virgil requested. Every molecule of his being resisted, but his sense of survival, financial and political, prevailed.

A pool camera crew had been invited to WHQ and were set up and waiting in Old Carolina's media room.

Anna Maria Trichina and public relations consultant Arnold Northrup sat with Pratt in the Executive Suite. Surrounding them, propped up on aluminum easels, were poster-sized excerpts of the specified passage from the Surgeon General's report.

Northrup cleared his throat. "You re on the air in fifty minutes, Nick. You'll be on for a max of five minutes, basically within the time frame of local newscasts on the West Coast and prime time elsewhere. I can guarantee that every network will wrap your presentation with reports summarizing other Virgil publicity, including experts who will be commenting on what you're about to say or what you've just said." Northrup shouted toward Pratt's open office door, "Where's the makeup guy?"

Pratt fumed. "You're trying to tell me it doesn't matter. The CEO of the biggest tobacco company in the world announces to two billion people in every country on the planet that cigarettes will, contrary to previous statements, give them cancer, heart disease, everything, and it doesn't matter?"

"No, Nick," Northrup said. "I'm not saying it doesn't matter. I'm saying you don't have a choice, and we're doing it this way to control the damage."

"Of course I have a choice. There's nothing that says I have to push the company I'm responsible for out the window."

161

Northrup chuckled nervously. "Get it out of your system, Nick. The hardest thing for men in high places is to get over the illusion that they can control events like this. You can scream all you want at the flunkies you see every day, including me, and we'll do anything you want. Let me put it in plain English for you. Everybody in the country knows what's in the Surgeon General's report. Everybody knows cigarettes damage you. That's not your exposure here. If you don't do what this guy demands, everyone he kills after this is going to be seen as your victim. Not his."

Pratt's upper lip quivered. "Anna Maria, get me coffee."

She rose stiffly and left the room.

"I ought to play my voicemail for you. Every other CEO in the business has plenty of guts when it comes to me taking a brave stand and telling Virgil to go hump himself."

"That's another reason to play along. Don't forget Pensacola."

A makeup artist appeared and set his box full of cosmetics on Pratt's desk.

Pratt eyed him without amusement. "I just had an idea," he said. "Let's slip ads into the *New York Times* and the *Los Angeles Times* and the *Wall Street Journal*. The headline will read, 'We will never negotiate with terrorists.' Then we sign the ad, R.J.R. and Philip Morris!"

"Not funny, Nick." Northrup sat down in a leather chair, crossed and uncrossed his legs, and got up. He paced, thinking.

"Listen," said Northrup. "We have to get all this into perspective. This is nothing but packaging. You put little warning labels on every package of cigarettes, but you use tiny type against a dark background and the words just fade away. We can do the same with this. We write a preamble expressing your personal grief and sorrow over these insane murders. Make it clear that you are bowing to extortion only to save lives. You read the damned thing, then you close with a reminder about psychotic serial killers, victims, orphaned children."

Pratt glared. "And what about Virgil's specific instruction about appearing contrite?"

"What will he care? He'll be in the spotlight again."

"And the other CEOs riding me?"

"Make them regret it. Take the lead. Publicly call them to an industry conference to establish standards for preventing product tampering and for response to future situations like this one. Let this never happen again. That kind of thing."

The makeup artist went to work and Pratt stared at the easels, shaking his head.

53

Valzmann, dressed as a deliveryman, sat casing the Dallaness house from the driver's seat of a pizza truck parked half a block away. After several minutes, he spoke into a radio then exited his truck with a pizza in a cardboard box, walked to the house, up the path, and rang the bell. Anthony Dallaness, out of breath, went to the door in a bathrobe, pajamas, and slippers. A sitcom theme song blared from a television in the background.

"Hold on! Hold on!" Anthony said. He opened the door and saw the pizza deliveryman. Valzmann stepped in and kicked door closed behind him.

"Hey! Nobody ordered anything here."

At that, Valzmann drew a switchblade from his windbreaker. It snapped open.

"Sit down, Anthony."

Anthony, hair stuck in sweaty clumps, hadn't shaved for days. It was difficult for him to breathe, but he gamely drew himself up.

"Oh, get real, Anthony. Look at yourself. You're a wreck. Sit down."

He stood still. Valzmann slapped him across the face.

Anthony stepped back and sat down on the sofa, already wheezing loudly in fear.

"All right. What do you want, sir?" Anthony's eyes fixed on the man's tiny white earring. He'd describe that to the police for sure. Some kind of junkie or something.

"I'm afraid your wife Mary has been a bad girl. She took something that didn't belong to her, and I'm going to get it back. I think you know what I need, Anthony. Tell me where the computer disks are, we'll have a slice of pepperoni, and I'll be on to my next delivery." Valzmann smiled. "Where are they?"

Anthony's increasingly heavy breathing made it seem like he was about to cry.

"Look, I'll tell you, you got me scared. Maybe someone gave you some wrong information. Mary wouldn't be involved in anything like stealing."

"Anthony?"

"I'd tell you. I swear it. And I don't know anything about any disks. Do you want money?" Anthony reached toward his wallet on the end table next to him.

"Anthony." The tone was menacing. Valzmann relaxed and smiled. "I really don't have time to screw around with you."

Swiftly, Valzmann drew a clear plastic trash bag from an inside pocket. With virtually no resistance, he yanked it down over Anthony's head. Anthony hardly moved, like a kid resigned to take the hypodermic in the arm from the school nurse. Valzmann held the bag closed with his gloved fist at the neck.

Anthony's eyes grew large, distorted by the plastic.

Valzmann slapped him through the bag. Anthony's face twisted in pain. His chest heaved and his arms flailed.

Valzmann removed the bag from Anthony's head. Anthony hunched forward into a paroxysm of coughing.

"Raise your hand when you're ready to tell me." He wanted to let Anthony catch his breath. "I'm counting to three, and then we'll do it again. Where ... are ... the disks?"

Wild eyed, Anthony shrugged. "I don't know. Please. Can't you call back? Mary will know. There may be some confusion."

I told Pratt she'd never confide in this jerk, Valzmann thought.

"You're not making any sense, Anthony." Valzmann put the bag back on. This time Anthony resisted, reaching up and grabbing at the gloved hand that held the bag tight around his throat.

Valzmann laughed.

Anthony turned purple and after several moments, his flailing and flapping quieted down, then ceased. Valzmann removed the bag and pushed Anthony backward to an upright sitting position. He put his head close to Anthony's and examined the fixed and dilated pupils. After returning the bag to his pocket, Valzmann pulled out a cell phone. He pressed a button.

It rang twice.

"Sir. I know this isn't your private line, but may I report? Thank you. I tried to get the tickets from the first scalper. But we got canceled for lack of participation. We expected as much. Are you sure you don't want me to try for the second? I know she'll be here shortly. I've been told she's just left the store."

He listened for a beat.

"Yes I know you're in a rush. Oh, it's that late already? Okay. No, sir. I won't try for the second game until we know for sure we can get the tickets. I know. It would be stupid to. Yes, sir. Goodbye."

He hung up and glanced at a wall clock. It was 8:59 p.m. Valzmann picked up the TV remote and changed the channel to CNN. He sat down next to Anthony, whose still-warm body slumped to the side. Valzmann reached over and again adjusted Anthony into an upright position facing the television. Valzmann then picked up Anthony's wallet, flipped through it, found his driver's license, and removed it.

Light from the television flickered on Anthony Dallaness's dead, staring eyes. Valzmann looked toward the television just as Pratt's image appeared on the screen. At that moment, headlights played across the living-room window, distracting him. A half-minute later, he heard the sound of a garage door grinding open. Then it began closing.

"That's my music," Valzmann said, raising his index finger.

"Got to go, Anthony." He rose and casually left through the front door. He walked to the truck, got in, rolled down the window, fastened his seat belt, and started the engine.

He drove away at the posted speed limit.

54

Mary Dallaness opened the door that connected the garage to the kitchen and walked in. She kicked off her shoes on the mud mat and dropped her purse and briefcase on the Formica counter. She could hear the broadcast. She walked into the hallway and stood there. The television was flickering with Nick Pratt's image.

"Anthony?"

No answer. She stepped forward into the living room. Her boss was on screen, delivering his prepared remarks.

"... Eight days ago on October 5, the murderer who calls himself Virgil demanded that I read an excerpt from a document titled 'The Surgeon General's Report on Smoking and Health.' While it has always been contrary to the policy of my company and the tobacco industry to repeat rumor and inflammatory rhetoric of this kind, we at Old Carolina Tobacco, Inc. have decided to make an exception in this case in order to prevent any further deaths. Therefore, I will read the material specified by the killer, although I do so with no endorsement of the content."

She took a few more steps into the living room and stood behind the couch, directly opposite the television screen.

"I'm so sorry I'm late again," she said to Anthony, fixing her attention on the television. "Wow. How long has he been on?"

Mary watched Pratt. He had begun to read the text from The Surgeon General's Report. After a moment, she circled around the right side of the sofa, still watching raptly, and settled down next to her husband.

She reached out with her hand and placed it affectionately on his knee. Something was terribly wrong. For an instant, all the muscles of her face twitched. Her head jerked from the television toward Anthony, and she shrieked.

"Anthony! Anthony! Oh my dear Lord, help us!" She dove across him and grabbed for the telephone. The handset clattered on the end table. She punched the keys. "9-1-1! Please! My husband. He's dying ..."

Mary sobbed and cradled her husband in her arms, her tears splashing down onto his face.

On the television screen, Pratt had finished reading the excerpt and concluded his announcement with additional remarks.

"... *only to do our part in preventing more senseless slaughter of innocents. The terrible tragedies of recent days are the work of a sick, perverted animal, not the tobacco industry or the good people who work in it. Nothing should persuade us otherwise. Thank you, and good night.*"

55

Philadelphia

Dr. Trice had a consulting conference with the director of the Employee Assistance Program at a South Philadelphia Coca-Cola bottling facility, and it would be no trouble, she said, to meet Rhoads at Primo Pasta at Philadelphia International Airport.

After her conference and a taxi ride to the airport, she hurried on her short legs to the restaurant. She took a seat at a booth with a window looking out onto the tarmac, told a waitress she was waiting for someone, ordered a cup of coffee, and went to work on the bag of hot roasted toffee-covered peanuts she had bought at the airport.

Ten minutes later, Rhoads slid into the booth and shook Dr. Trice's hand. The plate-glass window provided a view of the north light-craft runways. He watched Dr. Trice as she put four heaping teaspoons of sugar into her coffee.

"I thought you doctors were supposed to know better than that."

"Why do I know what is right but do what is wrong? Who said that, Rhoads?"

He shrugged.

"Some so-called saint. I can't remember, either. I love sugar." She took a sip of her coffee and reached into the crumpled white paper bag holding the peanuts. "You're back like a stray cat who once got milk at the alley door. I take it, therefore, that you've reason to believe there was validity to my prediction."

"Yes, ma'am. Old Carolina owns the StarCity hotels. Your star idea. The FBI set up surveillance at both StarCity properties. Virgil showed up at the gift shop in StarCity's Princeton hotel, but he was too slick — and too lucky. Somehow, the FBI kept it from getting into the news. You couldn't have been any more on the money. Needless to say, everyone was impressed as hell."

"Yes," was all Dr. Trice said. Then she added, "Why is Virgil still free?"

"He gave us the slip, and he's not going to give us another chance like that again."

The waitress returned, set down two glasses of ice water, and took Rhoads's coffee order.

"Obviously," Rhoads continued, "I'm interested in any more predictions you have."

"Good. But first I have to go out to short-term parking. I left the Ouija board in my trunk." She laughed at the expression on Rhoads's face. "Well, that is what you thought, isn't it?"

"I'm past that now, Dr. Trice." The waitress brought the coffee, and he took a sip. "But you did have some trick up your sleeve. How'd you do it?"

"Now it's my turn to play dumb," she said.

"First of all, I don't play dumb. I am dumb. If I ever have an expression on my face that makes you think I don't get something, I probably don't. There is one thing, though, that separates me from the mass of dumb men. I know I'm dumb. And dumb as I am, I'm just smart enough to know you weren't completely straight with me. You didn't use a Ouija board, so how did you figure out the star angle?"

Dr. Trice went into the bag for more nuts. Her fingers stuck to the paper. She held the bag out toward Rhoads who simply shook his head. She chewed a handful and started speaking before they cleared her palate.

"Institutions like the FBI tend to be categorical in their thinking," she said. "In the FBI's eyes, chemists know about chemistry. The Hair and Fiber Section experts know about the material tailors use. Pathologists know about cadavers. Psychiatrists know about psychology. In such organizations, intelligence outside one's official area of expertise is distrusted mightily."

She took another nut and chewed it thoroughly.

"My deduction," she said, "was not psychiatric. It was literary."

"Literary? As in a book?"

Dr. Trice resisted rolling her eyes. "Yes, handsome, from classical literature. You see, our friend calls himself Virgil. Virgil was a Roman poet who wrote ..."

"We already thought of that. The FBI looked up everything that guy wrote. Couldn't find anything that clicked."

"There's that categorical thinking again. Virgil, you see, was more than a poet. He was also a character in a work written by someone else. The greatest poem ever written, for my money. Written seven hundred years ago by Dante Alighieri. Called *The Divine Comedy*. In it, Virgil takes Dante on a grand tour of hell — the inferno. Well, what do you know? Our Virgil is giving us the same treatment."

"Oh, okay. I can see that," Rhoads said nodding. "But what does that have to do with the StarBright gift shop?"

"*The Divine Comedy* is a poem divided into three parts, three canticles. *Inferno*, *Purgatorio*, and *Paradiso*. Each one ends with exactly the same word ..."

"Which is?" he asked.

"You tell me."

He shrugged.

"It's an easy one, Rhoads. Take a guess."

Rhoads wouldn't even make a serious try. "Mayonnaise?"

"Close. The word is 'star.';"

Rhoads regretted the stupid joke. Then he imagined explaining to Franklin that the poem thing was the key to catching Virgil.

"Do you think we can get some literature professors to study the poem and help us figure out what he's going to do?"

"That I don't know," Dr. Trice said. "This is where I become a psychiatrist again. Your Virgil has a connection to Dante's Virgil, who, in the *Comedy*, is already dead. He is merely the shadow of the man he once was, doomed to live in hell and guiding the education of Dante. Later, Dante will return to the world of the living and communicate what he's learned about the penalties for misbehaving, for forgetting God."

"That super-personality thing?"

"Whatever our Virgil once was, he now sees himself as dead, as a transformed spirit beyond the reach of mere mortals. He feels wise and invulnerable. And condemned. That's why he is so incredibly dangerous.

There's a very good chance he has passed beyond the conception that what he's doing is murder. In a sense, he no longer believes in death."

Rhoads nodded and whispered *shit* under his breath. That hundred-grand bonus was looking a long way off. "Would it be pressing my luck to ask you what you think he's going to do next?"

"This one isn't a prediction, Rhoads, just a probability. Actually, nothing more than an educated guess."

Rhoads reached into an inside pocket and took out his notepad.

"Our Virgil's working on his own epic," Dr. Trice said. "And in every good story, there is a continuous building of tension, drama, risk, and excitement. All that leads to some kind of a climax, the grand finale he's mentioned in the few, very few," she shot him a glance, "transcripts you've been willing to share with me. So, I don't know if the grand finale is what he's going to do next, I just have a strong feeling it's what all this is leading up to. I have no idea what sort of surprise he has in mind."

"I think the Deputy Director might be prepared to relax his grip on those transcripts for you," Rhoads said, making a note. "I'll see what I can do."

56

DALLANESS, ANTHONY A., on October 11, of Asheville, formerly of Vineland, New Jersey, passed away at age 46 after a lengthy illness. Beloved husband of Mary (née Steelman), brother of Michael. Friends and family are invited to funeral services to be held …

57

Anna Maria Trichina unlocked the door of her red Alfa Romeo Spider and got in. She pulled out of the main entrance of WHQ, drove half a mile, and entered the eastbound lanes of I-240.

She tuned in to an oldies station and accelerated. Then, without warning, her rearview mirror began to pulse with red and blue lights from the police cruiser behind her.

"Merde," she whispered to herself when she realized the cop meant her. She pulled over on the shoulder. The cruiser pulled up close behind her. The officer exited his car and approached hers. She rolled down her window.

"Officer, I ..."

"Please turn your ignition off, miss. Then let me see your license, registration, and insurance card."

Well, he's no fun. She reached into her glove compartment and re-moved the leather folder that held the registration and insurance card. She handed them to the policeman, pulled her arm back in, and rum-maged through her handbag for her driver's license.

"Hang on for my license. I know it's here," she said, flashing a thin smile. "Somewhere."

The policeman glanced at the documents. "I stopped you because you seem to have a couple of lights out in the rear. Both your brake lights are out. You know that?"

"That's weird. Both lights? Yes, here it is." She had found the edge of the license in the card section of her wallet, plucked it out, and handed it to the policeman. "The car was just inspected a couple of weeks ago. Could be the electrical system blowing them out."

"Maybe you backed into something. They're smashed."

Or maybe someone hit me, she thought.

He examined the documents more closely. When he got to the driver's license, he wrinkled his brow.

"Miss? Is your name Dallaness?"

Oh, good, she thought. *He noticed the Old Carolina parking sticker, and he knows Mary Dallaness. I'll milk this and get away without a ticket.*

"Dallaness? No. It's Trichina. Anna Maria Trichina. Do you know Mary? She reports to me at Old Carolina. I love having her work for me. If you know her, then you must know her husband Anthony passed away."

The cop took half a step back in order to see into the car better. He looked Trichina in the face. "Say that again."

"Oh, I'm sorry. You hadn't heard. Anthony succumbed to emphysema last night. It was sad."

"I don't know what you're talking about, Miss. But I think you need to tell me why you just handed me a driver's license in the name of ... Anthony Dallaness."

Like someone who's been shot but isn't yet aware of the wound, Trichina didn't understand. "Anthony Dallaness? What? Can I see that?"

The policeman showed her the license but didn't let go of it. She squinted, trying to read it. The policeman switched on a flashlight and shone the beam onto the license.

Now she got it.

She gasped and heard her heartbeat in her ears.

"What I'd really like is to see your driver's license. Do you have it in the vehicle?"

She dived into her handbag and rooted feverishly with shaking hands. The purse slipped from her lap and its contents spilled between her legs and onto the floor. She sat back in her seat, panting, staring.

"Are you all right in there, Miss?"

Trichina didn't respond.

"Miss, I said are you all right?"

58

Friday, October 13
Bala Cynwyd, Pennsylvania

"Wow. Look at this place," one of the FBI agents said as their unmarked van pulled up in front of Dr. Trice's Main Line residence. Autumn leaves stood in several huge piles on the full-acre front lawn. Ivy climbed up the stone face of the mansion and the glass-framed greenhouse next to it. "It's like the Ponderosa."

Two agents exited the van, each carrying a large cardboard box filled with copies of files and transcripts, interviews, audiotapes, and behavioral assessments.

Dr. Trice, still in her bathrobe, watched at the open front door. She showed the men in. They entered her home and put the boxes on the dining-room table. Neither of the agents had eaten yet, and they both sniffed the air. Something spicy and garlicky filled the house.

"Please sign the receipt right there, Dr. Trice," one of the agents said, pointing to the signature line with the pen he was handing her. "And the Deputy Director said that for your convenience, a sealed, duplicate set of this information will be delivered to your office at the Hospital of the University of Pennsylvania. Is someone there to accept the delivery?"

She looked at her watch. "No, not this early."

"When, then?"

"Usually by eight forty-five. Ask for Carol Frederick. She'll lock them up."

"Fine. Thank you. We'll deliver them then. Eight forty-five."

"Thank you."

"One last detail, Dr. Trice."

"Yes?"

"You've been informed that these documents are confidential and sensitive, and that by accepting them, you agree not to discuss them, now or at any time in the future, with anyone other than FBI personnel."

"This is the third time I've been advised."

"Okay," the agent said. "Thank you."

Dr. Trice watched the two men get back into the van. She shook her head and hummed. *Nobody loves you when you're right*, she thought.

59

Asheville

In the Dallaness kitchen, Rhoads and Mary sat at an oak table drinking coffee. Rain streamed down the windows and drummed on the glass. Mary had intended to make copies of the Midas files for Rhoads, but she had forgotten in the aftermath of Anthony's death. "I'll get those to you tomorrow, okay?" she said.

"When you can," he said. "It can wait."

Mary's head was tilted slightly up, like she was trying to remember something. "They said he could go at any moment, but I thought it would be so much more gradually."

"Emphysema's tricky. I had a granduncle and great grandfather who both had it. They went fast."

"Smokers?"

"What do you think?"

She shook her head mournfully. "All those hateful, endless details of dying. Any minute, I keep thinking I'm going to have to run upstairs and make sure he's taken his medication. Like when our beagle ran away. I kept thinking he was curled up next to the couch."

"The phantom limb idea, Mary. That will pass." He reached across the table and put his hand on hers.

"I never should have married. It didn't work from the beginning."

"Don't do that to yourself," Rhoads said.

"You're not married. You're smart."

"The loneliness stays with you like an old bathrobe," he said "That's the fine print you don't bother to read when they tell you all about the exhilarating freedom of flying solo."

Mary turned to watch the raindrops hit the window above the sink. "Well, still, I'm not sorry he's gone. Though I did love him."

"You know, once I was on business in Chicago and stopped into Dalesford's and bought a wallet. You know those stupid pictures of models they put in new wallets? I walked around for a month with a woman's picture in my wallet, the woman who came with the wallet. It wasn't to fool the guys, it was to fool me. I told myself that if I had some-one I loved, that's where she'd be, right there in the wallet. I wanted to see what it felt like."

"What did it feel like?"

"It felt like my life was counterfeit. That's what it's felt like ever since my wife died. Until I met you."

Mary smiled the smile people use to hold back tears, the smile that crinkles their eyes. "But what about your brother. And his family?"

"They're all I have, and I'll do anything to take care of them, but it's not the same. I talked to Teddy the other day. He says rehab's okay and that he's working the program, so that's good."

"So you think he's going to be all right?" she asked.

"If all right means all better, no, not in the long run. But I do think that with a little help he'll make it. He'll do okay, and sometimes, okay is all you can hope for." Rhoads went on. "I thought about that wallet and that photo the other day when we met for coffee."

"Why?"

"You were the girl who came with the wallet. There you were, in my life. We're talking to each other, not at each other, about something im-portant. Yet, you were the girl in the wallet. You weren't mine, you were going home. You had a husband you loved and had to care for. It gave me an idea for a business. You see, I could start something like a prostitu-tion ring, except instead of sending a woman to screw a guy, the woman calls you up and asks you over to her house for dinner. And after dinner, she'd fake affection, pretend she liked you, and not let you help wash the dishes."

"Oh, T.R.," she said, standing up and taking a step toward him. He remained seated. "I know the timing's terrible, but here it is anyway. I think about you all the time. I don't have to be the girl in the wallet. I want to be the girl."

Mary stepped closer still and took Rhoads by the hand. He got up and started to reach out to embrace her. She stopped him and led him out of the kitchen and into the den. The air was chilly and damp. Several big, old blankets were on the floor.

Logs sat piled over a thatch of kindling in the fireplace, waiting for a match.

"Light a fire, T.R.," Mary said. "Make it warm in here."

Outside, the mist swirled in the wind and leaves fell from trees, fluttering down onto soaked lawns and slick, black asphalt driveways.

60

New Jersey

Muntor drove for hours, across the Pennsylvania Turnpike, over to the New Jersey Turnpike, and north toward New York. He intended to go home, but he couldn't yet, not until he was far enough away to make another telephone call.

First, though, he stopped at a turnpike service plaza. He thought he needed coffee, but once inside, he knew he needed more. Muntor shot up in a grimy bathroom stall. His energy level and mood skyrocketed as soon as the syringe left his arm. He forgot about the coffee.

Back in his car, seeing the road became difficult. The lights from oncoming cars were beginning to get bright, too bright, in contrast to the darkening sky. The Biphetamine had the effect of hypersensitivity to light. Muntor finally arrived at JFK Airport with a stunning headache and difficulty breathing. He found an outdoor pay phone and double-parked there with his flashers on.

What if a cop drives by and makes a note of my license plate? Muntor surveyed the scene. He didn't think it was very likely.

He dialed the telephone number on the scrap of paper he removed from his pants pocket and spoke fast as he left his message with the WWW-FM newsroom on Long Island. He told the person who answered that he would be calling FBI Headquarters at noon Saturday, the next day. He had a big announcement, he said, and he wanted Tom Rhoads to be available.

The news intern who answered was a Cigarette Maniac news addict, and after receiving the call from someone purporting to be the Maniac himself, he dialed the home number of the news director and let the telephone ring barely three times. Then he hung up, glad his boss didn't answer. He relished the idea of becoming involved in the case. The news director would have insisted on handling the matter himself, or worse, snorting and assuring the intern that the call was a phony. And even if the call was a prank, the intern was still well within reason to sound the alarm to the FBI.

The intern took a piece of printer paper and wrote out, as best as he could remember, the exact text of what the caller had told him. He called directory assistance in Washington and asked for the FBI's emergency number. He said, "Wow," when informed that the Federal Bureau of Investigation has no public emergency number, just a main switchboard number. The operator gave him the number — 202–324–3000 — without comment. The intern really wondered about the kind of people the telephone company hires. Couldn't she appreciate the gravity of the matter that was clearly evident in his voice?

He called. He told the FBI switchboard operator he had information "of the most urgent nature" on the cigarette-tampering case. He smiled at his legitimate use of such a phrase. The operator, flushed with panic, paused a full second before activating the Centrex circuit-seize key. Had the caller disconnected during her moment of hesitation, investigators would have lost an opportunity to identify the call origin site.

"Please remain on this line, sir," she said and connected him to the CYCIG Task Force in the ERC.

A special agent, monitoring a bank of eight television screens, each attached to a VCR, was watching *SportsDay* on CNN when the telephone rang.

His headset had been pushed back so he could hear the sportscast better. In one quick motion, he pulled the headphone ear tabs into place, tapped the mute key on the audio-system remote, and picked up the telephone. The switchboard operator announced the call on line 6260.

Without comment, he disconnected her and finger-punched the button.

The special agent asked the intern whether the radio station automatically records calls to its newsroom. The answer was no. The agent asked many more hurried questions, determined that nothing ultra-time-sensitive had been said, made two pages of quick notes, thanked the intern, and told him to sit tight, that FBI investigators would be there shortly to interview him. They'd want to know, he said, among other information, if the intern had any idea whether Virgil called WWW-FM, or him, for any particular reason.

The special agent sat up straight and spun his chair around toward the three other special agents clustered in conversation half a room away.

"Call from Smokey!" he shouted, running his finger across the supervisors' schedule. He had prepared himself to awaken Franklin if anything significant happened, but the three-card schedule told him Brandon was to be called first. He thanked the Lord he hadn't called Franklin in error.

The other agents looked over, wondering what had happened.

"He called a radio station on Long Island then hung up," the special agent told them. "Said he's going to call here noon tomorrow with some sort of important message. The station's news intern called us. Sounds real."

One of the other agents jogged out of the room in shirtsleeves to the Telecommunications Section, where they probably were already duping the recording of the intern's call onto cassettes.

The Director and Deputy Director would get one, and copies would go to the Behavioral Science Section, the Investigative Support Unit, and the case agent serving as liaison with the consultants. Within the next few days, the FBI planned to release a montage of Virgil's various calls, hoping the public might be able identify the voice despite his various vocal disguises.

Franklin entered the ERC and silence swept in with him.

"What do you say to keeping Virgil from communicating with Rhoads?" Franklin asked Dr. Myron Sorken, the linguistics expert from Johns Hopkins who had arrived minutes earlier. Franklin ignored Rhoads, who was there as well. "That's what I'm inclined to do."

Sorken objected, saying he agreed, in part, with Dr. Trice's idea about nurturing the relationship between them. Franklin countered with the lost-ground argument. The FBI, he said, was playing along, but the killings were continuing, maybe even escalating. In a losing battle, change tactics.

Sorken threw in a complicating assessment. "Virgil's dying. You can hear it in his voice. Whatever his announcement's going to be, you can bet it will be consistent with someone who is well aware that he's getting weaker. That can be good news or bad. Virgil will in some way, maybe some very subtle way, give away something that confirms he's fading fast."

61

Virgil telephoned one minute after noon. Franklin instructed Rhoads to answer.

"Good morning, Mr. Rhoads," the gruff voice began, speaking too quickly for Rhoads to respond. Excessive static crackled on the line. "I haven't seen anything on CNN about upstate Pennsylvania. Didn't hear about it yet? Or is the FBI trying a strategy of a news blackout? If so, it's ill advised. Everything I do should be duly noted by the media."

The communications tech wearing the headset had the approximate call-origin location. He scribbled "cell phone, Long Island" in large black-marker letters on the pad he had for that purpose and held it up.

"Did you visit somewhere in Pennsylvania?"

"Sure I did. Groundhog Day, sort of. You'll find out. Anyway, I'm calling to make another fair trade agreement. I can't stay on the line too long. I borrowed someone's car phone without asking, and I don't want to run up too big a tab, so here's the deal. You get in touch with the Association of Tobacco Marketers and see to it that the Big Eight tobacco companies begin a promotion offering postage-paid money-back refunds for any customers who wish to quit smoking and mail in their unsmoked cigarettes. I'll let the tobacco companies figure out the logistics. And since I currently work in corporate America myself, in the entertainment industry, I know that it could take a few days to organize such a promo. I'm not unreasonable, I'll give them time, on the condition that they publicly announce no later than nine o'clock Monday night that they are preparing the offer."

It sounded as if Virgil was calling from a cell phone in a moving vehicle.

"You said 'fair trade.' What are you offering?" Rhoads asked, referring to the script prepared by the Behavioral Science Section. BSS had predicted some kind of deal would be offered. "Because what we need is to put a stop to the killings. Otherwise, we have no more room to negotiate. As a matter of fact, if you won't give me that, the FBI is taking me off this investigation altogether. Virgil, you don't want to make a fool out of an ally, do you? You make me look bad to the guys here. Can you agree to a cease-fire?"

Muntor did not want Rhoads and the FBI to see this refund deal as just one more in a relentless stream of demands. If they thought they were just digging deeper and deeper holes, they'd soon quit playing along. He needed to make them think his requests came from a very short list.

"Oh, come on, T.R., they're just bluffing you. They wouldn't take you away from me. You're the one who's most intimate with me. They need you. Don't put up with their silly threats. Nevertheless, you just made a deal. I'll take a break. I believe I have a well-deserved vacation coming to me. How's that?"

"Great," Rhoads said. "That's just great."

Virgil continued. "I'll tell you what. Maybe I'll even bail out of this ugliness early. It's tempting, it's very tempting, the way I feel, completely beat. Maybe I'll just fade away."

The agents and consultants wanted the killings to end, but only by apprehending Virgil. If he simply quit, they might never find him. For how many years did the Unabomber suspect remain free?

While Rhoads spoke, Franklin listened on a headset. He thought the refund arrangement would be no problem. Didn't the cigarette manufacturers offer automatic refunds anyway as part of their standard customer-satisfaction policy?

Virgil wasn't finished. "My vacation, however, won't begin until Monday night after the announcement. Then, no more action until further notice, provided I see the refund plan moving along. If it is a nicely conceived refund deal, I may throw in a bonus. But we'll see. Shall I commit myself to more mayhem in the event the ATM is not inspired to launch the refund deal?"

"That won't be necessary," Rhoads said. "We'll contact them immediately."

"All right, thank ..."

Rhoads thought fast and diverged from the script. He needed more, and he sensed he had only seconds left before the line would go dead.

"Wait, Virgil. One more thing. You want to help me personally?"

"Such as?"

"Such as no more trick-packs, beginning right now. That will demonstrate you and I have a working relationship. Please."

"Nope. Sorry."

"Please? I'm working with you here."

"Deal's a deal. You're an honest man, Rhoads. I know you'll stick to the deal even if the FBI won't," Virgil said and disconnected. His voice sounded as natural as they had ever heard it.

The collective mood in the ERC turned somber. Rhoads could picture the sick bastard grinning.

"You believe him?" Franklin asked, removing his headset.

"So far, he's done what he's promised," Rhoads said.

"What about that 'working in corporate America' line? I think we have a hit on the VoiceStressor."

"If that's his idea of a red herring, we'd have caught him by now. He's just throwing in an obvious phony lead."

Sorken interrupted them.

"Which means his mind is in the deception and misdirection realm," the professor said, "instead of the strategize-and-attack realm."

"What does that mean to you, Doctor?" Franklin asked.

"Like the rest of it. It may mean absolutely nothing. How innocuous a lead is 'working in corporate America'? Or on the other hand, should this be a precursor to a change in his behavior, I would say that it suggests a turn toward more risk-taking and more violence. This man is not the emotional Rock of Gibraltar. In him, changes are like pre-quake tremors. In most cases, they foretell an imminent, more powerful transformation."

Franklin rubbed his beard stubble. He hadn't been home for thirty hours. "What do you make of his refusal to cease planting his trick-packs until Monday night?" he asked.

While Sorken pondered the question, Rhoads spoke up. He narrowed his eyes as if he were focusing on something in the far distance.

"You know," Rhoads said, "Virgil may be even smarter than we think. He has never asked for something that we could have had reason to deny him. He's playing public sentiment like an experienced PR pro. We ought to check the Big Eight's public relations departments for unhappy employees, past and present. Guys laid off, et cetera. He knows that if we refuse him, he can simply report us to the media as uncooperative, then he kills fifty kids and signs it, 'Your Friendly Tobacco Companies.' We already know the bastard's tape recording his calls to us."

The communications tech spoke. "With a suction-cup mike and the wire run up his sleeve into a compact recorder in his pocket, he could stick it on the receiver of a pay phone or cell phone without being seen and remove it just as easily. That'd be no problem."

"Can't our communications people do something with the modulation of the phone calls to make taping us more difficult for him?" asked one of the Behavioral Science psych team members.

"Veto!" Franklin said. "Get off that track. No games like that. I need ideas on what he might do next and where he might do it. If we can assume he's going to keep his promise and put the brakes on, at least temporarily after Monday night, wouldn't it be safe to assume that he will want at least one last fling?"

"It's impossible to put every cigarette retailer under surveillance," an agent said.

Rhoads was busy figuring something in his notebook. "Why don't we go to the media and say that we expect an attack, or a series of attacks, between now and Monday night?" he said, looking at his notes. "That will serve the cause three ways. First, it will put smokers on alert. Two, it will make an assumption that the manufacturers will float the refund deal. That will squeeze them into a 'yes' position. And three, it may force Virgil to perform, to take a risk that he wouldn't normally take." Rhoads turned to the members of the psych team who sat next to each other at the conference table.

"Rhoads has a point," an FBI behaviorist said, "We can't just keep reacting to him. We need to do something, make him react to us."

"Exactly," Rhoads said. "There's a risk, yes, but we have to assume he won't stop. The best we can do is try to push him in a direction where we can anticipate him."

"He can only place so many cigarette packs," the psychologist said. "Practically everyone on the planet is on the lookout for him. He's probably not quite ready for his grand finale. We have him mapped to a probable home base in the metro areas of New York, Philadelphia, Baltimore, or Washington."

"There's a risk," Franklin said. "He said he thinks Rhoads is an honest guy. If we push him, we might lose him. He might stop calling us, and the calls are our best leads at this point."

"What's that all about? How does he know Rhoads?" the psychologist asked.

"I don't know him," said Rhoads. "But he thinks he knows me. Look, if he objects to our play, I'll just say you overrode me. It's a risk, but we can't just follow his lead."

"He's right," Franklin said. "We need to grab the reins while we can. We go with Rhoads's plan."

62

Old Carolina Tobacco, Inc. World Headquarters
Asheville

Rhoads flew to Asheville. In the Executive Suite, he sat down, lit an Easy, and watched while Pratt paced and cursed.

Pratt took a seat in a guest chair next to Rhoads, crossed his legs, and steepled his fingers, lost in thought.

"Damn it, Rhoads, what the hell is going on with the FBI investigation? You haven't given me anything. Why do you think I assigned you to this thing?"

"I can tell you what the FBI thinks about that."

Pratt stood up impatiently and began pacing again. "Go on."

"They're hung up on the Midas and Benedict thing," Rhoads said. "That's all they want to talk about with me. All they have from Old Carolina is that three-page executive summary you or Trichina wrote. They think you whipped it up off the top of your head to pacify them."

"Essentially, that's what I did," said Pratt.

"So, if you want them to give information to me, how about helping me out with something I can give to Franklin? Give them the project files. What could be so bad in them? Otherwise all I can do is follow them around."

Rhoads knew he had to remind Mary to get him the copies of the files. Pratt wasn't going to hand them over.

"Or work that shrink angle, the doctor in Philadelphia," Pratt said.

"I'm on top of that. She's important."

Pratt sighed and sat down behind his desk.

"I know this is difficult for you, T.R.," said Pratt. "Don't think I don't appreciate it. And I've been remiss in telling you this, but whatever happens, you can write your own ticket here. Any kind of job you want, you name it. I've already instructed Anna Maria to see to it. But this is not a simple situation. You've been around long enough to know that there are always eight sides to every story. I'm convinced that wherever Benedict is, he has nothing to do with what's happening. He couldn't be involved in killing hundreds of innocent people. Benedict's not a problem. But Midas? That's a problem. It's an embarrassment that could kick the legs out of our stock. The stock's sliding deeper into the sewer every day. The whole industry is getting creamed. Rhoads, I'd give Virgil one hundred million dollars to surrender himself. But no matter what happens, we can't afford to let the public know what Midas was."

Rhoads looked at Pratt. "Is it as embarrassing as having people puking blood onto the sidewalk while clutching a pack of Easy Lights every night on the six o'clock news?"

"I'm going to confide in you, Rhoads. I've never told you what Midas was because, candidly, I didn't know if I could trust you. Now I think I can. Midas was a rather ill-conceived project."

Rhoads sat up. He knew Pratt must be feeling especially desperate to confide in him. He knew it wouldn't be all of the truth — especially about what had become of Benedict — but it would be something he could use. Once he read the documents Mary had copied, he'd know exactly what Pratt was trying to hide.

"We thought better of it, late perhaps, but we did think better of it," said Pratt. "That's why I killed it. The idea was, broadly speaking, to study the relationship between nicotine doses in cigarettes and brand loyalty. You get the picture?"

"Yes." Rhoads got it. They were planning on upping the nicotine in their products beyond legal levels to ensure their customers would never be satisfied with another brand.

"It was one thousand percent banned, we knew that. But we thought we'd develop the products and then figure out how to get them into the marketplace, legally. But things went awry before we got to that stage."

"So you're talking legally embarrassing, as in Senate subcommittee investigation embarrassing."

Pratt sighed again. He looked weary, his bravado of minutes earlier dissipated. "Something like that."

"And that's why Benedict ... quit?"

"Yeah. He got a major attack of Holier-Than-Thou-itis, which, if truth be told, had a lot to do with our decision to disband the Midas team."

Rhoads thought, *And to eliminate Benedict, no doubt.* He couldn't wait to deliver Pratt to the FBI.

"So why did Benedict take off?" Rhoads said.

"Who knows why these PhDs do what they do? But it wasn't to take a walk on the wild side as a freelance domestic terrorist. He didn't have the nerve for something like what Virgil's doing. He used to just about pee himself when he had to make a presentation to the Executive Committee."

"So what is it you want from me?" said Rhoads. "The FBI's not sharing. They won't as long as they think we're holding out. I've been doing the only thing I can, which is try to get info from Franklin and take it a step further. But I haven't had a chance. This shrink in Philadelphia has been the only decent thing I've developed."

"Of course, I know you're doing your best. I'm going to send Franklin an expanded file on Midas. Now you know why I can't give him everything, and I need you to stay in closer touch."

"Listen, Nick, all I know is that the FBI's treading water. They've got a huge army of agents working all the physical evidence. But that's useless. This guy is very smart. The cyanide is untraceable. When he calls, it's always from someplace he can get away from. He's obviously a master of disguise. And he's patient as a cat at a rat hole."

Pratt brightened. "That's why they're so mesmerized by Benedict. They have nothing else going. They'll catch him. The FBI usually does. Do you know what the arrest rate for bank robberies in this country is? It's over ninety percent. They'll find Virgil, so all we have to do is keep them from digging into Midas while they do it. It seems like they're chasing the wrong leads. I need you to point them in the right direction."

"I don't think you're wrong, but if they're that focused on Benedict, it would be a tremendous help if we could dig him up, wherever he is, and show him to the Feds and say, 'Look, this guy's a harmless nerd.'"

"I know, I know," said Pratt. "That's what's killing me. Let's say we do find him. The last thing I need is some born-again humanitarian spilling his guts about private company business at a mass-media feeding frenzy."

"But people are dying, Nick, and that'll make the feeding frenzy worse. Without Benedict, it'll only get worse. You want two things — you want the FBI to catch the real killer, but you don't want to give them enough to figure out Benedict isn't the guy."

"Yeah," Pratt said, grimacing. "That's a problem."

63

From the October 14 edition of the *Daily Spirit*, Punxsutawney, PA:

"He Seemed Like a Nice Old Man"
VIRGIL STRIKES LOCALLY
PUNX'Y WAITRESS DIES
Found a Pack of Camels on Table

64

Sunday, October 15

The rain had stopped.

Mary and Rhoads woke while it was still dark and quiet. They held each other and listened to the rain. A little after dawn, he kissed her goodbye and left. In his briefcase was a printout of all the Midas files, hundreds of pages of truth, the rarest commodity at Old Carolina Tobacco, Inc.

"I have to read this stuff, but I'll call you," Rhoads said.

The doorbell rang so soon after he left that Mary thought he had forgotten something.

She looked through the peephole anyway, and in the fish-eye lens, she saw Anna Maria Trichina. She opened the door.

"I know it's early, but we have to talk," Trichina said, stepping in. Mary tensed and blocked the way. She smelled alcohol and fear on Trichina.

"First," Trichina said, "my sincere sympathy. I didn't know Anthony. But I know this. I've never lost anyone close to me. I don't know how I'd handle it."

Saying nothing, Mary stepped back and let Trichina come in. Trichina continued. "So, for whatever it's worth, I imagine it must be like a limb torn away. Unbearable."

Mary didn't want to discuss her emotional state with Trichina, but felt she had to say something. "The second-guessing myself is what I have to get over. Anyway, I know that's not why you came. Come on in, I have some coffee."

"I know this may seem inappropriate, considering ... that you are in mourning, but ..."

"But?"

Trichina dropped her voice to a whisper. "But we have to talk and it'd be safer in my car. I'll explain. I'm sorry, I know this is inconvenient. Plus, it's cold. Throw something on."

I'm not going out now. Not with her, Mary thought.

"Can't we talk here? I have something on the stove and ..."

"Put something on and turn the stove off. We'll only be a few minutes."

Mary did not know how to say no. She just stood there and blinked defiantly.

"Please," Trichina said.

A minute later, Mary found herself sitting in the passenger seat of Trichina's Alfa Romeo. Trichina started the car.

"Don't look so nervous. We're not going anywhere," Trichina said. "Just around the corner. It's just that your house may be bugged."

"My house?" Mary hesitated. "I think you better tell me what this is all about right now."

Trichina put the car in gear and drove a couple of blocks until she came to a playground adjacent to an elementary school. Mary glared the entire way. Trichina parked the car and lit a cigarette. Mary had to ask her to turn on the key so her window could be opened.

"Sorry," Trichina said, lowering the window. "I've been a bitch to you, Mary, I know. Don't take it personally. I am a bitch. But if we don't work together now, we may both wind up like your husband."

Mary had her head turned toward the window, avoiding the smoke. Her head snapped around to Trichina.

"What in the hell are you saying?"

Trichina looked Mary in the eye. "Mary. They murdered him. Whatever it looked like, it was a deliberate killing."

Mary shook her head and smiled, relieved. *What a paranoid little fool you are, Anna Maria. So beautiful, so stupid.*

Like a patient grade-school teacher with a kid who keeps making the same mistake, Mary said, "Sorry Charlie. Anthony had emphysema. He lived way past the time they predicted. He couldn't breathe, his heart worked too hard, it just stopped. What reason could anybody have had to kill him?"

"Because of the copies of the Midas documents you sneaked. They must have thought Anthony would know where you put them. When he didn't tell them ... well ..."

Mary squirmed. Dread coursed through her. Her eyes filled. "I don't know what you're talking about."

"Sure you do. You made a fake directory when no one was watching you, and then you erased it instead of the directory you were supposed to erase. Smart. You fooled me, but you don't know Nick Pratt. He's got everything covered."

Mary shook her head, refusing to believe Trichina. "Anthony died from complications of chronic pulmonary emphysema. That's the certified cause of death. You're trying to say that I'm responsible for Anthony's death. I won't listen to that. Take me home."

For a moment, Trichina didn't say a word. "Mary, listen carefully. I'm being straight with you. You may not know it, but you've got a tiger by the tail." She paused. "You've got two tigers by their tails. If you want to get out of this ..."

"Get out of what?"

"... then you have to stop lying to me. You made your own copies of the Midas financials. They know that. How do you think I know all this? Pratt told me. He wants me to get them back from you. He told me I'm supposed to act like I'm in danger just like you. But the truth is, I am." Trichina's eyes opened wide. "You don't know these men, Mary."

Trichina took hold of Mary's wrist and unintentionally squeezed hard. "You're hurting me."

Trichina saw what she had been doing and immediately let go.

"Mary, listen. Pratt and his gang, they're like bank robbers. The number one rule they teach bank teller trainees is, if you're being robbed, don't look at the gunmen's faces. You avert your eyes. Don't let them know you've seen their faces. If you can identify them, you have to assume they're going to kill you because they can't risk leaving any witnesses. Mary, we both have seen those documents. We've seen their faces. Now your husband is dead, and both our lives depend on what you do next. Where are the documents?"

Mary's mind reeled. Was any of this true? Was all of it true? Where was T.R.? He'd tell her what to do. It took her a full minute to be able to speak. She could barely get her words out louder than a whisper.

"My copies are safe," Mary said. "What happened to the copies you had me make for you?"

"I deposited mine with an attorney who had instructions to use them should anything happen to me. But, again, the bastard Pratt found out. I imagine his man waved enough money in the lawyer's face, and the lawyer sold me out."

This is unbelievable. She's an actress, and she's acting scared. She's not in danger from Pratt, she's working for him.

Trichina grabbed Mary's wrist again.

"Stop it, damn you. Don't play the dumb broad with me now," she practically screamed in Mary's ear. "You read between the lines of those documents. You're no fool. You must know that Pratt gave T.R. two hundred thousand dollars to pay Benedict to keep his mouth shut about Midas, but something went wrong. Maybe Benedict threatened T.R. with the police or something. So T.R. killed Benedict, kept the money, and then told Pratt that Benedict was gone when he got there. Or something like that. Who knows? I'm piecing this together by myself. All I know is that if we can't figure out how to use those documents to protect ourselves from Pratt and his jackboots, we're both going to die."

Mary held up her hands in surrender. Her head was spinning. T.R. up to his neck in it? How could that be? This was too much for her, too fast. She trembled.

"All right," she said, sobbing. "All right. What do you propose we do?"

65

October 15
Headline in _La Suisse_

U.S. Terrorist Targets Geneva

CYANIDE-LACED CIGARETTES
SHIPPED TO DAVIDOFF
"I Knew What They Were Straight Off," Clerk Says

66

Trichina opened her door and admitted Pratt. He stepped across the threshold and swung the door closed behind him. His upper lip twitched. Trichina read fury, rage, resentment.

"What's the big idea, Anna Maria?" he said, working to control his voice. "You call my chauffeur and tell him that it's for my own good to come here immediately. The one weekend you know my son's back in the U.S. What's the matter with you?"

Trichina turned her back to him and walked into the dining room. She wore a short skirt, a bulky blue sweater and was barefoot. Yellowing flowers stood in a vase. "Then why are you here?"

Pratt started to sputter.

She cut him off. *I have Mary running scared. Now let's see if I can get Nick to blink.*

"Shut up, Nick. You sit down. You listen for a change."

He regarded her narrowly and sat down on the sofa. He knew her well enough to know this, whatever it was, wasn't a bluff. Trichina retrieved her briefcase from the dining-room table, returned to the living room, and sat in a chair opposite Pratt.

"From now on, Nick," she said, opening her briefcase, "things are going to be a little different for me. I'll be designing my own career path. We're going to do things my way."

"Silly rabbit. What do you think you have?" In one compartment of his mind, Pratt was fantasizing about what he'd tell Valzmann to do to her.

"Or I'll put you in prison."

Pratt looked at her, saying nothing, his face blank.

"I have all the evidence I need about Midas and the Benedict disappearance to convince a grand jury that you should be personally indicted for first degree murder. The evidence is safe. I don't have to do a thing. Anything happens to me and the evidence will be sent where it will do the most damage. I know you got through to my lawyer Finch, but he wasn't the only man on base. Sloppy of you, Nick. But then again, you suspected I had a backup or else I'd probably be at the bottom of some landfill with Benedict right now."

"First degree murder, Anna Maria," Pratt said, controlling himself. "That's a pretty dramatic claim."

He rose and turned his back to her. He didn't want her to see his face. A vicious twitch materialized and clambered across his face beneath his flesh like a lizard on hot sand. Images of the bamboo tiger's cage the Viet Cong kept him in flashed in his mind. The facial spasm moved from left to right. The skin above his right eye twitched uncontrollably as if someone had taken a pinch of the flesh and twisted it. His breath came in short bursts.

What happened to his mouth was most terrifying of all. It snapped open wide and silent as if under the command of a dentist, held its pose, and then snapped back down again. Trichina heard the sound, but it didn't register as tooth on tooth. She looked up to see his head shake from side to side three or four times with such force, so fast and hard, that she feared it might tear itself off and fall forward through the picture window.

And as fast as it had begun, the massive twitch stopped, like a sudden cloudburst giving way to sun. Pratt gasped again, nostrils flaring. Trichina looked away. She did not want him to see her watching. His face now burned a brilliant crimson. He turned slowly and mechanically, like a mannequin on a revolving display. Unable to speak just yet, Nicholas Pratt concentrated all of his rage and focused it on the invisible spot he drew on the back of Anna Maria Trichina's head.

Frightened by the little scene out of *The Exorcist*, Trichina feigned composure by flipping through pages of a blue notebook she had taken from her briefcase. She wanted to take back control of this meeting.

"No small talk, Nick. Exactly one week before you terminated Midas, you pushed through a post-allocation budget increase request for two hundred thousand dollars. Which you actually signed off on! Sloppy, sloppy, sloppy. Or would that be cocky, cocky, cocky? Didn't Richard

Nixon make the same mistake thinking no one would ever get to listen to those Oval Office tapes?" She raised her eyebrows in mock surprise.

"Anyway, your little budget increase was turned into cash through a variety of transactions. One way or another, all two hundred thousand wound up in the pocket of a fellow by the name of Thomas Rhoads. Rhoads went to Denver, officially to meet with a security alarm contractor to write up specs for the Old Carolina facility in Denver. But he had something else he was going to do for you, didn't he? Right around that time, Benedict disappeared. That must be a coincidence."

Trichina closed the notebook as if it was the last page in a bedtime story and turned to face Pratt. "The End," she said.

Pratt glared and said nothing.

"Now, Nick," Trichina said softly, "if you're innocent, why don't you just walk out right now? Otherwise, we are going to go over the list of my new job benefits, the conditions for my silence." Trichina swallowed hard. "Don't look so sour, Nick," she said, her tone dripping like warm honey. "I'm a reasonable woman. I can be had."

"I'll admit no guilt, Anna Maria. What I admit to is being curious to hear about the rest of this ... this delirium. So I'll remain seated."

Trichina smiled." "Call it what you will, Nick. Nevertheless," she said, holding up her hand and raising one finger as she ticked off each demand, "I am to be promoted to position of Executive Vice President of Marketing, named an officer of the corporation, and given the compensation that goes with that rank. All retro to the first of the year."

"Anna Maria? Have you any idea what an executive vice presidency at a company like Old Carolina pays? In excess of a quarter million dollars a year."

"As a matter of fact, I did know that, Nick."

"Even if this whole conversation weren't ludicrous, your demands are impossible. I have a board of directors and shareholders to report to. Executive vice presidencies aren't handed out on the basis of long legs and..."

Pratt crudely put his thumb in his mouth.

"You can explain it to the board any lying way you want," she said. "And thanks for reminding me. That's another change. You will never lay your leathery hands on me again."

Pratt rose. "Anna Maria, I'm leaving now. By virtue of this very conversation, you've proven yourself to be reckless and irresponsible. Perhaps you're under too much pressure, I don't know. I had big plans for you. They're dead now. And although you may imagine in some girlish fantasy that you have me at some disadvantage, I assure you, you do not. I encourage you, for your own good, not to expose yourself to ... to legal action, Anna Maria."

"Save the euphemisms, Nick. I don't need to tape record you. I have you by the nuts already. You have a week to set it up and announce my promotion. After that, I go directly to the Justice Department. And if I wind up dead before then, I'll see your raggedy ass in hell."

"Why are you doing this, Anna Maria?"

"Lots of reasons, Nick. But I'll give you one for starters. Remember the marketing awards trip to Acapulco? Your lie about a vasectomy? How'd you phrase it? Oh, yeah. *Don't worry, beautiful, all the little swimmers have been cut off at the pass?* Nice, and I wind up pregnant. Then that other ... incident, the ..."

"Oh for crying out loud, Anna Maria. I paid for the goddamned abortion. It didn't cost you a dime. I saw to it you had two weeks' vacation to recover from a twenty-minute procedure. I ..."

"You sad, pathetic sack of shit, Nick. Is that all you got from that episode? That you saved me a few bucks for the surgery? I didn't realize it at the time, Nick, but that child that I got rid of ..." She broke off. She was not going to let herself get emotional, not now. She took a deep breath and a different tactic. "...don't you underestimate the power of the maternal instinct, Nick? You'd be a lot better off if you did."

At that, Pratt laughed and started for the door. Another idea was forming. Trichina, he realized, could be helpful in retrieving all the runaway Midas documents and computer disks. If she were properly motivated.

Pratt faked a slump of shoulders, as if he was beaten, resigning to see it her way. He walked back and sat down on the leather sofa.

"I don't mind helping you, Anna Maria," he said. "But why wouldn't you think to discuss this idea with me? Why this irrational attack out of left field?"

Pratt's conciliatory tone succeeded in leading Trichina to think she had won. At least this battle. She moved toward him.

"I'm so glad we don't have to leave this on an unpleasant note," she said. She stepped closer and looked Pratt in the face. Thirty years ago, he was probably damn good-looking, kind of a Sean Connery type, she thought.

She took one more step closer and sat slowly on the sofa, separated from Pratt only by a white pillow. He inhaled her musky perfume. She looked straight ahead, not at the CEO. Her hand moved toward him and stopped, resting on the pillow. Her deep maroon fingernails dug into the soft leather. She picked up the pillow and put it carefully on the floor in front of her. Her knees parted ever so slightly.

"Mr. Pratt," she said softly, caressing her thigh through the skirt's material. "I've got a very sensitive situation here, and it's fairly crying out for the skill of a man of experience."

She continued looking straight ahead but could feel Pratt watching her.

"You said you wouldn't mind helping me, Nick."

Trichina closed her eyes and leaned back. It was Pratt's turn.

67

Chicago Sun-Times headline
Tuesday October 17

CIGARETTE REFUNDS COULD REACH $200 MILLION

**ALL BIG 8 TOBACCO FIRMS IN NATIONWIDE
MONEY-BACK REFUND PROGRAM**
Execs Acknowledge Move Is "Virgil-Inspired"

68

Bucks County, Pennsylvania
Wednesday, October 18

Muntor needed a remote place to stage a dress rehearsal for the grand finale, and he knew a realtor could help him find one. He loved hiding behind real estate agents. The way they preferred to control the relationship by insisting that they drove you in their cars while you sat back and enjoyed the view, the way they lead you about, as if you had a ring through your nose. The whole routine served as a perfect cover.

Muntor dressed as a country gentleman in a good seersucker jacket he had found in the closet. He bought a wide-brimmed sky-blue hat, cordovan wing tips and cotton pants to imitate the wardrobe he had seen in an ancient copy of an *Esquire* Fall Fashion Review.

At the realtor's office in Doylestown, Pennsylvania, Muntor misrepresented himself as a serious prospect. He told her he was interested in farmland, preferably with an old farmhouse and a barn or stable. Something he could convert into an office. A spring or pond would be a plus. They spent hours Wednesday afternoon looking at properties.

Working from a list she had compiled, the agent eventually drove by a property with an old school building on it. They went up and around the long driveway. Muntor said he didn't like the looks of it. As they drove away, the realtor told him how the county had tried to sell the school at auction, but none of the bidders offered the minimum, and the sale was canceled.

"Interesting," was all he remarked. He tried to seem bored.

At about 3:30 p.m., after driving to two other properties, Muntor announced that he had seen enough for the day. On the ride to be dropped off at his car, he made a careful mental note of how to return to the school.

Now that he knew where he could practice for the big event, Muntor drove to a diner and killed time reading and drinking coffee until 4:30 p.m. That would give him an hour or so of light — more than enough time for a quick dress rehearsal.

He returned to the school. The vacant building was more than secluded enough for Muntor's purposes.

He proceeded up the gravel driveway to the sprawling 1930s-era fieldstone schoolhouse. The wall on the north side had caved in winters ago, the realtor had said, and part of the roof had rotted through and was ready to collapse. Every pane of glass, hundreds of them, had been broken.

Muntor, confident that no one was around, stood in the driveway next to his car and changed from his prospect's costume, carefully putting the slacks and shirt and jacket onto the wooden hangers he had brought. He changed into jeans and a flannel shirt, yanked a heavy duffel bag from the floor behind the driver's seat, another from the trunk, and took two trips to half-drag, half-carry them into what remained of the school. In his exhausted state, the effort required was extreme.

Muntor set the duffel bags down. He walked through the crumbling halls until he found the giant auditorium. Wrecked and mostly empty, the high-arched ceilings seemed more fitting for an airplane hangar than an assembly hall. It was exactly as he had imagined.

The pain in his chest ripped at him, sharp and steady. He didn't have enough strength to get the equipment from the duffel bags. He leaned back against a dusty tile wall, reached into his shirt pocket, and withdrew a small brown envelope containing a syringe. He removed his jacket, took off his belt, and rolled up his sleeve.

Invigorated and recharged, in both mood and energy, Muntor walked briskly and retrieved the duffel bags. He brought them into the auditorium. From one bag, he removed bright yellow fire-department hazardous-materials protective clothing, boots, suspendered-trousers, a full, knee-length tent-style overcoat, and a special helmet with a hood that protected the entire face, the kind firemen use when responding to chemical fires or encountering heavy smoke. Muntor laid all these articles out on the dusty floor that had once been gleaming tile and waxed hardwood.

Then, using both hands, he removed another article from the second bag. Out came an orchard-fogger, a green-and-white-striped steel cylinder designed to generate thick clouds of insecticide, and an oversized fire extinguisher whose hose was attached to a long, curved, black gunmetal trigger nozzle. Liquid sloshed around inside the cylinder.

Muntor put on the protective clothing, all but the hooded helmet, carefully and quickly. He had practiced this part. As usual, he struggled a bit, wriggling the tank and its cobweb of straps into position on his back, but finally positioned it snugly without too much delay. He was getting faster at putting it on.

Then he took his video camera and tripod from the duffel bag. He attached the camera to the tripod's mount and set it up in a far corner of the huge room. He looked around at the hundreds of broken, splintered wooden auditorium seats that had been screwed into the floor. He imagined them filled with the movers and shakers of the tobacco industry.

There was still enough light left for what he needed to do, but he had to work fast.

He was nearly out of breath and had almost forgotten a critical part of the drill. Muntor set the orchard-fogger down and removed a folded piece of paper from his pants pocket. He looked at the diagram he had drawn. Referring to it, he measured off a large rectangular area, sixty paces up, forty-five to the right, sixty paces down, and forty-five more, back to the spot from which he had begun. At each corner, to show him the rectangle's perimeter, he had stopped and marked an X into the dusty floor with the tip of his yellow rubber boot.

Muntor noticed a dozen wrens perched high on a rotting beam above him. He stooped and picked up a broken wooden seat leg and threw it toward the birds. He aimed wide, not wanting to hit them. The splintered wood crashed into the wall behind the birds and sent them scattering in a wild flutter of wings. A few feathers spun lazily to the floor.

"No need to get you guys involved," he said as they flew out of the auditorium through the missing roof slats. He hadn't spoken in hours. His voice was a croak.

Next, Muntor retrieved a bath towel wrapped around two small wire cages, each containing a young white laboratory rat, from the second duffel. Muntor walked the rats to the two farthest corners and set them down. An old joke popped into his head — laboratory rats are the primary cause of statistics.

He walked back to the duffel bags and orchard-fogger. One wren had returned to the beam above. Muntor picked up another piece of wood and tossed it toward the bird.

"Last chance," he shouted to it. "Get out of town."

Muntor pulled on the hooded helmet.

Later, Muntor would watch the video.

The sequence would open with billows of white-gray, like threatening storm clouds. Then the image of a man. And for the end of the sequence, a long shot, starting from the driveway, encompassing the entire building, the white-gray fog rising from holes in the roof and through the glassless windows.

69

Harrisburg, Pennsylvania
Saturday, October 21

Outside, it was cold enough to snow.

Inside, Muntor sat at a booth in Bob Diner in Harrisburg.

Bob Diner? That can't be a typo, Muntor thought, sitting under fluorescent lighting that was too bright, amid the noisy people and the clatter of dishes, waiting for the waitress to bring the coffee he ordered. A previous customer had left a newspaper folded open to the stock quotes. He nudged the paper into a position so he could see the Old Carolina Tobacco, Inc. price.

The stock was down another three dollars.

Beautiful! he thought. Then the pain in his chest distracted him and killed his appetite, and nothing on the menu interested him except the restaurant's name. Bob Diner? Didn't someone forget the apostrophe and the "s" somewhere along the line? But no, that's what it said on the menu, that's what it said on the paper placemats, and that's what it said on the illuminated blue letters atop the brick-and-chrome restaurant.

He wanted to ask the waitress about the diner's name, but he could not afford to draw any attention to himself. He missed small talk with strangers. It was true he had no close friends, but he loved to engage people in conversation on topics in the news, upon which he could be impressively authoritative.

Now, though, he was cold and tired and he wanted strong, hot coffee.

The waitress brought the cup. He sipped it. Tepid, damn it. He tried to get her attention, but she had disappeared into the back.

Muntor looked around and reluctantly sipped more from the cup while he stole glimpses of the patrons.

He held a pack of Winstons in his hand. He was waiting for the all-clear moment when he could wedge the trick-pack between the seat cushion and booth back. He had looked in the crevice earlier and noticed the crust of a slice of rye bread and several small squares of the wax paper that comes on pats of butter. Muntor knew that even in good restaurants, not that this place was one, all you have to do to find something disgusting is to look.

In this planting, Muntor chose to remove most of the cigarettes from the pack and leave the ace inside with the remaining ones. That method, he reasoned, suggested a *bona fide* pack left behind by chance by an inattentive customer. He'd used the ploy, successfully, several times before.

Just after wedging the pack in the cushion behind him, Muntor looked up. A man and woman, the female facing Muntor, sat several booths away. Blue-collaresque features in business garb. They didn't seem to be husband and wife, or brother and sister, or casual acquaintances. They looked more like colleagues.

But they could be the cops.

Muntor tried to make a slight furrow of worry creep across his brow. He was acting now, psyching himself for what he was going to do. *I have this damned briefcase full of cyanided cigarettes*, he said to himself, almost as if reading from a script.

The thin line between paranoia and faking paranoia blurred. To Muntor, it was possible that the man in the booth could be looking at him out of the corner of his eye.

I'm getting out of here, and I have to get rid of this briefcase. But not too quickly, not too slowly. This has to be handled subtly. This has to look good. Take it easy.

Muntor left two quarters on the table and took his check to the cashier. She was a bosomy woman about sixty who wore the kind of sequin-decorated eyeglasses that opticians should be prohibited from selling. A copy of the *Harrisburg Patriot-News* lay spread out on the rubber counter-mat used by cashiers to drop change. A front-page headline described the latest activity of "The Tobacco Terrorist." An FBI composite sketch, vague enough to fit ten million men, was displayed in a black-bordered box. The cashier moved the paper in order to accept Muntor's check and money.

"Everything all right?" she asked. She did not await a substantive answer but instead squinted at the waitress's penmanship and began to make change for the crumpled five Muntor handed her.

To stifle the urge to cough, Muntor took a deep breath. A musical wheeze issued from his chest. The woman looked up, aimed her squint at him, held it for a beat, and then returned to her change-making task.

He swallowed hard and looked around toward the couple whose demeanor could be that of undercover police. Was the male turning away from him at that instant or just engaged in animated conversation?

Muntor left Bob Diner, walked fast but paced himself and got into his car. A young couple walked past his car as he drove off. *They didn't seem to notice me, though they may have.* Muntor didn't like that possibility. *And now, should a police cruiser come down the street or around the corner and ask them if a guy walked by in the past few minutes, theoretically, they could describe me and my car.*

Muntor drove for several blocks and then turned into an alley. He saw what he had been looking for. The dumpster, green-gray in the poor light, one of its two steel lids raised and beckoning. To make it easier to find at night, he had used reflective spray-paint earlier to draw a yellow smiley face on it. Muntor lowered his window as he inched his car close to the dumpster and, without stopping, tossed in the briefcase.

He drove out of the alley onto the street and accelerated steadily.

70

FEDERAL BUREAU OF INVESTIGATION SECURED TELEX TRANSMISSION
TX2156191095HB05
URGENT/CYCIG EVENT REPORTED TO:
DUTY CHIEF.WX
COPY PHILADELPHIA.FX
FROM: WIREROOM SUPERVISOR.WX
T&D:2156 HOURS 21OCTOBER

MESSAGE: *THE ASSOCIATED PRESS BUREAU OUT OF HARRISBURG RELEASED A STORY AT 9:53 P.M. THIS DATE REPORTING LOCAL PX RADIO DISPATCH OF A POSSIBLE FIND OF ADULTERATED CIGARETTE PACK IN BOB DINER [NOTE: CORRECT SPELLING OF ESTABLISHMENT IS "BOB DINER"], 4545 W. CAPITOL DRIVE, HARRISBURG. NO FLASH SUSPECT DESCRIPTION, NO VEHICLE DESCRIPTION, NO DIRECTION TAKEN. CONFIRMATION PENDING. SA/D. EDMONDS.*
END OF URGENT.

71

FBI Headquarters

The telephone rang at the duty officer's desk. The officer spoke quietly for several minutes before making a note in the daybook. Then he called Franklin.

"Another copycat, sir," the officer said. "Detained in West Hollywood. Tried a Virgil-type switch in a grocery store at the checkout counter. We have a team en route now to interrogate him."

72

Sunday, October 22
Harrisburg, Pennsylvania

Just after dawn, a Harrisburg Police Department patrol car responded to the anonymous 9-1-1 call complaining about a bum making noise rummaging through a dumpster. The car stopped in front of a side street several blocks from Bob Diner. Two policemen got out and walked into the alley behind the Blue Note Cafe and approached the dumpster.

A pair of spindly, baggy-panted legs stuck out of the dented metal container, waving and kicking in the air. The left foot wore a white Nike, the right foot some sort of dirty sky-blue deck shoe. The two policemen stood watching with crossed arms and bored grins.

"Looks like Jeeter legs," one of the cops said. "He must have struck pay dirt this time."

"Looks like he's drowning in there."

"Yeah. I guess we ought to pull him out."

Each policeman grabbed a leg and pulled hard. The rest of Lester Jeeter was jerked into the dim morning light and deposited, standing, on the cement. He was black, rail thin, wild-eyed. In his right hand, he held a briefcase, which he swung blindly at his attackers.

"Whoa, Jeeter!" the first cop said, ducking.

Knocked off balance by the swing of the briefcase, Jeeter fell to the ground. When he looked up and saw that he had swung at the police, he cowered and clutched at the briefcase.

"Don't hit me, man! I thought you was that jitterbug again."

The policemen ignored him. They stared at his shoes.

"Jeeter, who dressed you today? You dress like a fifty-year-old crack-head wino," the first cop said. "Wait a second. You are a fifty-year-old crack-head wino."

The other officer, a sergeant, straightened up. A no-nonsense expression lurched across his face.

"Hey, Keith? Wasn't there a briefcase in the description of the cigarette guy last night?"

At that, Jeeter drew the briefcase tighter to his chest.

"Get away from that, Jeeter," the sergeant said, holding out a hand. "Hand it over. Now."

Jeeter ignored him. "Shit! This is my suitcase. I found it."

The cop stepped forward and yanked the case out of Jeeter's arms.

"Dang, man."

"Cuff him," the sergeant said. And then, into a hand-held radio, "Sixteen-two to dispatch. I'm at Westgrove in the alley, behind the Blue Note. I need the Virgil team back here. Might have something."

"Now look what you've done, Jeeter," the first cop said. All the excitement bewildered Jeeter.

"Don't talk to him, jackweed, cuff him! I know you don't pay attention to Donnelly in the shift briefing, but don't you even watch the news? If this briefcase here has anything to with that Virgil guy, this place is going to be wall-to-wall white-shirts, wall-to-wall Feds, and wall-to-wall reporters in about eight seconds. We screw this up and they'll be laughing at us coast to coast on Dan Rather tonight."

"I was the one who spotted his legs, you know."

Jeeter looked like he was going to cry. "I don't give a rat's ass about no damn Rather tonight. I want my $100 now! What about my $100?"

"What $100?" asked the first cop.

Jeeter paused, not knowing what to say. Then he thought of something. "Hey, it's a nice case, man. It's made out of eels. That's worth a Ben at least! Ain't there some kind of reward for the cigarette man?"

"Eels? You're full of shit, Jeeter."

"Damn, it, Keith. Will you cuff his ass and put him in the car! How many times do I have to tell you? And get the yellow tape out of the trunk."

73

Ben Brandon called Rhoads at 10:00 a.m. and thoroughly enjoyed knowing he had woken him.

"The Deputy Director asked me to call you," he said when Rhoads turned surly. "But I don't know why."

Brandon, who had been up almost four hours already, summarized the facts surrounding the possible recovery of Virgil's briefcase in Harrisburg. He described the events the FBI and Pennsylvania State Police believed may have precipitated Virgil's abandonment of the briefcase.

When Rhoads's conversation with Brandon concluded, Rhoads called Dr. Trice and told her the story. While he spoke with her on his cordless telephone, he walked through the rooms of his apartment, water bottle in hand, misting his trees.

"Remember this, T.R.," she said. "If you have something, if you have anything, you have it because Virgil gave it to you. Don't ever think otherwise, or you'll be sending yourself headlong down a primrose path."

Rhoads nodded, then realized she couldn't see the nod.

"T.R.? You there?"

"Yes."

"You remember what Br'er Rabbit said to Br'er Fox, don't you?"

"Refresh my memory, ma'am."

"It's an old story by Joel Chandler Harris. You see, Br'er Rabbit finds himself being held by the scruff of his neck by the nasty Br'er Fox who is trying to think of something unpleasant to do to Br'er Rabbit. So what Br'er Rabbit does is say, 'Do anything you want, but please don't throw me in the briar patch, it's all stickers and thorns.' So, Br'er Fox, not a deep thinker, but a very categorical thinker, throws Br'er Rabbit into the briar patch and laughs and laughs — until he gets the surprise of his life. Br'er Rabbit jumps up with nary a scratch and deftly makes his way out of the briar patch, dancing and singing. As he's tearing away, Br'er Rabbit looks over his shoulder and with his own laugh shouts, 'Born and bred in a briar patch, Br'er Fox. Born and bred.'"

Rhoads made a mental note to ask Mary if she knew what in the hell Dr. Trice was talking about and what the hell a Br'er Rabbit was.

74

The FBI's Evidence Response Team flew into Harrisburg on a Learjet from Washington. In practically all investigations, crime-scene evidence collection is conducted by local police or the forensic specialists from the nearest FBI field office. Evidence is then shipped directly to the lab in Washington for analysis and often in nothing more secure than FedEx envelopes. In high-priority cases, a courier will hand-carry the material. Only in the rarest of cases would lab technicians come from FBIHQ to supervise evidence gathering. The Washington-based forensics team arrived two hours behind the one from the Philadelphia field office. Franklin instructed the Philadelphia team to do nothing more than protect the scenes at Bob Diner and the dumpster.

The parking lot entrance to the Harrisburg Central police station sat at the end of a peeling, gray corridor tiled with ancient gray linoleum.

With a loud slam, the double-doors of the parking lot entrance burst open. A half-dozen Harrisburg policemen strode in at a pace somewhere between marching and running. Two of them held a cuffed and frantic Jeeter.

From the station's street entrance, at the other end of a nearly identical corridor, another set of double doors burst open. Leaves blew in as a throng of trench-coated federal agents, led by Franklin, strode in. Rhoads's lanky figure was among them.

The two columns of serious men met in the middle and stopped abruptly, face to face.

Franklin produced his badge. "Deputy Director Oakley Franklin, FBI. I need Captain Mulcahy."

"Follow me," one of the Harrisburg officers said.

In an observation area adjacent to the interrogation room, Franklin, Mulcahy, and Rhoads stood together holding coffee cups. They looked through the one-way glass at Jeeter being questioned by Brandon and a black plainclothes Harrisburg detective.

"Don't get your hopes up, Director," Captain Mulcahy said as he leaned against the smudged glass. "I can tell you right now this Q and A is kind of pointless."

"I understand Lester Jeeter is well known to you," Franklin said.

"Yes. The sector guys roust him out of that dumpster every couple of days. His mind is shot. Crack. And vino. A nice combo. Do you want to hear them?"

"Please."

Mulcahy flicked a switch on a battered old speaker mounted on the wall.

Inside the interrogation room, Jeeter sat, now uncuffed, across a plain wooden table from the Harrisburg detective and Brandon.

Brandon was in the midst of speaking. "So, you admit you are now, and have been for many years, an alcoholic, Mr. Jeeter. Is that right?"

Jeeter turned to the detective, incredulous. "What's he talking about? Can't I just sit back in the cage like always?"

"Sure you can, Jeeter." The detective offered him a cigarette and he accepted, nodding thank you. "But the briefcase you found is very important. Can you just tell us what you did this morning, beginning when ... and where ... you woke up."

Brandon rolled his eyes, not approving of the detective's approach.

While Jeeter thought about the question, Brandon grew increasingly impatient. Unable to contain himself any longer, Brandon butted in and pointed at Jeeter. "Yes or no, did you see the perpetrator?"

"Perp-a-what?" Jeeter asked, again looking at the Harrisburg detective. The detective looked toward the one-way mirror hoping the captain would come in and yank out the FBI jerk.

"He wants to know if you saw who put the briefcase in the dumpster," the detective explained.

"I didn't see nobody. Somebody just threw it away. You should see all the stuff you can get from a dumpster. Chairs, half a big bucket full of warm Colonel Sanders. Once I got a computer, and I took it to a guy who just plugged it in and it worked. He gave me a hundred. Now this case, I found it. I found it and if you want it, I want to get paid for it."

"Are you aware, Mr. Jeeter," Brandon said, "that if this is your briefcase, you could be charged with more than 370 counts of first degree murder?"

Jeeter's eyes rolled, terrified. "I didn't kill nobody, man. All I did is find a damn suitcase in the trash." He appealed to the detective. "Bill. Just put me in the cage. Please."

"It's okay, Jeeter. We know you didn't hurt anybody. We're just trying to find the man who put it in the dumpster. The man who put it there is a dangerous killer."

"I told you, I didn't kill nobody, man," Jeeter said and turned away.

From the other side of the one-way glass, Mulcahy, Franklin, and Rhoads watched. Mulcahy looked disgusted, Franklin wore a sour expression, and Rhoads smirked.

"Oh well. Every 'no' brings us closer to a 'yes,'" Franklin said. "Let's call an end to this. Let Mr. Jeeter go. Let him calm down. We can always talk to him later. Do you agree?"

"Yeah," Mulcahy said. He spoke into the intercom. "Wrap it up, Bill." He turned to Franklin. "I don't think it would have gone any differently even if your man hadn't interfered. We'll keep our eye on Jeeter for you. If you ever need him again, just let us know. He won't go far. He's a creature of habit."

"Well, thanks, Captain," Franklin said. "I'm going back to Washington. My lab boys are prepping the evidence for transport to the FBI lab in D.C. First they need to X-ray it. The Pennsylvania State Police Bomb Unit's doing that now. They'll probably need another hour or so. If you don't mind, an Investigative Support Unit crew will be working out of Bob Diner for another twenty-four hours or so. I've asked them to clear everything with you."

The captain nodded.

"And please, thank your men for not giving in to the temptation to open that case," Franklin said. "We won't open it until we get it into a sterile room at the lab. The right speck of dust can speak volumes."

"Every now and then, we get it right."

"By the way," Franklin said. "What's with that name? Bob Diner?"

"Once owned by a man named Charles Avery Bob. It annoys everybody. Part of Harrisburg's charm, don't you think?"

"Not really," Franklin said and turned to Rhoads. "You want to fly back with me?"

"Actually, I thought I'd stick around to see what I can learn from the officer in there," he said, nodding to Brandon in the interrogation room.

"Suit yourself," the Deputy Director said.

75

Rhoads had no intention of hanging around to talk to the cops. He wanted to stay in Harrisburg and nose around without chaperones. He had gotten the call soon after he had gotten the files from Mary. He had hidden the disks in his house, but he hadn't had time to read through the paper copy still in his briefcase.

He was out of cigarettes and couldn't find a vending machine in the station house. He walked down the main corridor and approached several policemen engaged in conversation by the processing desk.

"... by the dumpster behind the diner," one of the officers was saying. "So Louie says 'What do you want with all them cups of coleslaw you take out of the garbage, Jeeter?' And Jeeter says, 'What do you think? I'm having homeless folk over for a buffet, asswipe.'"

The police laughed.

"That don't beat what we saw this morning. You should have seen them legs kicking around in that dumpster," the sergeant said. "Looked like a cartoon."

Imitating Jeeter's voice, the junior officer said, "That's my case, man. It made out of eels, man, eels!"

They all laughed again.

Rhoads jumped in. "Any of you guys tell me where I can get a pack of smokes?"

"If you don't mind Easy Lights, try the diner," a red-faced middle-aged cop said. "They got a fresh batch in last night."

Another officer, embarrassed at his colleague's rudeness to a well-dressed stranger, pointed down the hallway to the street entrance. "There's a Seven-Eleven half a block away. Make a left when you get out front. The machine in the cafeteria here's busted."

Rhoads said thanks and walked toward the exit. He nodded to two special agents. They carried an evidence bag containing the briefcase on their way to Washington.

Rhoads stopped in his tracks, turned back toward the FBI men, and ran to catch up.

"Hey. Hold up."

The men stopped.

"Can I take a peek at the briefcase for a second?" Rhoads asked.

"Who's he?" one of the agents asked.

"Rhoads, the guy from Old Carolina," the other agent said. He turned to Rhoads. "Sorry, it's already sealed."

"Shit," he paused, thinking. Then, to the one who knew him, "You have an inventory sheet?"

"Rhoads, what do you want to know about it? We're late."

"Just a basic description."

The agent closed his eyes to remember what he had written on the sheet. "It's twenty-two inches by eighteen inches by four inches. Hard-side. Leather handle and a three-reel brass combo lock. Worn, brown eel skin covering."

"What kind of covering?"

"Worn. Brown. Eel skin."

"Okay, thank you."

Rhoads struggled to contain himself until he was out of sight of the FBI men and the Harrisburg cops.

Outside, he skipped down the stone steps and along the street toward the Seven-Eleven. He thought, *this is it: seventy-five grand and the boat.*

Rhoads knew a guy like Jeeter wouldn't know eel skin from Sanskrit unless someone told him first. And Rhoads knew who that had to have been. *Virgil. Making sure the briefcase was found.*

Now Rhoads had something the FBI didn't. It felt like a million bucks. He didn't know how to make use of the information, but he was going to protect it with his life until he could figure out what it meant. The closer he got to Virgil, the closer he was getting to the *Deep Blue*. He could see the trawler drifting and bobbing gently out there on the Atlantic under a hot sun with a capacity crowd of rich New Yorkers fishing for yellowfin. *Yeah, baby, I'm getting seasick already. Me and Teddy, trolling for wealthy fishermen.*

He had talked to Teddy at rehab again, and it sounded like he was still doing well. Rhoads knew that rehab wasn't the end of Teddy's troubles, but he still believed that it could be managed if they were together every day. He had thought a lot about solutions to Teddy's money problems, and the boat still seemed to be the best one.

As soon as he had a free minute, he'd dig further into the Midas files. He didn't know exactly what he'd find, but he knew they would be gold. Pratt was careful, but no doubt there was enough there to put him away. Now all he had to do was catch the killer, get the bonus, and only then hand Franklin the files. He laughed to himself. *Yeah, that's all I have to do.*

And he pictured Virgil in his mind's eye. *Come here, you dying son of a bitch. You're the answer to all my problems.*

76

Rhoads walked into the Seven-Eleven and got in line behind a heavy, flustered mother whose three noisy kids were tugging at her jacket. The youngest, a boy of about four, held up a popsicle.

"Ma! Can I have this?"

"Where'd you get that? I told you no candy. You put that back."

"This isn't candy."

"Put it back."

The boy pointed toward a freezer in the rear of the store. "I can't. It's too high."

"Stop it!" she screeched. "You got it out, you put it back. Now."

The boy pouted and did not move.

"You got it out, you put it back," his mother repeated through clenched teeth.

Rhoads watched as the boy slouched tragically back to the freezer. After a backward look at his mother, now busy paying the cashier, the boy managed to slide open the glass lid.

Unable to see in over the top, he stood on tiptoes and felt around in the cold.

Rhoads watched, fascinated by the boy's determination. It wasn't obedience that motivated him, Rhoads realized, but the challenge.

The boy clambered onto the edge of the freezer, leaned forward, and his head and shoulders disappeared inside.

He lost his balance momentarily, fell in another few inches, and flailed his legs wildly in the air to regain control. He found a place to drop the popsicle and tumbled out of the freezer, quietly proud of his effort. He returned to his mother empty-handed and breathing hard.

Something the boy's mother said stood out, hard and cool, the way smooth stones do in a rushing stream. The words repeated themselves to Rhoads like a chant.

"You got it out, you put it back."

Rhoads looked at the boy intently.

"You got it out, you put it back."

He didn't know why the words had such a pull. Another thought flew to him — Dr. Trice's caveat. *Thoughts or ideas that have a different texture about them*, she had said. *They are usually gifts from the universe.*

Outside, he took out his notebook and wrote down the mother's words.

Then he went looking for a telephone booth in a quiet place.

Rhoads hung up after talking to Dr. Trice fifteen minutes later. He took credit for figuring it out, but he knew he never would have even gotten close if it hadn't been for Dr. Trice's guidance.

She had steered him away from the mother's words, though, when the puzzle was solved, it was the words that told the story. Dr. Trice had known somehow to focus on the boy. She had asked Rhoads to describe what stuck out in his mind's eye about him.

"How much I liked him," Rhoads had answered. "The boy forgot all about not being allowed to have the popsicle, and all of a sudden, he had this huge determination to find a way to put it back."

"That was your emotional reaction to him," Dr. Trice had said. "You admire him. Tell me about your mind's eye image of him. What picture do you see?"

Rhoads had to think. Then he laughed. He came around to saying that when the kid slipped and fell further into the freezer, he just kicked and wriggled that much harder, fighting to regain his balance.

The kicking legs.

That's how the police described finding Jeeter. Then Rhoads saw it.

All he said was, "Yes!" That was enough to spark loud laughter from Dr. Trice on her end of the line.

Earlier, the eel skin clue gave Rhoads the idea that Muntor had given the briefcase to Jeeter.

Now he knew why. *Son of a bitch.*

77

After an hour's delay while detectives processed the paperwork, Jeeter left the police station. On his way home, he crossed the street to avoid walking past the dumpster and the two FBI agents who stood on the other side of the yellow tape that cordoned off a section of the alley.

He walked furtively, glancing backward frequently as he hurried along. When he got to a vacant building at the end of a certain block, he crouched down, raised a cardboard flap over a basement window, and crawled through headfirst.

Inside, he lighted a candle he had placed there earlier. He made his way through a series of collapsing, debris-laden rooms, rounded a corner, and lighted two more candles before sitting down on a bed made of wooden crates and plywood loading skids.

The only illumination Jeeter had in the dark rooms were wax candle stubs stuck into wine bottles. He regularly retrieved the stubs from the trash behind an Italian restaurant on State Street. Picture frames without pictures had been crudely nailed over photos carefully cut from *National Geographic* and glued with Elmer's to the water-stained walls. Jeeter collected pictures of tropical beaches.

What served as his bed was a disarranged bedspread atop a stack of several coarse wooden skids. In one corner, a battered television set with a broken antenna sat on the case of a malfunctioning VCR. The lone table featured a standing frame filled with a generic print of a blonde woman and toddler. They both beamed.

This makeshift residence, without heat, without running water, without electricity, was what, in his own mind, made Jeeter a class apart from the homeless.

Jeeter's ears pricked up at quiet footsteps outside. In the near dark, he froze, listening. Another scuffle and the sound of someone lifting the cardboard flap. He held his breath, his eyes showing alarm.

He heard someone lower himself into the back room. Jeeter looked for a hiding place and stooped in a corner behind a corrugated box to pull the bedspread over himself. He knew he could look like the rest of the junk. *There's nothing wrong with you 'cause God don't make no junk*, his big sister used to tell him a long time ago.

He heard a sound behind him, like a faint sigh. He was too frightened to stay hidden. He tore the bedspread off and whirled to look, his face knotted in fear.

There, leaning against the doorway, was one of the FBI men, somberly observing him and his dirty bedspread shawl.

Still fearful, but not quite so terrified, Jeeter stammered, "Who you?"

"Who did you think I was, Jeeter?"

"I didn't think you was nobody."

Rhoads just watched him, then spoke. "You thought I was him. Didn't you?"

Jeeter wagged his head "no" with great force. "No. I don't know who you talking about."

Rhoads took half a step closer. Jeeter tried to move back but found himself against a wall. The candlelight flickered.

"I'm not here to hurt you," Rhoads said. "I'm an investigator. I was on the other side of the glass in the police station. I saw that jerk from the FBI treating you disrespectfully. I just want to talk to you some more about what happened this morning at the dumpster."

Rhoads calmly entered the room. Jeeter, still crouching with his skinny back pressed against the wall, remained still. Without approaching him, Rhoads moved around, looking at the few possessions on the walls and floor.

"You're a cop. This is my home. You got a warrant?" Rhoads did not answer. Jeeter said, "I said all I got to about it this morning. I told it all already."

Rhoads picked up the picture of the blonde mother and child and ran his finger along the frame picking up dust. "I don't think so, Jeeter. You told them you found the case this morning. That isn't true."

"Is too. I was taking it out. They saw me taking it out."

"When the cops grabbed you, you weren't pulling it out, were you?"

"I sure was!" Jeeter shrugged off the silly bedspread, stood upright, and took a tentative half-step away from the wall. "They my witness! Go back and ask them. The sarge and that rookie Keith."

"Jeeter. Tell me the truth." Rhoads reached into his pocket and took out a rubber-banded clump of cash, driver's license, credit cards, ATM card, and the assorted business cards he'd collected but never discarded.

"Jeeter, you're not in any trouble. But I have to find the man who ..." Rhoads flipped through the clump and found what he was looking for, a one hundred dollar bill. He removed it and put the rest of the money and cards back into his pocket.

Jeeter's eyes fixed on the bill. "I'd sure like that hundred dollars, but still, I'm not going to lie. Nobody told me where to look."

Strike one, Rhoads thought.

He held up the bill by one corner and slowly crumpled it until it was a compressed wad completely concealed in his fist. "Ben Franklin's in jail, Jeeter," he said, "and only the truth can set him free."

Jeeter shook his head. Whatever was frightening him was real, Rhoads saw.

"The truth, Jeeter. I need the truth." Rhoads kept the bill hidden in his fist and extended his arm. "Whoever he was, Jeeter, you're the last guy in the whole world he ever wants to see again. He won't be back to bother you."

"You know that minimum-wage black-assed security guard in Washington, D.C.?" said Jeeter. "The one who found the adhesive tape on the door at the Watergate back in the Nixon days?"

"Sure. The one man who all the ex-CIA burglars didn't count on."

"Yeah, him. What'd he ever get out of it?"

Strike two, baby.

"I imagine he's a pretty proud man."

"Dirt poor, too, I bet. I read about how he lives now." Jeeter took a pack of cigarettes out of his pocket and lit one.

"Still ..." Rhoads began.

Jeeter cut him off.

"Look, I just found it, man. I just found the damned case." Jeeter sat down on the bed. Boards creaked. "Now, I told you the truth. Give me the money."

"Not until you tell me what you were really doing back at that dumpster, Jeeter."

"I just did."

"No."

"I just found it."

"You were putting it back," Rhoads whispered.

Jeeter shivered. "Oh, no. No sir! I was taking it out. They even saw me. You can ask them."

"You used that one already."

Rhoads uncrumpled the bill, then slowly crumpled it in his fist again. "Let me help you get old Ben out of the can," he said. "You just nod when I tell you how it really was."

Jeeter shook his head "no," but Rhoads continued.

"He approached you two or three days ago. Right?"

Jeeter wouldn't nod.

"He told you what to look for, a brown eel skin briefcase."

Jeeter looked away.

That's as good as a nod, Rhoads thought.

"He told you where to look for it, or maybe you suggested the dumpster. I mean it's your dumpster, right?"

Jeeter gave a tentative nod coupled with a small shrug.

"And he told you when it would be there. And he gave you money, and he promised you more, didn't he?"

Another tiny nod.

"He also told you if you brought it to the cops, you could get a few bucks from them, too, didn't he? He was the one who told you they'd part with one hundred dollars."

Jeeter averted his eyes and looked down at his two mismatched shoes.

Strike three.

"Then you heard all the excitement last night at Bob Diner, all the commotion. And you couldn't wait. Maybe somebody else, some homeless bum, was going to poach on your dumpster. So you went to the dumpster, and you got the briefcase out, sooner than the man told you to. Right?"

Jeeter looked up at the ceiling like a kid getting a lecture.

"You brought it back here. Right? But you didn't think it would matter, because you were going to put it back and then find it later when he wanted you to."

Jeeter lowered his eyes, looked over at Rhoads, and nodded again, even more slowly. Rhoads let a small smile play across his face as he moved about the room, casually examining things.

"Good, Jeeter. Thank you. This is between us, Jeeter. Now, there are just three simple things I need from you," Rhoads said. He handed Jeeter the $100 bill.

"One, a description of the guy, as detailed as you can. And two, as much as you can remember about what he said to you, word for word. And three, whatever it was that you took from the briefcase."

Rhoads had worked his way over to the fractured television and VCR near Jeeter's bed. He looked at them closely. Neither had worked in years, but next to them there was a stack of six or eight dusty, sun-warped videocassettes waiting to be played someday when things were better.

"I didn't take nothing, man," Jeeter said. "Just kept the suitcase here so nobody else'd get it. Just like you said."

Rhoads looked through the stack of cassettes.

Jeeter pointed a finger at Rhoads and shouted. "Hey!" That startled Rhoads.

"Hey!" Jeeter said. "I got a idea. How 'bout a drink, man? Gooood stuff." He went toward a wooden cabinet. "Special stuff for a special occasion. And real clean glasses, too."

Jeeter moved a box and from behind it retrieved a dirty shopping bag, but inside the bag was a wooden gift box. When he opened it, Rhoads saw it was lined in red felt. Two spotless crystal long-stemmed goblets and a bottle of Wild Turkey sat nestled inside.

Nice try. Rhoads could spot a decoy maneuver a mile away.

Where was I when he interrupted? Rhoads thought. He furrowed his brow. *I was at the stack of videos.* He went back, reached out, and took one cassette from the middle of the stack, the clean, new cassette. It had a label, hand-lettered, that read, "Six-minute scene from *Paradiso*, shot Bucks County, Oct. 20."

Jeeter's face twitched. He swallowed hard and moistened his thick chapped lips. He looked away.

"Okay," Rhoads said. "Let's have that drink, Mr. Jeeter. And you can tell me all about it."

78

Forty-five minutes later, Rhoads left Jeeter's, stuck a cigarette in his mouth, and walked back toward the police station.

He stopped before he arrived there. He wanted to see the video before the FBI did. He turned and walked in another direction. He had no idea where he was going. He walked past a liquor store, a pawnshop, a grocery store with a Korean name, a couple of abandoned storefronts. He stopped in front of a sign that read "Beaverly Hills Video." A porno arcade.

He went in and faced the clerk. "Do you have a booth here where you can watch full-length videos?" Rhoads half-hoped no such booths were available. He worried about sitting in something sticky.

The place reeked of disinfectant and smoke. The clerk nodded to a row of freshly painted booths at the far end of the store.

"Five bucks an hour for the booth, five ninety-five for a full-length adult film," the clerk said. "You can pick any one of those." He pointed toward a wall of shelves holding hundreds of porno films classified alphabetically by perversion.

"I brought my own tape."

"Nope. You can't do it."

"I'll give you the extra five ninety-five anyway."

"I said no." He stood up from the bar stool he had been on.

"What's the difference? I'm paying the same as if I rented one."

"Because last year some asshole comes in here with the same story and I say okay. Next thing I know, I'm closed down for thirty days. Asshole's watching some imported kiddie porn, and that's the same day the state's got some undercover inspector in here. So that's why."

Rhoads put thirty dollars on the counter.

"Ten for the shop, twenty for you. This isn't even porno. I'm a cop."

Inside the musty booth, after some fancy footwork explaining why he didn't have his badge, Rhoads slid the videocassette into the VCR. Rhoads could hear the machine running, and he could see the counter on the VCR clicking away, but the screen remained blank.

Virgil's idea of a joke?

Then a sputter of white static and something not quite discernible.

Roiling clouds of gray. Thick, turbulent, opaque. Then, gradually, like an image appearing in a film developer's tray, Rhoads began to see the shape and features of a human figure becoming visible among the clouds. The ambient light increased steadily. At last Rhoads was able to make out the details of a fireman's helmet, a full-face gas mask, a fluorescent yellow tent-like parka, and the long curved snout of an orchard-fogger belching gas from the green-and-white-tank strapped onto a man's back.

The scene was interrupted by a break and sputter of static. Another shot.

From one hundred yards back, a dilapidated building, perhaps an old school or hospital building in the countryside. Broken windows and a partially caved-in roof. At the near end of the building, everywhere, between the shattered panes of glass and the broken slats of the roof, the gray fog escaped, bleeding heavily into the sky.

What was it? Some kind of smoke? Steam?

Oh Lord, no, Rhoads realized.

It was gas.

Rhoads found himself walking on the street, his mind reeling.

He sighed when he realized he'd have to turn the video over to the FBI. He hated having to lose his advantage, but he thought that what he had found would go a long way towards earning the bonus from Pratt.

79

ASSOCIATED PRESS
ATTN.: ALL EDITORS, ALL MEDIA
BREAKING STORY UPDATE MONDAY, OCTOBER 23, 2:15 P.M. EST.
HARRISBURG, PA.
SLUG: **VIRGIL BRIEFCASE RECOVERED?**

ART AVAILABLE: 2 COLOR PIX.
1. *Crime scene. Dumpster in Harrisburg, PA, where briefcase was recovered.*
2. *Close-up of briefcase that may have been abandoned by 'Virgil' in Harrisburg, PA.*
(Xmit of FBI photo)

FBI: "VIRGIL EVIDENCE FOUND
IN HARRISBURG, PA."
By Fred Bird
Associated Press Staff Reporter

[Sunday, October 22-Harrisburg, PA.] In what may be the most significant evidence recovered so far in the cigarette-tampering investigation, the FBI today announced that technicians are analyzing an eel skin briefcase that may have been abandoned by a skittish "Virgil" who is suspected of fleeing from a diner here. A pack of tainted cigarettes was also recovered from the diner.

The Virgil investigation began 20 days ago when an unknown person or persons poisoned seven hundred packs of Easy Lights cigarettes and shipped them to tobacco shops all over the United States. More than 300 died. Since then, at least 30 others have died in subsequent tampering incidents authorities believe were perpetrated by the original killer.

As of noon today, 376 people have died and 41 remain hospitalized from injuries received when they smoked cigarettes laced with the residue of a sodium cyanide solution. Five people across the U.S. have been arrested in separate copycatting incidents, none fatal.

"We have not yet had enough time to confirm whether or not the briefcase is indeed Virgil's," an FBI spokesman said. "The evidence has been transported to the FBI Lab in Washington where it is under intense scrutiny at this moment. The FBI has released an updated description and sketch of the man believed to be Virgil. If anyone wishes to provide the FBI with information regarding this investigation, they are urged to call 202–324–3000. Agents are standing by now. There is no question about it. We need the public's help in apprehending Virgil, who has now reached the dubious status of the country's most heinous serial murderer."

80

FBI Headquarters

In Lab One on the third floor of FBI headquarters, an FBI agent who specialized in locks used a steel tool to roll the reels of the lock on the eel-skin briefcase, feeling for the tumblers to click. He did not need the stethoscope in his tool kit. He knew as soon as he saw it that the three-reel lock would be easy to open.

"Got it," he said as he found the number on the last reel. A latex-covered index finger tested the two side latches. He looked up at Franklin, who loomed over his shoulder. "Want me to pop it?"

"Go ahead. *Slowly.*"

His gloved hands carefully released latches, thumbs in place to catch the tiny brass plates from springing back with the familiar snap. Franklin and various agents and technicians clustered around the table on which the briefcase sat.

"Gee. How creative," the lock-picking technician said. "The combo was one-zero-zero."

"At least it didn't explode," Franklin said.

The lead technician looked at him with surprise. "Sir. We X-rayed it thoroughly before picking it up off of the detective's desk in Harrisburg."

"Just a joke, Galton. Disregard it. What have we got?"

Galton rose and another technician slid into the seat. With the aid of a large magnifying glass, he began looking through the briefcase, comparing items to images on 8x10 glossy photographs he had removed from a file folder.

"I'm ninety-nine point nine nine nine certain it's his," the other technician said after a moment. He counted under his breath. "Fourteen packs of cigarettes, various brands. Four Aimsco Ultra-Thin half-cc twenty-eight-gauge syringes, one plastic jar of one hundred tablets of Vitamin C ... but ... wait," he said, gently shaking the jar, "there seems to be a loose powder inside. I imagine we'll be taking a close look at that." He leaned farther into the open briefcase. "Three disposable Bic lighters and ... Damn, sir! I think he may have blown it this time. I can see smudged prints all over the place. All over the place."

The men look at each other with tentative grins.

"Are you sure?" Franklin asked.

"Yes. I am. They're everywhere in here. I don't think he was expecting anyone to get hold of the briefcase. You know how meticulous he's been."

Two agents high-fived each other.

One of the agents leaned in over the technician's shoulder to get a better look. Then he shrugged and said, "I got twenty bucks to anybody's ten that says those prints index to one Loren D. Benedict."

Galton spent the next four hours taking apart the briefcase, molecule by molecule. As soon as he noted his initial impressions, he called Franklin, who had gone home for a few hours' sleep. The Deputy Director was just stepping out of the shower when the telephone rang.

"Good news and bad," Galton said. "First, there's no question about it, the briefcase is a bonanza. It's definitely him, Oak, or someone using the identical batch of sodium cyanide, the stuff from Tellman Chemicals & Supplies in Baton Rouge. And in the briefcase, we found seven newspaper clippings stapled together. All but one of the articles were Virgil stories. But the bad news is the prints belong to Lester Jeeter."

An alarm went off in Franklin's brain. "Something's wrong, Galton. Jeeter never opened the case. The police made that clear."

"Unless he opened it before he got caught, somehow."

"No. The police were definite about that. They saw him inside the dumpster before he got it out. We have to pick him up. Damn it. We had a material witness, and I released him! Hold on Galton." Galton heard Franklin shout for his wife. "Lydia!" Louder. "Lydia!" A woman shouted back from somewhere far off. Then Franklin again. "Lydia! Call my office. Tell them it's urgent and to pick up Jeeter in Harrisburg." The far-off voice said something in reply. Franklin repeated himself. "Pick up Jeeter in Harrisburg. They'll know. I'm on a call, tell them I'll call them in five minutes."

"Okay, Galton. I had to get that rolling."

"Also, Oak, there's a slight chance we may learn something about the water he used in mixing the cyanide solution. If he used tap water from a major municipal utility, there may be some markers. But don't get your hopes up. Back to the sodium cyanide, it's not likely someone else is using the Tellman batch. And there's something else, I don't know if it helps or not. A hair fragment."

"A hair fragment?"

"Not human."

"Canine?"

"Feline. The question is, when did it get in there? Are our evidence experts still up there in Harrisburg?"

"Yes."

"I'll call them, tell them I'm looking for any hint that a cat or cats have been in Jeeter's residence or anywhere else he may have opened the case. Ask Jeeter if he has a cat or if cats come into his place."

"Where was the hair?"

"Behind the built-in fanfold compartment in the side of the case. The little belt buckle thing was buckled closed. We unbuckled it and looked around."

Franklin thought. "How flat is the fanfold compartment when it's empty and buckled closed?"

"Like a file folder with nothing in it. Pretty flat."

"Tight enough that a junkie would figure there's nothing in there worth taking the time to unbuckle a fastener for?"

"Unless he's a crack addict desperate for cash. He wouldn't have cared how flat it was."

"Okay. You've made a case for him opening it. You know many drug addicts jonesing for the glass pipe who would take the time to re-buckle?"

Galton thought about that then said, "Good point."

"I'd say then whatever you found behind there probably belongs to Virgil, not Jeeter. And I doubt anyone would think to plant anything that subtle. Too much of a long shot that we'd even find it."

"Okay, Oakley. The problem is, is I'm not sure what we could do with a garden-variety cat hair."

"I know. In the meantime, get some extreme close-up color photos of the hair made while we try to figure how if it can help us."

"That's already being done."

"Galton? What was the subject of that other newspaper article?"

"A sheet torn out of *Adweek* magazine listing a bunch of ad industry events taking place in Las Vegas. We're working on that, too."

81

Harrisburg, Pennsylvania

Six FBI agents peeled out of the driveway at Bob Diner after getting word, relayed from Washington, about Jeeter. The message had been terse. *Priority. Get to Lester Jeeter's residence and take him into custody and seize the building.*

Harrisburg homicide's day-work One-Squad got the call from the FBI. The fire department arrived simultaneously in response to a report of smoke in the building.

The officers discovered Lester Jeeter dead on his side, lying on the floor by the front door of what seemed to be his living room. A section of greasy rug under Jeeter's head smoldered from a cigarette that had apparently fallen out of his mouth, sending acrid smoke throughout the rooms and out onto the street where someone had noticed and called it in.

The fire department started an electrical generator and brought in a set of lights to illuminate the crime scene.

"What a loser," a Harrisburg homicide detective said to one of the FBI agents. The FBI agent gazed at Jeeter and shook his head. Cyanotic skin is tougher to determine by sight on the body of a black man than on a lighter-skinned person. But there wasn't much question about it. Virgil had struck again.

The homicide detective stooped close to Jeeter's body and continued his inspection. "Can I ask you something?" he said to the FBI agent. "I mean how fucking stupid do you have to be to steal cigarettes from the guy who's known all over the universe for poisoning them. You got to laugh. You really got to."

The FBI forensic experts who had taken the briefcase to the FBI Lab in Washington were ordered back to Harrisburg.

Within minutes after landing, they would begin tearing the place apart.

The experts found mostly what they expected. A lot of filth, and, right there on the kitchen counter, a pack of Montgomerys, the lot number of which indicated it had been distributed by Old Carolina Tobacco, Inc. to a retailer in Atlanta. The lot number matched that of another pack recovered from a previous CYCIG crime scene. Residue on the cigarette paper showed a water stain, as had other cigarettes recovered from earlier crime scenes. Occasionally, Virgil had gotten sloppy while injecting the cyanide solution, and the solution would leave its mark.

The county coroner signed the custody form that officially turned the decedent's body over to the FBI. The FBI's experts were not ready yet to have Jeeter shipped to the morgue.

The coroner took a last glance at the body and raised his hand to the others in a silent goodbye as he left the crumbling building Lester Jeeter had called home.

82

Asheville

"Why go overboard? Why take any additional risk?" Pratt said to Valzmann, who sat across from him in the Executive Suite. Pratt took a scrap of paper from his pocket and looked at it. Genevieve's handwriting. She had given it to him earlier when the market closed at four o'clock.

Closing price, Old Carolina Tobacco, Inc.
184 –1 1/4, Volume 4,940,000.
Third most active stock

He crumbled the paper and put it back in his pocket. He looked up at Valzmann.

"Look," Pratt said, raising his eyebrows to emphasize that it was all Easy Street from here on in. "You've already, in effect, buried him. There's no need to do anything else. First they'll find the cash in his apartment, with a nice chunk missing. Then with a little help, if necessary, they'll get the idea to search his uncle's mountain lodge. And the stink that will greet them when they open that canvas bag." Pratt stopped speaking. His mouth parted into a white-toothed grin that burst into an ugly, raucous laugh. It took him some time to regain control of himself.

Valzmann smiled and nodded in agreement. He had a sudden thought. "Mr. Pratt? What about the security violation copies Dallaness made? They're live grenades."

"Dallaness!" Pratt said and laughed again. He rose and walked over to the telescope that stood trained on a particularly scenic crest of the Blue Ridge Mountains. "Mary Dallaness?" he said, squinting into the eyepiece. "That mouse. She's nothing to worry about."

"Then why'd she make them in the first place?"

"Who knows? Because Rhoads told her to."

Pratt walked over and slapped Valzmann on the back.

Valzmann took his cue to leave and made it as far as Pratt's door before the CEO called to him.

"Hang on for a second," Pratt said. "Come back in here. And close the door."

Valzmann liked the sound of this.

Pratt took a seat on the gray leather sofa.

"You gave me an idea, Valzmann. If you were Mary Dallaness and if you were Tommy Rhoads and if you had stolen some critically important documents from a bunch of ruthless bastards, who would you give them to for safekeeping?"

"Exactly," Valzmann said, closing his eyes, already considering how he'd handle it.

"Wait." Pratt worried about a possible complication. "If Rhoads had an accident now, instead of later as we've planned, how would that affect his role as fall guy for Benedict's disappearance?"

"I believe it would enhance it. He wouldn't be available to complain to his new friends at Tenth and Pennsylvania."

Pratt's countenance darkened. "Okay," he said. Scenes from the movie he was directing played on the screen before his mind's eye. He turned and pointed his long, tan finger in Valzmann's face. "Listen carefully. Here's what you do."

83

New York

At 9:45 p.m., with ample time for overnight editors to use the material in morning editions or early newscasts, the Dow Jones news service released two stories analyzing the financial impact of Virgil's "public awareness campaign" on the tobacco industry and related business sectors.

The market's gut reaction when the news broke twenty-one days earlier had been negative speculation and wild selling by private share-holders and skittish institutional investors. That backlash had, over the following days, been counterbalanced by investors who thought the recent erosion of industry stock prices presented outstanding buying opportunities. Although prices continued to fall, rumors abounded that institutional investors were planning to buy huge blocks of stock in the immediate future.

The Dow Jones stories were based on what staff reporters were able to sniff out from contacts at Wall Street's brokerage firms.

Since the Virgil story broke, the brokerage house analysts who covered the tobacco industry had been pressed into overdrive. They worked anxiously at terminals to be the first to forecast the correct direction of tobacco stock prices and beat competing investment firms who would offer similar investment advice to their customers. The analysts dug into just-released tobacco industry retail sales data looking for Virgil's impact on company earnings, market trends, and insider transactions.

The internal auditors at the Big Eight cigarette manufacturers worked overtime as well to tabulate retail sales reports and other data as it became available. Projections were in demand in the executive suites. Demographic experts from the Association of Tobacco Marketers were placed conspicuously in 250 retail sales locations throughout the U.S. to observe buying behavior, conduct exit interviews with cigarette customers, and distribute cigarette safety tip sheets, advising smokers how to search for telltale signs of package tampering.

Publicly, Big Eight media spokespeople stated that not only had sales not decreased, they had increased as a result of kneejerk hoarding, a typical consumer buying behavior. Some people feared that cigarettes would be temporarily de-shelved until the tampering incidents could be controlled. Big Eight management was only vaguely concerned about the quirky drop in ten-day sales trends in the east and southeast. Sales were down 0.6 percent, something that had never happened in the fall. Cooler weather brought higher sales. Meteorological reports showed that temperatures had been lower than average so far for the season. Typically, sales rose 2 to 3 percent in comparable ten-day periods.

The research division of the Gallup Organization, retained in secrecy by the ATM, worked to analyze reports calculating how many smokers, if any, had been inspired by Virgil's behavior to try to quit smoking. The ATM found the early numbers unsettlingly high. Twenty-one percent of survey respondents said they intended to quit smoking within the next two weeks. Typically 18 percent of those responding said they intended to quit "now or in the near future," when asked the week before New Year's Eve.

In confidential memorandums, the industry's own experts determined that 8.9 percent of "serious" quitters never resumed smoking, and from that they computed a model of a permanent loss-of-revenue. The numbers got a grim reception in tobacco industry executive suites.

And there was more bad news for the industry. The twelve-step programs at the heart of support groups such as Alcoholics Anonymous were reported to be exceptionally effective for motivated cigarette quitters.

Sponsored by the National Respiratory Health Foundation, Smokers Anonymous meetings were launched in 325 locations across the United States.

84

Clipping from Monday's *New York Post*:

SIX ARRESTED IN "VIRGIL" SIT-IN AT R.J. REYNOLDS IN NEW YORK
Crowds Jeer, Throw Bottles as Police Arrest Demonstrators

85

From the *Pittsburgh Post-Gazette*:

Man Described as Thin, Grey, Sickly
Scalper at Three Rivers Sounds Virgil Alarm
"The Guy's Coughing Made Me Suspicious"

86

Tuesday, October 24
Asheville

It was Rhoads's turn to wake Fallscroft. The pilot answered groggily.

"Can I be at FBI Headquarters in D.C. by 6 a.m.?"

"I imagine this is serious," Fallscroft said.

"Can I be there?"

"If this is serious, sure."

"The FBI called. There's been a significant development," Rhoads said. "Virgil wants money. Meet you at the helipad in how long?"

"What time is it now?"

"Three."

"Three in the morning?"

"That's the one."

Rhoads heard Fallscroft release a long sigh. "We can take off at four o'clock straight up."

"I'll be there."

"T.R., you're not drunk, are you?"

"Not yet. You in?"

"It's what they pay me for."

87

New York

A stock quotation from the *Wall Street Journal*:

> Closing price, Old Carolina Tobacco, Inc.
> 182 –2 1/4, Volume 11,162,000.
> Second most active stock

88

From the *Cincinnati Star*:

Terrorist Stole Vending Machine Keys from Delivery Van
**VIRGIL FILLS BUS TERMINAL VENDING MACHINE
WITH CYANIDE CIGARETTES**
Four Cincinnati Fatalities Bring Death Toll to 385

89

The national news editors of *USA Daily* sat around the huge budget table and tried to figure out how to handle the wild reaction to Virgil's $1.5 billion demand.

The publisher, an obnoxious, self-absorbed country-clubber who forced his inane twice-weekly conservative column on the paper and its readers, came late and disrupted the meeting in progress.

"We want to be super careful that how we handle this does not encourage Virgil to up the ante," he said.

"Any more than we already have," a senior reporter added.

The publisher ignored the remark. "Let's see the headline candidates," he said.

An assistant held up an oversized sheet.

Authorities Believe Surrender Offer Is Legit
VIRGIL TO GIVE UP IF CIG FIRMS DONATE
$1.5 BILLION TO RESEARCH
Staggering Sum "Pocket Change" for $45 Billion Industry

The publisher read it and looked at the picture of the FBI press conference announcing the demand Virgil made in an interview with a *Washington Post* reporter. The publisher nodded. The assistant held up another headline.

Killer Made $1.5 Billion Demand via *Washington Post*
A DYING VIRGIL WANTS TO GIVE UP
IF CIG FIRMS 'DONATE' TO RESEARCH
Experts Say Virgil's Cancer Is Likely Weakening Him

The publisher rolled his eyes. "You're plugging the *Washington Post?* Are we going to include one of their subscription forms, too?"

90

Event Response Center
FBI Headquarters

The room was filled with FBI agents, terrorism experts from the United States Army and CIA, state police representatives, technicians, and other specialists.

Franklin, Brandon, Rhoads and a dozen others sat and stood around a conference table.

A huge map depicting all CYCIG crime scenes hung on the wall behind them.

Franklin, at the head of the table, held up a newspaper. "I take it everyone has seen this. The early edition of today's *Washington Post*."

The *Washington Post's* Exclusive Interview with Virgil
VIRGIL: "I WILL QUIT FOR $1.5 BILLION"
Money to Fund Medical Research

"We'll get to specifics of that situation later," Franklin said. "But first, let's get caught up on exactly where we are."

Rhoads had finally come through and delivered what he claimed were the secret Midas files. They were exactly what Franklin had been looking for, and they corroborated the information Benedict had mailed to the DOJ. They probably wouldn't help catch Virgil, but he was already looking past the CYCIG case to a major prosecution of Old Carolina and Pratt.

Franklin knew Rhoads had kept some of the best information back as a kind of insurance, but he had learned to trust him. Rhoads had delivered them the best lead so far, and if he wanted to make sure he got his payday, Franklin didn't blame him. The guy had been a good cop, and now he was a private citizen with a family to take care of. Franklin didn't see any problem with making it a win-win for both of them.

"It's been twenty-three days since Event Day One, we have three hundred and eighty-seven dead, including three school-age kids," said Franklin. "And about one hundred hospitalized, most with permanent respiratory damage. Plenty of them will die. There have been victims in thirty-six states. But the concentration of fatality sites, not including the FedEx barrage at the beginning, has been focused more heavily in the northeast corridor. We've had a total of two verified sightings. The man can walk into a crowded bus terminal in Cincinnati, refill a cigarette vending machine, and no one can say what he looks like. He's Mr. Average, Mr. Unremarkable, the Invisible Man. Not even a consistent physical description, as you can see from the sketches."

Franklin indicated a series of oversized wall-mounted posters. "You all have tapes and transcripts and reports of all of Virgil's telephone calls, both to us and to other individuals and organizations. As a bonus, we've now had a total of twenty-one copycat incidents, mostly pranks just to frighten people, and none lethal, not even any serious injuries. For most of this period, our primary suspect has been Loren Benedict, a former scientist at the Old Carolina Tobacco, Inc. facility in Denver. Benedict disappeared from Old Carolina on 17 January, two years ago. Five days before that, someone, presumably Benedict, called the Department of Justice and then mailed in three pounds of files claiming that they were proof of Old Carolina's conspiracy to covertly increase the nicotine levels in three of its major cigarette brands.

"As a bonus, Benedict included a copy of a secret internal report showing that Old Carolina held indisputable scientific evidence linking cigarette smoke to a dozen types of cancer. No one has heard from him since. And Virgil uses a gruff articulation to disguise his voice, so no one who knows Benedict can say Virgil is or isn't Benedict. For what it's worth, we've played the tapes for his mother and sister, and they're convinced the caller is not Benedict. This is in line with what we've concluded independently. As of now, Benedict is no longer our prime suspect."

Franklin took a sip of water from a coffee mug.

"Now," he continued, "it's time for reports on the most recent incidents and evidence. Assistant Section Chief Danny Maharis of the Forensics Unit will update us on the briefcase. And I should point out that much of this evidence is due to the efforts of our consultant, Mr. Rhoads."

Franklin sat down and Maharis, a sandy-haired man with wire-rimmed glasses, rose.

"The evidence," Maharis began, "was recovered from a dumpster in Harrisburg, Pennsylvania, following a sighting of Virgil on Saturday, four days ago. Initially we believed that he had been pressured by some circumstance into abandoning the briefcase because of fear of apprehension, but subsequent events," he said as he shot Rhoads a dark glance, "lead us to believe that the briefcase was, in fact, a plant intended, apparently, as communication of some sort. But we are not certain about that. However, thanks to the outstanding efforts of Frank Galton, we believe we've recovered two items of substantial forensic value that Virgil, we're praying, doesn't know he let us have."

Maharis clicked a slide projector's remote. An enlargement of a partial fingerprint appeared.

"The first of these items is a partial print, still unidentified, which all but eliminates Benedict as Virgil. Frank had the good sense to take apart the three-reel combination lock and scan partial prints from the unexposed surfaces of the reels. Virgil hadn't wiped those surfaces clean. Then Frank compared them with known Benedict prints. Not even close. The second item..."

He clicked the remote again, and an image of a Bengal house cat appeared.

"... was a single cat hair. We traced it to a rare and exotic breed of house cat known as a Bengal. This turns out to be the most significant lead we have so far. There are fewer than thirty approved breeders of Bengals in the U.S., and maybe fifty or sixty who are unregistered. As we speak, we are talking to every Bengal breeder we can find. And an additional item that was in the briefcase ..."

Maharis leveled a scowl at Rhoads.

"... a videocassette, will be discussed by Dr. Myron Sorken, who is working in conjunction with the Behavioral Science Section.

"Based on analysis of the videotape and what the subject recorded, we are confident that the images were indeed recorded in Bucks County, Pennsylvania. We also think the date and time noted were at least fairly accurate, based on our study of the angle of the sun and shadows and the visible flora."

Sorken rose slowly and walked to the podium, adjusted the microphone, and began. "Due to the attention focused on the suspect Benedict, my involvement with BSS in this investigation had, unfortunately, been limited prior to the recovery of the briefcase. We had been developing a profile that has been further enhanced and revised in light of the videotape. We are prepared to state positively that the perpetrator is a white male, of mid- to late middle age, perhaps of genius level I.Q., almost certainly afflicted with a terminal lung condition. His latent tendencies toward paranoid schizophrenia have been amplified considerably by his medical condition. He is, we believe, in a partially or wholly dissociated state and believes himself to be a kind of Messiah or avenger who is above human morality. To put it more simply, he believes he's doing the right thing."

A murmur, then someone whispered something about a Spike Lee movie.

"And," Sorken continued, "his determination is fueled by that conviction. The content of the videotape is hopeless, forbidding, threatening. From the little we have to work with, Virgil appears to be planning a mass murder event modeled on the Nazi gas-chamber atrocities. The scope of which ..." Sorken said with high drama in his voice, punching out each word with a finger jab to the table, "... we do-not-know."

Franklin nodded to Sorken and raised the newspaper he had previously exhibited. "Dr. Sorken, how does the *Washington Post* demand fit into your profile? Is this consistent?"

"As a manifestation of the overall delusion, his seeing himself as divine, or nearly divine, he affirms it to himself, and to us, through acts of control and intimidation. It is not nearly so important what the demand is, but that we obey it, as the unfortunate follow-up to Mr. Pratt's failure to make the required broadcast on 6 October makes clear."

"If I can cut through some of your language here, you're telling us he's on a divine mission and he can't be reasoned with, and he won't stop until he's had his holocaust," Franklin said.

Sorken was pleased. "That's right."

"But he's dying. Won't it catch up with him at some point?"

"It's always a possibility he'll just expire, but many schizophrenics are capable of extraordinary feats of physical endurance regardless of their actual state of health. And if, as may well be the case, he is resorting to chemical stimulants, these will have a concomitant effect, increasing the psychosis and thereby further increasing both physical strength and stamina. At present, our judgment is that he is an exceedingly dangerous and formidable person and far from running out of gas."

Franklin turned from Sorken and addressed the rest of the ERC. "The demand issued through his *Washington Post* interview was, of course, targeted at the tobacco companies, and Mr. Thomas Rhoads, chief security consultant at Old Carolina, will report on the steps being taken in those quarters."

Brandon cleared his throat and shifted in his seat. He had confronted Franklin earlier and said, "What I'd like to know is why Rhoads is here and not in a cell charged with obstruction of justice, destruction of evidence, and accessory to first- degree murder."

Franklin said, "You're out of order, Brandon. Rhoads is here because I made the decision to include him, and because he's helped us make significant inroads in the case. Understood?"

"Understood," Brandon said.

Rhoads grinned and winked at Brandon before rising to speak. "Nicholas Pratt and the CEOs of the other seven leading cigarette manufacturers will be holding a joint press conference later in the week to announce how best to meet the terms and conditions for the transfer of one point five billion dollars to the research organizations Virgil specified. Their plans will be closely coordinated with you guys. I'm the go-between. Now, there is something that I'd like to say about the way you all have interpreted the evidence."

Several agents sat up to listen, but many more shot each other mocking looks.

Rhoads let them settle down and said, "You are still underestimating him."

"Oh come on!" Brandon said, slapping his palm on the table and looking toward the ceiling.

Rhoads enjoyed the outburst but didn't register it outwardly. "A.S.C. Danny Maharis said the cat hair is the most important lead we've come up with. No way. If we have a cat hair," he continued, "it's because Virgil gave us a cat hair. The worst mistake we can make is to kid ourselves that we have any advantage over this guy. He's made fools of all of us, every step of the way. I appreciate Director Franklin recognizing my contribution, but what have we really learned? We've learned that Virgil is feeding us information. He's leading us. All I discovered is that fact. He intended for us to find the briefcase, and we now know that he intended it to tell us something about the evidence it contains. Every bit of it is part of his plan."

Rhoads sat down. No one said anything.

Franklin walked to the podium. "There are differences of opinion in every investigation. The hardest thing for all of us is to remain objective. What we need to do is keep open minds about the evidence. We have two primary approaches at this point — first is that we have legitimate, solid leads on how to find Virgil, and that we are still a step behind. We may not like the second option — I know I don't — but Mr. Rhoads has a point. One thing we can all agree on, just by looking at the map, is that Virgil is heading west. Okay. Thank you everyone, that is all for this meeting. Starting tomorrow, we will convene here each morning at oh-seven-hundred hours until further notice."

The room cleared out with the exception of Franklin and Rhoads.

"Thanks for getting Deputy Fife off my ass," said Rhoads.

"Brandon's a good agent. You may not see eye to eye, but you're both developing solid leads, so give him a break."

"Oh come on, I got Jeeter's videocassette to you within five hours. And you wouldn't have gotten that tape at all without me. I'm sorry the Benedict angle didn't pan out. But now you've got the Midas files, so no matter what happens, Pratt's in your sights."

"Some of the Midas files, maybe most. Thank you for that. You're going to let me have the rest when this is over, right? Unless you have something to hide."

"When you tell Pratt I did my part in solving the case and I get my money, you'll get it all. And you won't find anything that points a finger at me."

"Good enough, then," Franklin said.

Rhoads started out the door.

"One more thing, Rhoads. Something for you to think about. If Benedict isn't Virgil, then I have to start thinking that Benedict is dead. That means, after we've stopped Virgil, a few folks at Old Carolina are going to have a lot of questions to answer about Midas and the missing scientist. You're sure you don't want to let me in on anything now, something that might make things swing your way later?"

"I told you — it wasn't me. You need to be looking at Pratt and Valzmann. Hell, if it were me, I'd have people on Valzmann already." Rhoads had read the rest of the files on the way to the FBI meeting as Fallscroft flew the helicopter. The specific details were missing, but it was clear to any trained investigator that Valzmann had been paid to make Benedict disappear. He had delivered the paper files, minus the most damning parts, and was happy that the disks were hidden at his house.

"You know we're stretched thin as it is," Franklin said.

"I know. Look, I'll tell you most of it now. When they sent me to find Benedict, they gave me $200,000 to pay him off, to keep him quiet. When I didn't find him, I gave Pratt the money back. But what happened to the money? When you get the rest of the files, you'll see what I mean."

91

Asheville

The jet-black limo eased up silently to the curb. Valzmann stepped out of a shadow and leaned his head in as the tinted window slid down.

"Nothing to worry about, sir," Valzmann said, patting an envelope inside his jacket. "Rhoads didn't disappoint us. He's still as big a fuckup as ever. It took me two minutes to find the disks. They were just sitting out on his kitchen table under a pile of unopened bills."

"You just took them?"

"There are four disks, none labeled. I had to leave, go to an office supply store in the mall and buy the same brand of disks, same color, and come back and switch them."

"You sure the disks you took are the ones we want?"

"I'm going to go check right now, but I'm sure they're the ones."

"Good," said Pratt. "Next step — find out if they have other copies."

"That will require... personal interviews and, in all likelihood, application of pressure."

"Let's change the plans slightly. Instead of one at a time, you go get Rhoads and Dallaness. You go get them both as soon as you can set it up. Any minute one or the other will get the idea that there's no time like the present to let the media have the disks. It's important you get them together in the same room. And be careful, he's so damned stupid, he might get ... heroic. But you get them and bind them in chairs, turn Rhoads so he can't see what you're doing to her. Then you go to work on her with the pliers. Pinch a bit of the flesh along the underside of her arm to the thickness of tissue paper, and she'll react. I know what that feels like. Rhoads will soon volunteer to answer your questions."

Valzmann nodded that he understood.

Pratt seemed satisfied with his plan and exhaled slowly through his nose. "Then he'll talk."

"You want me to video it?"

"Of course."

"And after they've had a chance to express themselves?"

"'And days of mourning shall follow.'"

Pratt expected Valzmann to applaud the plan. Instead, there was an awkward silence.

"You don't like that approach?" Pratt asked.

"No, I do like it. It's excellent."

"Well? There's something else?"

"Sir, on my own time, I've been following Mrs. Dallaness via the security cameras."

"Yes?"

The man kicked at the cement underfoot. "I find her lean little body very... very appealing."

Pratt nodded. "Be my guest."

"Thank you. Just getting prior approval."

Pratt nodded again, then had a thought and reached out and touched the man's sleeve. "When it's time for dessert, make sure you turn Rhoads's chair around so he has a clear view."

"That's SOP, sir." The man sighed. "It's a shame, though, that we have to give Rhoads Retirement Plan 86."

"You're getting soft, old boy."

"I mean it's a shame that we'll never get to see the expression on his face when the police show up and tell him they just spent six hours digging up a dead scientist named Benedict behind his uncle's cabin at Deer Mountain. I pulled a neck muscle planting him."

Pratt thought for a moment. "You're right, Valzmann. It is too bad. But remember, nothing's perfect."

Without saying another word, Pratt pressed the button that raised the window between them.

Valzmann turned and began walking away when Pratt again lowered the window.

"Valzmann, come here."

Valzmann returned, hands thrust into his coat pockets.

Pratt grinned. "This guy's feeling terrible for weeks and weeks and finally goes to see his doctor, right?"

Valzmann nodded, masking his irritation at another joke.

"So," Pratt continues, "the doctor runs a battery of tests and tells the patient to come back to get the results the next day. So the next day, the patient comes back. The doctor calls him into his office, closes the door, and says, 'Well, I have good news, and I have bad news.' The patient says, 'Give the bad news first.' The doctors says, 'Okay, you've got lung cancer from smoking three packs a day for thirty years. You have a month to live.' The patient turns white. 'Oh my God,' he says. 'What's the good news?' The doctor leans across the desk to the patient,'" Pratt leaned out the limo window, imitating the doctor, "'and whispers, 'Did you get a load of the red-headed receptionist out there — the one with the great legs and big tits?' The patient says, 'Yes ... yes, I saw her.' Now the doctor leans in even closer and grins proudly, 'I'm screwing her!'"

92

After the meeting in Washington, Rhoads flew to Cincinnati with Brandon to check out the crime scene at the Trailways terminal.

After less than ninety minutes there, he left for Asheville. Why he needed to accompany Brandon was a mystery to him.

Probably Franklin's idea of a joke. But no, Franklin was devoid of humor. They worked the scene and flew back that evening.

He got to Mary's house at midnight.

She seemed strangely distant, worried about something she wouldn't discuss. But by one in the morning, they were in bed, under a flannel sheet, glistening with the sweat of exertion. The day had exhausted Rhoads, and what little energy he had left, Mary wanted. He tried, but soon she realized how tired he was.

She took over.

"Don't move a muscle," she whispered. "Let me drive."

Later, he lay on his back, eyes open, staring into nowhere, and she on her side, against him, tracing the words "Mary and Tommy" on his abdomen. She formed the letters in an inexact way so he wouldn't know what she was spelling.

She was about to suggest they go again when his breathing told her he had fallen asleep

An hour later, his beeper went off.

"Do you have to get it?" Mary asked, as he got out of bed.

He used the telephone downstairs in the kitchen for a long time, long enough for him to smoke three Camels. When he came back up and got into bed, he told Mary nothing.

She just sighed.

Rhoads rolled away to sleep.

"What's the matter?" she asked. "You tired of me already?"

"No. Just tired."

"Thinking about Virgil?" she asked.

"No. Just tired."

"I am," she said.

"Tired?"

"No. Thinking about Virgil."

"Virgil himself? Or the whole Virgil mess?"

"I can't believe Pratt's going to hand over a billion and a half dollars to a certified madman."

"Why are you talking like that? You know Virgil's not getting a dime. It's going to fund heart, lung, and cancer research grants. And secondly, Pratt's only coughing up seven hundred and fifty million. The other tobacco companies are kicking in the other half. And nothing's definite yet."

"It's still negotiating with a terrorist in my book."

"Mary, tell me you don't get a kick out of seeing Pratt's face rubbed in it."

"You can't know Pratt and not laugh at that."

"And tell me you don't think Virgil has a point," Rhoads said. "Maybe his etiquette needs a little tune-up, but the man's got a point. It's not that I sympathize with him. He's a killer. But he's got a point. He's claimed the moral high ground, and plenty of the public's with him. That's something nobody counted on."

"Moral high ground! Virgil? Are you crazy?"

"Yeah, Virgil. He's raised the equivalent of a million dollars fifteen hundred times to heal the diseases Old Carolina sells by the pack. That's a lot of money."

She wanted to turn away but stopped herself. "Don't talk like that. Even to joke."

"Who's joking? You've seen the news. Bastard's got people quitting left and right. Clubs and seminars. Smokers Anonymous is the fastest growing self-help support group in the world. Free university-sponsored wholesale hypnosis sessions. Tobacco sales are down, especially in kids, the kids the tobacco business hopes are too stupid to see Virgil as their folk hero. If he doesn't want them to smoke, plenty of them are going to play along. He's created more converts than thirty years of surgeon general's warnings."

Mary sat up, wrapped the sheet around her, and glared at him. "You make it sound like we're the villains. Tobacco is a legal product, T.R."

"So is sodium cyanide."

For a few minutes, they were just there, next to each other, breathing. Then Mary started in again.

"Hundreds of thousands of decent, hard-working men and women earn their daily bread working in our industry. Including me."

"Four hundred and thirty thousand decent, hard-working men and women drop dead annually from smoking-related diseases. Including a guy named Anthony Dallaness."

That did it. Mary got out of bed and stood over him pointing a trembling finger. "Maybe to you it's nothing more than a bad case of rudeness, but to me, your friend Virgil would love nothing more than a news story about twelve-year-olds vomiting their lungs up all over the playground."

"You know that's not what I meant. Get back in bed. Come on."

"You agree with Virgil!"

"Come on, forget it. I'm just playing devil's advocate."

"No, you're not. You agree with Virgil! Admit it! You think he's better than we are. You're sick to twist the situation that way. I've never killed anybody, but I'm not sure about..." She stopped herself.

"About what?" Rhoads glared.

"What about your trip to Denver? They sent you after Benedict and paid you two hundred thousand dollars."

"You think I had something to do with Benedict's death?" Rhoads laughed at the idea that he'd kill for Pratt. He stopped. He didn't want her to think he was laughing at her. "Where'd you get that idea?"

She felt a chill.

Rhoads lowered his voice. "Is that what Trichina told you?"

She took a step forward and straightened up. "You're sure he's dead, so what am I supposed to think? I don't know you well enough to know what you're capable of, T.R. What about the two hundred thousand Pratt signed for, in cash, the day before you went to Denver? Where's that money?"

"That was to pay off Benedict, to shut him up. He was going to open his yap to the government about Midas. I was to offer him a fifty-thousand dollar-a-year consulting contract for the rest of his life plus the two hundred grand in cash plus Pratt's promise that none of the data Benedict developed would ever be used to sell cigarettes. But by the time I got there, he was already gone."

Trichina had cautioned Mary about confronting Rhoads. He was a convincing liar, she said. She knew that, she said, from personal experience.

Mary looked at Rhoads and realized how much she really didn't know him. She wanted to believe him, but the money concerned her. And now that he was siding with Virgil, she thought that his sense of right and wrong might be very different from hers.

"I think you'd better go," she said, her voice colder and more distant than he had ever heard it before. She took a step back and her warm skin shuddered against the cool tile of the bathroom wall. "This was all a mistake. You and me." She turned her back.

"You don't believe me? Don't you know yet I would never, ever lie to you?"

She stared straight at the wall in front of her. "I don't know anything anymore."

He tried to turn her around, to look into her eyes. When he touched her, she jerked away, as if she was about to be attacked.

He dropped his arms submissively.

"I'm sorry," she said. "You have to go."

"Fine with me," he said. He got into his clothes as fast as he could and tore down the stairs. Mary winced when the door slammed.

PART THREE

93

Wednesday, October 25
Asheville

"T.R.?" Mary Dallaness's voice said hesitantly as it crackled over the speaker on Rhoads's answering machine. "Listen, I know I was upset last night. And I know I shouldn't be talking to you on your answering machine. But I don't know what to do. I don't know who to turn to. I just got a call from Corporate Travel. They're having a courier deliver plane tickets and a memo that sends me and a few others from Documentation to some investor relations meeting in New York. They want me to leave right away, tomorrow. I think it's an excuse to get us out of here so they can, uh, you know, adjust the computers. I'd better talk to you in person, T.R. Call me as soon as you can. Please. I'm scared. Really scared."

94

The Royal Carland Hotel
New York

"I go to bed early, very early," Valzmann said to the registration clerk. He registered at the Royal Carland under the name of Jonathan Conrad. "Eight p.m. And I get up early, very early. Four a.m. I don't want to be hearing elevators banging and clanging."

"No sir, that's why we gave you 2502, the room you asked for. Very, very quiet there, sir."

"And who did you put me next to? The percussion section of Herb Alpert and the Tijuana Brass?"

"No sir. On one side of your room, there's a linen closet. The housekeepers use it only during the day. The guest room on the other side has been reserved by a woman who won't be arriving until tomorrow. And once she does check in, I'm sure she'll be very quiet, sir. She's here on business."

"The kind of business where she'll be bringing customers in and out all night long, probably."

"No sir. She's here for a tobacco industry meeting. Serious people."

"Well, you just make sure. You won't like it if I have to call down here and speak to your superior."

"No sir. You'll see, sir. There'll be nothing to disturb you. You'll get quality sleep here at the Royal Carland, sir."

95

Baltimore

Without the knowledge of Franklin or Pratt, Rhoads met Dr. Trice at the Inner Harbor Aquarium in Baltimore. She had called and said she wanted to show him something. She took the Metroliner down from 30th Street Station in Philadelphia.

They walked through the exhibits, stopping twice at refreshment stands. Rhoads ordered nothing. At the first stand Dr. Trice bought soft pretzels that left splotches of yellow mustard at the corners of her mouth. The stain remained visible until the second stop, where the doctor ordered a large cola, insisting that no ice be added to the cup, and an ice cream sandwich in the shape of a taco.

When they got to the crustacean tanks, Trice winked at Rhoads, stretching her arm in the direction of the large glass wall that separated them from the sea creatures.

"Observe, if you will, the primitive Cordozo," she said, cutting the air with a wide wave of her arm, directing Rhoads's attention to something moving on the other side of a brilliant red coral — a glistening, silvery fish that appeared to him to be a large, bulky version of a minnow. Dr. Trice had the demeanor now not of a respected academic, but of a stage magician. "This species has few physical advantages to recommend it for natural selection. It is large, weak, and slow, though note its substantial set of incisor-like teeth and protruding lower jaw. What it does have going for it is its ability to apply stealth and deception to mislead predators. This fish, when under apprehension of attack, will rub itself against an abrasive object, a rock or piece of coral, leaving a trace of its own blood, even bits of its own flesh.

"Predators' olfactory glands draw them to the blood while the Cordozo circles back around the object from the rear and attacks the distracted pursuer, restating the terms of engagement," she continued.

Rhoads tapped on the glass with his knuckle. None of the sea creatures seemed to notice.

Dr. Trice rolled her eyes. Everyone knows not to disturb the fish by banging on the aquarium.

"For the first time," she said, "you find yourselves able to predict Virgil's movement. Doesn't that strike you as odd? Or, has the bureau suddenly gotten a whole lot cleverer? Because with men like Franklin near the top of the heap, I doubt it. Is that what they think, that they know this man? I think otherwise. You think you've gotten smarter, and he's gotten weaker. I don't think so. I think he's going to circle back on you."

Rhoads listened carefully and stared into the tank. The three or four Cordozo swam lazily over a bed of crawling black lobsters. "What's he done that makes you think that?" Rhoads asked.

"He is moving steadily west. And he's moving slowly. That may be because he is tiring. He is most likely out of breath. Literally. He knows he hasn't much time left, despite his stated ambition of four hundred and thirty victims. I say he never intended to make that number, although he's gotten shockingly close. If he is truly seeking glory, nothing more than the attention he sought but never received from his mother or father, then you can be assured he will stage his 'grand finale' before the cancer and emphysema take much more strength out of him."

Rhoads withdrew a folded piece of printer paper, a list of the FBI's Likely Vectors analysis of Virgil's potential geographical targets and the most probable, most vulnerable upcoming events. Anything the FBI thought might interest Virgil. Rhoads took the list from Brandon's desk and made a copy. He scanned the page now.

"He seems to be heading toward a Specialty Retailers Symposium at the Brasilia Hotel and Casino in Las Vegas. Nick Pratt's going to speak there. That's confidential, doctor. They know that from a schedule of retail marketing events they found with newspaper articles in the brief-case recovered in Harrisburg. At least that's what they're all figuring. And, from what I know, it makes sense. If he is headed there, then it will be all over. That is where we will grab him. They've got the Mother of All Stakeouts planned for Las Vegas."

"What else is on that list?" Trice demanded as she snatched the confidential memorandum from Rhoads's hand. She ran her eyes over it quickly before Rhoads pulled it back.

Then he read to her. "The American Advertising Association meeting, that's today in Los Angeles. Either of the StarCity properties, even though he's been to one already. They're both currently under constant surveillance. The American Vending Service Association, San Francisco. Their members operate vending machines. And the PAM Technologies seminar in Seattle, whatever that is."

"PAM? I think they're involved in the development of smokeless tobacco products and cleaner-burning cigarette paper."

Rhoads looked as if he thought she made that up. "Now how would you know that, doctor?"

"I follow the stock market, buster. They've been losing money for five or six years, running around patenting everything their engineers dream up. Too much development, not enough marketing. Now it looks as if they're a bit more organized." She pointed to the paper in his hand. "What else do you have there?"

"Nothing else in the next few weeks."

"Your list mentions events in the east. Name them."

"They don't count, Dr. Trice. Virgil's moving west now. That's documented."

"What's on the list out east?"

Rhoads shook his head. "Okay. A special investor relations meeting set up by Old Carolina this Friday in New York. A nicotine patch medical seminar for family practice physicians in Boston on November 2. An EPA conference on office environment health issues in Washington on November 5 and 6 ... but, given what's known about Virgil's whereabouts, put together with the retailers meeting in Vegas, the events in the east have just about been ruled out."

Saying that, Rhoads folded up the list and put it in his pocket. Dr. Trice did not look convinced.

"Look," Rhoads said. "The man is westbound. We know that for a fact. I didn't read you the events that are scheduled back east because the man's not in the east, is he? Las Vegas is the place. We know approximately where he is, and now we know where he's going. He's calling us more and more frequently, and it's easier to know where he is."

Dr. Trice dropped her handbag to the floor and reached up to grab Rhoads by each lapel. She exhaled through her nose like a snorting bull. He smelled her too-sweet perfume and the mustard on her breath. She burned her eyes into his.

"Rhoads! Listen to me. I'm telling you. Whatever he's going to do, he's going to do it soon, and he's going to do it back east. He's going to do it soon because he's almost used up. He's going to do it back east because you always build your snowman on your own front lawn. No one wants to spend all day building a snowman at someone else's house, and if you do, you wish you were doing it at home. He lives in the east, so does the cat that was the source of the hair in the briefcase. He's emotionally attached to that animal. He doesn't leave it alone for long. Did the Behavioral Science guy write a report about that? I'll bet you he goes home regularly to hold his cat, talk to his cat, overfeed the cat out of guilt. No, there's no question in my mind. The grand finale will be in his hometown. If not his hometown, then the nearest big city."

Trice paused only long enough to catch her breath.

"Now, think, Rhoads. He's changed something. He let you find what appears to be a clue. He's never done that before. But anything new in this behavior model means something has changed, and that is when you have to tread very, very carefully. What do changes in any one element of the behavior model suggest?" Trice asked.

Rhoads shrugged. He knew Virgil was leading them, but he thought that the trail still pointed west.

"Mr. Rhoads!" the doctor shouted, glaring at him like he was a sleepy student. "I asked you, what do changes in any one element of the behavior model suggest?"

Rhoads thought for a moment, then half-answered and half-asked, "Cause-and-effect changes in other elements?"

"Right, laddy! The grand finale is near. Forget about that four hundred and thirty people nonsense. That's just a cod. If he is leading you to the west, I urge you to look to the east. I tell you, he is going to circle back on you. And he's not going to wait much longer. I think the time is now."

96

Asheville

Valzmann's assistant, feeling full of himself because Valzmann was in New York, strolled in hours late to work. He leisurely read the paper, then donned the headset to review the audiotapes of the night before.

"Shit!" he said. There was something on one tape that he should have reported right away. He removed his headset and pressed a speed dial number on his telephone. Valzmann's voicemail system automatically routed the call to Valzmann's room at the Royal Carland.

"They've had a big fight, sir," the assistant said. Judging from the sounds of a television in the background, Valzmann had been watching professional wrestling. Valzmann clicked off the sound. "She kicked him out and he drove away pissed as hell. He burned rubber so loud I could pick it up off the bedroom bug."

Valzmann listened to his inarticulate assistant's interpretation of what he had heard. Then Valzmann called Pratt.

"With Dallaness being sent to New York," Valzmann said, "I came up ahead of her. I figured it was a good possibility Rhoads would join her. Now this fight."

"That will complicate getting at them when they're together," Pratt said. "You might have to do them separately."

Valzmann didn't like this. "Separate deaths will be more difficult to explain."

"Yes," Pratt said, "but much easier than facing a grand jury."

"Remember your joke about the hit man who was able to get two birds with one stone?"

"Yes, Valzmann, I remember. The problem is, you've told me that they've had a serious fight."

"People make up."

Pratt was silent, then excited, "Why wait? I'll come up with some reason for sending Rhoads to New York. A strategy meeting with other tobacco security chiefs. Something."

Valzmann lit up. "Yeah, then I'll set it up to look like they were in bed and Rhoads fell asleep with a cigarette in his big mouth. A hotel room fire with two fatalities."

Pratt sighed. "No, Valzmann. Don't you think cigarettes have suffered enough bad publicity?"

Valzmann winced at the gaffe. "Okay. Then what?"

"This is the story you have to stage. Rhoads knows he's going down for killing Benedict. Rhoads knows Dallaness has the goods on him. He kills her then feels bad about it and ..."

"Kills himself."

"Enjoy New York," Pratt said, hanging up.

97

New York

Valzmann called Pratt back within the hour.

"Dallaness checked in half an hour ago, sir," he reported to the CEO. "But it will be tough to get Rhoads up here. He's in Asheville, all excited about going to Las Vegas where the Feds are setting their trap. What do you want me to do?"

"Okay, then," Pratt said without a moment's hesitation. "Go get her. Forget about getting them simultaneously. Kill her now. I can't take any more chances that she'll open her mouth to the Feds or the media. Trichina was right. Anyone can bully Dallaness into anything."

"Yes sir, I'll let you know when it's done." A rush of excitement shot through Valzmann. No matter how many times he'd done it, it remained the ultimate trip.

Valzmann hung up and moved to the bed. He sat down, removed his leather shoes and placed them on the rug, side by side. He reached down and found his sneakers and stepped into them. He tied them quickly and snugly, his mind working out the logistics.

He relished the science of meticulous planning, reducing his personal risk to three places to the right of the decimal point. That was a luxury he didn't have today. On the other hand, pulling off a successful spontaneous job was a mark of the gifted professional.

Nevertheless, he shook his head in quiet disappointment. He'd have to use a method he detested, that of the lumbering brute, and he'd have to move fast. One quick motion, into the room, seize her from behind and get his hand, the one wearing the padded glove he had stitched together himself, over her mouth. Instantly. He'd have to pick her up by turning and thrusting his hip into the small of her back so she couldn't kick effectively and then he'd carry her into the bathroom. Then, boom, throw her as hard as he could, head first, like a ripe tomato against a tree trunk, against the porcelain edge of the tub. He'd only have one shot. Multiple concussions would not appear consistent with an accidental fall in the bathroom. He'd have to make it hard enough, but not too hard.

Then, if he did it well, she'd be inactive but still alive, still breathing. That would be essential. Next, he'd strip her down, turn the shower on, and set her body in a position that made sense. The drain would have to be blocked with a washcloth under her so the water would rise in the tub high enough to drown her.

Not very artful, he thought, *but any port in a storm.*

He looked forward to removing her clothes, but that pleasure would be muted. She'd be unconscious, and there'd be no fear for him to inhale.

Valzmann walked to the wall his room shared with hers and pressed his ear against it. The wallpaper felt cool, the wall dense and solid. He could hear nothing, but, he reasoned, she should still be in there.

Maybe asleep. Napping would be perfect. He'd be on her before her brain could organize a scream.

He picked up the key to her door, dropped it in his pocket, and let himself out of his room. No one was in the hallway to see him.

98

Mary Dallaness sat on the bed in her room wearing only panties and pink polish on her fingernails and toenails. Anthony had hated pink. She carefully poured saline solution onto her contact lenses in the tiny matched cups of the plastic case balanced on her knee.

Outside in the hallway, Valzmann listened at her door.

Again, he heard nothing. He stepped back and checked the hallway in both directions. Still no one coming or going. He reached into his pocket and withdrew the key. He steadied himself and positioned the key to slide into the lock. Then, using only lateral pressure from his thumb, he slid the key forward as slowly and gently as he could.

He cringed at a tiny click.

Mary heard it, too, or heard something, and turned reflexively toward the door. The movement of her torso was enough to disturb the balance of the contact lens case. It fell from her knee.

Shit! She shot her hand out to catch it. Too late. The case had fallen to the carpet and under the bed. In an instant, she was down on her hands and knees in the narrow space between the bed and the wall, searching the carpet fibers with her fingertips for the transparent lenses.

The door crashed open with a deafening boom.

The sound startled her so that she convulsed as if shocked by an electrical current.

In an instant, Valzmann's trained eyes had taken in the entire room, including the open closet. The heavy entrance door bounced back and slammed closed. *Where the hell is she?* He took one long stride and was in the bathroom. In another instant, his hand found the light switch. He looked behind the shower curtain.

Not in there either.

His adrenaline pumped at high pressure. If she wasn't in her room, where had she gone?

That didn't matter. In a second he'd be out of there. She wouldn't have been alerted. A free peek, but he would have preferred to have accomplished the mission.

Valzmann reached for the doorknob.

He opened the door, stepped out into the hallway, and scanned for people.

All clear.

He began to pull the door closed behind him when he abruptly stopped. Valzmann closed his eyes for a second, smiled, and went back in. He had almost left the bathroom light on.

99

The hotel security people insisted to Mary that what she heard had to have been the slamming of a nearby room door.

"What about the bathroom light going on and then off?"

The security people looked at each other and shrugged, saying sometimes power surges could be the culprit.

She still hadn't heard back from Rhoads.

100

**Amtrak Station
Indianapolis, Indiana**

Muntor, wearing a fake mustache, looked out the lounge car window as the train creaked to a halt at Track 5. A moment later, the door hissed open and Muntor disembarked wearily, carrying a doctor's black bag.

A conductor offered him help. Muntor shook his head.

The conductor saw that in the elderly all day long. Independent. Don't want assistance unless they ask for it, and when they do, don't dawdle. The conductor watched the old doctor make his way slowly to the escalator, holding his bag, until he heard shouts coming from several cars down the track. The lounge car.

"Get an ambulance!" someone shouted. "Some guy's choking to death back here. Call 9-1-1!"

The conductor took a step in the direction of the escalator, but it was too late. The doctor had disappeared.

Muntor intended to find a decent hotel and get some much-needed sleep. Maybe he'd even stay a day or two in Indianapolis. He didn't want to think about Bozzie. He'd never see the sleek, leopard-spotted cat again. What a beautiful cat, what a smart cat. How it used to wake Muntor by tap-tap-tapping one of its velvet paw pads on Muntor's nose.

Maybe they'd put Bozzie's picture on the news after they found the house, some kind of psychological ploy. That'd be a dirty trick. That'd be a damned dirty trick, taunting me with my own cat. But I'd love to see him.

101

"Mary," Rhoads said into her voice mail.

He didn't give a damn who was eavesdropping or what kind of laugh Pratt and his goons might have when they heard what he was about to say.

"I got your message. Thank God you're all right. I don't know what I'd do if something happened to you. And I know this is a hell of thing to say over the phone, but I'm saying it now. I'm falling in love with you, Mary, and I didn't know it until I heard your message, heard how frightened you were. I want to be with you. The minute this Virgil mess is over, I'm going to disappear from Asheville, and I'm going to take you with me. Now, be careful. And I mean what I said. I want you, Mary. Focus on that — and you be careful."

102

St. Louis, Missouri

Alvin DeSotis, a clean-cut young recruiter for the Army Reserve in Montgomery City, stood in the shadow of the St. Louis Gateway to the West arch, accompanied by his two young boys.

One of the kids held a half-eaten fluff of blue cotton candy, and the other had his hands wrapped around a large soda cup.

DeSotis pulled a cigarette pack from his shirt pocket, looked inside, and made a face. Empty. He dropped it in a nearby trash receptacle.

He looked around. There was no cigarette machine or newsstand in sight. What he did see, however, was a well-dressed man wearing sunglasses and smoking a cigarette.

"I hate to bother you, sir, but could I bum a cigarette?"

The old man coughed, swallowed, and reached into his overcoat pocket.

"My pleasure," he said. He had an odd, strained voice. "They're generic. Do you mind?"

"Not at all," DeSotis said, taking one. "My brand. Thanks. Mind if I bum a light, too?"

"Can't help you there. I had to stop someone to get this one lit," he said.

"All right," DeSotis waved. "Thanks again."

DeSotis returned to his kids waiting at a wooden bench. One wanted to find a bathroom, the other sat glumly, swinging his legs back and forth.

"We're not going anywhere until I find someone with a lighter," he said, "so just relax."

A middle-aged couple approached. The woman held a cigarette. "Stay here," he said to his kids and got up, heading to intercept the couple.

The kids watched as the woman handed their father a matchbook and kept walking. Sitting back on the bench, DeSotis struck a match, brought the flame to the cigarette, and drew in deeply.

The youngest of the boys looked up at DeSotis and screamed.

"Daddy? Daddy? Daddy!"

The other child began to cry.

A passing bicyclist turned toward the screeching. "What now?" the father said, exhaling.

"I'm going to pee right now if we don't get to a bathroom."

DeSotis turned to his other son. "And what are you screaming about?"

"Billy's pinching me."

"No, I'm not."

Then DeSotis turned to the first child. "Well, you'll have to wet yourself then. Because I'm going to finish this cigarette." He closed his eyes and took in five or six deep drags.

When he finished, he rose, dropped the butt on the pavement, and stepped on it.

"Let's go," he commanded. "I have to pee, too."

En route to the public restroom, the trio passed an open-air snack stand. Several people were there, some sipping sodas, others standing in line. Muntor sat on one of the snack-stand stools, his back to the passers-by. He had seen the father and his sons coming and did not want to make eye contact again. He allowed enough time for them to pass, then got up from the stool and walked away.

A few minutes later, one of the snack-stand employees noticed that the man had forgotten a pack of cigarettes, a lighter, and a few dollar bills all bound together by a red rubber band.

103

Brandon's finger trembled slightly as he stood in Bengal breeder Angela Rail's kitchen and dialed Franklin on his cell phone. His heart beat so fast he worried about the possibility of following in the footsteps of two maternal uncles who died from sudden myocardial infarctions, both before the age of thirty-five. He had concealed that family history from FBI doctors during the pre-employment physicals.

"Franklin," the Deputy Director said, simultaneously picking up the telephone in his kitchen and lowering the flame under his crepe pan. Mrs. Franklin sat in the dinette reading *Meeting Evil* for the third time. She kept rereading it just for the subtle glory in the last paragraph.

"Sir, it's Brandon."

"Go, Ben."

"I've got the name of the man who is probably Virgil."

Franklin snapped his fingers and pointed to the phone, signaling to his wife that this could be the call they'd been waiting for.

"Go on."

"Two summers ago, on August 1, a man from Philadelphia roughly fitting our physical profile of Virgil bought a male Bengal kitten. He paid Mrs. Rail with a check drawn on the Mellon Bank."

"You've alerted the Philadelphia field office?"

"They just came back with the preliminary information. His name is Martin Muntor. He's fifty-six. He lives in Northeast Philadelphia on Roosevelt Boulevard. Used to be a reporter and editor for the ANS wire service, the American News Syndicate. Forced into early retirement. Eight weeks ago, sir. Perfect timing. No NCIC hit on him. We don't have much more than that right now, but we are scrambling."

"This is the guy Mrs. Rail thought had emphysema?"

"Yes, sir."

"Where's he now?"

"That's the question."

"You like him?"

"So far, I love him. Especially the news bureau experience. It fits. In late August, ANS laid him off and closed their Philadelphia operation a week later. Haskell's on the phone right now with a reporter who used to work with him in Philly. We'll have more shortly. Another thing — the breeder said he was a strange guy with a stiff, peculiar gait. Paranoid. Talked to himself under his breath, accused her of ripping him off without rational basis."

"What have you told the breeder?"

"She and her husband know it's obstruction of justice if they discuss what they've told us with the media or anyone else."

Franklin picked up the remote and turned off his television.

"Kick a Code One, Brandon."

"Did it."

"Call VICAR?"

"Did it."

"Put everything on the hot line?" Franklin heard a bell ringing upstairs in his home office. It was the telex coming in.

"Did it."

"Fire up the Tactical Assault Team?"

"They're rolling now."

Franklin turned to Mrs. Franklin and pointed. "Get my driver."

"Call me in my car in five minutes," he said to Brandon, and he hung up.

He found himself standing.

He turned to a worried-looking Mrs. Franklin. "Here we go."

104

Dawn
Friday, October 27
Philadelphia

The houses along the stretch of Roosevelt Boulevard where Martin Muntor lived had been built in the 1920s on poorly compacted soil. Three-quarters of a century later, the houses were aslant and collapsing. Many had been condemned by the city.

The bright orange No Trespassing signs were invitations to crack heads and their dealers. They moved in as residents moved out. Some homeowners stayed, mostly the older ones, die-hards, because they wanted to. The neighborhood was theirs. Others, like Martin Muntor, stayed because they had nowhere else to go.

Neighbors on both sides of Muntor's house were quietly evacuated by the authorities. All telephone service on the block was temporarily interrupted to prevent a neighbor from calling Muntor or the media.

The FBI's Tactical Assault Team assembled in predawn darkness on a side street just off the boulevard. The team commander told his men that their entry should be safe and surgical. The plan was to use stun grenades to temporarily incapacitate Muntor and reduce the risk of him destroying evidence. Even if Muntor was not there, he said, fragile evidence needed to be protected.

"Preserve your own asses first, evidence second, subject third," he said and made each man repeat it to his face. Then his men got ready and checked their equipment. The VHF headsets, the thirty-pound Door-Down sledgehammer, the plastic rope, the ballistic armor, the firearms with night scopes.

If Martin Muntor was home, he was theirs.

Franklin and Rhoads stood together next to an unmarked FBI van a quarter-block away from the Tactical Assault Team staging area.

"A cat hair. Good work, Rhoads."

Rhoads nodded. "Thanks. But do you really think he's going to be sitting in his kitchen wearing his slippers and eating Rice Crispies? Give me the word, and I'll go up and knock on his front door."

"Okay, thanks for the information," said Franklin. "I'll order eighteen highly trained members of the T.A.T. to stand down because Rhoads has X-ray vision."

"I hope he's in there, I really do. But he's been ahead of us the whole time. He's dying. What's he going to be doing at home? This is a man with a mission. I'll be surprised if he's not still out there somewhere trying to complete it."

"Even the best of them slip up. You know the profile as well as I do — most serial killers want to be caught, either because they want someone to stop them, or because they want to brag to the cops."

Rhoads lit a cigarette. "He gave us the cat hair. What are there, four or five thousand of these Bengal kitties in the U.S.? How many breeders? Twenty, thirty? It's inevitable that somebody would remember a nasty, wheezing man. Especially a nasty, wheezing man who calls up the breeder, a breeder who knows who he is and where he lives, and reminds her that he's a nasty wheezing old man. Therefore," Rhoads said, flicking ashes into the street, "you can bet he isn't coming back here."

"Everything suggests that he keeps coming back home after each incident, probably to feed his cat. And we know he just hit St. Louis."

"Okay, I'll stand out here quietly. You do your big SWAT number. If he isn't there, you let me see the place. Deal?"

"Deal."

At first light, the team commander gave the signal. A climber on the roof dropped three percussion grenades down the chimney that rocked the houses near Muntor's. Besides a number of broken windows, there was no other damage. T.A.T. members moved through the house, the first floor, second floor, basement, attic, garage, checking behind every door and in every room and closet, every possible place a human could hide. The premises were unoccupied. By the second hand on the team commander's diving watch, thirty-nine seconds later the Two Squad leader radioed that no humans were in the house, although they did find a cowering, spotted silver cat.

In the kitchen, Franklin, Rhoads, and one other agent, an evidence technician, all wearing latex gloves, examined the room, touching as little as possible. Franklin lifted the lid off a pot on the stove.

An agent popped his head into the kitchen. "There's a small stack of newspapers on the floor in the dining room," he announced. "Don't step on it. It covers a hole that'll drop you ten feet into the garage below. Might have been part of some escape plan. But it hasn't been disturbed. Be careful."

"Right," Franklin said. Rhoads went out into the dining room to see the newspaper-camouflaged hole, then returned to the kitchen. Without looking up from where he stood at the stove, Franklin said, "Muntor's fussy."

Rhoads and the evidence tech turned to him.

"What?" Rhoads asked.

"Remember that Virgil mailed a disposable syringe to the *Wall Street Journal* reporter? Disposables are good enough for the cigarettes. But not for whatever it is he's shooting up."

Rhoads walked over and looked into the pot.

A glass syringe and several needles sat in an inch of water. Rhoads shrugged, distracted by something he had noticed before Franklin called his attention to the pot. He went back to the telephone mounted on the wall near the door that lead into the dining room. Next to the telephone, also affixed to the wall, was a message board with an erasable marker. A coupon for a Jiffy Lube oil change was thumbtacked to it, as well as an 800-number for the local branch of the auto club.

"Franklin!" Rhoads half-shouted. "He's got this note board here. I think I've got a partially erased telephone number."

105

Old Carolina Tobacco, Inc.
World Headquarters

At Old Carolina Tobacco, Inc., the news that the FBI had found the residence of the man suspected to be Virgil roared from the Fifth Floor down like a boulder in a rockslide.

Anna Maria Trichina was at her desk, getting last-minute details out of the way before going to New York for the investor relations meeting.

A company electrician popped his head into her office and interrupted her train of thought by shouting, "Ms. Trichina. They found Virgil! The FBI found a guy up in Philadelphia! Just heard it on the radio."

It was not a wholly accurate report.

Trichina reached Arnold Northrup and learned that the FBI had raided a property believed to be the residence of Virgil.

She resisted the implication. It sunk in slowly and reached her consciousness with the same jolt that wakes you up when you've overslept through an important event. Now that Virgil's house had been found, she assumed, his capture wouldn't be far behind. That meant Pratt's paranoia would crest as the FBI intensified its investigation into Benedict's whereabouts.

There'd be nothing stopping Pratt from going berserk, sending his mad dogs to search every possible person and place for copies of Midas documents. And, Trichina realized, there'd be little to stop him from silencing anyone who knew what they contained forever.

Trichina chastised herself for not going all out earlier, when she had the chance, to find the Midas disks Mary took and bring them to Pratt.

She was going to do something about it. Right now.

She screamed for her secretary. "Get me Mary Dallaness. She's in New York at the Royal Carland."

While she waited for the call to go through, Trichina fantasized about reaching through the phone. taking Mary by the throat and squeezing the truth out of her. This was, after all, a matter of life and death.

In New York, a steady undercurrent of anxiety distracted Mary. She fought it by busying herself in her room with the material for the investor relations meeting.

The telephone rang. It was Trichina.

"There you are. I've left you a thousand messages, Mary, but you haven't returned my calls." There was a pause, and the soft tone came off Trichina's voice like a sheath being pulled off a knife. "If you're too idiotic to protect yourself, why stop me from protecting myself? The disks you have can save us both. Now tell me where they are."

"I'm hanging up," Mary said.

Trichina lowered her voice. "Mary, don't. Listen. With this Muntor lunatic about to be arrested, Pratt will stop at nothing to protect himself. At nothing! He knows the FBI is going ballistic trying to figure out what happened to Benedict, and Pratt will risk anything to protect himself."

"I told you. I don't have the disks."

"Who does?"

Mary didn't answer.

"It's T.R.," Trichina said.

"No."

"Liar."

"He doesn't have them, and I won't tell you who does."

"Bitch," Trichina shrieked. "How stupid can you get? Our only chance is to give them back. And even that might not be much of a chance."

"You can't even keep your story straight," Mary said. "One minute we need them to protect ourselves, the next minute we need to return them. What plan will you have for tomorrow? Sell them to the *National Enquirer*?"

"You'll get us both killed."

"Good!" Mary said. "What would you do with the disks? Turn them over to Mr. Pratt? I think you're the one who'll get us killed."

Mary slammed down the telephone before Trichina could say anything else.

106

FBI Headquarters

On one wall in the ERC, there was a huge poster of a three-year-old Commonwealth of Pennsylvania driver's license photo of Martin Muntor. On another wall, an enlargement of the partial telephone number lifted from Muntor's kitchen message board, and next to it an equally large print of a thoroughly burned sheet of newsprint, developed in high enough contrast to be somewhat legible.

The conference table was more crowded than ever with agents, consultants, and representatives of other federal, state and local agencies. Franklin spoke from a podium at the front of the room.

"I want to be cautious about this," he said, "but I think things are starting to break our way. As you all know, we now have a name, a face, and a house. We're still working on it, of course, but the subject's house was remarkably clean. This is a very careful man. His name is Martin Muntor. M-U-N-T-O-R. Here's what else we've learned. The Bengal cat hair recovered from the briefcase in Harrisburg is an exact match with that of a Bengal cat we took out of Muntor's house. Muntor has an ex-wife, two daughters — we're talking to them now — and a mother in a nursing home in Long Island. The mother's dementia is profound, and she's not likely to be able to help to us whatsoever."

Several late-arriving agents entered the room and found seats. Another agent approached the podium, a file folder in hand, waiting to be introduced.

"That's not bad, that's not bad at all," Franklin said. "And, I believe, that A.S.C. Maharis is going to show us that we have even more than that."

Maharis stood up and opened a folder. "Until eight weeks ago, Muntor was a reporter for the American News Syndicate in its Philadelphia bureau. Then the roof fell in on him. In the course of a single week, he got laid off, found out his health insurance was in jeopardy, and received diagnoses of terminal lung cancer and emphysema. Obviously, this made him mad."

Dr. Sorken slammed his open palm down on the table. "I'll handle the psych profile if you don't mind."

Most of the room laughed. Franklin saw the laughter as a sign the agents were, for the first time since CYCIG began, beginning to feel relieved and hopeful. Except for Rhoads. He sat stone-faced.

Maharis ignored Sorken and went on. "We even have his cat in custody. Also a wild animal."

Maharis rolled back his shirtsleeve to show claw marks. "A neighbor's boy had been feeding it. But the really good news is it is very likely that we now know the target of Muntor's so-called grand finale."

Rhoads frowned. Maharis saw it.

With the click of a slide-projector remote control, Maharis displayed an extreme close-up of the partially erased telephone number Rhoads had discovered in Muntor's kitchen.

"Our friend Mr. Rhoads," Maharis said, "found this on a message board in Muntor's kitchen next to the telephone. I know it doesn't look like much, but based on characters taken from samples of Muntor's handwriting, we've been able to reconstruct the telephone number. These first three digits are seven-oh-two, the area code that includes Las Vegas. The remaining digits are two-five-two, seven-seven-seven-seven. That's the number of the Brasilia Hotel and Casino in Vegas."

He clicked the remote again. An enlargement of a piece of charred paper appeared. Maharis picked up a laser pointer.

"The telephone number alone tells us very little. However, we also found the remains of a sheaf of papers in the fireplace. And these papers were burned pretty thoroughly. If Muntor had even touched them once with a poker, we'd be out of luck. But our Identification Section, with the aid of high-contrast photography, was able to read some of them. All but one of the pages contained newspaper or magazine stories about Virgil and the murders. The exception was a page from a brochure that included a registration form for attendance at the Specialty Retailers

Marketing Symposium tomorrow. We've heard about that event before. It's being sponsored by the Association of Tobacco Marketers. Retailers who attend will be trained in positioning tobacco products in their stores to bring in more customer traffic. And guess what. It's taking place in Las Vegas. At the Brasilia Hotel and Casino."

The noise level in the room rose as those present commented to one another.

"Hang on, hang on," Maharis said, quieting them down. "As a final confirmation, it's clear he's working his way west right now. He may have been seen in Pittsburgh. He's hit Cincinnati, Indianapolis, and St. Louis in the last four days. He won't get too many more before we get him."

Rhoads, uncharacteristically, raised his hand. Maharis nodded at him. "Mr. Rhoads?"

"It's a false trail."

"We're aware of your reservations, Rhoads," Franklin said.

"I know. But hear me out. The house was devoid of clues except the phone number and the paper. Do we really believe that a guy this careful would leave such perfect clues? They're just tough enough that we get to feel we achieved something by figuring them out, but both of them point to Vegas. Really? He burned the page from the brochure but left it so we can read it? Why not just put it in the trash and take it out to the curb? Can you really imagine a man this careful tossing the brochure into the fire and not sticking around long enough to make sure it was reduced to ash?"

"As I said, we're familiar with your theory. But this is a solid lead, and we're going to chase it down," Franklin said.

"I'm not saying you shouldn't. But you should also keep looking at other scenarios in case we're wrong. Virgil is a murderer. That's his sin. You know what ours is? Pride. He knows that, and he's using it to lead us in the wrong direction."

"Noted. How about this — you think Vegas is a dead end? Don't come. Follow the case wherever you think it leads. I can't give you field agents, but Bureau techs and analysts will do whatever you ask while you're chasing Virgil. Fair?"

"Fair," Rhoads said. "Thank you. And good luck in Vegas. I hope I'm wrong."

107

From the *Boston Globe*, Friday, October 27

FBI: 'VIRGIL' IS PHILADELPHIA JOURNALIST MARTIN MUNTOR
Former Reporter Dying of Lung Cancer

108

Old Carolina Tobacco, Inc.
World Headquarters

The main auditorium had been crammed with all the apparatus of a major press conference — microphones, cameras, lights, and more than one hundred reporters, cameramen, and audio technicians from news organizations all over the world.

On the stage, Nicholas Pratt stood flanked by four other Old Carolina Tobacco, Inc. executives sitting in chairs. He fumbled with a slip of paper an aide had handed him before he entered the auditorium. Old Carolina common stock had been falling precipitously.

> Closing price, Old Carolina Tobacco, Inc. Common Stock
> 169 –3 1/4, Volume 20,588,000.
> Most active stock

Pratt calculated he had now personally lost thirty-six million dollars in common stock value since Virgil's first attack, and that figure did not include the beating his bonus contract would sustain. Knowing that Virgil — Muntor — was probably making the same calculation intensified his wrath.

In front of him, at the podium before a multitude of microphones, stood Anna Maria Trichina, looking somewhat drawn.

"I thank you all for coming," she said. "Allow me to introduce myself. I am Anna Maria Trichina, executive vice president of marketing for Old Carolina Tobacco, Inc."

Pratt camouflaged his grimace with a small smile.

"As you know," she continued, "the terrible crimes of the past twenty-five days have rocked the tobacco industry and the rest of the world. But our concern at this time is not for the business impact of recent events, but, like everyone else, to find a way to bring this nightmare to an end. That's why we are pleased to be able to announce today that the CEOs of the eight leading tobacco companies have agreed in principle to a bold plan for restoring the peace of mind and physical safety of people everywhere. To provide you with the specific details of the plan, I'd like to introduce W. Nicholas Pratt, president and chief executive officer of Old Carolina Tobacco, Incorporated."

Trichina stepped to one side. Pratt moved forward and centered himself in front of the podium.

"Thank you, Anna Maria," he said. "As the media has reported so widely and wildly, it is no secret that Martin Muntor, the man who calls himself Virgil, has offered to surrender to the authorities in exchange for a one-and-a-half *billion* dollar charitable contribution by tobacco companies to seven named university and private medical research organizations.

"This is not a time for rhetoric, political statement, or discussion of any kind. This is a time for clear, direct, and decisive action. Today, I am taking that action. For the past two days, the CEOs of seven other companies and I have been meeting to determine how best to satisfy Mr. Muntor's demands. We have agreed to make the transfer of funds to the research institutions no later than Monday, November 1, at 2 p.m. The agreement I will now describe would normally be subject to official approval by the shareholders of Old Carolina for reasons that will be obvious in a moment. Collectively, the other seven companies will contribute seven hundred and fifty million dollars. Old Carolina Tobacco, Inc. will also contribute seven hundred and fifty million dollars."

Pratt swallowed hard at the mention of that amount, then continued.

"This is a considerable amount of money for one company," he said. "The means of financing it are complex. But drastic times call for drastic deeds. The minimum time needed to get shareholder approval exceeds the amount of time available. Another, fiercer wave of fatal attacks has been threatened, and the FBI believes the threats are real and unstoppable. Neither Old Carolina nor other companies in the industry dares to risk ignoring Muntor's demands. I am confident that Old Carolina shareholders will support my decision and ratify the course I have chosen. The only condition we require is that Muntor surrender himself to the authorities, on or before midnight on Monday, November 1. He will have ten hours to satisfy himself that the funds have, in fact, been transferred as directed. The tobacco companies have been legally committed to the transfer, and no *ex post facto* reversal or cancellation of the transaction is possible. Mr. Muntor is invited to call his contact at the FBI for more information about that. The transfer cannot be voided if he surrenders and is in custody by the deadline. Now, are there any questions?"

Scores of reporters jumped to their feet, discharging a roar of shouted questions.

109

Brasilia Hotel and Casino
Las Vegas

Muntor, wearing a mustache and baseball cap, sat in the auditorium-sized Race and Sports betting area in the Brasilia Hotel and Casino. He had an hour to kill until he had to be at the airport. He was in town under the name B. Doyle and had told the front desk to page him when the airport van was ready. He had to remember to listen for that name. Planting the decoy device in the ballroom off the mezzanine had been easy. The whole contraption cost him less than two hundred dollars, and most of that went to buying an electronic timer at a hobby shop on Maryland Parkway.

In front of him was a wall of giant televisions. Many of the screens showed horse races and football games. Many of the sets, however, were tuned to a local television station broadcasting the Old Carolina news conference. Muntor sat drinking chamomile tea. The air conditioning was too cold for his thin blood. His hands and feet were like ice, and he coughed hard and painfully.

On the screen, an unseen reporter shouted a question. "Mr. Pratt, do you have any personal message you wish to convey to Virgil?"

"Yes, I do." Pratt looked down at the podium as if he were collecting his thoughts. "We are acting in good faith solely in the interest of putting an end to this unprecedented number of product-tampering homicides."

Pratt hesitated for a long moment and looked straight toward the cameras. "I implore you, sir, in the name of all that is holy, to abide by the terms you yourself established. A tremendous number of people, now and in the future, will be well served by the medical advances that will inevitably occur as a result of this transfer of funds. You have gotten what you wanted. You will be treated fairly by the authorities."

Muntor sipped the tea, his face impassive, thinking, *who are you to tell me what is holy? You who have sold poison? You are the moneychangers in the temple, and I will root you out.*

110

Philadelphia

As darkness fell on West Philadelphia, Dr. Trice sat at her desk, just about to take the first bite out of a wedge of cheesecake layered with dark chocolate fudge.

Rhoads poked his head in.

"Hello, Dr. Trice."

"T.R.! You're in Philadelphia? You caught me," she said, nodding at her cheesecake.

"I won't tell anybody." Rhoads entered almost sheepishly, took off his jacket, and sat down in the chair facing her desk.

"The FBI is setting a trap for Virgil in Las Vegas. We raided his house and found clues that point to a casino there."

"Las Vegas?"

"They're convinced he'll be there."

She grimaced. "If you found evidence pointing to Vegas, he's not going to Vegas."

"That's what I think too, but all we have is you and me. On the outside, looking in. Trying to see what we can see through a foggy window."

"Maybe what needs to be seen isn't on the inside," she said. "Maybe we have a better view from out here."

"Bea, I know Muntor is the bad guy, he's killed close to four hundred people. He's obviously insane, and he has to be stopped. But the other night, I got into a fight with the woman I'm in love with because there I was, curled up with her in bed, defending Muntor."

"Go on."

"The thing is, more and more, I find myself agreeing with him. I understand his rage at the tobacco business, at all of us who work in it and don't think we're doing anything wrong because we're not pulling a trigger or killing people instantly. I mean, he's made me think about things I've done in the past, or things I should have done and didn't. If he's so evil, why do I feel like he's got more courage than I have? Like I'm the guilty one?"

Dr. Trice put down her fork.

"Do you believe in God, T.R.?"

Rhoads paused. "Not the kind of God they teach you about in Sunday school, anyway. I don't know. Maybe."

"You don't sound very convinced."

Rhoads shrugged and looked into his lap at his hands. He had interlaced his fingers.

"No one can tell you what to believe," Dr. Trice said. "And I'm certainly not going to. But I can tell you what I believe. I believe without a doubt that there's some kind of ... consciousness ... at work in the universe. It's nothing anyone can understand very well, nothing we need to understand very well. I believe there's a tiny spark of that consciousness in each one of us. I believe that it is the physical world itself that comes between all the sparks and separates them, breaks the connection. When the connection is lost, we spin out of control. Sometimes more or less subtly, like your zeros. Sometimes wildly, like Muntor. Being separated hurts. The horror some infants experience at separation from their mothers catapults them over the edge into the abyss labeled schizophrenia. But for most of us, it is through faith, hope, and charity that we can diminish the gap. If we work hard enough, we can reconnect with that consciousness. In some quarters, they call that salvation. I call it going home again."

Rhoads took a deep breath. He tried to listen. It was difficult for him. God-talk always had been. But Dr. Trice wasn't preaching. She was trying to make a point. He could see that.

"I know, T.R., that you believe, on one level or another, that you have a part to play in this matter, that you feel some bond with Muntor. Something beyond the fact that you are both lost and lonely men. And that gives you a special responsibility. And you hate that. It's work, and you'd rather play."

Rhoads swallowed and looked again at his hands. He couldn't recall arranging his fingers that way since he was child, instructed by his father to kneel beside the bed and say bedtime prayers.

He looked up. "So what am I supposed to do about it? I've got a lot riding on being there when Muntor goes down. All I have to do is be there, and Pratt gives me my seventy-five thousand dollars. You know what that means? That means I get my boat. I refloat *The Deep Blue* if I'm there. I save my brother, maybe save myself, whatever that means."

"I understand the impulse, and it's a noble one. And still, you're not on a plane to Vegas."

"Yeah."

"Then common sense suggests that you should follow your gut, not the percentages."

"How's that?"

"If you're not in Las Vegas, and Muntor is, I agree, you lose," Dr. Trice admitted. "You lose the seventy-five thousand and that will hurt. However, if Muntor does show up in New York while you're standing around in Las Vegas, you lose. And that will cost lives, plenty of innocent lives along with the few guilty ones Muntor's gunning for. That will cost you something else, something much more precious. If Muntor shows in Las Vegas and you're not there, you're no worse off than you are right now. But if he shows in New York and you lose because you were playing it safe, well, it could finish you. By trying to risk little, you find you are risking much. You'll never forgive yourself. In a way, T.R., this is your big chance to believe in yourself. Trust your hunch."

Rhoads took a backwards step toward the door. "One of the most important decisions of my life, and I haven't the slightest clue which way to go. Isn't that pitiful?"

"No, it's not. We all want to be on the winning side. It takes real guts to risk being wrong. If Virgil's in Vegas, the FBI will get him. All you have to do is decide what to do if they're wrong."

"That's all, huh?"

"You think they're wrong, and you have to act on that. You're the only one who has that freedom. Maybe because if you know something, you have a responsibility to act. If you know nothing, you have no responsibility. Responsibility's a burden most of us like to minimize. I remember once reading a book review by the psychologist Bruno Bettelheim. The

New York Times assigned him a book called *The Nazi Doctors*. In the review, Bettelheim wrote he didn't know if he could do the book justice because its author believed that to understand is to forgive, and Bettelheim said he didn't subscribe to that belief."

"I don't understand."

"I didn't believe Bettelheim. I think he does subscribe to that belief — that to understand is to forgive, but in his mind he didn't want to forgive the Nazi doctors. Through the book, he had acquired a greater understanding of them and then found himself accountable in God's eyes to forgive them. And he resented having to do that."

"Now how does that relate to me?" said Rhoads.

"If you know something, you have a responsibility to act. If you have a gut feeling, you have the responsibility to act on it. You may not like it, just as Bettelheim didn't like his conflicting feelings about forgiving Nazi doctors."

Rhoads stood in the hallway, awaiting the elevator, when Dr. Trice stepped out.

"I didn't want to make it part of our conversation in my office there, T.R., but now that you're leaving, how's it going with the drinking?"

Rhoads looked down at the mat in front of the elevator. "Not so hot, Doc. I got pretty thirsty last weekend."

"And since then? Today's Friday."

"Bone dry. And now I'm going to find an AA meeting here in Philly and take the first flight to New York tomorrow morning."

"Is that how you plan to celebrate finding Muntor's house? Going to a meeting?"

Rhoads hadn't thought of it that way. "Yeah, Doc. I guess so."

"That's my boy," Dr. Trice said. "That's my boy."

111

"Ms. Trichina," Larry the doorman said over the intercom. "Sorry to bother you, but there's a deliveryman here from Really Good who insists Unit 1202 ordered a pizza. But I know you always tell me if you're expecting a delivery. Is it yours?"

"Not guilty, Larry."

Trichina could hear the deliveryman arguing with Larry.

"Ms. Trichina," Larry said. "This guy says the pie's been out too long to take back, and he wants to know if you want it. Large, onion and green pepper. Half price."

She took her finger off the intercom button and thought about it. She hadn't eaten a thing since lunch.

"How much is half price?"

Larry consulted the man from Really Good. "He says four-fifty."

"Tell him two bucks and a buck tip. Take it or leave it."

Larry repeated the offer.

"He says he'll take it," Larry said into the intercom.

"Okay," Trichina said. "Let him in."

On the way up to Trichina's, Valzmann's assistant pressed himself into the one corner of the elevator the security camera couldn't focus on. He snapped on a pair of surgical gloves and felt like a million bucks.

112

30th Street Station
Philadelphia

Dr. Trice entered 30th Street Station, bought a muffin, a cup of coffee, and a newspaper, and sat down. The terminal was mobbed with Northeast Corridor business travelers, students, and local passengers.

Several pigeons had gotten into the building and flew about high overhead. An indigent man walked up to Dr. Trice and held out an empty soda cup, begging for change. Dr. Trice shook her head "no," and the man moved on. She donated to the city's twenty-four-hour shelter instead of handing out money to those who'd likely buy a bottle of cheap wine or a cap of crack.

The Amtrak information board updated itself electronically and indicated Dr. Trice's train would be ten minutes late.

That meant time enough for another muffin.

113

The Royal Carland Hotel
New York

Getting dressed in the cab from the airport was awkward and inconvenient. Rhoads changed from his jeans and turtleneck to his most expensive business suit, an Italian-cut black wool job. He had brought a light gray tie and an out-of-character thick-linked gold ID bracelet and polarized sunglasses. He had borrowed the bracelet from an attorney who lived in his apartment building.

The suit jacket fit snugly. He certainly was not packing a weapon on his hip or under his arm. Anyone could see that.

The cab pulled up at the Royal Carland. Rhoads gathered his wallet, carry-on, and the leather portfolio that contained a nine-millimeter semiautomatic, a pair of plastic handcuffs, and his mini-aerosol container of PinPoint Mace. He paid the cab fare and jumped out.

Outside the Grand Imperial Ballroom, at a quarter past ten, Rhoads tried to walk the way he imagined a successful big-portfolio investor would. Strides that were long and fast, supremely confident. At least in a bull market.

He had a little less than an hour until the meeting was to begin.

He glanced at the headlines in the *USA Daily* and other papers in the racks in the lobby newsstand. The FBI had successfully kept the Las Vegas angle out of the news.

As Rhoads turned away from the newsstand to make an informal perimeter observation of the property, he noticed the open cigarette display. How simple it must be for Muntor. Maybe that would all be coming to an end. Rhoads moved around the inside of the hotel in a methodical concentric circle. Working the two elements of luck — preparation and attentiveness — Rhoads studied a brochure that provided a simplified floor plan of the Royal Carland.

Someone once told Rhoads that belief in luck was nothing more than lack of confidence. With that in mind, he walked faster to cover more ground.

114

The attendees filed in, packing the Majestic Ballroom. A banner displayed near the head table announced the Specialty Retailers Marketing Symposium. Beyond the four or five armed hotel security officers, there was no sign of other precautions.

In a corner at the back of the room, Franklin, dressed in the uniform of the hotel's maintenance workers, first listened then spoke softly into a cell phone.

"… Received. A no-show at the airport. He hasn't been spotted here, either. The situation here is Condition A-Andy. Nothing happening. Out," Franklin said and punched a button on the phone, then snapped it closed and slid it into one of the deep pockets in his overalls. Almost immediately, the unit chirped again. He retrieved it.

"Black Jack here. Talk to me."

"This is Bandit. Urgent. Repeat. Urgent. We're on the third floor, directly above the ballroom along the west wall. We're showing a hit on the meter. We're showing a hit on the meter."

Franklin whispered urgently. "Black Jack to all even-number units. GO! GO! GO!"

Simultaneously throughout the ballroom, from out of nowhere, fifteen or twenty figures, all undercover agents, began moving, then running, toward the exit. They headed for the third floor.

Franklin snapped his fingers and Brandon, wearing a business suit and sitting in the back row of folding chairs, looked up. A second later, he and Franklin were racing from the room as well. Franklin and Brandon took a stairway to the third floor.

They burst into a nearly vacant ballroom, much smaller than the Majestic. Agents in jumpsuits were huddled several feet back from a tablecloth-covered banquet table they had upended. A large black cardboard box sat there, a humming, grinding sound coming from within.

"Where's my bomb team?" Franklin bellowed.

"Any second, sir, they'll be here any second," an agent said.

Franklin stepped forward. Sweat formed and glistened on his massive dark brow. He turned and looked around. "All you people out of here. I'm opening it. Muntor probably put together a pretty primitive bomb. Maybe it'll be simple to disarm."

No one moved.

"I said out of here!"

His men stayed with him. Franklin took a step closer and reached out toward the flap that obscured the box's contents from view.

The sound of a gun cocking caused everyone to look up and freeze. Except Franklin. He had taken another step closer to the box.

"Move another inch toward the box, and I'll blow your fucking arm off."

Franklin looked up. He didn't recognize the man with the gun, but he knew the uniform. The ATF Bomb Disposal Unit. The man did not lower the weapon when he realized he was pointing it at the FBI Deputy Director.

"I'm operating under the assumption that you're stone crazy, sir, and I can't let you near that box. Step back."

Franklin half-raised his hands and did as he was told.

The bomb disposal personnel moved in and the other FBI agents backed farther away. Franklin ordered his men to leave.

This time they did.

"The device's display reads seven minutes and twenty-two seconds and counting," the bomb team leader said, crouching next to the box. "My guess is someone started the clock twenty-two minutes and thirty-eight seconds ago, giving himself a full thirty minutes to get out. I don't see a receiver or a timer. That means either one or the other's hidden inside and therefore not visible, or..."

"Or what?" Franklin bellowed.

"Or twenty-two minutes and," the bomb team leader looked at the still-counting display, "now forty-four seconds ago, someone stood right here, right in this room, and started the countdown manually."

"Then he could still be in the hotel," Brandon shouted. "Oak, broadcast an evacuation order. Get everyone out of this building now."

"No," Franklin said, turning to a senior agent. "Seal the building first. I'm not letting Muntor get out of here. Once we're airtight, broadcast the evacuation. Every human being leaving this building gets eyeballed. Regardless of age, sex, race. Go."

Franklin turned to another agent. "You. Call FBIHQ. Tell them we've found a device."

"And Brandon ..." Franklin said, waving for him to join him in a sprint toward the elevators.

"What, sir?"

"And, Brandon, you were right," Franklin said, already half-winded. "Rhoads is a damned jinx. He's not here, we get lucky."

The elevator arrived and Franklin slipped in as soon as the doors parted enough for him to fit. Brandon grinned and banged his shoulder painfully on the still-opening elevator door as he squeezed in after his boss.

115

In a fifteenth-floor hotel room, Martin Muntor awoke. He did not know how long he had slept. It could have been ten hours, it could have been forty-five minutes. When the injections wore off, they had that disorienting effect. All he knew for certain was that today was the day.

What woke him finally and got him out of bed was a splinter of daylight that fell across his closed eyes. The rays had seeped in through the space in the heavy opaque drapes where he had failed to draw them tightly enough together.

He moved weakly into the bathroom, bumping his knee into the doorframe and then steadying himself at the bathroom sink. He chose not to look at himself in the mirror.

The cold water he splashed on his face ran down his neck and onto the perspiration-soaked crew neck T-shirt he had worn to bed. He ineffectually toweled himself off. He had barely enough energy to make it back to the suitcase stand in the bedroom. He searched frantically, tearing a sweatshirt, maps, socks and underwear out of his suitcase.

Then he found the leather kit bag and lovingly removed the contents, setting each object carefully on the dresser.

He prepared another injection quickly. There was no time for his full ritual.

Muntor closed his eyes for several minutes while the drugs began their course through his veins and gave him new life and new, indomitable power.

Invigorated, Muntor took a shower, changed into clean clothes and sat down on the easy chair facing the television. He pulled a brochure out of a file folder and stared at the floor plan of the ballroom, studying it for the hundredth time.

"All ye who enter here," he said to the floor plan, jabbing a finger at the entrance of the Grand Imperial Ballroom, "abandon hope."

Muntor put the brochure on a table and slid open the closet door. He removed first one, then the other, large duffel bag — the same ones he had at the dilapidated schoolhouse in Pennsylvania. He unzipped them both, removed the equipment and dressed in the fireman's gear, the bright yellow protective overcoat, and the full-face helmet and hood.

Dizzy with excitement and fatigue and drug-induced energy, Muntor sat on the unmade bed to pull on his protective leggings and high rubber boots, then rose to wrestle the orchard-fogger tank onto his back. He leaned over toward the telephone, opened the faceplate, and dialed the hotel operator.

"Help! I just got off the elevator. I was upstairs at the observation deck with the kids," he said, not attempting to disguise his voice. "A policeman's been shot, and another one's just lying there on the floor. You need to help them. I'm going back up to see what I can do. Send help!"

The observation deck, Muntor thought as he hung up. *A long, slow ride on the elevators, on the other side of the hotel from where the meeting is. And every available man will be sent, far away from me. While they're coming up, I'll be going down.*

Muntor pulled the faceplate back into place and adjusted the oxygen supply to the mask. He took the orchard-fogger's long, silver nozzle in his hand. He wrapped his finger around its trigger and teased it. It felt good. He knew he'd be able to use it. The trigger and trigger-guard assembly reminded him of the big-bore hunting rifle he had used to shoot up junkyard cars as a kid. Funny he hadn't thought of that until now.

He walked quickly into the hallway to get an elevator down before the police and security people commandeered them all rushing to the aid of their fallen comrades. He reached the bank of elevators. He pressed the "Down" button and waited to descend.

116

The American Investor Relations Society meeting had begun precisely at eleven in the Grand Imperial Ballroom. Rhoads, holding his leather portfolio, entered the room and looked around.

Three entrance doors gave access to the small ballroom. Inside, under a dozen sparkling chandeliers, a field of elegant luncheon tables had been set. One of the tables, flanked by a podium, had been hurriedly reserved for Pratt when it was learned he would attend.

Rhoads took a seat at one of the tables near the swinging doors that led into the banquet kitchen. The position afforded a view of the entire room and all entrances.

Forty of the nation's most influential tobacco business leaders were present, including the CEOs of three other Big Eight companies, heads of mutual funds, investment houses, a cadre of handpicked journalists, the president of the world's largest agricultural conglomerate, congressional supporters, and two tobacco state governors.

Pratt wasn't scheduled to speak for another fifteen minutes, and Rhoads knew he wouldn't arrive until a couple of minutes before then.

Rhoads scanned the room methodically. Either the FBI's covert surveillance teams were so good that Rhoads couldn't pick them out from nearly forty multimillionaires, or they simply weren't there. In any case, he felt exposed.

He continued scanning and soon spotted two Old Carolina security people. He had provided them with explicit instructions. "No matter what happens, ignore me. I'm no one you know," he had said.

Several times, Rhoads's heart leaped out of his chest when a man attired in a suit — what Rhoads thought Muntor would be wearing — appeared and seemed to be about the same size as Muntor. One by one, Rhoads eliminated them.

When ear-splitting electronic fire-alarm bells began to clamor from recessed public address speakers in the ballroom ceiling, Rhoads's body switched into a fight-or-flight level of adrenaline and muscle tension. Heavily oxygenated blood rushed into his eyes and ears to make those organs acutely sensitive. His nostrils flared back imperceptibly, a biological hat-tip to a mammalian history when sense of scent weighed heavily in the survival formula.

Had Muntor set the building on fire or tossed a bomb? Rhoads had not anticipated that. Muntor was a product tamperer, not a Hamas guerrilla. Rhoads's gut instinct was to race to one of the hotel security people to find out what was being broadcast on their radios. Instead, he decided to stay still, keep low and alert. He thought of the lesson learned too late by the quarry of the Cordozo fish in the crustacean tank in Baltimore. *When you least expect it — expect it.*

After a minute, the alarm's deafening noise was interrupted by a recorded electronic female voice instructing occupants to exit the building and avoid using the elevators. Some conference attendees rose slowly, wondering if the alarm was real. Several minutes passed before firemen appeared wearing fluorescent yellow coats with "NYFD" marked in bold, reflective letters across their backs. They trudged through the crowded room in high rubber boots, burdened under heavy white helmets, steel air tanks strapped behind them like scuba gear, and aerator hose mouthpieces strung like medallions around their necks.

"Just hang in here for a few moments, please," one of the Old Carolina employees announced from the head table. "We're getting information that this is probably a false alarm."

Something about the firemen nagged at Rhoads.

A battalion chief spoke into a radio and a reply crackled back. The men waded across the floor and disappeared behind the swinging doors leading into the banquet kitchen. A few attendees rose to get coffee from an urn attended by a white-coated member of the kitchen staff. The firemen's casual demeanor encouraged everyone to pay little attention to the incident.

The firemen, Rhoads wondered. *What was it about them?*

He remembered Dr. Trice's alert. "Thoughts or ideas that have a different texture about them ... they are usually gifts from the universe."

He remembered a part from the transcript of Muntor's call to the radio program *National Talk*. Something like, "I'm just starting a backfire, fighting a huge fire with well-placed little ones."

Bingo!

Rhoads knew. Muntor thought of himself as a fireman. He had sent them here. His little game. A little foreshadowing. Of course! Muntor called in the alarm. From his seat, Rhoads craned his neck, seeing little. Impatient attendees rose and milled.

Rhoads began to doubt himself. He used a pen to write "RESERVED" on the back of an envelope and left it on his seat.

Am I imagining a Muntor who isn't here? Did someone in the kitchen trigger the alarm?

He took his portfolio in hand and headed toward the kitchen to find out.

A dozen kitchen workers stood outside the door talking and yawning. They waited for the firemen to leave.

Rhoads walked past them. He felt the weight of his gun in the portfolio. Inside, six or eight firemen were spread about examining various sections of the huge, gleaming stainless steel-filled kitchen. The area was lit brightly like an operating room.

Wide, tiled aisles dotted every few feet with small drainage grates lying between rows of steel food-prep tables and sinks. Banks of ovens lined one wall, and hooded grills and scores of giant pots and pans and baking trays were stacked on top of a long row of refrigerators and freezers. The aroma of brewing coffee and the strong odor of commercial disinfectant wafted together, confusing the olfactory senses.

Rhoads moved forward. One of the firemen turned to him at the sound of the swinging door.

"We need you back on the other side of those doors," he said, pointing a finger.

"Security," Rhoads answered and kept coming. The fireman shrugged and turned back to the others in his troop.

The fire department battalion chief was satisfied that the call, made from a house phone in the hotel, had been a hoax. One of seventy or eighty false alarms each day in New York. He was about to radio the dispatcher and report that the alarm was unfounded but waited on one of his men for the last report — the results of a gas leak analysis.

One of the firemen took a metering device from his pocket and stood over a field of gas burners built into the top bank of ovens. He waved the device like a wand above the burners and with his thumb pressing a button on the meter. In a moment, he looked at the meter's display and then snapped it off, putting the device back into his pocket. He gave a thumbs-down to the captain, who then spoke into the radio. Another fireman used a key to open a utility box on the wall. He reached in and flipped a switch. The clanging alarms went silent. The swarm of firemen left, walking past Rhoads, saying nothing to him.

As the last fireman passed through the large doors, several kitchen staffers entered.

"We need you to stay outside for a couple more minutes," Rhoads said, raising his hand. The worker did not recognize him but assumed he had the authority to make the command.

"Okay, but the firemen said ..."

"Just another couple of minutes." The workers left.

Everything seemed to be in order, but Rhoads wanted one quick look around.

He strode quickly across the floor, carefully stepping over a puddle of greasy liquid that had dripped from packages of defrosting ground meat, and inspected a door on one side of the kitchen.

Securely locked.

He turned back the other way, just as quickly, toward the conveyor belts rattling silverware and saucers and cups through the dishwashing steamers. He squatted down and peered under them.

Nothing there either.

He exhaled as he rose.

Better possibilities in the ballroom. Better get out there.

As he walked toward the swinging doors, in an alcove behind the wall of refrigeration units, Rhoads heard something, a heavy, labored breathing, someone trying to catch his breath. He stopped and froze, then, silently, tiptoed closer, pressing his back to the cold ceramic that lined the wall. He steadied himself with a flat palm pressed against the wall in order to lean forward as far as possible, trying to cock his ear and hear around the comer.

He heard it again. Something like a wheeze, like a musical sound coming from an off-key human accordion. At first, he thought maybe a fireman had been abandoned by his fellows.

No, he realized, they had all left together.

He moved forward another few inches. He heard the sound again, then someone grunted softly. Rhoads got down on his hands and knees, his portfolio under him, lowering his head almost to the floor. The tiles were clammy and ice cold. He moved his head another inch forward, just enough for one eye to see back into the semi-darkness of the alcove. There it was, a figure squatting down, pushing or pulling a box. Rhoads couldn't see. He eased back, straining to keep his balance. He drew a deep breath, steadily, slowly. He edged slightly forward, to see a little more deeply into the alcove. In close quarters, an inch was a mile.

There it was again, now he heard it quite clearly.

A wheeze.

He pulled his head back, feeling for the portfolio. He opened it, reached in, and got a grip on his nine-millimeter with his right hand. He crouched lower on his hands and knees. He couldn't, of course, be sure that it was Muntor. *Err on the side of caution.*

Still on all fours, Rhoads hunched awkwardly over the portfolio, wanting to slide it out of his way, but that would make noise. He could move himself more quietly than he could slip a leather portfolio over a floor. He moved forward a bit.

With a surge of cold panic emptying itself into his gut, Rhoads asked himself the question he should have asked a full minute earlier. *What's in that box?*

Rhoads wanted to get a lay of the kitchen. As he eased back to improve his view, the heavy steel-lipped rim of a fire extinguisher smashed into the side of his head and sent him flying forward, stunned. Head bathed in blood, his right eye swelled shut instantly. Rhoads had held on to his gun, but he was acutely disoriented. In the next instant, he covered his head with his left arm and rolled away. Tiny sparks of white light poured into his brain from the tear in his scalp. He felt blood drip behind his ear in a warm rivulet. Rhoads found himself half under the shelf of a food preparation table. He crawled out and stood up, eyes burning into that dark alcove, trying to ignore the clanging in his head.

He inched forward, gun pointed into the dark. He saw no figure there now. He could not cry out for help. He heard his own panicked breathing.

The fireman stepped forward, facemask awry, a fire extinguisher held between both hands.

Why did he hit me?

The form moved toward him. The sound of labored, wheezing gasps grew louder. Rhoads stood up now, coming back to himself. He looked at the fireman. The uniform was bright yellow but different than those of the firemen who had just left.

Rhoads understood.

This was Martin Muntor.

Rhoads began to bring the automatic up but lost his balance as a wave of dizziness washed over him. He was fading out, knees unable to support the weight of his body. The warm wet dripped from his head. Without a word, the man in the fireman's uniform bolted back into the dark alcove. Rhoads heard a heavy door slam. He regained his balance and followed, stumbling over a large cardboard box. Glass jars filled with something rolled against each other.

Rhoads easily caught up with him. The man, almost unable to breathe, had braced himself against a storage shelf. The man turned to Rhoads, eyes wide and wild behind the protective faceplate, able only to concentrate on catching his breath. He had no capacity to resist Rhoads.

Rhoads raised his gun and started to speak when everything slowed down and grew dim like the settling of a sudden fog.

Dizzy, dizzy. His knees weakened, and he felt himself slowly, slowly sinking, fading, melting into the floor. Rhoads was passing out and he knew it, and there was nothing he could do.

117

Dr. Trice took a cab from Penn Station to the Royal Carland. She checked her coat and. carrying her handbag, followed the signs to the Grand Imperial Ballroom.

Although uninvited to the event, she felt that as a stockholder in Old Carolina Tobacco, Inc. she had every right to be there.

At one of the ballroom doors, a greeter handed her a schedule and a large information packet emblazoned with the Old Carolina logo. No one questioned her presence. She entered the ballroom and, without realizing it, took the seat next to the one Rhoads had been sitting in.

When she looked at the word "RESERVED" on the Old Carolina envelope next to her and saw the peculiar, childish block letters, she recognized them instantly as Rhoads's handwriting.

"Have you seen the person who was sitting here?" she asked a man seated nearby, pointing to the empty chair next to her.

"I think he went in there," the man said, indicating the banquet kitchen's swinging doors.

Dr. Trice nodded. "Thank you."

She rose and headed toward the swinging doors.

118

The ice numbed Valzmann's hip. He kept reaching under his jacket to make certain nothing was leaking. What a mess that would be. Stuffed into one of the Royal Carland's huge industrial trash dumpsters out back by the service dock was the body of a hotel plumber, minus an appendage. They'd probably never find him. Valzmann had the man's severed right hand in his pocket, wrapped in plastic and enclosed in a bag filled with ice. The fingers would leave convincing fingerprints on Dallaness's body. He hoped the plumber's prints were on record.

Valzmann made his way through the service corridors behind the banquet kitchen. His cell phone chirped and he answered it before it rang a second time.

"What's the situation with Mrs. Dallaness?" Pratt asked quietly. "I'm pulling up to the hotel now. My presentation begins in a few minutes."

"I'm ready sir," he said. "At the next break, I imagine she'll need the john. If she uses the one in her room, I'll do it then."

"What about Rhoads?"

"He's here. In the audience. Playing undercover."

"He's here? Perfect." Pratt laughed softly. "Prick's supposed to be in Vegas. He walked into a buzz saw this time. Now you can work your magic on both of them and make sure we've got all the disks."

"I don't think that'll be necessary, sir. Late word from Asheville. Trichina had only one set, and we got those from her lawyer Finch. She tried to bluff when she said she had a second set. I was able to verify that the disks I took from Rhoads's apartment were the actual ones Dallaness made."

"And is our executive vice president moping today?"

Valzmann paused. "I'm sorry, sir. The operation was a success, but the patient died."

Pratt exhaled from his mouth like a kid blowing out candles on a cake.

"You sure?" Pratt asked.

"Sir? She's dead."

"No, Valzmann. You sure we learned the truth? I'd hate to think ..."

"Billy took care of it, Mr. Pratt. He said she fought hard, much harder than he expected. But no one can withstand the blowtorch."

119

A long black limousine pulled up at the Royal Carland's main entrance. Pratt emerged in the company of Arnold Northrup and three security men. Two doormen opened glass doors and they entered the lobby, taking took note of the greeting sign.

American Investor Relations Society
Welcomes
the Visionaries of the Tobacco Industry
Second floor, Grand Imperial Ballroom

Earlier, Pratt's attorneys had circumvented Franklin and gone straight to the Director of the FBI to complain, considering Virgil's unimpeded progress, about the inadequate security plans for the conference. The Director personally assured the attorneys that there would be more than met the eye at both the Brasilia and the Royal Carland.

Hotel personnel led Pratt and North to a private elevator that arrived instantly and took only a few seconds to deliver them to the second floor. As they stepped off the elevator, Northrup pulled out a chirping cell phone and answered it.

"Hold on, please." Then, handing the phone to Pratt, he said, "The FBI." Pratt took the phone. "Yeah?"

He listened. He beamed, snapped the telephone closed and handed it back to Northrup. He leaned in toward him and spoke out of the corner of his mouth.

"Looks like we finally got someplace Virgil was headed before he got there. The FBI was waiting for him to show up at the Specialty Retailers' show in Las Vegas. They've found some kind of a device they think he planted in the Brasilia, and they've got the building sealed off. Arnie!" Pratt said, thinking that there was suddenly an excellent chance he wasn't going to have to spend seven hundred and fifty million dollars at two o'clock on Monday. "They don't think he had time to get out. They think they have him cornered."

Pratt lit up like a kid on Christmas morning.

Like a dog and its master, Northrup walked behind Pratt. At a respectful distance, Northrup stopped and stood still. Pratt continued to the podium by the head table. A roar of applause greeted him.

120

In darkness and freezing cold, Rhoads came to.

His head pounded with excruciating pain, and his arms and hands were tied with something to an icy pole behind him.

Shit! My head. It pounded and ached.

He had no way to reach up to stop the bleeding bruise, his blood warm as it ran down the cold skin of his forehead. Somehow, he reasoned, Muntor had dragged him here and bound his arms behind him.

The scent of food. Frozen meat. Locked in a freezer, freezing to death. He thought of the freezers on the boat he and Teddy had meant to buy. The clients would catch fish and their catch would be held in the freezers for them to take home. The dream of the boat evaporated. He would never buy the boat, and Teddy's family would have no one to look out for them.

Instead, he thought, he'd die right here, in a frozen puddle of his own blood. Locked in here with the flesh of the butchered.

121

"Step aside," the uniformed Martin Muntor said to one of the young models hired to greet the American Investor Relations Society conference attendees. "Building safety violation inspection."

Muntor's words made no sense — they were intended only to confuse. His fire department hazardous materials outfit had authority. The model did as ordered.

Muntor stepped forward, pulled the doors to the ballroom closed, and laced heavy chains through the handles of the exit. He secured the chains with a heavy padlock he took from one of his pockets. Then he strode as fast as his Biphetamine- and Dilaudid-fortified body would go to the second of the three ballroom exits. He chained those doors, too.

Only the main entrance remained accessible.

122

"Thank you," Pratt said, nodding to a few people. "Thank you. Ladies and gentleman, I don't think anyone will mind if I depart from the scheduled agenda to make an important announcement." Pratt hadn't smiled like this in almost a month. The audience hummed and grew excited. "We have just learned that, at this very moment in Las Vegas, the FBI is closing in on Martin Muntor. And, we are all hoping that ..."

Boom.

Boom. Boom.

From the back of the room, something banged loudly three times, breaking the mood.

Pratt looked up.

All heads turned. Martin Muntor announced himself by hammering on the doorframe with the long black gunmetal trigger nozzle attached to the tank strapped on his back.

"Excuse me, ladies and gentlemen. And law enforcement officers," he said, his voice both strained and strong. The faceplate of his gas mask was flipped up, enabling him to be heard.

Some could see the large green-and-white tank strapped to his back. He held the orchard-fogger's trigger nozzle by his side.

He raised his free hand high. He held a small object. "A dead-man switch," he said. "This is a mechanical engineering term for any device similar to the one I have here in my hand." His arm straightened and jutted forward in a kind of *Sieg Heil* salute. "It's designed to take care of business if its operator loses consciousness."

A frightened murmur rippled through the room.

The six or eight FBI agents seated at the tables tensed, ready for instructions from the command post through their earphones.

They all slipped their weapons from their holsters and into their hands without any obvious movement of body or limb.

Conference attendees seated near Muntor could see that the device he held was no larger than a deck of cards. With his right arm high, Muntor took two steps forward into the ballroom.

"Should I be harmed or rendered unconscious before I complete my presentation ..."

From somewhere behind him in the hallway, a uniformed New York City policeman had been watching. Instead of calling for backup, he charged in, gun drawn. He stood four feet from Muntor. Muntor turned toward him and snapped down the gas mask's faceplate with a brush of his right forearm and, with his left hand, raised the long black trigger nozzle and squeezed once. A small puff of white gas shot into the policeman's face. He dropped his gun and crumpled to the floor in a spasm of choking. In a moment, he was still.

No one else dared rise.

Muntor trudged back two paces and pulled the doors behind him closed, slamming them in fury. As if there had been no disturbance, he raised his faceplate, held out the dead-man switch, and continued. "Should I be harmed or rendered unconscious before I complete my presentation, my thumb will come off the button I am depressing here, there will be a massive explosion, and I will perish. And so will everyone in this room and most of those in this hotel. In a moment, I'll give a harmless demonstration to prove my capability. In the meantime, remain seated. And you over there by the swinging doors," he pointed to the kitchen staff, "you all move over toward the head table, away from the kitchen."

The workers moved as one. A small shriek came from one of them. At the head table, Pratt's face had turned bone white.

Two FBI agents rose in defiance of Muntor's instructions to remain seated. Another agent, apparently their superior, shouted out to them. "All posts, do as the man says. Take your seats."

The agents sank back into their chairs.

"And no radio communication," Muntor warned. "A device has been activated, and radio transmission could trigger it."

Without turning away from the people in the ballroom, Muntor tucked the nozzle under his arm, took a third chain from one of his suit's oversized pockets, and secured it to the door behind him.

123

Dr. Trice, out of breath and shivering, knelt beside Rhoads in the frozen-food locker and struggled with the nylon rope that bound his hands to the pole. She couldn't get it loose.

While she worked, Rhoads spoke to her in a calm voice. "I thought I was going to die. That I'd never get that boat."

"Can we talk about this later, T.R.?" she said, jerking with little success at the rope. "You're not dying so soon. But I can't get your wrists free."

"Leave me here and go find a knife. Over by the prep tables."

The seventy-two-year-old woman stood up uncertainly and stumbled out of the locker, her hands numb after only a long minute in the freezer. The prep tables were on the other side of the huge food service area. Rhoads listened forever to the clicks Dr. Trice's heels made on the kitchen tile until they faded.

Then he heard other steps approaching. Whoever was out there stopped.

A moment later, from beyond the freezer door, a large man entered, holding a gun.

"Here you are, Rhoads." He grinned. "Looks like your day's had a poor start. And it's about to get worse."

A bright light streamed in from the kitchen behind the man.

Rhoads squinted. "Valzmann."

"Quiet, Rhoads. You are about to die. There's a loose end down in Asheville that has put Mr. Pratt at risk. And I'm going to tie it up — with you."

Rhoads's head spun. "This is about Benedict..."

"Good boy, Rhoads. Now, before I ice you, I'm dying to ask you something." Valzmann grinned. "If you want to hide something, why hide it in your house? You're smarter than that. It didn't take me ten minutes to find the disks."

As he spoke, Rhoads noticed a shadow flit by behind Valzmann.

"Flying here, flying there," said Valzmann, "chasing that bonus so you could buy your boat. Too busy to take care of the details. Sloppy."

"You're going to pin Benedict's death on me."

"Already done," Valzmann said. "Last words?"

Rhoads mumbled.

"Speak up, Rhoads," Valzmann said. "Make your last words meaningful. You want to give me a message for your brother?"

From beyond the freezer door, a woman spoke. "Excuse me, sir. Where do you want me to put these salmon hors d'oeuvres?"

Valzmann turned towards the voice.

Dr. Trice, an arm extended forward, stepped boldly into the locker.

Valzmann screamed and dropped his gun. He turned, putting his shoulder between himself and the woman. His hands flew to his face and eyes. He coughed and spat.

Dr. Trice stood firm, emptying her canister of cayenne pepper spray at Valzmann, trying to hit his upper lip where he'd breathe the spray through his mouth or nose. Getting the eyes wasn't as important as making him choke. A blinded attacker can still grab hold of you and break your neck, but one choking half to death is effectively incapacitated.

"You whore!" he gurgled through the saliva and mucous flooding his eyes and nose and mouth. She had gotten him square in the face. He couldn't see.

Dr. Trice advanced with a serrated kitchen knife and plunged it hard and high into Valzmann's leg. She aimed for the external iliac artery she knew ran from the groin down the front of the leg. She twisted the knife resolutely. The blade had hit bone, and it stuck. She pulled her hand away. He was a broad, solid man. If she had hit the femoral artery too, his blood pressure would drop like a rock in a pond. He'd go down fast. She had had big men, patients, go berserk on her and knew from training to keep her thinking under control. It gave her a vastly superior position.

"Ahhhh..." Valzmann screamed and clutched at the wound.

He fell to the floor.

"Get over here with that knife," Rhoads yelled, jerking against the rope. His breath condensed in the cold air.

"I can't, it's in his leg."

Valzmann screamed in pain and tore the knife out. It fell from his hands.

Very accommodating, Dr. Trice thought. This is a man who wants to be punished.

She picked it up. "I have it now."

Valzmann started to move.

"You keep pressure on that wound, or you'll be dead in three minutes," she told the coughing, choking man. Valzmann slumped over onto his back, doing as told. She walked around him, crouched by Rhoads and felt behind him for the rope. She found a place with her fingers where it would be safe to cut. She freed Rhoads with a few quick flicks of the gory knife.

Rhoads was up in a second, one eye swollen shut and warm blood still dripping. In the dark, he stumbled on Valzmann's gun, stooped, and took it.

Dr. Trice found a cloth and handed it to him. "It's not sterile, but pressure, Rhoads, pressure. Head wounds bleed."

Rhoads looked at Valzmann. "You sure he's down?"

"He'll stay for a while," she said.

Valzmann made a fruitless effort to get up. "Get the paramedics, Rhoads." The man was crying. "Please. I'm bleeding to death."

"Yeah. That's not tops on my to-do list."

Rhoads and Dr. Trice hurried out of the locker, toward the ballroom. Rhoads looked through one of the round windows in the swinging doors.

"Go the other way," he said. "There's got to be another exit back here."

"Find a phone," Rhoads said. "Call 9-1-1. Tell them Virgil's sealed the Grand Imperial Ballroom. Then hang up, call back, tell them again. They take multiple calls seriously."

"What are you going to do?"

"I don't know."

124

"Are you rolling? I want you to roll tape," Muntor ordered the trembling cameraman who stood on a platform in the corner of the room, hired to videotape the conference. The man was a freelancer who earned his living recording business events for free — and then selling an edited tape back to the company involved. "You make sure you get everything."

The man nodded and put his eye to the camera, training it on Muntor in his yellow hazardous materials garb. Out of Muntor's view, an FBI agent leaned over at his table and whispered urgent words into a hand-held radio.

Muntor moved away from the chained door and trudged forward several paces. He kept his arm raised, clutching the dead-man switch.

Panic was in the air.

Those nearest him cringed.

"Do not move!" he shouted at them. With his faceplate open, they could see his sallow, sweaty face, his agitated eyes. He moved towards the entrance to the banquet kitchen. Muntor knew he had secured Rhoads adequately, but was worried that other security people may have gotten in through a rear entrance. It would have been easy enough to kill him, but Muntor knew Rhoads. He would get to the bottom of all of it. With Muntor dead, Rhoads would turn his focus to Old Carolina and bring them down, the same thing Muntor had tried to do with his exposé of the tobacco companies.

Keeping his back to the wall, Muntor reached the doors and regarded them with concern as he stood between them and a small plastic trash can.

"Now for that demonstration," he said. He eyed the people near him. One middle-aged man in particular stood out. Was it his build or the quiet way he watched? Muntor did not know, but he was certain the man was some kind of agent. Muntor looked right at him but spoke loudly enough for everyone to hear. "You are about to hear a small explosion. It is harmless. Keep your eyes on my thumb."

Muntor narrowed his eyes and looked toward the cameraman. "Are you getting this?"

The cameraman nodded several times too many.

"Good," Muntor said to him. "Because if you continue to obey, you'll keep on living. And you'll keep on living with a lot more money than you have now. Why? Because I, at this very moment, give you ... what's your name?"

"Alex S. Taylor," the cameraman, said, barely audibly.

Muntor looked into the camera from across the room. "I hereby give Alex S. Taylor all rights to my video documentary, *Muntor's Last Stand*. You can find a copy of it in my house in Philadelphia. In my basement in a fireproof steel safe. Make sure you get yourself a good, tough lawyer who will work on contingency and be able to fight the Feds, force them at least to make you a copy of the tape I'm sure they'll say they need for evidence against me. But they won't. The consideration is that you must agree to edit today's affair into the film as its grand finale. Do you understand, Alex S. Taylor? Do you agree?"

The cameraman again nodded rapidly many times.

"Out loud," Muntor instructed.

"Yes, sir. Yes sir, I understand."

Muntor then stretched his arm high and faced the device towards the ballroom. He lifted his thumb and beside him the trashcan exploded with a loud blast and fell over, smoking. Most people ducked and screamed, others merely flinched. This was happening so fast. No one quite believed it. Moans of fear and hysterical cries rose toward the ceiling along with the odor of sulfur and a column of blue-black smoke.

"Just a firecracker," Muntor said. "But it detonates when my thumb comes off the switch."

One woman murmured, "Please, God, please."

At once, Muntor's hand was again raised high. He had taken another device from his pocket.

"This one," Muntor said, looking towards the new dead-man switch he held, "makes a boom you don't want to hear."

Despite the powerful injection he had administered a little more than an hour earlier, the weight of the protective clothing and the bulky steel tank began wearing on him.

Near Muntor, a woman stood up at her table. Her voice trembled as she said, "Mister, before you kill us all, I'm going to say something."

Muntor turned and shouted back, his voice breaking. "Sit down. You have nothing to say. This is my day."

"I don't care. I'm saying it." She turned and faced the rest of the room. She shook. Terror flashed in her eyes. "I have to say it. I don't care if I die, as long as I get to say that Mr. W. Nicholas Pratt," she glared at him across the room, "the high and mighty CEO of Old Carolina Tobacco, Inc., is responsible for the death of my husband, Anthony Dallaness, and the death of Dr. Loren Benedict. And I have evidence that proves at least one of those killings. My name is Mary Dallaness, and I have worked at Old Carolina for ten years." She turned to Muntor. "You give me that hose, and I'll kill him myself."

"Mary!" Pratt's voice boomed. He had shouted into the microphone at the podium and startled even himself. The sound echoed through the ballroom.

"Sit down, I say!" Muntor screamed. He snapped the faceplate down and raised the trigger nozzle as high as the dead-man switch in his other hand. A half-dozen people threw themselves to the floor.

"No, you've got to listen to me," Mary cried.

"Silence!" Muntor said.

Pratt's heart pounded. He gripped the comers of the podium, determined to remain standing.

A man stood up and raised his empty hands to show Muntor he held no weapon. He turned to Mary and bellowed, "FBI, lady. You sit down. Right now. That's an order. You're endangering everyone in this hotel. This man doesn't want to harm us. Don't push him."

The agent quickly sat down.

In the kitchen, directly behind Muntor, Rhoads's head appeared, partially visible through one of the round windows in the swinging doors.

Muntor couldn't see him, but he must have noticed the movement of someone's eyes to the window at his back.

By instinct, Muntor threw himself backward. The heavy door swung back violently and knocked Rhoads down onto the kitchen floor.

Muntor, weighted by all the equipment, came through the doors and stood over Rhoads. "I let go of this," Muntor said, showing Rhoads the dead-man switch, "and everyone's gone. Get out there. Damn it, Mr. Rhoads, I didn't want you involved in this. You had a bigger role to play. But I suppose you've made your choice."

Rhoads, stunned by the blow of the door, crawled into the ballroom. Mary rushed to him and knelt by his side.

Muntor performed a quick survey of the kitchen area and returned to the ballroom holding the dead-man switch high. He had been gone only five or six seconds. Everyone was still seated.

He stepped out and faced the people in the ballroom, moving along solid wall, keeping his back to it, moving away from the swinging doors. From his new position, as long as everyone remained seated, he could see all three chained exit doors, the kitchen doors, and the head table.

"Here's what's going to happen," he said. "There's an excellent chance all of you, with one small exception, will be out of here in a few minutes. Out of here, alive and unharmed," he added. "If... if Nick Pratt cooperates."

On the other side of the room, Northrup whispered to Pratt. "Do as he says, Nick. He's crazy. But I think he's about to surrender. He just wants maximum attention."

Muntor cleared his throat. "Nick Pratt will trade himself for the lives of every man and woman in this room. He's going to stand up there at that table and smoke one of these."

Muntor slipped the orchard-fogger's trigger nozzle into one of the fireman uniform's giant pockets and produced a pack of Easy Lights. He waved them around for show before putting them back in his pocket. Muntor's upright arm ached. He carefully transferred the dead-man switch from one hand to other, keeping steady thumb pressure on the black button, and raised it, this time only for a moment, for all to see. Its function was now well known, and he no longer needed to keep it elevated.

Muntor, remembering the cameraman, turned to him and pointed. "Are you still getting all this?"

"Yes, sir."

"How soon until you run out of tape?"

The man looked at the back of the camera. "I've got five minutes and thirty-three seconds."

"More than enough," Muntor said. "More than enough."

The room was deadly silent save for Muntor's wheezing. He advanced slowly toward Pratt.

"An eye for an eye, Pratt," Muntor said. He used his other hand to show the pack of cigarettes again. "I'm dying of cancer and emphysema, but I've never smoked a day in my life. You have spent your life selling this poison, and you're going to reap what you've sown. The body is a temple, and you've desecrated it by the millions."

Pratt, a third of the room's span away, took a step back from the podium, shaking his head "no." A collective shudder rolled through the room.

"Come on, Pratt," Muntor's voice creaked.

"No!" Pratt said. He took half a step behind Arnold Northrup.

"Come on, Pratt. You light up, and I'll surrender. I'll surrender over your dead body." There was no humor in the remark.

Pratt took another step backward. "No! No! No!"

"Come on, Pratt. You light up, and I let everyone go. Shall I ask the crowd what they want? Because before the tape runs out, we're settling this. One way or another."

"Martin Muntor, sir," the FBI agent said, standing again, hands raised. "Let me use the house phone to tell my people what's happening. They don't know about the dead-man control, and ... and it might be better if they did."

That made sense to Muntor. He dropped the cigarettes back into a pocket and took hold of the orchard-fogger's trigger.

"Good. Use that phone there," he said, using the nozzle to point to a telephone on a wall by the coffee service area. "First, take off your jacket. Do everything slowly, except when you get to that telephone. Then you've got thirty seconds. When you're finished, pull the phone out of the wall. Remember this: I'm already dead, so play it smart and these people here may live. Go now."

The FBI agent did as Muntor instructed. When he got to the telephone, Muntor glanced at a wall clock and shouted a reminder to the agent that he had no more than thirty seconds. The agent dialed a number.

No one except the agent moved or spoke until Muntor told him his time was up. The FBI agent disconnected. Then, with one swift punch with the heel of his hand, he knocked the telephone off of the wall and sent it crashing to the floor before returning to his seat.

"How much time, cameraman?" Muntor asked.

"Four minutes, ten seconds."

125

"Hello, Martin, I'm coming out through here."

Muntor jerked his body around toward the sound coming from the kitchen. He raised the nozzle toward the sound.

"I'm unarmed," said Dr. Trice. "I'm an old lady back here in food prep. I'm coming out. Don't hurt me."

Muntor looked toward the slowly opening doors and the short, heavy woman who came through. That she knew his name seemed natural to him. In his delusion of grandeur, he presumed everyone now knew of Martin Muntor. She stood no more than ten feet away, looking directly at him. Her calm demeanor confused him. He thrust the dead-man switch toward her threateningly. She half-raised her hands and then dropped them to her side.

"Who are you?" Muntor asked. Without waiting for a reply, he said, "Take a seat. Take any seat, now."

"Martin. I'm Dr. Trice." She looked at his eyes in the shadow of the faceplate. Dull and wet. His respiration was rapid and shallow.

Rhoads spoke from the floor. Mary cradled him in her arms, the bloody cloth pressed against his head. "Bea, please. Sit down like he says. That switch in his hand can blow the place up. Let the professionals handle this."

Dr. Trice looked away from Rhoads. She looked at Muntor.

"Look, Martin," she said. She hadn't moved an inch toward a seat. "I heard what you said to Pratt, and he deserves to die that way. But I've got something better for you."

"Please take a seat, lady," Muntor said. "I'm too tired to tell you again."

She pointed a finger up at him. "Look, Martin," she said, eyeing the tank strapped on his back. "I imagine you have the equipment necessary to kill Pratt and anyone else in this room. But if you want to make more of an impact on the world, you want to hear me out."

"Three minutes, thirty seconds!" the cameraman shouted, an edge of hysteria in his voice.

"Please shut up, lady," said Muntor.

"Martin, listen," Dr. Trice continued. "Turn off that switch. Surrender. Make sure the one and a half billion dollars gets to where it's supposed to go. You said you want a public-awareness campaign. This is the greatest one in history. You kill Pratt, and no money gets transferred. You kill Pratt and all of us, in six months, maybe a year, maybe even two, after they've made the movie and A&E or HBO does an hour-long biography on you and five or six jerks write instant books about you, it'll all fade into oblivion. The tobacco industry will still be here, people will still be dying of lung cancer and heart disease and having low birth-weight babies.

"But, you let Pratt live? Every time he shows his face, they'll remember today and what you did. Every time people see the Old Carolina logo or Old Carolina cigarettes, they'll think about Martin Muntor and Virgil and what you did and the money you squeezed out of them for medical research. You kill everyone, and you go down as just another pathetic lunatic seeking a moment of glory. You surrender now, you'll have a story a thousand times better than if everyone perishes."

Muntor looked at a wall clock and then at the cameraman. "How much?"

The cameraman sobbed. "Two minutes, twenty seconds. Oh, God, please, God."

"I've already killed hundreds," Muntor said to Dr. Trice. "I'm already that dismissible pathetic lunatic."

"No! It's not so." Her face grew red. "You surrender now, and the money transfer changes everything. You've accomplished something. You've accomplished something positive. As you said in one of your calls to the FBI, 'I'm going to accomplish something of value before I die.' Who among us can say that? Very few of us can say that, Martin. Distinguish yourself. You said the body is a temple. You want others to treat their bodies with love and respect. And their minds, too. This is the lesson you've been trying to teach. But who will hear it if you kill more innocents?"

Muntor thought. He bit at his lower lip.

He looked across the room at Pratt who had backed himself into a corner by the coffee service table and a towering dieffenbachia. Pratt's shoulders pressed against the white wall. He shivered.

Muntor took a step toward him. A tiny squeak came out of Pratt's mouth. Muntor took several more steps in that direction and stopped just as he stood over Rhoads and Mary on the floor. He looked down.

"Nice try in Princeton, Mr. Rhoads," he said. Before Rhoads could speak, Muntor moved forward, advancing toward Pratt.

The room was as quiet as heavy snow falling in the woods. He stopped three feet from the quaking CEO. He took the long nozzle from his pocket and wrapped his index finger around the trigger. He raised it and moved it up, very slowly, to Pratt's face.

"Oh, Lord," Pratt said, arms folded across his chest. He tried to step backward, but he was already as far as he could go. He shook.

Muntor didn't turn his head from Pratt but shouted to the cameraman, "How much time?" He tightened his grip on the dead-man switch.

"Fifty-five seconds," the voice said, barely audible to Muntor under the helmet. Muntor withdrew the pack of Easy Lights from a pocket. It was difficult to do with one hand, but he succeeded in removing a single cigarette from the pack. He put it between his lips and held it there. With his free hand, he removed his helmet and gas mask. Muntor dropped them. Pratt flinched at the sound.

Muntor's hair had matted under the helmet, and a clump stuck straight up. Perspiration beaded his forehead and soaked the back of his neck. "Fifty-five seconds, Pratt?" Muntor spoke softly. This was just between them. "Not a lot of time to make such an important decision. You want this?" Muntor said, wiggling the cigarette tauntingly between his teeth. "Or this?" He moved the nozzle in closer, pressing its gunmetal lip painfully against Pratt's mouth. "Cancer really hurts, Pratt. Tumors are painful. Like a hand in there that knows how to grab a fistful of nerves. It squeezes and squeezes till you go out of your mind."

Pratt's legs gave out from under him. He sank back against the wall and slid down, slowly, to the floor. He sobbed.

"Oh no, please. You've made your point, sir. Haven't you cost me enough already? Please. No."

Muntor made a half-turn and positioned himself so that no one else in the auditorium could see him drop the dead-man switch into his pocket. He crouched down and took Pratt by his hair, forcing him to look up. Pratt squealed and threw his hands up to protect himself. They were close enough to feel the heat of each other's breath. The people seated at nearby tables screamed when Muntor leaned in. It seemed he was killing Pratt.

"Pratt," Muntor whispered, "if I ever find out that you've somehow stopped the funds transfer, I'm going to track you down in hell."

Pratt's cries revealed to the others that he was still alive.

Muntor struggled to his feet and turned to face all those present. His hand that had held the dead-man switch was thrust deep in his pocket.

"Rhoads, over here," Muntor tried to shout in the direction of Rhoads. His voice came out crackling and breaking. "And hurry up." He clutched the cigarette between his teeth. Pratt, on the floor behind Muntor, whimpered.

Mary fought to hold Rhoads down, but he threw her off, got up, and stumbled as fast as he could across the ballroom to where Muntor had cornered Pratt.

Muntor shouted to the cameraman over his shoulder. "How much time?"

"Twenty-one seconds," a teary voice said.

When Rhoads got within two paces of Muntor, Muntor held out the trigger nozzle to stop him.

"Close enough, friend," Muntor said. "Ladies and gentlemen and law enforcement authorities." Muntor struggled to speak loud enough for everyone to hear. He moved a half-pace to his right, making sure Rhoads was not blocking him from the camera's view of the scene. "In accordance with the terms of a binding agreement between me and Old Carolina Tobacco, Inc. of Asheville, North Carolina, I hereby surrender myself to Thomas Rhoads."

Muntor still held the cigarette clenched between his teeth. He held up his hand for silence. "And may God see fit to have mercy upon my soul."

Rhoads did not move a muscle.

No one in the room said a word.

Without warning, Martin Muntor's right hand came swiftly out of his pocket. He held a disposable lighter. He flicked it and raised the flame in a swift arc toward the cigarette he held between his teeth.

The crowd shuddered. Rhoads heard the rustle of what had to be security people leaping out of their seats, launching themselves toward Muntor.

Rhoads lunged forward and grabbed the frail man's wrist with one hand and pressed the palm of his other hand against Muntor's forehead. Rhoads kept him from leaning forward and bringing the flame to the cigarette. It was no contest. Rhoads stopped the flame an inch from the cigarette.

Muntor invoked all his strength and pulled hard, bringing his wrist toward his face, the lighter's flame now half an inch from the end of the cigarette. Rhoads tightened his grip and braced himself against Muntor's forehead. He held the position. Muntor kept his thumb on the lighter to keep the flame alive.

Muntor's and Rhoads's eyes met, and all the world fell away.

With the last of his strength, Muntor tried again to pull the lighter to the cigarette. "Please," he said so quietly only Rhoads heard him. "Let me go." He peered into Rhoads's eyes, searching for charity.

Rhoads stared back. He needed a glimpse of the lost soul behind Muntor's drawn, wild face.

"It's all right, Rhoads," wheezed Muntor.

Rhoads turned away for an instant, his hand firmly holding Muntor's frail wrist. Then he looked back, straight into Muntor's eyes, and swallowed.

Muntor knew this was it. He acknowledged Rhoads's gift with a tiny nod. He almost smiled. He had come a long way, and now it was over. Muntor exhaled thoroughly, so he could take in a deeper, fuller puff of smoke.

He closed his eyes.

Rhoads relaxed his grip imperceptibly, and the gap between the cigarette and the flame ceased to be.

With a sharp gasp, Muntor drew his last breath.

126

Ten days later
Off the coast of Barnegat Light, New Jersey

Rhoads set down his red-stained paintbrush and leaned on the side of the gently bobbing *Second Chance*. A dirty rag hung from his jeans pocket. He looked up to where Teddy stood, painting the roof of the boat's pilothouse. The sun shone high and hot.

"Teddy," said Rhoads. "Time for a drink?"

Teddy's throat was dry. A cold beer would be perfect. Teddy looked down at his brother and pressed his sleeve against his forehead to absorb the sweat.

"I've been ready for hours," Teddy said. "I'm parched. I never thought you'd ask."

"So come on down," said Rhoads. "If we can't have a drink on our own damned boat, then what's the point?"

Teddy dropped his brush in the nearly empty paint can and jumped onto the deck.

From below, where Rhoads and Mary had been making their temporary home, Mary climbed the wooden rungs of the ladder and, once on deck, positioned herself carefully on the slippery boards. She squinted into the sun and inhaled the salty air. She carried a tray with lunch, tall glasses, and a pitcher of iced tea.

"How about sandwiches, sailor boys?"

"You're a mind reader," Rhoads said, moving toward her. He gripped her shoulders and saw the sea reflected in her eyes. He beamed.

"Go wash up," she said to both men. "I think you've accomplished enough for now."

About the Author

Frank Freudberg is a novelist and ghostwriter. He's contributed to the Associated Press, Reuters, *Time, Newsweek*, the *Los Angeles Times, USA Today, Der Spiegel, Christian Science Monitor,* and *The Guardian*.